Kay Brellend, the third of six children, was born in North London but now lives in a Victorian farmhouse in Suffolk. Under a pseudonym she has written sixteen historical novels published in England and North America. This is her third novel set in the twentieth century and was inspired by her grandmother's reminiscences about her life in Campbell Road, Islington.

KAY BRELLEND

Coronation Day

HARPER

This novel is entirely a work of fiction.
The names, characters and incidents portrayed in it are
the work of the author's imagination. Any resemblance to
actual persons, living or dead, events or localities is
entirely coincidental.

Harper
An imprint of HarperCollins*Publishers*
77–85 Fulham Palace Road,
Hammersmith, London W6 8JB

www.harpercollins.co.uk

A Paperback Original 2012

East End Coronation Party © Hulton-Deutsch Collection/Corbis
East Ender Cleaning Doorstep © Hulton-Deautsch Collection/Corbis
Queen's Coronation Procession © Hulton-Deutsch Collection/Corbis
Party Smiles © Getty Images
Jolly Time © Getty Images
Sweet Gift © Getty Images
Coronation Party © Getty Images

3

A catalogue record for this book
is available from the British Library

ISBN: 978-0-00-746018-2

Set in Meridien by Palimpsest Book Production Limited, Falkirk, Stirlingshire

Printed and bound in Great Britain by
Clays Ltd, St Ives plc

Find out more about HarperCollins and the environment at
www.harpercollins.co.uk/green

*MAH and GCH, much love to you both
and wishing you well, now and always.*

ACKNOWLEDGEMENTS

Thanks to:
HBS for some amusing tales about building site shenanigans. Juliet Burton, Susan Opie, and last but by no means least, the great HarperCollins editorial team that commissioned this book to tie-in with our marvellous Queen's Diamond Jubilee Celebrations.

PROLOGUE

Summer 1939: Park Road Pool, Hornsey

'Leave her alone, Vic, fer Gawd's sake. You make her blub again and we'll all get chucked out. Lifeguard's got his eye on us.' Christopher Wild jerked his head towards a tanned, brawny fellow, garbed in swimming trunks. From his vantage point, seated at the top of an A-frame ladder, the lifeguard had a clear view over the lido and at present had his stern expression fixed on them.

Vic shrugged off the warning, intent on swaggering over to the group of schoolgirls to continue teasing them. Christopher grabbed his pal's arm and yanked him back. The youngest girl was crying, and being comforted by her bathing-costumed friends. At intervals the group was throwing dirty looks at the party of youths.

'Only having a bit of a lark with her, bleedin' cry baby she is.'

'Ain't a lark if she's hurt, is it?' Christopher pointed out and shoved Vic Wilson down onto the grass next to some of their pals. He'd just prevented him again trying to creep up behind Grace Coleman to nudge her into the deep end of the pool. The first time he'd done it Vic had given the lame excuse that he was teaching her to swim. Christopher thought Vic a good pal on the whole, but knew he could be spiteful, and stupid too.

Christopher sat down next to Vic. Most of the members of their little gang were lying back, basking in the July sun's warmth. Christopher remained seated on the parched grass with his arms clasped around his raised knees. He subtly watched the group of girls and, in particular, Grace who was knuckling her bloodshot eyes and pushing rats' tails of drenched hair back from her forehead. She'd managed to hang onto the side of the pool after Vic had given her a hefty bump, sending her off balance and into the water. Although she'd disappeared beneath the surface, her friends had hauled her out almost immediately.

Grace Coleman was a skinny little thing with long fair hair. She was usually quite loud and confident and was popular too. In other respects, she was quite sporty, and could outrun all the boys in kiss chase. But she couldn't swim.

The Colemans lived in the next street to Christopher in Islington and their families knew each other well. For a reason he couldn't fathom, he'd always quite liked her. At ten years old she was two years younger than he was, and in Christopher's opinion Vic Wilson was a prat for tormenting her so he could show off.

Noticing the direction of his friend's gaze Vic said, 'Dunno why she comes here if she don't like getting wet.'

'She don't mind getting wet, it's drowning she ain't keen on.'

'I'm getting a drink.' Bill Bright, one of Christopher's

2

other friends, got up and strolled off in his swimming trunks in the direction of the cafeteria.

'Get us one 'n' all,' Vic called after him.

'Give us the money then,' Bill sent back over a shoulder.

'Give it yer when you get back.' Vic grinned cheekily.

Bill showed him two fingers and put on a swagger as he came level with the group of girls.

Christopher noticed that Grace was about to be left on her own again. Now she'd quietened down, her friends were jumping back into the pool, intent on enjoying themselves. He levered himself up and went over to sit down on the grass beside her.

'You alright?'

She nodded and sniffed. Her red-rimmed eyes narrowed on Vic, who was watching them. 'If he tries to push me in again I'm gonna tell on him. Me dad'll give him such a hiding.'

'He's just an idiot. Don't mind him.' Christopher thought it was unlikely that old man Coleman would stir himself enough to do any such thing. When Wilf Coleman wasn't working in a meat factory he spent his time slouched in the betting shop or in the pub.

'You're a good swimmer,' Grace said enviously. 'I was watching you earlier diving off the board.'

'Got taught when I was little by me dad.'

'Bet he didn't push you in. My dad did. When we went on holiday to Clacton he tried teaching me to swim like Vic just did. He got annoyed and pushed me off the edge of the pool 'cos I wouldn't get in. Was only the shallow end though,' she added in mitigation.

'S'pose me dad might have done that to me.' Christopher narrowed his eyes at her. 'You ought to learn, y'know, 'cos if you don't you'll get teased every time you come here with yer friends. Can't just hang about on the side, can you?' He nodded at the girls frolicking in the pool. 'None of them offered to hold your chin so's you can do a few strokes to and fro?'

She nodded. 'Yeah, they have. I just don't like it though. Don't like feeling the water stinging me nose and me eyes.'

'Gotta hold yer breath and keep yer eyes shut,' he explained. 'Soon as yer head's up and out, blink and take a big breath.'

''S'alright fer you to say.'

'I'll show you if you like.'

'He's sent you over to try and push me in, hasn't he!' Grace glared at Christopher and shuffled away on her skinny posterior.

'Please yourself . . .' Christopher sighed and got up.

A moment later Grace was at his side, her small hands wringing water from her long hair. 'You could show me another time . . . when they're not about . . . they'll just laugh.' Her eyes slid sideways towards the watching youths.

'Might not be coming again for a while.' Christopher grimaced and stepped away.

'Alright . . . show me . . .' Grace caught at his hand to stop him leaving. 'But round the other side, away from them.'

Christopher disentangled his fingers from hers and ambled around the perimeter of the pool with Grace traipsing in his wake. He stopped by an area of water that wasn't quite as populated.

Grace nervously assessed the rocking blue waves. 'How deep is it?'

'Come to about the top of your head. Don't worry, I'll hold you up, won't let go . . . honest. Then you've just got to do a bit of doggie paddle towards the shallow end and you'll be able to stand up . . . or carry on if you like.'

Grace took a deep breath, trudging forward.

'Ready?' he said, standing by her side at the edge of the pool.

He got no reply. He cast a look down on her wet head. 'Once you've done it, nobody's gonna tease you no more.'

She nodded her agreement. She could see her friends larking about. They hadn't even noticed she'd moved away and was about to make a momentous effort.

'Ready?' Christopher asked again.

She nodded, sucked in a shaky breath and in the split second he moved she grabbed at one of his hands, launching herself forward with him.

CHAPTER ONE

February 1952

'Touch any of them tools again and it'll be the last thing you ever do, you thievin' toerag.'

Christopher Wild stuck a threatening finger close to the man's bristly chin, his face contorted into a savage mask. A moment ago he'd been knocking down a partition wall inside a derelict property when, from the corner of an eye, he'd seen a suspicious movement through a gaping hole in brickwork where a window frame had once been.

'Wasn't stealin', was I now,' the fellow muttered in his guttural Irish accent. 'Was just gonna borrer the pick for a little while, that's all it was . . .' He propped the pick back against the front wall of the house, next to a fourteen-pound hammer, then stuffed his hands into his donkey-jacket pockets. He was a large individual with wildly unkempt black hair and a ruddy complexion.

'Yeah, 'course . . . just gonna borrow it, weren't yer . . .' Christopher mimicked sarcastically. He grabbed several implements by their battered wooden handles and sent them hurtling, one after the other, along the hallway of the house where they thudded against bare boards. 'Piss off and borrow stuff off yer mates.' Christopher flicked his head at the contingent of navvies working a distance away along the street. Some of them had heard what was going on and had come out of the tenement to watch. A couple started to approach.

The Irishman spread calloused hands, gesturing for a truce as he retreated. Despite his attempt at nonchalance his small eyes were shifting to and fro. Christopher knew if the navvy had managed to filch the pick, Wild Brothers Builders would never have seen it again . . . not without a fight anyhow. And they'd had one of those earlier in the week when a couple of shovels went missing. The week before that there had been an almighty bust-up when his colleague, Bill, got a tooth smashed in a fight. A new high-reach ladder had disappeared from where it had been tied on the top of one of their vans. Of course, the pikeys had denied all knowledge of any of it, they always did, but now Christopher had caught one of them red-handed he knew that every accusation, every punch landed, had been well deserved.

'What's up?'

'Nuthin' I can't handle,' Christopher mumbled to a middle-aged man who'd sprinted up to him, looking agitated.

Stephen Wild, Christopher's father, had been sitting in one of the vehicles scribbling with a pencil in his notebook when he'd noticed a confrontation between his son and one of Declan O'Connor's crew. He'd stuck the pencil behind his ear, dropped the ledger, and sprung immediately from the Bedford van to rush over. He was well aware that things could turn very nasty at any time.

7

The Irishman started to amble away and Christopher put a hand on his father's shoulder and steered him over the threshold of the door-less house. He didn't want another fight erupting so soon after the last. And thankfully they hadn't lost any more equipment.

Christopher worked for his uncle's construction firm as a foreman when his father wasn't about to take charge. Although it was called Wild Brothers, his father was more or less just another employee and his uncle Rob was the guvnor. Rob was certainly the one with the money and the business nous. Stephen Wild was the brawn, or he had been in his younger years when he'd had better health and vigour. Now it was Christopher's turn to take on the brunt of the donkeywork, and to chivvy the lads into action so contracts were finished on time.

Since tempers had started running high due to the Irish crew muscling in on their territory Wild Brothers' few employees seemed to be working less and moaning more. Stephen took a glance along the street and noticed that their rivals were carrying on a heated discussion, with much gesticulating.

Alert to trouble brewing, Christopher's colleagues started emerging from the bowels of the derelict tenement they'd been demolishing in Whadcoat Street. The men were carrying the tools they'd been using. Hammers and jemmies were swinging in fists as they approached to stand about their boss in a show of solidarity.

'Nuthin' goin' on here. Get back about yer work,' Christopher told them. They remained where they were, covered in brick dust, looking belligerent and ready to get stuck in.

'They on the thieve again?' Vic Wilson demanded indignantly, glaring along the street.

'They're having a go at it. Keep stuff inside the house, or locked in the vans.'

'Fuckin' Micks,' Bill Bright said, flattening his lips against the gap in his teeth. 'Should've put me 'ammer over that pikey's crust earlier in the week.'

'Yeah . . . then we'll all be out of work, and sitting in the nick, won't we,' Christopher stated dryly. 'Just what they want, ain't it? Us doing something stupid so they can have the work all to themselves.'

'We let 'em push us around then, do we?' Ted Potts suggested sarcastically.

'Get back to work,' Christopher snapped impatiently.

He watched his crew peel off one by one and go back inside the property. He waited until banging and crashing resumed before he turned to his father.

'Ted's got a point,' Stephen Wild muttered, squinting at the group of labourers along the road. 'Declan O'Connor'll be laughing his bollocks off alright if we let 'em keep getting away with it.'

Declan was the Paddies' guvnor and would turn up about once a day to check on his crew and taunt Wild Brothers' boys with a few yelled insults.

Most of the navvies had gone about their business. But a couple were still leaning on shovels, chin-wagging, and throwing dirty looks their way.

'A real bust-up's brewing and it'd be as well to get this out of the way now rather than later when O'Connor turns up.' Stevie jutted his chin belligerently.

Christopher turned a jaundiced eye on his father. He was a reasonably fit man for his forty-five years, but in no shape to be taking on burly Irish navvies in a fistfight . . . or worse. If things kicked off it might not just be punches doing damage. Bill's threat to use a hammer

9

had been in retaliation to O'Connor swinging a shovel at his head two weeks ago. Luckily it had missed or he wouldn't have ended up with just a broken tooth and bruises. But things were getting serious. The fact that O'Connor's gang took a dinner break in the pub didn't help. When they ambled back in the afternoon a couple of them were always two parts pissed and up for a brawl – even amongst themselves.

Christopher was aware his uncle Robert had fingers in many other pies and might not be too bothered about the winding-up of his building concern. But if the pikeys took over in the street, the rest of them would suffer. A few other piddling contracts might come their way and keep him and his dad employed, but Vic, Bill and Ted would have to go.

'Just need to keep calm,' Christopher said. He quirked a rueful smile. 'Keep calm and carry on . . .' He quoted a wartime motto.

'They'd better stay on home ground then. The boys are getting to the end of their tethers. And so am I . . .' Stephen came to an abrupt halt, squinting at a house some distance away. Despite demolition work having started at one end of the long road, some families still lived in houses in Whadcoat Street.

It was February and bitterly cold but an elderly woman had just shoved up her sash window and stuck her head out to bawl something at them.

'Aunt Matilda's after you by the looks of things,' Christopher told his father as he noticed his great-aunt waving to gain their attention. 'You go and see what she wants; I'll make sure everything's under control here.'

Christopher was glad when his father immediately went loping off along the road. He didn't want him getting

10

geed up by the lads into confronting the pikeys. Christopher watched him come to a halt and angle his face up towards Matilda.

When his father reappeared Christopher was attacking the splintered remains of a doorframe with a hammer. Something about his father's shocked expression made him drop the tool to the ground.

'King's dead.'

'Eh?'

'Matilda just said it come over on the Home Service. King George has died.'

'Eh? What's that?'

Vic Wilson had appeared, wiping his grimy face with a handkerchief.

'Me aunt's just told us that the king's died.'

Bill and Ted trooped into the front room of the house.

'What's that?' Bill asked, frowning.

'King George has died . . .' Stephen repeated croakily, blinking rapidly. He looked close to tears.

Into the stunned silence came Vic Wilson's voice. 'Weren't unexpected I suppose.' He grimaced. 'Smoked like a chimney, didn't he?'

'Poor sod might not've needed 'em so much if his brother'd done his duty, 'stead of running off with that bloody American woman,' Stephen barked angrily. 'He weren't trained up for the job, was he.' He gestured with a hand as he sank down to his haunches then collapsed to sit on the bare boards. 'Just got chucked in at the deep end by that selfish git. Edward was the one brought up for it from when he was a kid and got taught all the right stuff. George just had to pick it up as he went along.' Stephen came to a sudden halt, his face florid from his impassioned outburst. His head dropped forward

11

and his fingers sank into his hair. He wasn't a royalist by any means but, like most Londoners, Stephen Wild had nothing but praise and respect for King George and Queen Elizabeth. They'd braved the dangers of the Luftwaffe bombings on the city along with everybody else instead of scurrying off to the comfort and protection of a mansion in the countryside.

Christopher perched on an upturned crate and shook his head. He agreed wholeheartedly with what his father had said. 'Yeah, good bloke he was. Did us proud during the war, considering he weren't really cut out fer the job. Queen Elizabeth too. She was a diamond.'

'He was only about ten years older'n me.' Stephen produced a packet of Weights and immediately took one out then threw the packet for Christopher to catch it.

'Makes yer think, don't it. Me dad's comin' up to sixty-five . . .' Vic sat on the floor next to Stephen and got out his own cigarettes.

Bill squatted down too and fished in Vic's packet of Weights when it was offered, then lobbed it towards Ted.

As a melancholy silence descended on the room Christopher drew smoke deep into his lungs then rested his head in his cupped hands.

'Can't believe it, y'know . . .' The woman's voice had come from the doorway and jerked them all to attention. 'He was only fifty-six. Weren't an old man at all, was he?'

'Were a sick man though, Aunt Tilly, weren't he,' Christopher said. 'S'pose we all knew fer a while it might be coming.' He stood up. 'Any more news come over on the wireless? Was it a heart attack took him in the end?'

Matilda came gingerly further into the debris-strewn property. 'Don't know . . . not said.' She shook her grey head, her wrinkled complexion creasing in a frown. She was seventy-one years old yet, considering what she'd been through in her life, in robust condition. 'BBC has cancelled all the programmes. Just gonna be sad music and news broadcasts. Bound to come out later today what caused it.'

'Won't get nuthin' done now. Everything'll be closing up out o' respect.' Billy nodded sombrely.

'Right 'n' all!' Stephen said forcefully, shoving himself to his feet. 'Ain't a man anywhere deservin' of more respect than him.'

'We off home then?' Ted asked optimistically.

'Yeah, go on, get going,' Stephen said. There was plenty of work left to do, and a good few hours in which to do it, but nobody had the heart now to get stuck in.

'Bet them Irish bastards don't show a bit o' respect and knock off early,' Vic said. He unhooked his jacket from the back of the door and shrugged it on over his overalls.

'Most Paddies can't stand the English at the best of times,' Bill interjected sourly. 'Probably be doin' a jig, they will.'

'Can't tar 'em all with the same brush.' Matilda wagged a finger. 'The Irish couple wot's just moved in along the road don't seem bad people. Spoke to the woman the other day when she was coming out of Smithie's shop and she was as polite as yer like. Introduced herself straight off. Noreen Murphy's her name and she said her husband's called Kieran.'

'Well, I don't reckon they should have camped in that dump in the first place,' Vic mumbled, slightly chastened. 'They've got a couple of young kids with 'em. It ain't right, livin' like that.'

'Couple of sweet little girls they are 'n' all,' Matilda remarked. 'But yer can't always pick 'n' choose when it comes to putting a roof over yer family's head.'

'As far as I'm concerned they can stop in the road as long as they like if they ain't causing trouble.' Chris chipped in his opinion.

'Well, I'm getting off home now,' Vic announced, sounding sulky.

'Winston Churchill's gonna make a broadcast to the nation tomorrow about King George.' Matilda's tone was solemn once more. 'Eight o'clock on the Home Service, just so's you know when to tune in.'

CHAPTER TWO

'Keep moving . . . keep moving . . . please . . .'

The crowd obediently shuffled away from the gates of Buckingham Palace to congregate instead on the nearby pavement. Nobody seemed to want to leave although it was bitterly cold and raining. In fact, as news had spread, people who'd been travelling home from their offices in the City had diverted to St James's, swelling the multitude mourning the death of the king.

People were huddling together, turning up collars and pulling hats firmly down over their ears. But they stayed where they were, staring solemnly through the gloom at the royal palace where the Union Jack was limply fluttering at half-mast. Above the politely insistent voices of the policemen could be heard the sound of men and women weeping.

'Come on now, over the road, please. Move away from the gates, madam . . .'

Matilda knuckled burning tears from her eyes and obeyed the constable's request. He looked to her to be

15

no more than a boy, but he had a nice face, and had kindly patted her shoulder on noticing her distress.

Having got a foothold on the packed kerb Matilda tried to wedge her stout body into a tight space. A woman in a luxurious fur coat unintentionally jostled her, knocking her back into the road. Matilda's arthritic joint gave her a jolt and she gasped aloud.

'So sorry, my dear,' the woman murmured in a cut-glass accent.

Matilda nodded acceptance of the apology, rubbing her knee.

'We're going to miss him terribly,' the woman added and shuffled sideways to make a space for Matilda next to her on the pavement.

Matilda settled beside her, aware of a floral scent wafting from the little lacy hanky the lady had held to her nose. 'Right 'n' all we are,' Matilda gruffly returned. 'His eldest gel's got big shoes to fill . . .' She broke off to watch as a sleek limousine drew up by the gates and was allowed through. She'd been outside the palace since five o'clock that afternoon, and during that time had seen many visitors arrive. A bobby on duty had explained to someone – and the information had rippled through the throng – that foreign diplomats were arriving to sign a book of condolences.

'King and queen helped get us through the war, didn't they?' Matilda carried on in her rough tone. 'Could've run and hid somewhere safe but they didn't.'

The fur-coated woman nodded her elegantly coiffed head and on impulse shared the protection of her umbrella with Matilda. 'Wonderful, steadfast people,' she agreed and again wiped her nose. 'She's in Kenya, you know . . .' At Matilda's quizzical look the lady

16

explained. 'Young Elizabeth . . . she's at the Royal Hunting Lodge in Kenya. But I've no doubt, she'll be flying straight home. What dreadfully sad tidings for her and Margaret.'

''S'pect she would have stayed with her dad had she known how grave it all were,' Matilda said. 'Can't change that now. Still, he got a peaceful end, so I heard on the wireless. That's a blessing and no more'n he deserved.'

'Amen to that,' the woman said and closed her eyes.

'Matilda Keiver?'

Matilda heard her name faintly called and pivoted about in surprise. Having looked this way and that she suddenly noticed a woman's face and neck stretching to gaze over a sea of hats. Matilda bobbed her head to and fro to try and guess the identity of the woman now waving at her. She squinted and then her lips parted in an astonished smile. 'Friend of mine's over there. Better go and say hello,' she told the well-to-do lady. 'Toodle-oo . . .' Her companion's sable sleeve got a pat before she departed. A moment later she was edging her way through the throng.

'Shirley Coleman!' Matilda exclaimed when she was standing next to the woman. 'Not seen you since . . .' Her eyes veered heavenwards as she calculated the years. 'Must've been 1941 when I last clapped eyes on you.'

'September 1941 I moved out of Crouch End,' Shirley confirmed. ''Course the kids had gone a bit earlier to Surrey. Got evacuated there, didn't they.'

'That's it, I *do* remember,' Matilda said. 'How've you been keeping?'

'So-so,' Shirley returned, mouth drooping down at the corners. 'Sad business about the king, isn't it?'

Matilda nodded sadly. 'Was only gonna come and stay

for a little while, but now I'm here . . .' She glanced about. 'Looks like nobody else wants to go home neither. S'pose it's the only way people like us can show how grateful we were fer what he did, and the queen 'n' all. Just saying to a lady over there . . .' Matilda jerked her head to the left. 'Could've hid during the Battle of Britain, couldn't they, but braved it out like the rest of us.'

'Yeah,' Shirley agreed. 'Got to show appreciation and respect.' She suddenly looked around. 'Grace is here somewhere. She came with one of her workmates but I think her friend's gone to catch the tube home.'

'You lot back living in London then, Shirley?' Shirley and her family had never been neighbours of Tilly's in Whadcoat Street but she'd got to know the family quite well.

'Grace and me are back. My son Paul is married and living Dorset way with his family. We've been back a year now. Wilf passed away, you wouldn't have known that.'

Matilda placed a woolly-gloved hand on her friend's shoulder. 'Sorry to hear that, Shirley.'

'Came back from Japan a very poorly soul, he did.' Shirley grimaced. 'Died in 1949, and after he'd been laid to rest, Grace and me carried on in Surrey for a while but then decided to come back to London. She's a typist, you know. Got a good job in an office in the City.'

'Sorry about Wilf,' Matilda repeated in a murmur. 'So whereabouts in London are you living?'

'Tottenham. Just off White Hart Lane. Close to where I grew up. Don't think you ever knew my mum, Ada Jackson, did you, Til? She's still about and not in bad health, all things considered.'

Matilda grinned. 'Never met her, Shirley. But I know that area well. My Alice ain't far from there. She lives

18

Wood Green way on the big council estate. Got a lovely little place, she has.'

'Bet you've got grandkids too, haven't you, Til?'

'Big family we are . . . grandkids, great-grandkids . . .' Tilly chuckled proudly. 'How about you, Shirley? Your Grace married, is she?'

Matilda knew that Shirley's children were a lot younger than her own because Shirley was more the age of her daughter Alice. But despite the age gap, Tilly had become quite friendly with Shirley because her great-nephew, Christopher, had grown up with the Coleman children.

Christopher had spent a good deal of his childhood being looked after by Matilda while his father was at work so his great-aunt had been acquainted with his friends, and some of their parents.

'Grace isn't married, but got grandkids all right. Paul's got three boys. But don't see a lot of them being as they're so far away. Grace . . .' She grimaced. 'Grace was engaged, but he was a wrong'un.' She shook her head, her expression turning ferocious. 'Did the dirty on her and went off with a widow who was nearly old enough to be his mother . . . oh, shhh . . . here she is. She doesn't like me talking about it,' Shirley whispered. She beckoned her daughter closer.

Matilda smiled at the pretty young woman who'd squashed a path through the crowd.

'You remember Mrs Keiver, don't you, Grace?'

Grace frowned and bit her lip, not wanting to appear rude.

'You know, young Christopher Wild's great-auntie . . . lived down Campbell Road . . . or Whadcoat Street as it turned into some years ago as I recall.'

A sweet smile parted Grace's lips. 'Oh yes, of course

19

I remember you . . .' She did remember too. Nobody who had visited Campbell Road, or The Bunk as it had been nicknamed thanks to its proliferation of doss houses, was ever likely to forget it. Neither would Grace ever forget the couple of times her friend Christopher had taken her on visit to his auntie, despite the fact it had been over a decade ago.

Her parents had constantly warned her to give Campbell Road, and the people who lived there, a wide berth. But when she'd found out from Christopher where his great-aunt lived she had, with the inquisitiveness of youth, begged him to take her there. She'd been astounded to discover one of Christopher's relatives lived in a dirty hovel. Christopher and his father had lived close to Grace's family and, while it certainly wasn't luxurious in Crouch End, their terraced homes were adequate in most respects. Grace recalled she had been about ten or eleven at the time of her secret visits to The Bunk, but even at that tender age she'd been thrillingly shocked that such a slum existed and it had left an indelible mark on her memory.

'Well . . . nice to see you both, but I suppose I should be making tracks.' Matilda glanced about. 'Bleedin' cold night, ain't it. I'm gonna be off and catch the bus back.'

'We'll walk with you to the bus stop.' Shirley and Grace settled into step beside her. They walked in silence for a short while, huddled in their coats, shoulders hunched up to their ears, hats pulled low, to protect against the drizzle.

The two Coleman women settled into a slower pace as they noticed Matilda walking with a slight limp.

'Got arthritis bad in one side,' Matilda brusquely explained. 'Damp don't help.'

'Wilf suffered with arthritis something chronic in the

winter,' Shirley remarked. 'Young man too he were when he first got afflicted.'

'Had a bad accident a long while ago,' Matilda offered up. 'Never been right since.'

'Oh . . . ?' Shirley said curiously.

'Don't talk about it,' Matilda answered bluntly.

'So where you living now then, Tilly? Did Reg come back from the war? I remember he went off to fight early on.'

Tilly shook her head. 'Died in 1943. Should never have gone. Told him he were too old. Lied about his age, didn't he, to get hisself enlisted.'

'Brave man . . .'

'Stupid man.' Tilly begged to differ, but with a soft smile twisting her lips.

'Two husbands you lost to the Germans then,' Shirley said sympathetically. She knew that Jack Keiver, Matilda's first husband, had been killed fighting on the Somme. She knew too that Matilda and Reg Donovan, although living as man and wife, hadn't taken a trip to the Town Hall to say their vows.

'Yeah,' Matilda confirmed with a wry grimace. 'Long, long while since I lost my Jack, God bless him.'

'So where you livin' then?'

'Same place,' Matilda replied a touch brusquely. She tended to be defensive when asked her address. People always followed that first question with another that began why . . . ? while gawping at her as though she'd lost her marbles.

Grace inclined forward to peer past her mother at Matilda. 'You're still in Campbell Road . . . I mean Whadcoat Street, Mrs Keiver?' Her voice was pitched high in surprise.

'Yeah . . . but not for long,' Matilda replied with a sour smile. 'Slum clearance has started up one end.' She dug her hands further into her pockets. 'So gonna be re-housed at some time. Don't know where.' She slanted a look sideways at her companions. 'You'd be surprised, there's still a good few people living there in the street. Remember the Whittons and the Lovats and old Beattie Evans? Some of them that are still alive are still about.' She gave an emphatic nod. 'Still got enough friends and neighbours left around me.'

'Bleedin' 'ell . . .' Shirley breathed, her astonishment causing her to revert to language she hadn't used in a long while. Having lived in Surrey, Shirley liked to think she'd travelled up in the world. 'Never would have guessed it. Thought you'd all be long gone from there. You must've lived there a time, Til.'

'Nearly all me life . . . over seventy years, bar a few years here and there, before I turned twenty, when me parents moved about London a bit. But we always come back to Campbell Road . . . usually 'cos it was the only place we could afford to kip, it's true.' She sighed. 'But had some good times in amongst the bad. Me 'n' Jack settled there just after we was married. Had all me kids there, with old Lou Perkins' help.' She broke off to grin. 'She's still about Islington somewhere, too. I intended to be carted off from The Bunk in me pine box but seems like the Council's got other ideas for me.'

Grace exchanged a furtive look with her mother.

'So how is Christopher doing, Mrs Keiver?' she blurted. She was a sensitive young woman, not one to deliberately cause offence to another, and she knew Matilda had spotted the glance, clearly questioning her sanity.

'Yeah . . . he's doing alright. Works in his dad's

22

building firm as a foreman. In fact their firm, Wild Brothers it's called,' she informed them proudly, 'is doing the demolition work that's started at the top end of Whadcoat Street. *Whadcoat Street,*' she repeated derisively. 'Daft name. It'll always be Campbell Road to me.'

Matilda halted as they reached the bus stop. 'Well, nice to see you both after all this time.'

'We'll keep in touch,' Shirley said quickly. 'Would you mind if I sort of popped by?' She had a morbid curiosity to see whether Matilda's hovel was better or worse than the one she remembered.

'Come any time. Sometimes go out for a little drink round the Duke, but that's it.' Matilda smiled. 'You'll be bound to catch me in.'

CHAPTER THREE

'You look like Rudolph the Red-Nosed Reindeer.' Matilda tapped Kathleen Murphy's cold nose playfully with a finger.

'Hello, Mrs Keiver.' Noreen Murphy gave Matilda a smile. 'It's bitter today, isn't it?' She pulled her daughter's hat down further over her ears then adjusted the collar of Kathleen's coat in an attempt to shield her cheeks from the sharp breeze.

'About time we had a bit more sunshine to warm us up now it's April,' Matilda said, clapping together her gloved palms. She'd been shopping for vegetables in the market when she'd spied Noreen pushing a pram and had ambled over to talk to her. Asleep inside the pram, swaddled to the chin with a woollen shawl, was baby Rosie. Little Kathleen was sitting on top of the coverlet, holding onto the handle to keep her balance, her little legs, bare above her socks, mottled purple with cold.

'You off home now?' Matilda asked. She'd noticed that a bag containing a very few potatoes was pegged on the pram handle, but Noreen seemed to be heading back in the direction of The Bunk.

Noreen nodded.

'I'll walk with you. I'm done here too.' Matilda fell in step with her neighbour. 'Has your husband had any luck finding a job?' Matilda had bumped into Noreen earlier in the week and discovered that Kieran Murphy was scratching around for work. Noreen had told her that since they'd turned up in The Bunk he'd only managed to pick up a bit of poorly paid casual labouring but wanted something permanent.

'He's out looking now,' Noreen sighed. She slanted a quick look at Matilda. 'Don't think I'm being cheeky, will you now, Mrs Keiver, but I remember you said your nephews were working on the demolition in the road, and I was wondering whether they might need an extra hand? Kieran's a good hard worker.' She praised her husband.

'Not sure if they do, luv, but it's always worth havin' a word. Tell Kieran to ask for Stephen or Christopher, they're the foremen in charge.' In fact Matilda knew her nephew, Robert, who owned the firm, considered Wild Brothers to be already overstaffed. She'd heard him grumbling about his lack of profits and too many wage packets to be found at the end of the week. 'How about the Irish gang working along there? Has your Kieran asked them for a shift or two?'

'He thinks they're up to no good, and I do too,' Noreen said quietly, wiping little Kathleen's runny nose with a hanky. 'We've heard them talking . . . troublemaking . . .' She broke off to rub at her daughter's chapped knees as Kathleen whimpered she was feeling cold.

'I reckon it's wise to give 'em a wide berth 'n' all,'

Matilda agreed with a nod. 'But being sensible don't help put grub on the table, do it?'

Noreen grimaced wryly at that.

'You thought of getting yourself a little job of some sort?' Matilda asked kindly. She guessed Noreen Murphy was about Christopher's age: mid-twenties. She was an attractive young woman with the same long black tresses and large grey eyes as her eldest daughter. But she made no effort with her looks. Her hair was simply scraped back into a straggly bun and her pretty features were pale and permanently set in an expression of exhaustion. Matilda guessed Kieran was probably the same age as his wife yet he looked equally haggard and a decade older.

'I think about a job a lot, but that's all I do.' Noreen gave Matilda a skewed smile. 'Kieran's not keen on me finding work. He thinks it's his place to provide for us.'

'Yeah, well, that's all fine and noble but it's an attitude that don't feed and clothe kids. Sometimes it takes the two of yers pullin' in a wage to make a decent life. If he ain't having any luck finding work, perhaps you might do a bit better.'

'I've said the same thing to him, and we always end up having a row about it, Mrs Keiver.'

'Call me Matilda, we're neighbours after all, and if you change yer mind I know of a woman down Tufnell Park way who's looking fer a cleanin' lady. I know she's alright 'cos I used to do a bit of charring for her mum, in me time.'

The baby coughed and mewed plaintively and Matilda leaned forward to look in the pram. 'Want to get that little 'un along to the doctor, don't you . . .'

'She's fine . . . she teeths with a bit of bronchitis, that's all it is,' Noreen said quickly. 'I have linctus at home.'

They turned into Whadcoat Street and ambled along in amiable quiet. As they drew close to the shop Matilda said, 'Better go 'n' pay something off me tab at Smithie's. Miserable old git'll be after me otherwise. You take care of yerselves . . .' Having ruffled Kathleeen's hair Matilda set off across the road.

'Ain't you had enough of hanging around in this stinking hole all week?'

'You don't have to hang about here if you don't want to.' Christopher ignored his friend's scowl and blew into his cupped palms to warm them. Despite the approach of spring a light sleet was descending and treacherously coating the pavement so he trod carefully in his smart leather shoes and stuffed his hands into his pockets to protect them from an icy breeze. He came to a halt in front of his aunt's dilapidated house. Once the door had been painted bottle green but now only a few flakes of colour clung to the splintery wood. Christopher turned to Ted Potts. He'd tried to shake him off earlier so he could visit his aunt on his own. 'Why don't you go and knock Vic up.' He jerked his head, hoping to hurry Ted on his way. 'I'll meet you both at the dog track at about seven o'clock.'

'Nah . . . 's'alright.' Ted gave a martyred sigh. 'I'm here now, ain't I. I'll stick around with you.' He didn't relish going into this fleapit to see Christopher's great-aunt, yet neither did he want to go to Vic's home. If Vic's wife were about he'd get an ear-bashing for luring Vic off out. Deirdre kept tabs on Vic and, considering that they'd only been married two years, and Vic had already been caught out with another woman, it wasn't surprising.

'Go on . . .' Christopher twitched his head again. But his friend seemed content to slouch against the doorjamb and fiddle with a penknife. Once he had it open he started idly cleaning his nails. Christopher scowled and raised a hand to hammer on the door. A window above was shoved up and he stepped back to grin at the wrinkled face, edged by two plaited grey buns, peering out.

'That you, Chris? Come on up. Door's open,' Matilda called down. 'See you've brought yer mate with yer.'

'Alright up there, Mrs K?' Ted Potts called in greeting, a wonky fag wagging between his lips. 'Brass monkeys out here, it is.'

'Got the kettle on,' Matilda informed them before ramming home the sash in its frame.

The two young men proceeded into a dingy damp hallway and up some perilously rickety stairs. Very few of the spindles remained and the handrail shuddered when touched. On the first-floor landing a door stood open and Christopher and Ted filed into Matilda's home.

It never failed to amaze Ted why anyone would choose to continue living here now that the Council was clearing the street and re-housing people elsewhere. But Christopher had told him that his aunt would hang on in her first-floor room till she was forced out. Chris had said in an odd way he understood Matilda's hankering to grip onto her past.

At present Matilda was the only person occupying this particular tenement house and Christopher had urged her to spread out a bit and make use of a couple of the other rooms too. The rent would be the same for one room or all nine of them. Mr Keane, the landlord, was glad to get paid anything at all. Over half of the properties in the street were now empty and producing no income for their owners. The worst examples had been abandoned completely by the freeholders.

But Matilda's view was that it was easier, in the winter months, for a person living alone to keep cosy in a small space. So she lived, slept, ate in a single first-floor front room, much as she had for a good part of her life. Fortunately, in a road of derelict houses she'd found one that was slightly better than the rest. Most had never been connected to electricity but she'd managed to get a property where she could plug in her precious wireless that had been a Christmas gift from her nephew, Rob.

'Kettle's just boiled,' Matilda said. 'Who's fer tea?'

There was no response to her offer because both her nephew and his friend were staring at the little girl sitting on the bed, chewing on a biscuit. The child gave them both a shy smile then ducked her face behind a curtain of long ebony hair.

Matilda grunted a laugh. 'Say hello to Kathleen, you two. I'm keepin' an eye on her for Noreen while she's off out doing a bit of cleaning to earn herself a couple o' bob.'

'I thought the Murphys had two little 'uns,' Chris said, recovering from the surprise of seeing his aunt doing a spot of babysitting.

'Noreen's taken Rosie with her in the pram. She's not walking yet and still sleeps a lot, so ain't a problem. But this little one gets fed up waiting fer her mum to finish work, don't yer, Kathleen?'

Kathleen nodded her small head. 'You'd sooner come and sit with yer Auntie Matilda, wouldn't yer? Like me biscuits, don't yer . . .' She gave the child an affectionate grin. 'Anyhow I know your daddy's home now 'cos I saw him walking up the street out the window. So do you want to go home or wait for Mummy to fetch you?'

Kathleen slanted a peek at Ted. 'Home . . .' she whispered.

Chris burst out laughing. 'That's your ugly mug scared her off. Told you to go off to Vince's, didn't I . . .'

'Take her back home fer us, Chris, would you, and I'll make the tea.'

'Me aunt saw you were back so asked me to drop Kathleen off home.' Chris had been holding the little girl's hand, but as Kieran Murphy cautiously opened the door to him, he offered it to her father to take.

Kieran Murphy continued staring at him, looking shocked. 'Mrs Keiver's been minding Kathleen?'

'Yeah . . . while Noreen's at work, didn't you know?' Chris could see the fellow's freckled cheeks reddening in embarrassment or anger.

'Please tell your aunt thank you very much,' Kieran returned stiffly, drawing his daughter to his side. He was about to shut the door but quickly stepped forward before Chris had gone too far. 'You work for Wild Brothers, don't you. I've seen you driving one of their vans.'

Chris retraced his steps. 'Yeah, I'm Chris Wild.'

'Is there any work going at all?'

Chris stuffed his hands in his pockets. He'd had a feeling he was soon going to have this question fired at him by Kieran Murphy. He'd seen the fellow watching them working, trying to pluck up the courage to come over and ask for a job. And now he was going to have to disappoint him.

'Sorry,' he grimaced ruefully. 'If me guvnor had his way he'd put someone off.'

Kieran gave a crisp nod and retreated back inside, mumbling his thanks.

'That tea brewed?' Christopher, now back at Matilda's, pulled out a chair, parking himself at the battered planked table.

'Not fer me, thanks, Mrs K,' Ted said quickly, having noted the grimy chips on some cups in an enamel bowl. He was seated on a chair that was losing its stuffing and was glad Chris had quickly returned from taking the kid home because he'd run out of small talk with Matilda. He gazed about at old mismatched furniture that he knew his parents would have been embarrassed to put out for the dustmen to cart off. The iron bedstead shoved in the corner was strewn with tatty clothes and other odds and ends. A large oval mirror in a gilt frame hung on the wall, above the hob grate where the kettle was puffing steam, and was reflecting Ted's expression of distaste back at him.

'So how you lads doing up the other end?' Matilda asked cheerily.

The last time she'd entered the demolition zone where the lads were working had been when she'd felt compelled to join her nephews in commiserating about the king's death.

She set two cups and saucers on the table and gave the teapot a swirl to mix the leaves then tested the brew by pouring a few drops. It looked strong enough so she filled the cups and dripped milk from a half-empty bottle into them before handing one to Christopher.

'Had another fight with the Paddies the other day,' Ted conversationally told Matilda, ignoring Christopher's quelling look. He took a peer in the biscuit box Matilda had stuck under his nose and selected a digestive. 'Pikeys got a right good kicking, Mrs K . . .' He blushed. 'No offence, o' course . . .' He'd just remembered that Matilda's second husband, Reg Donovan, had been a didicoi. And she also seemed fond of the Murphy family.

'My Reg knew what he was,' Matilda said with a fond smile, settling down at the table opposite her nephew. 'You lot better make sure you keep yer wits about you if there's punches getting thrown. Make sure yer dad keeps out of it,' Matilda told Christopher, wagging a finger close to his face. 'Stevie's getting on a bit and shouldn't be getting into scraps with younger men.'

'Don't you let me dad hear you say that, 'cos he still reckons he's a bit of an 'andful, y'know.' Joking aside, Christopher knew his aunt was right; his father should steer clear of getting involved in the worsening feud. But, worryingly, Stevie was allowing himself to get wound up by the Irishmen, and Declan O'Connor in particular.

'Must be bleedin' hard on you, having to work with them close by, but just ignore 'em best you can.' Having given her concise advice Matilda drank some tea. 'Wage packet at the end of the week's what matters.'

'Right 'n' all, Mrs K,' Ted stoutly agreed, and helped himself to another biscuit out of the box on the table.

A quiet descended on the musty room and Matilda turned up her paraffin lamp as it was a gloomy late afternoon. She twiddled the knob on the wireless set and some Light Programme music increased in volume. 'Was listening to them talking about the Coronation Day plans just as you knocked,' she explained. 'Prince Philip's the Chairman of the Commission doin' all the arranging. It's a while off till the big day but I'm reckoning on us all having a good old knees-up next June. Time'll fly by till then.' She paused, looked reflective. 'Don't seem five minutes since the old king died but it's well over a month since he took his final journey to Windsor. All done for him now, God rest him.'

Christopher and Ted murmured agreement.

'Speakin' of George, bless him, I never told you, did I, that I went up to the palace on the day of his death,' Matilda suddenly announced. 'I stood around by the gates with all the other people. Should've seen the crowds up there! Couldn't hardly get a foot on the pavement for somebody bumping you off again. Very sad atmosphere, it was; men and women crying their eyes out. Got a bit tearful meself, I don't mind admitting. Lots of cars were going in and out of the gates . . .' She broke off her rattling description to exclaim, with an emphasising thump on the table, 'Guess who I saw there! Surprised me, I can tell you!'

'Well, it weren't the king,' Ted weakly joked then fidgeted in embarrassment.

Christopher glowered at him. Like the majority of people, himself included, he knew Matilda was fiercely proud of late King George and wouldn't appreciate tasteless mockery. 'Who did you see?' he asked his aunt.

'Shirley Coleman and her daughter, Grace. They'd gone there as well to pay their respects.'

'Thought the Colemans had gone to Suffolk,' Christopher remarked, dunking his digestive in his tea.

'No! They moved to Surrey. Grace and her brother Paul got evacuated there to a farm. Then Shirley went that way 'n' all to live close to them when Wilf joined up.'

'Oh . . . right,' Christopher said and took a gulp from his cup.

'Anyhow they're back living in Tottenham . . . White Hart Lane way. And Grace's got a good job in the City as a typist.'

'What about old man Coleman?' Ted joined the conversation. 'Old Wilf were a bit of a miserable git as I recall. Used to play knock down ginger on him, didn't we, Chris?' He leaned forward to give Christopher's arm a nudge. 'Not that he ever stirred hisself to open the door. It was always his missus chasing us up the road, weren't it?'

'Oh, Wilf died some years ago. Never recovered from his war injuries, so Shirley said.'

The two young men exchanged a suitably solemn look.

'Pretty girl, she is.' Matilda gave her nephew a wink. 'I remember you brought her here once or twice.' She chuckled to herself. 'She seemed surprised to know I still live here.'

'Everybody's surprised to know you still live here, Aunt Til,' Christopher returned dryly.

'Suits me,' Tilly returned brusquely but with a twitch of a smile. After a silence she added, 'You two look smart.' She studied her nephew and his friend. They were both wearing sharp dark suits. But it was Christopher who redrew her admiring glance, and not just because he was her kin. He had a tall, muscular frame that suited the outfit whereas Ted was short and overweight.

The Wild men had always been handsome; even Chris's evil, long-departed grandfather, Jimmy, who Matilda had despised, had been a looker in his day. Christopher's lean, angular face, deep brown eyes and thick dark hair got him a lot of attention from the girls. In fact Matilda was surprised he hadn't been snapped up long ago. But her great-nephew seemed in no rush, at twenty-four, to give up life as a bachelor, even though some of his friends were now settling down.

'Where you off to then, all dolled up?' Tilly asked.

'Me 'n' Ted 'n' Vic are going to Harringay Stadium then to the Starlight Rooms,' Chris explained.

'Don't you go wasting yer money!' Matilda mockingly rebuked. 'You know I don't hold with drinkin' 'n' gamblin'!'

Christopher grinned at that. It was common knowledge in the family that his great-aunt Matilda had been a very heavy drinker and a bookie's runner in her time.

Christopher drew out his cigarettes and offered the pack to Ted. He knew his aunt had never smoked, which he found quite a surprise as she'd had plenty of other vices. Having lit up and taken a long drag he settled back. 'Any more tea in that pot?'

'Make a fresh lot if there ain't,' Matilda offered, giving the pot a shake.

Christopher was aware of his friend slanting an irritated look at him. Ted was eager to get going and Chris was equally eager to get shot of him. In fact he wished Ted hadn't accompanied him to his aunt's because he'd wanted to speak to her in private about something. But Ted could be thick-skinned, and not easy to shake off, when he had nothing else to do.

'Why don't you get off now, mate? I'm stopping a bit for another cup of tea with me Aunt Til. Didn't realise it was getting on.' Christopher very obviously checked his watch.

'Yeah . . . will do,' Ted mumbled. He'd had enough sitting around in Matilda's shithole. He got up with much shaking of his trouser legs and polished his shoes on the backs of his shins. 'See yer then, Mrs K. Thanks fer the biscuits.'

'Mind how you go, son,' Matilda called as he closed the door. 'What's on your mind, Chris?' she asked as soon as they were alone.

Christopher darted a look at her and shrugged, thinking she could be too cute and blunt at times. His aunt had realised straight away he had an ulterior motive in getting rid of Ted, but he'd not yet worked out how to go about things. What he wanted to talk about had always been a taboo subject in their family. 'Just wondering what you can tell me about me mum,' he blurted out.

Matilda dropped her eyes to her cup. She hadn't been expecting that! It had been some years since Christopher had last quizzed her over his mother, and she'd thought she'd satisfied him that she'd nothing more to reveal. 'What is it you want to know about yer mum that I ain't already told you?' she asked levelly.

'Well, that's just it . . . nobody's really told me anything much about her.' Christopher made an effort not to sound as if he was blaming anyone. 'Dad won't tell me nuthin'. Bleedin' hell, wanted me to think she was dead for years and years, didn't he!' He gestured in annoyance. 'You know what he's like. He just clams up and gets narky soon as I mention her.'

'Well . . . that's understandable. They've been divorced a very long time, y'know. Weren't married fer long in the first place.'

'Yeah, I know; but I don't see why he won't even talk about her,' Christopher insisted, his voice rising. 'Ain't I allowed to know anything other than her name was Pamela Plummer and they was only married a very short time?'

"'Course you are,' Matilda soothed gruffly. 'But it were all a long time ago now, Chris, and things get forgot. Yer dad probably can't remember a lot of what went on. Crikey . . . you're twenty-four. You was only a babe in arms when they broke up and yer dad took on looking after you.'

'Have *you* forgot everything about her?' Christopher asked.

'No . . . like I told you before, she was a pretty young woman, I thought so anyhow,' Matilda said carefully. 'Quite small and blonde, were Pamela, so nothing like you in looks.' She gave her tall, dark-haired nephew a fond smile. 'You're the spit of your dad and Uncle Rob.'

'Is there a photo of her, d'you know?'

'I've not seen one in years,' Matilda replied truthfully. 'But I saw a picture of them on their wedding day. I know yer dad gave it to Pam when they broke up. He didn't want it.'

That was a vital clue Christopher hadn't known and he pounced on the information. 'So me dad were the one wanted to split up?'

'Don't think it was *just* him,' Matilda said gently. 'As you know, yer mum 'n' dad didn't get on and both of 'em soon realised they'd made a mistake. They was too young, y'see. It just didn't work out between them. It happens sometimes; people get caught up in the excitement of weddings 'n' ferget that afterwards babies come along and it's not all a lark but bloody hard work.'

'So it was me that was the problem. When I come along . . .'

'Don't be daft!' Matilda ejected quickly, cursing herself for phrasing things badly. 'What I meant to say is: when money's tight, and work's tight, it puts pressures on people and . . .'

37

'And they couldn't be bothered to try and stick together, even though they had me . . .'

'Now I didn't say that, Chris!' Matilda gave him a stern look. She felt she'd dug herself into a hole and must be careful how she climbed out.

'And me mum never wanted to see me after that?' Christopher asked earnestly. 'Why not?'

'I'm not saying she didn't want to see you,' Matilda answered slowly. 'But I *do* know she went back home to live with her folks. Mr and Mrs Plummer moved away from round here shortly after the divorce came through. I think Pam went with them, and haven't seen nuthin' of her since. Could be she got herself hitched again.'

'So I might have half-brothers or -sisters?'

'S'pose you might . . .' Matilda agreed.

Christopher drew out his cigarette packet and Matilda pointed at them, glad of a reason to change the subject.

'And you can do with cutting down on them coffin nails, 'n' all, Christopher, or you'll be going the same way as poor old King George.'

She suddenly turned her head, frowning. The bang on the door was unexpected, but she was very glad of the distraction. She knew she'd have to say something to Stephen about Christopher's renewed interest in his mother. She wasn't too cowardly to get involved – in her time she'd upturned greater cans of worms within the family – but this truth was very personal and would be hurtful to Christopher. It was his father's place – or his mother's – to tell him the whole story about his past, not hers. The fact that Stevie avoided all mention of Pamela told Matilda he still harboured bitter memories about his brief marriage.

'Go down and see who it is, will yer, Chris. Paid me

rent so it can't be Podge,' she reassured him. Podge Peters had been collecting Mr Keane's rents for decades. Only Podge wasn't fat any more. He was a shadow of his former self now he had lung disease.

Chris shoved himself up out of his chair, a soundless sigh in his throat, knowing the conversation about his mother was finished and he'd discovered very little that was new, or might help him find her.

As Matilda heard him clattering down the stairs she shook her head sadly to herself.

CHAPTER FOUR

'Oh! Sorry! We were after Mrs Keiver.'

Being confronted by a dapper young man, rather than Matilda, had disconcerted Shirley Coleman. The door had only been open a matter of seconds but already an odour of damp was assaulting her nostrils and behind him, in the hallway, was a disgusting glimpse of decay.

'You've found her,' Christopher replied. His eyes lingered on the younger of the two women, thinking she was worth a second look and not just because she appeared vaguely familiar. They seemed neat and well-spoken and Christopher knew if they were Jehovah's witnesses, or rattling a tin for the Sally Army, they were in for a surprise.

'You ain't here to preach to her are you?' The warning mingled with faint amusement in his tone as he propped an elbow on the doorframe and drew on his cigarette. ''Cos, if you are, I'd advise you to clear off while you can or she might pelt you with winkle shells. I've seen her do it.'

He became aware that the pretty young woman had

been staring at him while he'd been fondly reminiscing on his auntie's method of dispersing unwanted do-gooders. He exhaled smoke, gazing right back, deepening the pink in her cold cheeks.

'Who is it, Chris?' Matilda yelled from the top of the stairs, bobbing to and fro for a glimpse of the callers. Her arthritis was playing her up and she didn't fancy going down to find out.

Invariably, when somebody came knocking on Matilda's door, she'd shove up the front window and converse with visitors through it. Sometimes she even chucked down her rent money at Podge Peters if she didn't feel inclined to make the effort to open up to him.

A dawning realisation lifted Grace's brow a moment after she heard Matilda bawl out the name. 'You must be Christopher Wild,' she garbled, wishing she hadn't stared so obviously at him. She could tell he'd noticed her gawping. In common with her mother, as soon as he'd opened the door, she'd thought him a fine specimen of a man, with a wholesome appearance that seemed out of place in a slum. 'You won't remember me,' she rushed on with a breathless smile. 'Grace Coleman, and this is my mum, Shirley.' She put a hand on her mother's arm then abruptly stuck it out for him to shake.

Christopher stopped lounging and dropped his cigarette butt on the floor. 'That's a coincidence; Matilda wasn't long ago talking about you two. She met you in London weeks ago, the day the king died.' He gave Grace's hand a firm shake, then extended the same courtesy to Shirley.

'Yeah . . . we were there,' Shirley confirmed, as she suddenly noticed that Grace and Christopher had locked eyes and she was being overlooked. She could understand why her daughter was mesmerised, she thought

41

sourly. Christopher Wild was a tall, dark handsome man
. . . but, in Shirley's opinion, he sounded a bit rough
and ready, and looked a bit too similar to that nasty
bastard who'd run off and left Grace in the lurch a few
years ago.

'We told Matilda we'd pop by at some time. So as we
were in the area we thought we'd make it today. Go up,
shall I?' Shirley enquired on hearing Matilda's raucous
shout to close the bleedin' door 'cos there was a draught.

Christopher shifted aside to let Shirley pass. Grace
would have followed, but he put a hand on the doorframe barring her way. 'Not seen you in ages. Must be
ten years or more . . .'

'Eleven, I think,' Grace calculated. 'I wasn't quite
twelve when I got evacuated to a farm in Surrey with
my brother.'

'Stop here a minute with me?' He shook the packet
of Weights. 'Me aunt ain't keen on me smoking; reckons
I'll get ill if I keep on. If I have one here I'll save meself
an ear-bashing about coffin nails. Want one?' he offered
politely. 'Catch up on old times for a minute or two,
shall we?'

'Yeah . . . thanks . . .' Grace said and took a cigarette.
After Christopher had lit it she turned to stand with her
back against the brick wall of the house. 'Cold out here,'
she burbled, aware he was studying her profile.

'Ain't much warmer inside,' he answered dryly.

'Did you get evacuated?' She slid a sideways look up
at him.

'Sort of . . . for a couple of years. But I was lucky in
that I got to choose where I went.'

'How did you swing that?' Grace asked interestedly.

'Got relatives Southend way so after the heavy

bombings on London I got sent off to stay with them. It was only for a couple of years. I was soon back in London working full-time.'

'You were lucky.'

'How did you get on in Surrey?'

Grace shrugged. 'I remember it was quiet, and boring, and a bit smelly. I liked the animals, especially the sheep. They were nice enough people . . . strict though and posh with it.'

'Thought they must've been,' Christopher said with a half-smile.

'Why's that?' she asked sharply.

'They've taught you to speak proper,' he teased, chuckling when she blushed and turned away. 'Sounds nice . . . I like it,' he added.

'Why's Matilda still live round here?' Grace swiftly changed the subject.

'Memories, I suppose. She's spent most of her life in The Bunk. Friends, enemies, two husbands, four kids – not counting me dad and uncle who she sort of adopted after their mum died – she's had 'em all right here.' He stared into the distance but it was a lengthy road and the kink at the Biggerstaff intersection robbed him of a complete view.

'But even so . . .' Grace began, a mystified look pinching her delicate features as she glanced about at the squalor.

When she and her mother had arrived at the turning into Whadcoat Street they'd been unsure of which house was Matilda's as Shirley had forgotten to ask for the number. So, before venturing into the bowels of The Bunk, they had stopped on the corner of Seven Sisters Road for a recce. Grace's swift, encompassing glance had led her to conclude the road hadn't improved. But it was different. She had been ready to turn around and head home, but her mother had been determined to visit Matilda.

As a tramp-like individual had scuttled up Grace had bravely accosted him. He'd known Matilda, right enough, and had pointed at a door and given them a gap-toothed grin, before ambling away with a bag in each fist and a shilling for his trouble.

When Grace had visited those few times over a decade ago, she'd stood gawping, transfixed, at the rotten houses, the majority of which had been people's homes. But now, interspersed with roughly boarded up residences, business names were pinned to the front of some of the terraces indicating these were buildings in commercial use.

'She ain't the only one living down here now, y'know.' Christopher was accustomed to seeing revolted interest animating the faces of people unused to the area. He pointed his cigarette at houses further along the terrace. 'You'd be surprised how many people are kipping inside some of them.' A sudden shriek of laughter from inside made Grace and Chris exchange a rueful smile.

'Nice of you and yer mum to come and visit her, being as you lost touch for a long while.'

'Didn't want to come here, to be truthful.' Grace pulled a little face. 'It was mum's idea. She's not stopped talking about Matilda Keiver, and the old days, since we ran into your aunt by the palace gates.' She shuffled her feet on the pavement to warm them and hunched her shoulders to her ears, tucking her long fair hair inside her collar. 'She'd have come sooner to see her but I've managed to put her off.'

As a light sleet started to fall, Christopher moved further inside the hallway. He took Grace's elbow and pulled her in to shelter so they stood face to face in semi-darkness.

'But I couldn't get rid of her today,' Grace continued. 'She just said she was coming with me when I told her I was visiting Wendy.' Seeing his puzzlement she explained, 'I've got a friend who lives off Muswell Hill. I knew when I told mum I was seeing her today, she'd want to come too just so's we could divert here.' She drew daintily on her cigarette and blew smoke out of her mouth at once. 'Me mum is here 'cos she's nosy, you see, not being kind . . . sorry about that.'

'No need to be,' Christopher replied. 'Matilda's obviously glad of her company . . .' As though to prove his point another rumble of laughter could be heard above.

'Just because people live like this doesn't mean it should be treated like a bloody freak show.' Grace glanced about at her dismal surroundings. 'They deserve some respect. I like your aunt. I did when I was younger too. I bet all the way home on the bus me mum'll be going on about the state of her place. Worse it is, better she'll like it.'

'Don't be so sensitive,' Chris soothed with a tinge of mockery. 'Matilda's the last person to feel sorry for herself, or ashamed of herself. She could move out of here tomorrow if she wanted.'

Grace avoided his eyes and stared off through the open doorway.

'You always was a soft touch, Grace Coleman.' He slipped a low-lidded look over her petite figure.

'You mean I was a cry baby,' she said tightly.

'Didn't say that. Don't remember you bawling often

45

but you was always trying to stop us tying tin cans to dogs' tails . . .'

'Well, it was bloody cruel!'

''Course it were, but as a boy I didn't know no better.'

'Your mother should've taught you not to torment dumb animals . . .' She bit her lip, having remembered that Christopher's mother was dead, and his father had brought him up. 'Sorry.' She blushed scarlet. 'Sorry . . . forgot your mum passed away, didn't she . . .'

'She ain't dead,' Christopher said unemotionally. 'I found out years ago that were a lie me dad told me to shut me up asking after her. They broke up when I was still a baby and me mum took off.'

'Really?' The information was so surprising Grace forgot to immediately exhale and she coughed and spluttered as smoke reached her lungs. 'Where is she now?' she squeaked.

Christopher shrugged with feigned nonchalance. 'Who bleedin' knows?' He made an exaggerated gesture with his arm. 'Mystery, ain't it, and looks like it'll stay that way, 'cos nobody seems to want to tell me.'

'Perhaps they don't want to hurt you,' Grace suggested, having recovered her breath. 'She might have got killed in the war or moved away and remarried.' She gave him a kind smile.'Your mum might have a new husband and family.'

'Well, she didn't want her old ones, so that's on the cards.'

Grace bit her lip, feeling awkward in the presence of his bitterness, but she knew whatever he was feeling about his parents hadn't stopped him studying her from beneath his long, low lashes.

'Why didn't you just say you don't smoke?'

'I do sometimes,' she retorted, having noticed humour far back in his deep brown eyes. 'Usually when I go out and have a drink.' She dropped the half-smoked cigarette onto the boards and put a foot on it.

Christopher could see she was edging away from him towards the stairs to join her mother. He didn't want to lose her company just yet. Grace Coleman had grown into a very attractive woman, and he knew he'd like to ask her out, but it was more than that. She had a sweet kindness about her and, as her presence eased more memories to the surface, he suspected he'd liked her years ago for the same reason.

'Matilda told me you work in the City as a typist,' Christopher said.

'She told me you do building work.'

'Another topic of conversation over?' he murmured with a half-smile as she took another step towards the stairs. 'What else did she tell you about me?'

'Nothing. And I didn't ask.' Grace gave him an old-fashioned look. 'I know it's ages since we saw each other, but I do remember you were a little bit conceited, even then, Christopher Wild.'

He took a couple of steps after her. 'I was sorry to hear about your dad.'

'Thanks,' Grace said huskily and halted by the banisters. 'It seems he's been gone ages, but it's only a few years.' She paused. 'How about your dad? Did he go off to fight?'

'He joined up in 1941,' Chris answered. 'He would've gone before but he didn't want to leave me.'

'Did you live alone when he went?'

'Sometimes. But I was with Matilda or me Uncle Rob in London so I wasn't really on me own. Rob was me

47

guvnor too. I started work in his warehouse in Holloway Road before I left school.'

'You had a lot of freedom . . .' Grace sounded a little envious.

'Yeah, it was great. I tried to join up meself when I was seventeen.' He grinned at the memory. 'Me and a couple of mates went down Euston Road recruiting office.'

'And?'

'They chucked two of us out for being too young even though we tried to blag our way in with a lot of chat about bringing our birth certificates back another day. Sammy Piper got took on though. He'd just turned nineteen. Never saw him again, but he might've come through alright.'

'Lots didn't,' Grace said sadly.

'Yeah . . .'

'Well, better go up and say hello . . .'

Chris watched her start up the stairs.

'First door on the left,' he called as she gingerly put a hand on the wobbly banister.

'Just saying to Shirley we had a reunion on a miserable old day all them weeks ago when the king died, but if she comes over here on Coronation Day it'll be a right good knees-up. Won't be in the doldrums then, will we, Shirl?'

'I'll say that for you, Aunt Til, you do know how to have a bit of a shindig in the street.' Chris chuckled.

'We'll have to get started on plans for a street party. It'll probably be the last one we have, too, now the demolition's well under way.' Matilda grimaced her regret at having to acknowledge that fact.

When Whadcoat Street replaced Campbell Road, and Biggerstaff Road took over as the name for Paddington Street, a death knell had sounded for the notorious Bunk. Oddly, Matilda – and many others too – still mourned its passing and were prepared to hang on in what was left of the street till the bitter end. Of course, Matilda realised the decaying terraces couldn't remain – the majority were beyond repair – yet still she felt a wrench at knowing the living stage, where a multitude of precious memories had been played out, was in terminal decline.

'We've got till next June to get everything ready for the big day and don't you lot go knocking down the houses this end till I say you can,' she jokingly scolded her nephew.

'No chance of that, Aunt Til; guvnor reckons there's a few years' worth of work here and he wants us to end up with the lot.'

'Glad to hear it,' Tilly nodded, satisfied. 'We'll make it the best party yet . . . go out on a bang, as it were,' she said emphatically. 'We could get some fireworks, and have a big bonfire . . . ask all the old crowd over for a final Bunk get-together.' She gleefully rubbed together her palms. 'Some of 'em, like the Whitton gels and the Lovats, ain't moved that far away and a lot turn up on Bonfire Night every year. 'Course all my lot'll be coming over. The little 'uns will love it. Not that some of 'em are so little any more. You couldn't move down here last November 5th: busier'n Piccadilly Circus, it were.'

'Well, of course, if we don't have a do going on down our street in Tottenham, I expect we might manage to come over for it.' Shirley had sent a startled look her daughter's way while listening to Matilda's enthusiastic plans. The idea of mingling socially with slum dwellers, past or present, horrified her.

Grace knew her mother would sooner stay indoors on her own on Queen Elizabeth's Coronation Day than be caught making merry with people from The Bunk. Yet, personally, she would be glad of an invitation to a street party in Whadcoat Street. Matilda was a wonderfully natural character, in Grace's estimation. She imagined the Keiver family had great, uninhibited fun when they got together.

'Ain't you gotta be off, Chris?' Matilda gently ribbed her nephew in the break in the conversation. She'd noticed he was having difficulty keeping his eyes off Shirley's daughter, unsurprisingly considering how pretty Grace was. Although she was in her early twenties Matilda reckoned the girl could have passed for a teenager because she was so small and slim. She ran an eye over her stylish coat and leather court shoes, admiring the elegant way Grace was turned out. Shirley, on the other hand, looked as though she was trying to recapture her youth: her coat barely reached her knobbly knees and her make-up looked too thick in Matilda's opinion. Her lips twitched in a private smile as she turned her attention to her nephew.

'Chris is meeting his pals soon 'n' going to Harringay dogs,' she announced.

'Plenty of time yet,' Christopher said and settled back in his chair. 'Do you remember Ted Potts?' he asked Grace.

Grace gladly put down her cup of tea. It had a slight tang to it as though the milk in it was on the turn. 'Yeah . . . I think I do. Quite short, wasn't he, when we were at school?'

'Yeah, that's him; he still is a shortarse. He was here this afternoon. You only just missed him. How about Vic Wilson? Do you remember him?'

'He was a rotten bully,' Grace stated, narrowing her eyes.

'Not any more.' Christopher choked a laugh. 'He's married to Deirdre Thorn and she's got him right under her thumb.'

'Oh . . . I remember her! She was in my class at school.'

'His wife only keeps tabs on him 'cos he's been playing around,' Matilda interjected. 'Can't blame the gel for doing that.'

'How about Bill Bright?'

'Remember Billy.' Grace nodded. 'My friend Maureen liked him.'

'He got engaged a few months ago to Bet Sweetman.'

'Sounds like you two have got some catching up to do another time,' Shirley said with an arch look at Matilda. She gathered up her coat and handbag. 'Anyway, time we got off, Grace. You ready?' She shrugged into her coat.

'Thanks for the tea, Mrs Keiver.' Grace got to her feet, pulled her gloves from her coat pocket, and put them on. 'It'd be nice to come over for your street party next year. Thanks for the invitation.' Grace knew her mother had shot her a quelling glance but she ignored her.

'You're very welcome, Grace, and if I need some help with me plans I reckon I can count on you as another pair of hands.' Matilda gave her a beam.

'Of course,' Grace said. 'I make good sandwiches, you know.'

'Well, got to get that bus,' Shirley interrupted in a strained voice.

'Want a lift back to Tottenham? I've only got the works van but you're welcome to a ride. It's only got one passenger seat in the front but you can squash together and I'll dust it off first.'

'No . . . it's alright; thanks all the same . . . don't want to put you out . . .' Grace murmured.

'No trouble . . . I'm going that way in any case.'

'Yeah, why not, Grace,' Shirley butted in. 'Save us the bus fare and I don't fancy hanging about waiting at the stop in this weather. Freeze to death out there, we will.'

'Right, that's settled then,' Chris said and went to drop a farewell kiss on his aunt's freckled brow.

Moments after pulling up at the kerb in front of their house Christopher had courteously jumped from the van to help them out as the passenger door wasn't easy to handle: it slid stiffly along rather than opening outwards.

'Have you got time to come in for a cup of tea, Christopher?'

'I'm drowning in tea, thanks all the same, Mrs Coleman.'

Shirley's eyes veered between her daughter and Christopher, noting they were standing close together.

'Well . . . I'm going in,' Shirley said with a significant look. 'And I could do with a hand getting tea ready.'

'D'you fancy coming out with me sometime next week? Say Thursday about seven?' asked Christopher as soon as she was gone.

'That was quick!' Grace exclaimed, suppressing a smile. 'No small talk first?'

'We've done all that this afternoon,' he returned. 'No point in wasting time as far as I'm concerned.' He tilted his head to look into her honey-coloured eyes. 'So I don't bother with small talk, and you don't play hard to get . . . deal?'

'Alright . . . but I can't be home late as I start work early and have to catch the tube at seven-thirty.'

Christopher caught her chin to kiss her but she held him off with a fist planted hard against his coat. 'We've not even been out yet,' she squeaked in indignation.

'Yeah . . . but I saved your life . . . and you still owe me . . .'

She giggled at the mock gravity in his voice, liking the way one of his fingers manoeuvred easily to stroke her cheek. 'So you remember, do you? Thought you'd forgotten about teaching me to swim.'

'It's all coming back to me,' he said softly and removing her controlling hand from his chest, he kissed her gently on the lips before strolling away.

CHAPTER FIVE

'Got a bone to pick with you, Stephen.'

Stephen watched his aunt stomp over his threshold and carry on straight into the kitchen. He closed the door and followed her, quite meekly and without comment. She'd made the trip to Crouch End to see him so he knew something was bugging her.

After their mum had died of Spanish flu this woman had been a substitute mother to Stephen and his brother Robert. They both loved her and respected her blunt wisdom and sense of fair play. Even now she'd advanced in years, and was no longer the bruiser she'd once been, she wasn't afraid to tackle any problem head on, especially if it involved family.

Stephen rocked the kettle to judge how much water was in it then put it on the gas stove and turned to face her, resigned to getting a lecture.

'It's time Christopher was told all about what went on between you 'n' Pam.' Matilda didn't believe in preamble.

The month of May had arrived in a blaze of sunshine and had seemed to fire Matilda into action. For weeks past she'd been playing over in her mind the conversation she'd had with Christopher and wondering whether it was best to speak up or let sleeping dogs lie. She'd been glad to see Shirley and Grace Coleman that afternoon, not simply for a nice chat about her Coronation Day plans, but because their appearance had cut short her awkward conversation with her nephew. From the moment they'd all left, Matilda had been cross with herself for being relieved about it. One thing Matilda Keiver had never been was a coward, and yet she'd felt like one that day. She knew Christopher had reached a point in his life where he was no longer going to let the matter of his mum's whereabouts drop. And that was brave of him. So she'd decided to be equally courageous and tackle his father, even though it was bound to cause ructions. It was a problem they could solve together because if he wanted help she was ready to offer it.

Stephen's jaw had sagged towards his chest. He hadn't been expecting that! He'd thought his aunt had probably got the pikeys on her mind, and was about to nag him to back off on further hostilities to protect his, and Christopher's, safety and livelihood.

'What the bleedin' hell's brought this on?' he barked, rattling cups and saucers onto the wooden draining board.

'Not what . . . *who* . . .' Matilda replied, arms akimbo. 'Few weeks ago Chris asked me again about his mum and I did me best to answer him. But I'm warning you, this time he's not gonna be fobbed off.' She dragged a chair out from under the small formica-topped table and sat down, sighing as she stretched out her aching legs. 'Been giving it a lot of thought, y'know, Stevie; I reckon you should come clean over it once 'n' fer all.'

Having conquered his shock Stephen made a dismissive gesture. 'He'll forget about it now he's got this new girlfriend. Right keen on Grace, he is . . .'

'He won't forget it,' Matilda contradicted him, undeterred by her nephew's effort to change the subject.

'What's he said then?' Stephen snapped testily.

'He wants to know anything I can tell him about her. He asked to see a photo of her.'

'Well, there ain't none.'

'I told him that,' Matilda replied levelly. 'I said there was a wedding photo but you gave it to Pam.'

'Shouldn't have told him nuthin' about photos,' Stevie returned harshly. He clattered teaspoons onto saucers and spun away from the sink to glare at his aunt.

'I've told you before, I ain't lying about any of it. Up to now I've just told him the bare bones and tried to make meself scarce quick as I could. But I'm done with that. He's a man and he's got a right to know. I care about him as much as I do about you, and don't you forget it!'

'Well, if you care that much, don't go upsetting him, and you will if you keep on and he finds out his mother was cruel to him. Should never have told him in the first place that she was alive. Were only you kept on about it made me tell him she weren't dead.'

'I went on about it because you'd told lies! And lies always come back to bite yer!' Matilda stormed.

'What's all the shouting about . . . ?'

Neither Matilda nor Stephen had heard the front door opening, or Christopher walking down the hall. He came further into the kitchen swinging a look between the guilty faces of his father and great-aunt.

And he knew, without either of them answering him. He drew in a deep breath. 'Glad you're both here, and talking about me mum, 'cos I've got something to say on that subject too.'

Stephen licked his lips and darted a look at Matilda. She was gazing earnestly at her great-nephew.

'I'm gonna start looking for her,' Chris announced. 'Fact is, I already have started.' He stuck his hands in his pockets. 'I've been to the place you told me she and her parents were last known to have lived.' He stared at his father for a comment but Stephen was tight-lipped, whitening in anger. 'The lady who now lives in that house remembers the Plummers. She reckoned they moved off to Cambridge over twenty years ago but ain't sure if their daughter went with them or stayed in London.' He watched his aunt and father exchange a look, but still neither of them said a word. 'If there's anything you can tell me I'd be grateful to hear it, but if you don't want to help, it don't matter 'cos I'm still gonna try and find her somehow, just to get things straight in me head.'

'Well get this straight in yer head,' Stephen suddenly bellowed. 'She didn't want you, I did! And I was the one took on the job of bringing you up, 'cos she was too bleedin' useless to be a mother . . .'

'That's enough!' Matilda had shoved herself to her feet. 'Christopher wants to find out what happened to his mum. That's natural enough . . .'

'She weren't never a natural mother; she was a lazy good-fer-nuthin' slut . . .'

'Shut up!' Matilda roared, swiping out at Stephen's arm with the back of her hand to quieten him. 'If Christopher manages to find Pam, and she's got the guts to have an honest talk with him, he can make up his own mind about her, and what went on.'

'No . . . let him carry on,' Christopher said quietly. 'Finding out more in a few minutes than I've learned in twenty-four fucking years.' He gazed at his father. 'Why didn't you tell me that before? Why didn't you say she was lazy and useless and we were better off without her?' he asked in a voice hoarse with emotion.

'Didn't want to upset you about any of it,' Stephen forced out. 'What kid wants to know that sort of thing about his mum?'

'Me . . . I'd've liked to know. D'you think she'd want to see me now? Did she ever try and see me after you broke up?'

Stephen clamped together his lips but gave a savage shake of his head. It was a lie. He'd had dozens of letters from Pamela over the first few years after their divorce. In them, she'd begged to see Christopher, but he hadn't allowed it. The letters had petered out and, after their son turned five, the birthday cards stopped arriving too. Everything had been burned, but Stephen could remember they'd all had a London postmark. It had been the first thing he'd checked: whether she was still living locally. But he'd never seen her, although he'd expected her to turn up on his doorstep and demand to see their son. Stephen had jumped to the cosy conclusion that when the chips were down, she just couldn't be bothered.

'Why wouldn't she want to see me? I wouldn't make a nuisance of meself. All I want to do is spend an afternoon talking to her about when I was little and what she's been up to . . . that's all . . .'

Matilda felt tears needle her eyes and she swung about and started fiddling with the teapot and crockery.

Stephen strode for the door, grim-faced, but Christopher

stepped in front of him to stop him leaving the kitchen. 'Did she go off with another man? Is that it?'

Stephen shoved at Christopher's arm to move him. But Christopher refused to budge, so he stuck a finger under his son's nose. 'The only thing you need to know is . . . who's looked after yer? Eh? Who's got you over bumps and scrapes and the bleedin' measles and all the rest of it? I've spent me life going without and bringing you up . . .'

'Yeah, I know. And I'm grateful to you fer making sacrifices. But it took the two of you to get me here in the first place. You ain't everything . . .'

Stephen swore beneath his breath. 'You'd better fuckin' move, son, or there's gonna be trouble,' he threatened softly.

'Christopher . . .' Matilda's grey head gestured for her great-nephew to move aside.

Stephen strode into the hallway and ripped his coat off the banisters before slamming out of the front door.

'Well . . . that went well,' Christopher said acidly. But his face was ashen with strain.

'Sit down,' Matilda said gently.

Once he was seated she put a cup of steaming tea in front of him and loaded sugar into it.

'Fer what it's worth, Chris,' she said quietly, 'I think you're doing the right thing.' She placed a rough hand on his broad shoulder and squeezed. 'Can tell you like Grace a lot, even though you've not been walking out long together. Sometimes things just seem right, don't they . . .'

He nodded and sipped from his tea.

'Things are changing for you, Chris. You're a man . . . oh, I know you have been fer quite a while, but comes a time when the larking about with yer mates gotta stop 'cos something far more important comes into your life.' She walked away to the draining board. 'Yer dad'll get over it; be good fer him 'n' all ter jump this hurdle, then perhaps he'll start thinking about settling down again himself. He's still a youngish man. No reason why him 'n' Pearl can't get married. Can't use the excuse of caring fer his boy for ever, can he?' she said lightly.

Christopher shook his head but didn't look up. 'D'you know where I could start looking?'

'Bexleyheath,' Matilda said. 'I reckon if you was to go there and make some enquiries you might find out something about Pam Plummer . . . or Pam Wild. She might have kept to her married name, but I know when it all happened, and the two of 'em was eaten up with bitterness, she didn't want to be known as a Wild. Then of course, she might have married again in the mean-time, which would make it all a bit harder.' She paused. 'And you've got to accept that she might be dead, Chris. Whole of London took a battering during the war and lots of casualties . . . so if she stuck around in town . . .'

'Yeah . . .' he sighed. 'Just be nice to know though. What makes you say Bexleyheath?'

'Ran into a friend of your mum's I hadn't seen in a while, before the war. Vicky Watson was her bridesmaid. She said she'd sort of lost touch with Pam but thought she'd gone south of the river, Bexleyheath way. I remember Vicky seemed a bit cagey. It made me think Pam might have a new man in her life. Or perhaps Vicky just thought I harboured grudges over what went on between yer mum and dad. But that weren't the case then and it ain't now.'

'Where does Vicky Watson live?' Christopher immediately asked.

'Ain't Vicky Watson now; she's married to David Green who works for the Water Board. Or he was working there when I spoke to her. But that were over thirteen years ago. I think they had a place in Clapham, but 'course they might've got bombed out.'

'Thanks, Aunt Til.'

Christopher had spoken so huskily, so gratefully, that Tilly dipped her head to conceal the tears in her eyes. 'I'll be getting off then,' she croaked, putting her empty cup down on the draining board.

'Want a lift back?'

'If you've got time it'd save me poor old legs,' Matilda answered with a smile.

'Don't reckon your old legs are as bad as you make out,' he ribbed her, glad to lighten the atmosphere.

'You try falling out a bleedin' first-floor winder and see how you feel,' she came back indignantly, but with a rueful chuckle.

When he was younger, Christopher had had a macabre fascination with knowing all the details about Matilda's narrow escape from death. It had never been kept a secret from him that his paternal grandfather had been the black sheep of the family and had tried to murder Matilda. There had been no point trying to cover up the scandal as many people knew it first-hand. The younger generation had had gruesome details passed down to them about the night Jimmy had a fight with a gangster and was mortally wounded. Rather than wait, and let nature take its course, Jimmy had committed suicide by falling from a window and dragging Matilda out with him. Jimmy had died that night, although his legend

61

lived on. He was still spoken about by some locals with a mixture of dread and awe. At school, Christopher had enjoyed his mates being envious of him because of his notorious ancestor. But those juvenile feelings had passed; now he felt an acute sense of loss at never having known even one of his grandparents.

'Did Mr and Mrs Plummer ever try to keep in touch with me? I suppose even if they had me dad wouldn't have allowed it.'

Matilda slowly walked to the front door. She turned to Christopher before opening it. 'They were ashamed, Chris. Not of you – of their daughter and what had gone on. They were strait-laced people . . . not like us. Staying respectable and not being gossiped about could've been more important to 'em than seeing their grandson.' She sighed. 'That's just my opinion. Could be there were other reasons they kept quiet. If you get to speak to yer mum she'll tell you about them, I expect.'

As Chris helped Matilda out of his van in Whadcoat Street he spied Kieran Murphy pushing a pram over the threshold of his house. The man raised a hand to them but didn't stop to talk; he immediately disappeared inside.

'Ain't seen much of Noreen lately; I reckon he's got her under lock 'n' key.' Matilda scowled.

'Not done no more babysitting?'

'He don't want her workin'. Thought Noreen had told Kieran she'd got a little job cleanin' but seems she went behind his back and he hit the rafters over it. He's made her promise to give it up and stay home with the kids. Know she ain't lyin' over his temper 'cos I've heard them going at it hammer 'n' tongs on a few occasions.' Matilda gave a sorrowful shake of her head. 'Pride's all well 'n' good when you can afford it. But that man can't.'

'Could tell he had the 'ump about you minding Kathleen the day I took her home. Asked me for work that day too.'

'Rob wouldn't wear it, would he?'

Chris barked a laugh. 'I didn't even bother asking him 'cos I didn't want me ears chewed off.'

Matilda gave her nephew a wave and proceeded towards her house. She knew Kieran was angry with her as well as his wife because he'd found out she'd put Noreen in touch with the client in Tufnell Park. Pigheaded men didn't intimidate Matilda; if Kieran Murphy had an axe to grind he could come right out and say what was on his mind. And she'd tell him his fortune in return.

But for now Matilda had more important people's troubles weighing on her mind. A short while ago Stevie had gone storming off with a face like thunder but, like Noreen's husband, he'd eventually realise not to ride roughshod over loved ones 'cos sometimes a battle led to all-out war.

CHAPTER SIX

'There's been an accident. You'd better get back up there fast.'

Smithie's general store was still trading on Whadcoat Street and Christopher had been inside buying cigarettes when Vic Wilson burst in to garble out his terrifying message.

'Accident?' Christopher parroted, staring at him, but he'd already moved towards the shop's exit. A knot of bystanders could be seen congregated outside the house they were working on close to the junction with Lennox Road.

'Yer dad's fallen off that bleedin' old ladder . . .'

Even before Vic mentioned his father, an instinctive dread had started churning Christopher's guts. He sprinted as fast as he could towards the scene with Vic puffing in his wake.

The first thing Christopher saw was the wooden ladder – the one nobody was supposed to be using at heights because a lot of top rungs were worn – lying in bits on the ground. Stephen was curled up close by, moaning, with Bill crouching over him looking petrified.

Christopher fell to his knees beside them. 'What you done?' He bellowed at his dad, gripping his arm. He shot a stare at Billy. 'Anyone called for an ambulance?'

'Ted's gone to telephone for help . . .' Bill burbled.

'What's he done? Where's he hurt? Where you hurt?' he demanded, leaning over his father in an effort to make him open his eyes, but they remained squeezed shut. Christopher could hear laboured breathing interspersed with chilling whimpers of pain.

'Come off that old ladder, he did,' Bill spluttered in shock. He raked shaking fingers through his hair. 'We was all inside working and he kept on about it was time to get started on the roof even though you'd said we'd gotta wait till we had a decent ladder 'fore tackling it.' He turned to Vic who was prowling in a circle, sucking desperately on a cigarette. 'We told him 'n' all, didn't we, Vic?' Vic nodded a vigorous response. 'Took no notice of us. He must've gone up to start on that fucking gutter without even asking anybody to foot it for him . . .' Billy tailed off, with a despairing shake of his head.

Christopher touched his father's scalp and felt hot stickiness on his fingertips. Having gently moved aside some of his hair he exposed blood pooling beneath his skull. An anguished groan tore at his throat. 'I told him not to go right up it! Told him not to!' he raged in a suffocated voice. He jumped to his feet and paced to and fro. 'Vic, go and see what the fuck Ted's up to. Where's the ambulance? Go and see what he's up to . . .'

The sound of a distant bell calmed him slightly and

he dropped back to his knees to soothe his father who'd started to cough and shake.

'S'alright . . . listen . . . ambulance is coming . . .' he whispered, grasping his father's icy hand and giving it a tight squeeze. 'You cold?' Whipping off his jacket he gently put it round Stephen's huddled form. The other two men immediately struggled out of their coats and offered them up.

'Can I help at all? Shall I fetch a blanket to cover him? Do you need cloths or water?' Kieran Murphy had just dashed across the road to offer assistance, having spotted the commotion in the street from his window. His wife appeared in the doorway of their house, holding Rosie in her arms while Kathleen clung to her legs, thumb in mouth.

Vic threw him a dirty look and muttered beneath his breath, but Chris glanced over a shoulder and gave an appreciative nod. 'His hands feel frozen. Blanket might keep him a bit warmer . . . thanks,' he croaked.

Kieran disappeared back inside the property and returned with a large blanket in a matter of minutes. He helped Chris spread it out and tuck it around Stephen before quietly retreating to stand with Noreen. Ted came racing back round the corner and stood gasping and holding the stitch in his side. 'Didn't know whether to stop at the chemist and get some stuff like bandages and paraffin gauze . . .' His voice tailed off as he read his colleagues' expressions. They all knew that bandages and paraffin gauze weren't likely to be of much use.

'Jayzus . . . now what's gone on here?' Declan O'Connor had just arrived in the street to check on his workforce. He'd noticed at once the little group gawping at the drama and had sprung from his van to run over.

His crew had congregated along the road and were watching from a distance. None of them had come down to offer help.

Christopher sprang up. 'What's gone on? *What's fuckin' gone on?* I'll tell you what's gone on, you bastard. Me dad's come off a fuckin' ladder and you know why? Because you bunch of thievin' cunts stole the new one he should've been using.' He gripped one-handed at the Irishman's throat and squeezed hard while Vic and Bill tugged at his arms and torso trying to prise them apart. Ted crouched beside Stephen holding out his arms, trying to shield the invalid and prevent him becoming aware of the fracas.

'It was untied from the top of his van and stolen, so don't make out you didn't know,' Christopher spat though his grinding teeth, as finally his men dragged him back. 'So he used this one and it's only fit fer fuckin' firewood.' He shook off imprisoning hands and strode to the ladder. He saw at once where a few of the wormy worn treads had given way at the top and kicked out at it in violent frustration. 'You'd best keep that lot away.' Christopher pointed a shaking finger at the approaching navvies. ''Cos if yer don't there's gonna be murders here today . . .'

O'Connor looked for a moment as though he might retaliate; his fingers were massaging his scratched throat, and his snarl had hoisted one side of his mouth up close to his nose. But instead he strode towards his men, arms outstretched, to pen them and prevent them coming any closer. A moment later the pikeys were retreating towards their own territory, throwing glances over their shoulders. They stood by the door of the house they were working on, and watched as an ambulance screeched around the corner and speeded up to the casualty.

'Want me to go and let the guvnor know what's gone on?' Vic asked in a hushed tone. He gave Christopher's arm a shake to gain his attention.

Christopher had been crouching by the medical team examining his father, but now he slowly and wearily stood up.

'Go and let Mr Wild know what's happened, shall I?' Vic repeated in a whisper.

Christopher's uncle was always known either as the guvnor, or Mr Wild. None of Wild Brothers' employees was under any illusions as to who ran the show, or where familiarity ended.

'Yeah,' Christopher said hoarsely. 'He'll be at the warehouse off Holloway Road.'

Vic nodded.

'Would you tell him to let Pearl know?' Christopher knew his father's girlfriend would be distraught to hear the news but she'd be even more upset if she were the last to find out. He dug in a pocket and brought out his van key and handed it over. In seconds Vic was reversing at speed out into Lennox Road.

'Woss gone on?' a woman's gravelly voice called.

Christopher turned to see old Beattie Evans, who still lived in the street, hobbling towards him leaning heavily on a stick.

'Me dad's had an accident,' he answered croakily. 'Would you let me aunt know he's gone to hospital when she gets back from the market?'

Beattie nodded, mouth agape. 'Bleedin' hell,' she muttered. 'Stevie don't look good.' She glanced about at the stricken faces. The shortarse looked as though he was about to collapse, or throw up. And she could see why: he'd got his eyes fixed on the blood escaping

68

from beneath Stevie's head and trickling towards the gutter.

Beattie had lived in The Bunk long enough not to be badly affected by the sight of a bit of claret. In Campbell Road's heyday she'd watched men caving each other's skulls in with iron bars. In fact, she'd seen Matilda Keiver, in her prime, put a poker over a bloke's head when he wouldn't pay his rent. But those days were gone and everybody had gone soft in her opinion. She knew that hot sweet tea often did the trick on such occasions. 'Get anybody a cuppa, can I?' she offered gamely.

'Coming in the ambulance?'

Christopher pivoted about to see one of the crew addressing him. They had his father on a stretcher in the back and were ready to go. He nodded and clambered in quickly. A moment later he'd sprung out again to talk to Ted and Billy.

'Get everything under lock and key before you leave.' He sent a stare of violent hatred along the road. 'I wouldn't put it past those pikeys to try and turn this to their advantage.'

'I bought new ladders just a few months ago. I know I fucking did. I bought a couple of step ladders and a high reach, and I know you had 'em, 'cos I delivered them to you myself when you was working on that extension in Tooley Street.'

'Yeah, I know.'

'So why was he up a fucking worm-eaten old ladder messing about with gutters?' Robert Wild turned a look of angry disbelief on his nephew. 'If you needed more ladders why didn't somebody just say so?'

Robert and Christopher were standing together in the

69

waiting room of the hospital, and attempting to keep their voices low during a fraught exchange. At intervals both men were darting glances at the double doors that led to the wards, praying that the doctor would reappear with reassuring news.

Chris's uncle had turned up just twenty minutes or so after the ambulance had arrived and Chris had been enormously relieved to see him. He didn't relish having this conversation with his guvnor, but he was glad to have somebody with him to prevent his imagination running riot. Every time he heard a hum of activity behind the doors his heart leapt to his throat. He was certain the doctor would rush out at any moment to tell him they hadn't been able to save his father. The waiting room was almost empty: just an elderly couple sat huddled together on chairs at the end of one row. They looked as anxious as Chris felt and he guessed they too were praying for good news from the staff about a relative.

Aware of his uncle's steady stare Christopher ran a hand across the back of his neck and dropped his chin. He knew he'd have to grass his dad up, and he was already feeling guilty as hell over his accident.

Stephen had told him not to let on to Robert that the new ladder had been stolen. He'd said he'd replace it himself without the guvnor ever finding out that the Irish crew had stolen it off his van. Christopher had suspected his dad had felt embarrassed, and also at fault for having forgotten to padlock the new ladder. In the past they'd been able to leave equipment unattended for a short while without risking losing it, but since the Paddies had turned up in The Bunk anything out in the open had needed nailing down. Christopher also understood that his dad didn't like feeling beholden to his brother, or that he was in his shadow, although, of course, he was, on both counts.

'Didicois working down Whadcoat Street have been stealing stuff,' Christopher admitted gruffly. 'We've lost shovels to 'em 'n' all. They nearly had a pick away too only I caught 'em red-handed.'

Robert's expression made words unnecessary.

'He didn't want you to know,' Christopher sighed out as two nurses bustled past in a rustle of starch. 'Said he'd replace the stuff we'd lost out of his wages when he could afford to. Felt it was his fault for not keeping a closer eye on it all.'

Robert spun away, his fingers splayed rigidly above his head in a gesture of sheer exasperation, as he hissed a string of curses that made Chris wince.

'Have you let Pearl know?' Chris swiftly changed the subject.

Robert nodded. 'Sent Gil round to the shop where she works to get her and bring her here straight away. Thought they'd have arrived by now. Traffic must be bad . . .' He glanced at the large round clock on the waiting-room wall. It was almost five o'clock in the afternoon and Chris realised he'd been here for over an hour already

'Came as soon as I heard off Beattie about the accident.' Matilda hurried in through the swing doors. 'How is he?'

'Don't know yet . . . waiting to hear.' Christopher drew his aunt towards the row of hard-backed chairs and made her sit down. He could see she was breathless and agitated. He sat beside her while his uncle paced to and fro.

Ten minutes later Pearl appeared, ashen-faced. She

71.

rushed over but Gil, the warehouseman who'd given her a lift, hung back by the door as though conscious he wasn't family and should keep to a respectful distance on such a solemn occasion.

'How bad is he? Is he going to die?' Pearl blurted out. She was a tubby woman and the tops of her arms were visibly quivering beneath her cardigan. She looked dishevelled, as though she'd dropped everything to race here. Suddenly she pulled a handkerchief from her sleeve to scrub at her watering eyes.

'Waiting for the doctor to come and give us his verdict.' Robert had put an arm around her trembling shoulders. 'He's strong as an ox, is Stevie,' he encouraged her. 'Take more'n a tumble to see him off . . .'

'He's been telling me about those pikeys in the street.' Pearl was generally easy-going but, at present, her face was puckered in anger at the thought that Stephen might have been set about. 'Have they done it to him? Was he in a fight?' She shoved at her sleeves in agitation, eyes narrowing vengefully.

'No, nothing like that,' Robert soothed. 'He's had a fall from a ladder . . .'

Pearl gulped in a startled breath. 'How high up was he . . . ?' she started.

Matilda was first to notice the white-coated doctor entering and she sprung from her chair, flinching at the sharp pain in her knee. The little group converged on the portly fellow.

'He's been very lucky.' The doctor addressed Christopher. 'All things considered, it's a miracle, young man, I'm not now writing your father's death certificate.' He waited until the information had sunk in and expressions of sheer thankfulness were transforming four faces. 'He's badly bruised and has a broken leg and collarbone and a few cracked ribs. The ladder probably saved him from worse injury. From the few words he's said, he remembers landing on top of part of it and it probably broke his fall.' He paused, aware of hungry eyes on him; the invalid's family was silently devouring every word he uttered. 'It's the nasty head injury that's most worrying,' the doctor continued. 'He's concussed . . . I'm hoping that's all it is. But we'll need to keep a careful eye on him.'

Christopher nodded vigorously, feeling so utterly relieved that he thought he might burst out crying. He could feel heat in his eyes and a stinging sensation attacking his nose. He tried to say a few words of thanks but his throat seemed to have closed so he let his uncle do the talking and sank down onto the chair next to the one Pearl had tottered to. He put his elbows on his grimy overall knees and let his forehead sink into his cupped palms.

'Can I go and see him?' Robert asked.

'I think just his son should see him today.' The doctor paused. 'And only for a few minutes; you mustn't excite him at all. He's drifting in and out of consciousness and needs to rest.'

Christopher nodded wordlessly and, as the doctor gave him a kind smile, he felt his eyes fill up again.

'You'll keep him in here for as long as necessary, won't you, doctor? Don't let him come out till you're sure he's ready.' Robert knew his brother well enough: Stevie would discharge himself as soon as he was able to get his feet to the ground.

'I'll sit by his bed and make sure he don't do a runner, if needs be,' Matilda announced, thrusting her shaking hands into her coat pockets.

A sob suddenly burst from Pearl and she wailed against Christopher's shoulder, 'Stupid sod, he is. What's he doing going up ladders at his age when there's you young men to do that . . .'

Robert went over and patted comfortingly at her back. 'Don't worry, luv,' he consoled her. 'Soon as he gets out of here I'm gonna have his guts fer garters over it.'

CHAPTER SEVEN

'It's not your fault.'

'Yeah . . . it is . . .' Christopher immediately spurned Grace's comfort. 'We'd argued again just this morning about me wanting to find me mum.' The tip of his cigarette glowed and, in the ensuing silence, smoke drifted through his nostrils to mingle with night air. He turned away from the van's open window to gaze at her. 'Made a change for us to speak actually, even if it were just a blazing row. He's been giving me the silent treatment for weeks. Hell it is trying to work with somebody all day long when they won't say a word to you.'

'It's not your fault he went up that ladder, Chris,' Grace gently persisted. 'Your dad decided to use it, and he should've known better.' One of her hands covered his fingers, resting idle on his thigh. 'You'd all told him it was dangerous. What more could any of you have done?'

'Could've kept quiet about me mum, that's what *I* could've done. Wish I'd never bloody mentioned anything about going looking for her. Me dad was right.

He's always been around for me. What's she done except made herself scarce for over twenty years?' The bitter outburst tailed away only to be resumed a moment later. 'I knew it'd upset him badly if I started going on about her, but still I did it.'

'You've got a right to know about your mother,' Grace quietly reasoned. 'Anyhow, rowing over your mum doesn't excuse him doing something stupid.' She huffed. 'For Heaven's sake, at his age, he should've known better than risk his life like that!'

Irritably, Christopher whipped his fingers out from under Grace's warm palm. He knew there was sense in what she was saying but anxiety and guilt continued gnawing at him. 'Neither of us has been able to concentrate properly since this blew up. He probably forgot the ladder were knackered because of everything else going round in his head.' Chris flicked the dog end out of the van window and immediately drew out another cigarette from the pack. 'And where was I, eh, when it happened?' His tone was viciously self-mocking. 'Buying fags down the shop, weren't I, 'cos I couldn't stand the bad atmosphere and needed a break. If I'd been where I should've been, and seen him hoisting it, I'd've put a fourteen-pound hammer through the poxy thing right there and then.'

Grace slid closer to him on the seat and leaned her cheek against the tightly bunched muscle in his shoulder. 'Come on . . . relax, don't blame yourself,' she softly urged, massaging his forearm with her small fingers. 'The doctor said he's been very lucky. Tomorrow when you get to the hospital you might find him sitting up having breakfast in bed.'

'Please God you're right about that . . .' Chris

mumbled. 'He didn't say a word to me. Don't know if he could hear me talking to him. Looked still as death and whiter'n the sheet tucked under his chin.'

At the hospital Christopher had stayed only briefly with his father yet he'd found the time ample. The sharp, sterile scent of the small side ward, and oppressive silence, had made him glad to spot the doctor beckoning him away after five minutes. Although Stephen's eyelids had flickered up once or twice he either couldn't, or wouldn't, speak to his son. Nevertheless Christopher intended to visit the hospital first thing tomorrow before carrying on to see his uncle Rob and sort out what was to be done about the work situation.

'He'll be fine after his breakages mend and he's had a good rest!' Grace whispered fiercely against his stubble. She rubbed a finger back and forth on his grimy jaw, realising it wasn't just his overalls that smelled mucky, but his skin too. 'You could do with a wash and shave.'

Christopher put an arm around her and eased his face against her sweetly scented skin. 'Don't know what I'd do without you to talk to,' he murmured.

'Thought you said your Aunt Tilly was a diamond at listening and giving advice,' she teased.

'She is . . .' Christopher paused, realising that a couple of months ago he'd have headed straight to Whadcoat Street to sift through the day's troubles with his aunt. But instinctively he'd come away from the hospital and headed towards Tottenham, without even returning home first to wash and change out of his work clothes. 'It's you I need to talk to now when bad things happen.' His wry smile turned sultry and his lips prowled after hers to claim a hungry kiss. 'Don't go in yet . . .' He murmured against her cheek as their lips unsealed.

'Got to . . .' she sighed. 'You know what me mum's like about getting me indoors before eleven during the week . . .' She glanced sideways at the house and noticed the front-room curtain twitch. 'Oh, God, she's watching us alright; probably heard the van pull up. Got to go, Chris, 'cos it's work in the morning.'

As soon as Grace had got in the van and seen Chris in his overalls, her pique at his late arrival had withered away. She'd realised at once something was wrong. After hearing the bare bones of Stephen's accident she'd no longer fancied going to the pictures even though he'd sweetly offered to speed home and smarten up so they wouldn't miss the main feature. Instead they'd gone for a drive and she'd allowed him his long silences while he inwardly battled to make sense of what had occurred. Then they'd parked up outside her house and, unprompted, he'd given her a detailed account of the calamity that afternoon. Grace's quietly adamant opinion that he wasn't to blame had started to calm his inner demons, if not completely tame them.

'Shall we go to the pictures on Saturday instead?'

'You asking me out, Grace Coleman?' Chris demanded, feigning surprise. ''Cos if you are you'd better not start getting fresh with me, y'know.'

She blushed but saucily squeezed his knee. 'It'll be a change for me to be the one taking liberties, Christopher Wild.' She playfully fended him off as he lunged for her with a growl. 'My treat this weekend as it's the end of the month and I get paid,' she squeaked while being crushed against his chest.

Christopher relaxed his predatory grip on her arms and smoothed one of her warm cheeks with the backs of his fingers. Something had occurred to him, and he

78

regretted bringing it to her attention and putting a dampener on their plans. 'I doubt if me dad'll be out of hospital
so soon, but if he is, I'm not sure I'll be going anywhere
if he's hobbling about and needs looking after.'

'Oh, yes, 'course . . . I should've realised . . .' Grace
grimaced in apology.

Pushing aside all thoughts of his father Chris concen-
trated on the warm woman resting against him. He
curved an arm about her, drawing her close so his hands
could caress her back, stroke at her nape until she was
pliant and curling her body against his. 'I know it's daft
to talk about this so soon, when we've only been going
out a couple of months, but . . .'

Grace shifted position and caught his face between
her palms, curtailing his diffident declaration of love.
'Shhh . . . time enough for that another day.' She smiled
wryly. 'I'd sooner hear it – if you still want to say it –
when you're over the shock of your dad's accident.'
Despite her husky rebuff she snuggled up to him encour-
agingly, tilting up her face to ask, 'Will you try and find
this woman in Clapham so you can ask her some questions?' His puzzled expression prompted her to explain.
'You told me your aunt Tilly gave you a tip about a
woman who knew your mum years ago. I think you
said her name was Vicky. Will you try and find her?'

'Nah . . . don't think so. Gonna just let it die a death.
Since I brought up the subject of me mum we've had
nothing but trouble.'

'I think you *should* keep on looking for her,' Grace
demurred, levering herself upright by using a fist on his
thigh. 'Otherwise, when everything's back to normal,
you'll start wondering whether you did the right thing
giving up. It'll niggle away at you.' She grimaced. 'Don't

want to sound callous, Chris, but perhaps you've been given a good opportunity to try and find this Vicky. While your dad's in hospital he won't know what's going on, and what he doesn't know, can't hurt him,' she pointed out.

'What if he comes out with it direct and asks whether I'm gonna carry on looking for me mum?' Christopher frowned, mulling over what she'd suggested. 'I don't want to lie to him yet, if I tell the truth, he might have a relapse.'

'Don't know the answers, Chris.' Grace shook her head, setting her long blonde hair swinging about her sharp little chin. Her honey-coloured eyes clung to his face. 'It's up to you what you do. But I know what I'd do . . . if it were me . . .' She glanced to her left and sighed as she saw her mother gesticulating at her through the window.

'Me mum's waving at me. Before I came out this evening she said to ask you in when you brought me home.'

'Yeah?' Chris stretched his neck to squint at the sight of Shirley's head bobbing behind the curtain. 'What's she want with me?'

'To know if you're likely to stay the course, I expect,' Grace muttered sourly, while scowling in her mother's direction. She was aware that secretly her mother hoped he *would* scarper. Shirley had been dropping hints she thought all Matilda's kith and kin beneath them.

'Thinks I'm a no-good cad, likely to get you in trouble then leave you in the lurch, does she?' Chris suggested with a dry chuckle.

Grace swerved a doe-eyed look at him and Chris realised his teasing had hit a raw nerve.

80

They hadn't had a serious talk about their respective past affairs. Given that they were in their twenties, they'd both assumed the other had previously been romantically involved, perhaps seriously. Christopher hadn't pried, although he was curious, as any man would be, about a girl he was falling in love with. He knew his Jack the Lad past wouldn't stand up to a lot of scrutiny, and he didn't want to be a liar or a hypocrite about it, so he'd decided to keep quiet and explain himself when he had to. But, a moment ago, a few bitter words from Grace had piqued him into forgetting his strategy.

'You had a bad experience with someone?' He caught her wrist lightly as she slid towards the door.

'Most of them,' she returned lightly, attempting to shrug off his hold. When she couldn't she turned back to challenge him. 'How about you? How many girls have you regretted going out with?'

'Can't think of any . . . not that I've gone out with many in the way you mean; just knocked about with most of them,' he answered flatly. 'So there's bound to be a few who wished they'd never clapped eyes on me.'

'Why?'

He shrugged, giving her an impenitent look. 'I've been called a selfish bastard, and a few other names, in my time.'

'Why?'

'Why do you think?' He choked a laugh. 'I'm no different to the next bloke when it comes to pushing his luck on a Saturday night . . . or I was . . .'

Their eyes locked and Grace nibbled at her lower lip.

'You're different,' he said quietly. It was the first time he'd seen her look vulnerable, as though the lustre in her eyes might be caused by tears. 'I was gonna tell you

I think you're special earlier but you stopped me.' He took out his cigarettes but she took the pack from him and closed the lid.

'Your aunt's right, you do smoke too much.' She blinked and sniffed.

'Who was he?'

Grace studied her hands, clasped in her lap. 'I'll tell you another time.'

'You'll tell me now.'

She twisted towards him, head cocked defiantly to one side, but he didn't flinch from her combatant stare.

'Tell me?' he requested softly.

She'd met Hugh at a local dance in Guildford when she was nineteen and they were engaged six months later, shortly before her dad died. Although Shirley was receiving a small widow's pension by the time they were planning the wedding, and had had a part-time job in a drapery, Grace had realised it wouldn't be fair to expect her mum to contribute much. She'd accepted that paying for her wedding would be, on the whole, her responsibility, and had been glad she'd heeded her parents' advice to save a little bit of her wages each week for her future. She'd done so from the moment she started work in a dress shop in Guildford after leaving school at the age of sixteen.

Her lovely nan had offered to give her some money towards the cake and the flowers, and had put down deposits as soon as the date was set. When it was called off, Grace had insisted her nan be repaid and had returned the deposits out of her own pocket. She couldn't bear the thought of her grandmother, existing on a meagre pension, having to suffer for her generosity because of a rat like Hugh Wilkins.

'Are you going to answer me, Grace?' Chris's quiet question broke into Grace's thoughts. 'When I was nineteen and still in Surrey, I got engaged,' she blurted. 'He was a . . . *selfish bastard*.' She gave an acid smile on using his term, but kept her eyes lowered. 'He was about your age and worked as a shipping clerk, close to my office in the City. After his boss died – or perhaps it was before, I'm not sure – he started comforting the man's widow. A few months later, just as we were due to get the banns read, he moved in with her and her two kids and told me it was over.' Grace glanced at him before resuming. 'Didn't seem to matter to him that she was only a year younger than my mum. I suppose the money left to her by her late husband might have been more attractive than she was . . . or I was, come to that.' She proudly tilted up her chin. 'I think they got married last year. Sound bitchy and bitter over it, don't I?'

'Reckon most people would feel the same if it happened to them,' Chris said quietly. 'What a prat he was,' he drawled in a way that was a greater compliment to her than any praise.

Grace rewarded him with a shadow of a smile.

'You over him now?'

She nodded and turned fully towards him. 'Yeah, I'm definitely over him.'

'Good . . . that's all I need to know.'

'Might not be all I need to know,' she returned waspishly. 'How many girls have you . . . *knocked about* with?'

He smiled at the Weights in his fist. 'Not that many . . .'

'You might as well tell me, Chris, 'cos eventually your mates'll drop you right in it.'

He started to laugh. 'Oh, yeah, gits'll do that all right.

Especially Vic.' He glanced up with boyish diffidence. 'Leave it for another time, shall we?'

'You're lucky me mum's on the prowl, and it's getting late, or I'd pin you down over it right now.'

'Yeah?' He slid predatorily closer. 'Sounds good . . .'

She whacked at his arm in mock disgust. 'You'd better come round and let me out.' She tugged at the stiff handle. 'If I try opening the door I know I'll risk losing me fingers in it.'

'That's all I need, another dash up the Casualty Department.' He got out and came round to help her from the van. He didn't move aside but kept her trapped close to him, his body shielding her from Shirley Coleman's spying.

'Don't matter about none of what's past, Grace,' Chris whispered gently. 'None of 'em matter.' He tilted up her chin. 'It's just us now.' He slid his lips against her cheek. 'And tell your mum I'm a decent chap and she needn't worry I'll chase her round the kitchen. I've never had a thing for mature women . . .'

Grace burst out laughing so spontaneously that her petite figure bumped suggestively against him. 'She might like you chasing her round the kitchen,' she gasped out. 'She's always hinting she's not too old for a boyfriend.' A moment later her humour had passed and she was gazing up at him with a serious expression. 'I'll come with you, you know. When you go looking for your mum, I'll come too, if you want, and give you all the support you need, promise.' Having gone onto tiptoe she kissed his dusty cheek then extricated herself from his embrace. 'Give your dad my best wishes for a speedy recovery, won't you?'

'Yeah . . . thanks.' He watched her go in and close

the door, filled with a sense of elation, before giving Shirley a cheeky wave.

It was only as he crashed the van into gear that he realised it would be the first time, since the war, he could recall going home to Crouch End to spend the night alone. His father had always been there.

CHAPTER EIGHT

'How's Stevie this morning?'

Christopher had barely got a foot over the threshold of Rob's office before his uncle fired that urgent question at him. He accepted the mug of tea Rob had just poured out and perched on the edge of a chair.

'He seemed a lot better. But he's not going to be out for a while yet, so the sister said.'

A smile of sheer relief animated Robert's face on hearing the good news.

'He's all bandaged up and got bruises coming up on one side of his face and on his arms.' Chris described a large circle on one of his own cheeks with a finger. 'Couldn't see his legs but I reckon they're black and blue as well. Matron said he's been sick a lot but apparently that happens with bangs on the head. He's not sitting up yet, but he had his eyes open and we had a bit of a chat.'

Christopher had called in at the hospital to see his father before eight o'clock and the staff sister – who looked like a forbidding battleaxe but in fact had been kind – had muttered about *breaking the rules* but had allowed him to see Stephen for a short while. Their chat had skirted around anything controversial and, thinking about it now, Chris realised he'd spent almost the whole ten minutes satisfying his father's curiosity about the weather.

'Be alright, d'you reckon, if I go up during visiting this afternoon?' Rob asked.

'Don't see why not. I'm gonna pop in this evening.'

'So what's been happening with this Irish crew, and how come nobody thought to tell me about it?' Now he'd satisfied himself his brother was on the mend, Rob immediately got down to business with his nephew.

'They turned up not long after we started there. Dad was keen to find out how they got a foot in the door, but Declan O'Connor don't give nuthin' away. He's a right sly bastard. We come to the conclusion a palm must be getting greased up the Council Office.' Chris had expected a cross-examination from his uncle and had resigned himself to telling Rob everything about the pikeys, and the accident, whether his father approved of it or not. In Chris's opinion it was time the navvies got paid back for what they'd done. If the new ladder hadn't been nicked, his father wouldn't be lying in hospital.

'Declan O'Connor never does much donkeywork himself; he just turns up to pay his men and gee them up. Can tell from the way he tries to wind us up, calling out stuff about us falling behind, and not knowing our business, that he'd like to see us off. He's after having all the work in the street.' Christopher paused, and took a swig of tea. 'Have to say though, he looked shocked when he saw what had happened to me dad.' He glanced up at Rob. 'I went for him over thieving the ladder and causing the accident and they all backed off. Hope it stays that way, 'cos I can do without any more trouble while dad's so poorly.' He sighed. 'On me mind all the time, he is.'

'Sounds like I need to have a little chat with somebody,' Rob said, looking thoughtful. 'Why's Stevie been keeping this to himself?'

Christopher shrugged, feeling a bit uneasy. He decided to give his honest opinion. 'You know what me dad's like . . . I'm guessing he felt bad about new stuff going walkies. Like I said yesterday, he was intending to replace it out of his own pocket.' Then he added, 'I don't reckon he wants you to think he's incapable of sorting stuff out himself, and that's why he decided to try and handle O'Connor on his own.'

A faint grimace of surprise flickered over Rob's features. He hadn't been expecting his nephew to be quite so perceptive, or truthful, about Stevie's insecurities. But Rob knew Chris's loyalty to his father was rock solid.

'You alright overseeing the Whadcoat Street job on your own now?'

''Course I am.'

'Right . . .' cos when your dad gets out of hospital he's gonna need a good rest, and then I'm gonna have a word with him about things. Perhaps it's time he eased up working on the tools and came and did a bit in the office instead. It'd relieve the pressure on me too. Your aunt Faye is always telling me to slow down and take a few days off. Perhaps she's right about that.'

Chris took a gulp from his mug. He wasn't sure how his dad would take to sitting behind a desk, but there was time enough to argue the toss about that another day. He knew he ought to get off to work to make sure the lads weren't taking liberties while they were unsupervised.

'Is it right that you and your dad have been arguing a lot lately?'

Chris put down his tea and frowned at his shoes. Rob was his uncle, and his guvnor, but he felt like telling him to mind his own business on this one.

'Anything I should know about?' Rob prompted.

Chris shook his head. 'Nah . . . personal stuff . . .'

'Right,' Rob said. In fact he knew very well what the problem was between his brother and his nephew. When he'd given Matilda a lift home from the hospital the previous evening his aunt, in her agitated state, had blurted out that Stevie probably hadn't been concentrating at work because he'd been in high dudgeon ever since Chris had mentioned finding his mum. She'd realised at once she'd spoken out of turn, and had threatened Rob with dire consequences if he repeated it to anyone else.

'Who told you we'd been arguing?' Chris demanded.

Rob pulled open a filing cabinet drawer. 'You know how it is with the lads . . . word gets round.'

'You know what it's about, don't you?' Chris wasn't fooled for a moment. None of the lads knew anything except that he and Stevie had been avoiding one another as best they could.

'Heard rumours that you want to find your mum.'

'And?'

'And . . . I'm not sure you should rock the boat on this one, Chris.' Rob tossed some papers that he'd pulled from the cabinet onto the desk. 'It's been a long time settled, why stir it up?'

'Because I'm a Plummer as well as a Wild, and there's things I want to know.'

Rob had detected the raw emotion in his nephew's voice and he put up his hands, gesturing for a truce. 'Just telling you what I think, mate. But it's not my opinion that counts, it's yours.'

'Yeah, that's right,' Chris said coolly. 'Better be off and get to work.'

'Come back later before you knock off. I'll write out a docket and you can take it to the merchants to get any stuff you need.'

Chris nodded.

'Make sure you buy a couple of bleedin' strong ladders, won't you?' Rob called dryly as Chris closed the door.

He was just getting into his van when a smart saloon car pulled up by the office and a woman got out from behind the wheel. Chris liked his aunt Faye so he strolled over to speak to her.

'Heard about your dad, Chris,' Faye said immediately, her features crumpling in sympathy. 'So sorry . . . how is he this morning?'

'Better,' Chris nodded and smiled, emphasising the good news.

A sigh of sheer relief was Faye's response. 'And how are you bearing up? And how's that lovely new girlfriend of yours?'

'Yeah, I'm alright, but can't keep any secrets, I see,' Chris muttered, but with a twitch of the lips.

'In this family?' Faye's tone had risen in feigned amazement. 'Matilda told me about Grace.' She tapped his arm. 'And when Matilda's impressed with somebody you know they're alright.'

'Yeah, Grace is alright,' Chris endorsed softly, proudly.

'You going to bring her with you when you come for

dinner? I don't know if your dad will be out of hospital by then and able to make it, but we're going ahead with a little do for Daisy's birthday.'

Chris had forgotten all about his aunt's invitation to his cousin Daisy's birthday lunch.

'I've invited Pearl and I hope she'll come. It'll take her mind off things if she comes over for the day.'

'I'll ask Grace, I'm sure she'd like to come,' Chris said as he pulled open the van door. 'And it'd be nice to introduce her to some of the family.'

'You don't know that family like I do! If you did, you might be having second thoughts about going steady with Christopher Wild, or meeting more of his lot.'

Grace shot her mother an exasperated look. Moments ago she'd got home from the office and, before she'd even shrugged off her coat, Shirley had resumed nagging. The same conversation had been echoing in her head at breakfast that morning and Grace had gladly escaped to go to work.

It had all started when she'd told her mother that she'd been invited to Sunday dinner in a few weeks' time with some of Chris's extended family.

'So what if the man I'm going out with isn't a middle-class clerk who goes to work in a suit! Thank God for that! I had one of those before, didn't I, Mum, and look where that got me.'

'I know Hugh Wilkins was no good.' Shirley gestured disdain at the memory of her daughter's ex-fiancé. 'I'm the first to admit there's good and bad in all walks of life, so I'm not tarring all working-class people with the same brush . . .'

'Well that's a bleeding relief!' Grace shouted with

intentional coarseness. ''Cos *we're* working class!' She spun away from her mother in disgust. 'My dad, your husband, worked in a factory all his life, in case you've forgotten.'

'See!' Shirley wagged a finger. 'Before you started knocking about with one of the Wilds you wouldn't have talked to me like that. Your language, miss!'

'Oh, for Heaven's sake,' Grace muttered. A moment later she'd swung back to her mother, unable to contain her annoyance. 'You're a snob and a hypocrite, d'you know that? Nice as pie to Matilda to her face, weren't you, then behind her back tearing her family to shreds. When we went to see her, why didn't you tell her straight out that she lives in a dump, instead of sitting drinking tea with her then running her down afterwards behind her back?' Grace paused for breath. 'And why didn't you tell her straight out you'd sooner sit in listening to the wireless than go to Islington and join in her street party on Coronation Day?'

'You can't tell me Whadcoat Street isn't a dump, and who in their right mind would want to socialise with people like that?'

'I would!' Grace shouted. 'And I'm going to.'

'Well, you lower yourself if you want to. I only went to see her and have a cup of tea with her to be polite. Didn't really fancy a cup, I can tell you.' Shirley's face was a study of distaste. 'And I'm only thinking of you and your future, miss, when I say stay away from them. I don't want to see you making more mistakes.' Shirley adopted a pious look. 'You know I've always been pleasant to Christopher. First time he came here I invited him in for a cup of tea to thank him for bringing us home. I know my manners.'

'And he's always been pleasant to you, 'cos he knows *his* manners,' Grace returned pithily. 'So his dad can't be that bad, can he? He's obviously brought him up properly.' She barely paused before adding, 'You've not even asked how Stephen Wild is, have you? Yet, know what? Every time I saw Chris's dad he would always say to me, *send yer mum me best, won't you, luv.'*

Shirley reddened. 'You told me yesterday he's well on the mend, and will soon be out of hospital. Can't be asking about his accident all the time. Anyhow, I've never said anything bad about Christopher's dad. His mum . . . now that's a different matter,' she finished in a mutter and, aware she was defeated, stomped off down the hall to the kitchen. 'Could do with a bit of help getting tea ready,' she called irritably.

Grace quickly pegged her coat on a hook on the wall then followed her mum into the kitchen with an urgent question hovering on the tip of her tongue. 'Did you know Chris's mum?' she burst out.

'Knew *her* alright,' Shirley said with a nod. She stuck an old pot under the cold tap and half-filled it with water.

Grace was quiet for a moment while digesting that exciting news. Her annoyance at her mother was ebbing away on realising Shirley held useful information. When her mother thrust a peeler at her, and a colander filled with potatoes, she automatically started to prepare them. 'Chris was only a baby when his parents split up.'

'Yes, I know,' Shirley replied, cutting into a cabbage and digging out the stalk. 'Barely a year they were married and nobody believed that Christopher was a honeymoon baby, if you know what I mean.' She gave her daughter an arch look. 'Being as they took the trouble to get married – quite a lavish do it was – it surprised a lot of people when they divorced. But I knew it wouldn't last.'

'How did you know that?' Grace speared a glance at her mother while halving the peeled potatoes and dropping them into the water in the pot.

'Friend of mine told me that Pam Plummer was always more interested in Rob Wild than his brother, Stevie. Can't blame her for that. We all had a pash for Rob Wild . . . regular heartthrob he was. Even when he was a young hound he had a business and a flash car and plenty of money. But Pam should have left him alone once she married his brother.'

Grace overlooked her mother's farcical, selective snobbery where the Wilds were concerned. A comfortable lifestyle, with a hound of a husband, obviously trumped middle-class morals every time. She had an unexpected opportunity to find out more about Christopher's mother, and that was far more important to Grace than taking her mother to task again for being a hypocrite. Just yesterday, when he'd brought her home, Chris had again seemed swayed towards resuming his search for Pamela.

'How did your friend know Pam was still after Rob Wild?'

'She made it her business to know,' Shirley said with an emphasising grunt. 'For a while, people reckoned that Vicky Watson had Rob Wild hooked. She certainly thought so, so she kept tabs on the opposition.'

'Vicky Watson?' Grace breathed. 'You knew her?'

'Yeah. Went to school together.'

'Where is she now, do you know?'

Shirley shot a suspicious look at her daughter. 'Why're you so interested in Vicky Watson?'

'Just . . . Chris mentioned her 'cos she was his mum's bridesmaid.'

'Yeah, she was,' Shirley confirmed, with a smile of recollection. 'That's how she knew Pam liked Rob. Pam and Vicky were good friends for a while and confided in one another. But Vicky found out that Pam, even after she was married to Stevie, was chasing after Robert on the sly.'

'And how did Robert feel about it all? Was he married then?'

'He was involved in a really bad fight,' Shirley said, putting down her knife to stare into space. 'Nothing to do with Stevie being jealous or anything like that, 'cos Rob never showed any interest in his sister-in-law,' she immediately explained, having seen the startled look in her daughter's eyes. 'Rob was beaten up by gangsters. Anyhow, as soon as he was well enough he surprised everybody and married Faye Greaves and nobody knew much about her as she'd lived in Kent most of her life. Vicky was not pleased about that, I can tell you.'

'So where's Vicky now?'

'A few years later she got married to a fellow worked for the Water Board, and they moved to Clapham. David Green seemed a weird sort for Vicky. He was a lot older than her, and it was a surprise when they got together. But Vicky and me sort of kept in touch. I used to send her Christmas cards, then during the war it tailed off.' Shirley placed the pot of potatoes on the gas stove. 'Used to visit her sometimes and we'd go down to the Lyons corner shop and have a cake and a cuppa and a natter about old times.'

'So you've got her address . . .'

'Somewhere, I expect. I used to have lots of friends.'

Shirley pouted out a sigh. "Course the war put paid to a lot of it . . . moving about . . . getting evacuated . . . you lost interest in people . . .' She suddenly turned around to find she was talking to herself.

CHAPTER NINE

'What's so urgent that it can't wait till after I finish work this evening?'

Apart from his wife, few people spoke to Robert Wild in that tone of voice and got away with it. But it wasn't only Walter Purvis's attitude that was pissing Rob off; he was also seriously narked because it had taken many weeks to get in contact with the crafty git.

Various toffee-nosed secretaries had told him that Mr Purvis was on holiday, or out on site, or in another department, or any other old pony Walter had told them to put forward as an excuse. The fact that the Council's Chief Contracts Manager had been determinedly incommunicado had convinced Rob the man knew why he was after him. He gave him a hard stare. 'Get in the car for a minute,' he said icily. 'I need to talk to you.'

Walter Purvis slid onto the passenger seat and dumped his battered briefcase down on the floor. 'I've had to delay an important contract meeting on the second phase of Whadcoat Street to come here,' he complained, shoving his poplin shirt over his paunch and into the straining waistband of his trousers. He knew enough about Rob Wild's reputation for dealing with those who crossed him not to ignore his summons. It had arrived in an envelope that morning, addressed to his home rather than his office, and he'd been infuriated to receive it.

'Delayed it, have you? That's quite convenient,' Robert drawled. Walter was already sweating from the July heat; Robert knew that in a moment the fat creep would be in a real lather. 'What I've got to say is gonna have some bearing on your contract meeting so listen very carefully.'

Purvis frowned at him and shoved his spectacles up the bridge of his nose. From behind the wire-rimmed glass his pale eyes blinked rapidly. He was a middle-aged man of about the same age as Rob, but there all similarity ended. Walter was overweight, lacking in personal hygiene, and thinning on top. Hardly a model Lothario, as no doubt his despising wife would have testified, yet he unfortunately had a liking for lithe young men, and the high life, that wasn't satisfied by the salary he drew. He thus supplemented it by taking backhanders in return for dishing out lucrative building contracts.

Robert had had a few illicit dealings with him previously. Those had gone very well and when Walter told him he was the only building contractor he trusted enough to accept sweeteners from Rob had tended to believe him. Walter was scrupulously careful in keeping everything under wraps and he paid him well.

Robert was now feeling annoyed that he'd been uncharacteristically naïve. It seemed Declan O'Connor had also cottoned on to Walter and the greedy bastard was trying to play both ends against the middle. Rob was about to impress on him it had been a bad move . . .

'I thought we had an agreement that the first phase of Whadcoat Street demolition was all mine.'

'It is,' Walter said, perplexed. 'Your brother started on it, surely, many months ago? Payments have been issued . . .'

'Stevie's started down there alright, and thank you for the cheques,' Rob added politely. 'Are you satisfied with the way things are going?'

'Of course . . .' Purvis looked apprehensive. He was starting to sense trouble.

'So why get in the competition?'

'What?'

'A gang of pikeys have started work there too, just yards away. So do you want to tell me why my money suddenly isn't enough, when we had a gentlemen's agreement?' Rob watched the fellow's chins sag. He smiled. 'Or perhaps you're intending to return my envelope . . . you remember, don't you? It was the one I gave you, stuffed with tenners.'

Purvis's eyes swivelled to and fro as though he believed somebody might have overheard their conversation, even though Rob's voice had been sinisterly soft. 'I don't know . . . I've no idea . . .' He suddenly blinked rapidly. 'It's got to be Kennedy,' he hissed. 'He's been brown-nosing and telling me had everything under control,' he explained. 'I recruited him some years ago when he was fresh out of college and brash as they come. He's not changed much.' In fact Walter had given him a job because he'd thought him easy on the eye. And that's all he had done, look, because he'd never be stupid enough to pursue a young work colleague, no matter how fit and handsome he was. 'I've been giving him a bit of a free hand for the past six months, and he's been covering for me when I'm on holiday. If I hadn't been seconded to another department to oversee it while some soppy prat's gone off to have a nervous breakdown . . .'

'Well, you'd better shift yourself right back where you belong, Walter, and sort this out, or I will, and then who knows what stones might get overturned . . .' Rob suddenly realised the toffee-nosed sorts answering the phones hadn't been giving him the runaround after all. But he felt not an iota of guilt on realising that Walter had probably just told the truth about the pikeys being nothing to do with him. He reached to start the ignition but the surveyor made no move to get out.

Walter wanted to stay and talk now. 'What's been happening down there?' he asked nervously. 'This Irish crew . . . have they been causing any trouble I should know about? Anything that might draw attention?'

'Yeah, you could say they've been causing trouble: my brother's in hospital, and there's a brawl down there every bleedin' day. So sooner or later the Black Marias are gonna be racing the ambulances to Whadcoat Street.' Rob smiled sardonically. ''Course that's nothing new for The Bunk, and I'd know 'cos I grew up there.' He suddenly leaned close to Walter and murmured, 'I paid you well for this contract, so I reckon I'm due some of my money back, don't you? Let's say twenty per cent for all the inconvenience.'

'You said your brother's in hospital,' Walter burbled, blanching. The thought of handing back some of his commission, as he liked to call it, was a secondary concern; his mind was racing ahead examining dreadful scenarios that might expose him as corrupt and depraved and put paid to his career and his marriage. Arrest, court, the boys who might be called as witnesses, were all lurid images whizzing through his mind. 'Did these navvies beat your brother up and put him in hospital?' he gasped.

'Might just as well have done. He had a fall off a ladder and it wouldn't have happened if the thieving gits hadn't been stealing all Wild Brothers' equipment.'

'You should have told me before,' Walter complained in a high-pitched squeak. 'I could have nipped it in the bud . . .'

'Well, you know now, so sort it out,' Rob announced before giving Walter a withering look. 'Or believe me I will sort it out and there'll be blood and guts all over the place . . . yours included, if your wife finds out about your habits.'

Walter shrank back against the leather upholstery, seeking protection from that image.

'D'you mind?' Rob asked, and nodded at the car door. 'I'm meeting my wife for a spot of lunch . . .'

'Who is it you're after, dear?' the old fellow asked again, cocking his good ear at Grace.

Grace raised her voice a little. 'Mrs Green . . . Vicky Green.' She was beginning to wish she hadn't wasted an afternoon to come on a wild-goose chase, especially as her friend Wendy had felt obliged to type an urgent report for her so Grace could tell their supervisor everything would be covered in her absence.

Fifteen minutes ago she'd arrived at the Clapham address that she'd covertly copied from her mother's notebook. The woman at the property had told her she believed the Greens had moved around the corner, close to Clapham Junction, just after the war. But it seemed the elderly occupant of this house was also on the point of sending her on her way. Grace glumly realised she was having no luck locating the woman who might know Pam Plummer's whereabouts.

'Ah . . . Mrs Green.' The grizzled face nodded at her, and the old gentleman indicated the house to his right with his thumb. He shuffled back inside, shutting the door, leaving Grace staring at its coloured glass panel. She retraced her steps along the path and carefully latched the creaky wooden gate. She'd reached her destination and, after all her efforts, felt her courage oddly draining away. It was tempting to turn around and head home rather than explain her business to a stranger. And she realised her faintheartedness sprang from the fact that it wasn't actually her business at all that had brought her here; it was Christopher's.

When she'd set out she'd been fired with confidence and certainty, but now she was having second thoughts and wondering whether Chris would think she was interfering, rather than helping.

He had no idea she'd come here, or that she'd got Vicky Green's address from her mum. Grace hadn't told him about it because he'd been shilly-shallying about looking for his mother since his father had had a setback. Stevie had fallen on a wet floor in the hospital bathroom and ever since Chris had been unwilling to discuss Pamela.

Yesterday evening, when Grace had tried to gently impress on him again that it was the right time to do some detective work without upsetting Stevie, they had ended up bickering. She'd spent a restless night turning things over in her mind but had decided Chris would be relieved if she took the initiative and resumed the search. His father couldn't then blame him for going behind his back. But now she was having second thoughts . . .

Grace surfaced from her reflection to see the old boy had lifted an edge of his net curtain and was watching her loitering on the pavement. He gave her a smile and again jabbed his thumb at number thirty-seven. Grace acknowledged him by wriggling a few fingers then, taking a deep breath, walked next door. She knocked and waited. She knocked again and felt a twinge of shame as her clenched hands began to relax because nobody was at home.

'Who are you?'

Grace pivoted about to find a woman in a floral summer dress, a shopping bag in each hand, crossing the road to hurry towards her. On reaching the gate she struggled, juggling bags, to lift the latch.

'Sorry . . .' Grace burbled with a faltering smile. 'Are you Mrs Green?'

'Who wants to know?'

'Well . . . I do . . .' Grace said, feeling intimidated by her brusque manner.

'And who are you?'

The woman was standing close to her on the path now, her head with its fading blonde hair cocked to one side. Grace could see that once she'd been an attractive woman and, in common with her mother, she was making an attempt to hang on to her youth by using a lot of make-up.

'I'm Grace Coleman and my mum used to know a woman called Vicky Watson who married a Mr Green . . .'

'Shirley Coleman's daughter, are you?'

Grace finally got a smile.

'Well, well . . . haven't heard that name for a good while. Sort of lost touch with Shirley.' She looked Grace up and down. 'Still in Islington, are you? I remember your dad joined up and the rest of you were off to Surrey to get away from the bombing.'

'We live in Tottenham now . . .'

Grace watched Vicky turn the key in the lock of her front door then edge in sideways with her bulky bags.

'Well, come in, then,' Vicky invited. 'Might as well have a cuppa as you've come all this way, although I've got to say, I'm not sure *why* you have,' she added bluntly. She suddenly dropped her shopping and twisted about. 'Oh, you've not come in person to tell me your mum . . .' She jerked her head twice, indicating she'd rather not utter the final word.

'Oh, no . . . no . . . she's fine,' Grace reassured the woman, and followed her inside.

'Pam Plummer . . . now there's another name from the past,' Vicky said, putting down her cup. 'I often wonder what happened to all those people I used to know in Islington.'

They were seated now, in a neat front room, in fireside chairs that had a square table wedged between them, holding a plate of rich tea biscuits.

Grace sipped her tea. 'My mum told me you all knew one another from your schooldays. So I wondered if you kept in touch with Pam and have her address.'

'Does Shirley want to get in touch with her?' Vicky asked in surprise.

Grace hesitated, not wanting to lie, but not wanting to tell the truth either. She knew Chris considered searching for his mother a very personal matter. 'Mum was going on the other day about once having lots of friends; I think she's a bit lonely since dad died a few years ago. He got injured in the war and never really recovered,' she explained, having noticed Vicky's enquiring look.

'Very sorry to hear that . . .' Vicky murmured.

'Anyway, I've been thinking about a street party for Coronation Day next June,' Grace said brightly. 'There's less than a year to go now till the big day. I thought it'd be a great idea to have a get-together . . . and that it might be nice to find a few of Mum's old friends.' Grace knew that it was best not to mention that Matilda Keiver was involved, or that the party would be held in The Bunk. That news would be sure to make Vicky fire some very awkward questions at her. 'Mum doesn't know I'm here,' Grace added carefully. If it came about that a reunion did take place at some time she didn't want her fibs causing her mum problems. 'So it would be a nice surprise for her if it goes ahead . . . 'Course I'll let people know in good time . . .'

Vicky stood up and went to a little bureau. 'Last I heard of Pam she was living in Bexleyheath with her husband. But that was before the war, so it's a while and they might have moved on.'

'Husband?' Grace echoed.

'Yeah . . . second husband, name of Stanley Riley. Your mum would know she got divorced when she was young, but probably not that she'd remarried. When we all lived around Islington, Pam got involved with a rough family. She married one of them, worse for her, and lived to regret it.' Vicky pursed her lips in thought. 'I remember she had a son, but her ex-husband brought the boy up. God knows what sort of tyke *he* turned into. You should ask your mum about the Wilds, she'll remember them, I'm sure, and tell you there wasn't a good one amongst them.'

105

Grace lowered her eyes and sipped from her tea but she felt her indignation burning. Her mum had told her that this woman had very much hoped to marry into that *rough family*. 'I think I've heard of Rob Wild,' she said. 'He's done well for himself, hasn't he?'

Vicky swung about to give her a hard stare. 'He's done well alright . . . by treading on other people. He was a horrible, selfish man; the worst of the lot of 'em.' She opened the small address book she'd fished out of the bureau. 'Shall I write down the address for you?'

'Oh, I can remember it, thanks . . .'

It seemed that twenty-five years on, Vicky Watson, as she'd been, still hadn't got over her pique at being dropped by Rob Wild. Grace felt relieved she'd not mentioned the Keivers or the Wilds when talking about Coronation Day street parties moments ago.

'Pam might have a telephone number, I suppose, but I haven't got it listed here,' Vicky said, turning the pages back and forth.

'Don't worry, the address will do; thanks a lot for helping out with that,' Grace said, standing up. 'Thanks for tea.'

As Grace was leaving the house Vicky muttered, 'Oh, my husband's home early.'

Grace glanced over a shoulder and saw a soberly dressed, balding gentleman marching along on the opposite pavement. He appeared to be close to retirement age and wore spectacles and a pinched expression. She turned to smile farewell and understood the sour look on Vicky's face. She'd not yet met Chris's uncle but if what her mother had said about him were true, Mr Green would have been a very poor substitute for Robert Wild.

CHAPTER TEN

'Will you work in your dad's business, when you finish school?'

'He wants me to, so does Mum.' Daisy Wild had tilted her dark head towards Grace to whisper her reply. 'Mum always wanted to be a secretary before she got married. They think I should do a commercial course so I can do the firm's books.' She dismissed it with a hand flick. 'I'd rather do hairdressing for a while then find a rich husband to look after me.'

'You've got a nice lot of qualifications and can get yourself a good job, young lady,' the birthday girl's mother told her from across the dining table. Despite her mild reprimand, Faye allowed her husband to pour their daughter a glass of Sauternes.

Daisy wrinkled her nose and continued attacking her roast potatoes. 'You've got lovely hair; it's an unusual colour . . . sort of caramel blonde, isn't it,' she chattered. 'I bet it'd look good in a bun. Do you wear it up much? I could do it for you later. I like to practise on my friends at school.'

'Leave poor Grace alone.' Faye smiled in wry apology. 'She's trying to eat.'

'Sometimes I put it in a bun,' Grace told Daisy as she tucked into her lamb. The meal was delicious and she'd already complimented their hostess on an excellent roast. Grace had been immediately made to feel welcome by the members of Chris's family she'd not previously met.

'You work in an office, don't you, Grace?' Faye sounded interested. 'Do you like secretarial work?'

'Yes, I do. I'm in a typing pool so it's a bit hectic but we're lucky to have a good boss. The work gets shared out fairly and we're paid for overtime.'

Faye gave her daughter a significant look.

'You listen to your mum, and to Grace, and you won't go far wrong.' Rob pointed his fork at Daisy in emphasis. 'And I don't want to hear talk of husbands, rich or otherwise, for a good while yet.'

'Mum wasn't much older than me when she married you,' Daisy chipped in with a saucy smile.

'That's enough backchat, young lady,' her father told her. 'You just concentrate on finishing your schooling. Eat your dinner.'

'Leave the girl alone,' Matilda growled, putting down her knife and fork. 'If she likes doing hair, let her do hair. It's a job. Ain't as if she's telling you she's planning to sit around on her backside and sponge off you.'

'Thanks, Auntie,' Daisy muttered with a glimmering look for her parents and a subtle smile for Matilda.

It made a refreshing change for Grace to listen to people airing their opinions without an atmosphere ensuing. At home, a prolonged silence would have been the result of a difference with her mother, not that

Shirley would ever allow anything so common to occur while they had company.

'Well, this is nice,' Faye said contentedly as there was a lull in conversation and only the chink of busy cutlery, and a stifled burp from Matilda, was heard. 'It's been a long time since we had a little get-together on a Sunday. Of course, it's a shame Stevie can't be here.'

It had been inevitable that talk would turn to the invalid.

'I went in to see him last night,' Rob informed them. 'He told me an Irish family have moved into the street.' He'd addressed the remark to his nephew but his aunt came back with an answer.

'They're called Murphy. Nice people,' was Matilda's succinct opinion. 'Noreen was in the shop getting a bit of bread and tea on the strap yesterday. Poor sods have got two little gels 'n' all to feed.'

'Causing any trouble?' Again Rob's question was directed at Chris.

'Told you they're nice people,' Matilda replied bluntly.

'They are nice enough.' Chris endorsed his aunt's view. 'Feel sorry for 'em if anything, having to make do with a dump like that . . . no offence, Auntie.'

'None taken.' Matilda grunted, and continued her conversation with Pearl.

'The fellow's called Kieran and he's started working with O'Connor's crew. He asked me for a job first but I knew you'd say nuthin' doing.' Chris realised it wasn't the time or place for a discussion about work so he simply let the subject drop.

He had guessed that Kieran would eventually be forced to take any offer of employment that came his way. But he hadn't caused Wild Brothers any problems. He didn't join in any catcalling that came from the rival gang, and seemed to want to keep his distance from his colleagues. Chris could tell he was the sort of man who simply wanted to keep his nose clean and provide for his family.

'Have you been in to visit Stevie today, Pearl?' Matilda asked, in between trying to dislodge something from her teeth.

Pearl shook her head, thrusting plump fingers through her hair in a gesture of exasperation. 'Popping in this evening. Driving me mad now, he is, going on about coming home. I reckon the doctor'll chuck him out in the end just for a quiet life.'

'He's been whingeing at me as well about it,' Chris said, spearing another roast potato from the bowl in the centre of the table. 'I reckon he's about to discharge himself.' He'd done justice to Faye's superb cooking. Even after second helpings, and a few extras, he'd cleared his plate. 'That's the best dinner I've had in a long while.'

'I know your dad can pull off a decent roast,' Faye remarked. 'I've tasted a few of his dinners and they're not half bad.'

'He *can* cook actually.' Chris praised his dad while Pearl endorsed the fact her boyfriend was a bit of a chef, by nodding. 'Got to admit I've been missing him in that respect,' Chris added.

'Shouldn't have brought that up, Faye,' Rob jokily complained. 'Chris'll be up the hospital with Stevie's clothes next time he's feeling peckish.'

'Better feed him up a bit more then. Who's for pudding?' Faye had noticed empty plates all round.

Rob got up and helped his wife clear the table of used crockery and cutlery.

'Stevie is a dab hand at a bit of catering. When we

have our Coronation Day party he can be in charge of the food,' Matilda announced. She did a little drum roll on the table with her fingers. 'And I've managed to already stash away a nice bit of booze. Old man Turner who works down the docks got me a case of Irish whiskey on the sly.' She put a finger to her lips. 'Don't go tellin' Faye though, 'cos you know she don't like any duckin' 'n' divin' and stuff wot falls off the back of lorries.'

Chris grinned at his aunt. 'You should know better at your age,' he ribbed her, glancing at Grace for her reaction to his aunt's confession to doing a bit of receiving. Behind a hand, raised to cover her mock outrage, she was laughing.

'And don't forget, Grace . . .' Matilda wagged a finger at her nephew's girlfriend. 'You're on me planning committee and soon we'll need to get things underway.'

"Course, be pleased to help out.' The mention of the Coronation Day street party reminded Grace of her meeting with Vicky Watson. She slid a glance at Chris . . . time enough later to think about owning up to that . . .

'And you're me second in command as far as table laying goes,' Matilda told Daisy.

'I'm going to bring me boyfriend to the street party,' Daisy whispered to Grace. 'But don't tell me dad . . .'

A moment later Rob came in, wearing a proud smile and carrying a huge glass bowl of sherry trifle.

'Perhaps I'm not as stuffed as I thought,' Chris said. Through the sparkling glass could be seen sumptuous layers of jam sponge and fruit and custard.

'You just might find your eyes are bigger than your belly, Christopher,' Daisy rebuked him, playfully whacking her cousin's abdomen and making him wince.

111

'Well, you can't have none 'cos you're watching yer figure,' Chris retaliated and moved the glass bowl along the tablecloth, out of her reach.

Grace was enjoying seeing a family so at ease with each other. Whenever her mother had family over everybody seemed to stand on ceremony. Not that they entertained often: Shirley had never liked any of her in-laws, so they rarely saw the Coleman side now her father had passed away. Her mother's lot were a bit thin on the ground: Shirley's younger brother had been killed during the Second World War, leaving his widow childless. Grace now felt quite sad that she'd never had an opportunity to grow close to any cousins. She rarely saw her older brother, Paul, so she hardly knew her young nephews. Their visits were limited to Christmas and birthday trips.

But Grace had her beloved nan to visit. Her maternal grandmother had lived in Tottenham all her life, and being close to Nan Jackson was the main reason she and her mother had chosen to settle there on returning from Surrey after her dad passed away.

Once the trifle bowl was empty, but for creamy smears, people began lazily stirring in their chairs.

'Well, off you all go and relax in the front room,' Faye said. 'Rob'll put on the wireless for a bit of light music and I'll bring in a nice cup of tea in a while.' She moved back her chair and started clearing the table.

Grace got up too. 'You must let me help,' she insisted. 'It's the least I can do after that wonderful meal.'

'Thanks,' Faye said with a smile. 'That's kind.'

Pearl and Matilda also started stacking dirty crockery.

'How about you giving a hand, young lady?' Faye suggested to her daughter.

'I'm sorting out records 'cos Chris wants to listen to

112

the new one I bought this week.' Daisy squinted mean-ingfully at her cousin.

'Oh . . . right . . . yeah, that's it,' he replied gamely, while an almost imperceptible shrug indicated he had no part in it.

'You've got him well-trained.' Pearl directed that at Faye, while watching Rob roll up his sleeves and fill a large bowl with hot water. 'Stevie might be able to cook but he ain't keen on doing a bit of washing-up.'

Rob gave the women assembled in the kitchen a smile of studied charm. 'I can be hired out very cheap, you know, ladies.'

'Don't take no notice of him,' Matilda warned them with a wink. 'Won't be yer washing-up he'll be wanting to do . . .'

'Matilda!' Faye exclaimed with mock indignation. 'You know he's a reformed character and has been for a long time.'

'A rogue's a rogue,' Matilda stated with a twinkling smile for her nephew.

At forty-eight years old, Rob Wild was still a hand-some man despite his dark hair having silvered at the temples, and a tracery of faint lines being visible on his close-shaven jaw. The scars were the result of a fight he'd had with gangsters almost twenty-five years ago. The facial marks didn't worry him, neither had his leg injury until his slight limp had prevented him being able to join up to fight for his country in 1939.

'If Matilda reckons I might have a relapse and start flirting perhaps I'd better leave you girls to it.' Rob shook his soapy hands and dropped a kiss on his wife's fair head of hair before leaving the kitchen.

'Any excuse to skive! Right, you're on washing-up

duty at Matilda's Coronation Day party,' Faye called after him.

'Makes yer sick, don't it.' Matilda wiped furiously at a plate with her cloth. 'Been married how long? And still turtle doves, the two of 'em.'

'You have a lovely house,' Grace said a few minutes later, when the washing and wiping was well under way. She glanced around the large, well-equipped kitchen.

When Chris had pulled up in the van outside his uncle and aunt's house Grace had felt her jaw drop. The imposing stucco-fronted villa was situated in a very nice part of Tufnell Park and the sleek Wolseley car parked on the driveway at the side had obviously cost a lot of money.

'I know we're lucky to live here,' Faye readily admitted. She pushed her damp hair back from her brow with the back of her wrist then set to scrubbing plates again. 'Rob used to rent this house when he was quite young. Then, as Matilda knows, things went sour for a while and we moved to a smaller place in Islington. But he always wanted to move back here, although I quite liked our cosy little cottage. When the freehold came up for sale, he was fortunate enough to snap it up.'

'I want to move in with Stevie,' Pearl suddenly announced.

Three pairs of eyes swivelled towards her.

'But whenever I bring the subject up, he cocks a deaf 'un,' she added with a grimace of disappointment.

'Well, could be things'll be changing soon,' Matilda said with a deliberate flick of a glance Grace's way. 'When Chris settles himself down, you might find Stevie won't be keen to be living on his own.'

'Let's get that tea made.' Faye noticed that Grace was looking bashful. She took the wet cloths and hung them on the cooking range rail to dry. 'Leave that lot on the kitchen table.' She nodded at the clean, stacked crockery. 'We'll need it again teatime anyway.'

'Fancy a stroll in the garden?' Chris asked Grace as they sat side-by-side, sipping tea, in the elegant front room.

She nodded enthusiastically, and put down her cup. She was keen to explore outside. Having followed Chris towards the French doors she stepped out onto a paved area that ran the width of the house, beyond which was an expanse of well-tended lawn. They strolled arm-in-arm down some steps and on to springy turf.

'Crikey, I'm full,' Grace murmured with a satiated sigh.

Chris slanted a smile down at her. 'Better not bring you here again in case you start getting fat,' he teased with an appreciative look at her figure. She was dressed in a sleeveless floral print dress that was skimpy enough to show off a little bit of creamy cleavage and her shapely legs.

She pinched his arm in response, making him give an exaggerated howl. In retaliation he lifted her up and carried her, squealing, a few feet before allowing her sandaled feet back onto the lawn.

'Wish I had a house like this,' Grace said dreamily, turning around to look at the back aspect of the handsome property.

'Me too,' Chris said with a wry chuckle. 'Don't come cheap, places like this.'

'It's a big house for just the three of them.'

'Oh, Adam comes home sometimes. Daisy's got a brother,' he explained. 'He's quite a bit older than her: about twenty-seven or so. Adam's an officer in the RAF.'

'Is he really?' Grace said, surprised.

'He was a bit of an ace towards the end of the war, and he was only twenty.' Chris sounded proud of his heroic cousin. 'At the moment he's stationed in Germany with his fiancée.'

'Must tell my mum,' Grace giggled. 'She'll be impressed.'

'Glad one of us impresses her 'cos I know I don't, do I?' Chris returned dryly.

'Don't mind her; she's a snob and I've told her so.' Grace patted his arm, consolingly. 'I hadn't realised your Aunt Matilda could be such a card.'

'Oh, Matilda's a character alright.' Chris took her hand and led her to a bench set under a weeping willow tree. 'I tend to think of her as my nan rather than my auntie. When I was younger I used to think of her as me mum. She's been everything to me, really . . .' Chris gazed off into the sunlit summer afternoon.

Grace hadn't been sure when to tell Chris she'd got some information from Vicky Green. He still didn't know she'd gone to Clapham and found his uncle Rob's old flame. He'd been avoiding talking about his mother and whenever she tried to bring the subject up he'd get quite sharp with her.

But Grace had brought the address with her today, in the hope an appropriate time might arise when she could slip into the conversation that she knew where Pamela might be. And as he'd just mentioned thinking of Matilda as his substitute mum . . .

'I've got something for you actually,' she began lightly after they were seated. She pulled a scrap of paper from her pocket. 'My mum told me that she used to know Vicky Watson . . . Vicky Green as she is now, 'cos she's married. I went to see her and got you this.'

Chris's eyes darted to her outstretched hand, then to her face.

'You needn't worry that I told my mum or Vicky anything about why I was interested in Pam Plummer.' She looked earnestly at him, noting disbelief and a hint of anger darkening his eyes. 'It came up in conversation that my mum used to go to school with Vicky. She was reminiscing about all the girls fancying your uncle Rob years ago, because he was a bit flash. Apparently, Vicky thought she'd got him hooked. Anyway, my mum kept in touch with Vicky and used to send her Christmas cards, and she had her address, so I copied it down without her knowing.' She paused, garnering courage. 'I went to see Vicky in Clapham and asked for Pamela's address. I said I wanted it to contact Mum's old friends for a Coronation Day get-together. It's not wholly a lie . . . it'd be wonderful if somehow or other your mum could come.'

'Why didn't you tell me what you was planning on doing?' Chris demanded hoarsely, staring at the paper as though it were something poisonous.

'Because you've been a bit narky lately, Chris,' Grace calmly pointed out. 'I understand why that is,' she added in the same even tone. 'You're naturally worried about your dad, but he's so much better now and due out of hospital soon.'

He licked his lips, staring off into space as though trying to marshal his thoughts.

'Stevie can't blame *you* for getting it, Chris, *I* went there . . .' Grace began.

'Yeah! And I never asked you to,' he growled, turning a fierce look on her.

Grace felt tears start in her eyes. She had always known what his reaction might be, and yet still it hurt.

'Her name is Riley now. Your mum married a Stanley Riley . . .'

'So bleedin' what?' Chris knew he sounded petulant and childish and he hung his head, propping it in cupped palms.

'Sorry . . . I shouldn't have interfered.' Grace sprang up to walk back towards the house. 'It's time I was getting home,' she said huskily. 'I'm just going to thank your aunt and uncle and say goodbye to the others . . .'

Chris caught her arm and dragged her back beside him. 'Sorry.' He leaned close to whisper against her hair. 'I know you've done it for the right reason . . . but . . . I'm scared of going there and being told to clear off.'

'Are you scared of being welcomed in too?' Grace asked, pushing back to search his eyes. 'You don't know how your mum'll react.'

'Me dad called her a useless lazy slut when he found out I wanted to find her; he'd never said anything like that before.'

'Perhaps he's as scared as you are,' Grace said gently. 'It'll be a big change for you all if you get to know your mum; and you might have brothers and sisters too. He could be still bitter about it all.'

'I reckon it's true, what he said.'

'Well, perhaps it *was* true, but people change over time, and if you give up, you won't ever know.'

'I'm not sure . . .' he croaked.

'Think about it, that's all you've got to do,' Grace urged him.

Chris wiped a hand across his mouth and stared into the distance.

'Your dad's not out of hospital yet, there's still time before he comes home . . .'

118

'Yeah, I know!' Immediately he closed his eyes and muttered an apology for sounding brusque, raking his fingers through his long dark hair. 'Me uncle Rob thinks I shouldn't rock the boat, and he always talks sense.' He choked a mirthless laugh. 'Don't know how he found out I'd been hoping to contact me mum. Probably Matilda blurted it out. I'm pretty sure me dad wouldn't have mentioned any of it to him.'

'It's up to you what you do, Chris . . .'

He suddenly got up and, taking her hand, pulled her onto her feet. 'There's a pond down here with a few fish in it, come and have a look.' He screwed up the paper in his fist, stuffed it into a pocket, and set off.

CHAPTER ELEVEN

'We've got to get away from here.' Noreen Murphy bounced the baby on her hip in an attempt to stop Rosie's coughing. 'Are you listening to me, Kieran?' she asked plaintively. 'I said we should get away from here now . . . this week. Rosie's chest is rattling, can't you hear it?' She dropped a kiss on the baby's soft dark curls. 'It's too damp and dirty in this place . . .'

'I heard you before, woman!'

'Well, what have you to say about any of it?' she asked in despair. 'I talk and talk. What do you say?'

'We'll move when I've money enough to get somewhere decent.' He continued climbing out of his dirty work clothes and took them to the window to shake the worst of the muck from them into the street. 'I'll not keep moving us from one dump to the next.' He sent that over his shoulder at her. 'It'll be a good room next time, Noreen, promise you, it will. I just need to keep working and saving and in a month or two . . .'

'We need somewhere clean *now*. I want to go away from here *now*.' She spun on the spot to look about at her depressing home. 'It's no place for young children.' Noreen lay the baby down on a filthy mattress then drew the tot, clutching at her knees, towards the iron bedstead and sat her down on it too. She opened a packet of biscuits and gave Kathleen a custard cream to chew on.

'We'll go back to Ireland then, shall we?' Kieran suggested softly.

'If only we could . . .' Noreen sighed. 'We came here to escape one lot of troubles but what have we got in its place?' She looked around at her squalid surroundings.

Kieran walked over in his underclothes to embrace his wife. 'We're better off here, you know we are.'

'You're in with bad men, Kieran.' Noreen shrugged off her husband's comfort and started pacing to and fro. It was a dull summer day and the recent rain had permeated the atmosphere with the odour of mildewed mortar. Noreen rubbed her bare arms with her palms as she stared at her husband's back. 'I've heard them talking, you know. They're always planning on setting about Christopher and his men working along the street.'

Kieran swung around and gave her a fierce look. 'You keep yourself to yourself, you hear me, Noreen? I'm doing just that. I do my work and then I come home. We'll not be taking sides or interfering in any feuds between people. We've had enough of that back in Ireland. I'm sick to me stomach of fighting and killing.'

'You'd be better off at the labour exchange than getting in with such as O'Connor. Has he paid you all of your wages yet?'

A brusque shake of the head was Noreen's answer.

In response she went to the child sitting on the bed and took the packet of custard creams from her, making

121

Kathleen whimper. She lobbed it her husband's way. 'There's your supper then, 'cos I'm not going back to that shop and begging for more credit until Rosie needs linctus.'

'I'll take her to the doctor's surgery for medicine.'

'You will not,' Noreen said, narrowing her eyes. 'You know as well as I do that the surgery will want to know our address. You know too what will happen when the authorities find out our home is a slum waiting to be pulled down.' Noreen rushed over to Kieran and grabbed his chin forcing him to look at her. 'They'll take our girls away if they find out we're living in such conditions as aren't fit for adults let alone little children.'

Kieran wrenched free of his wife's pinching fingers. But he had nothing to say because he realised Noreen's fears were valid.

'Shush that noise now, Kathleen,' Noreen told the little girl, who was still grizzling. Kathleen contented herself with sucking her sugary fingers to ease her hunger.

Kieran came towards his elder daughter, holding out a biscuit. 'Look what Daddy has for you. Good girl,' he crooned, stroking her long dark hair and sitting down beside her. 'I'll have me money off O'Connor tomorrow, or tell him I'll not work longer for him.'

'And what if he tells you to whistle for your wages? What will you do then, Kieran?'

'Give over about it, woman!'

'I'm getting work,' Noreen said abruptly. 'I can get a job cleaning again. The lady in Tufnell Park said I could go back any time . . .'

'You will not.'

'I will . . .'

'And who will look after Rosie and Kathleen?'

122

'You. You're just along the street working, are you not? And if O'Connor won't pay up you can stop home with the little ones for it's pointless getting calluses and covered in muck for no good reason.'

'I'll do no such thing!' Kieran looked outraged. 'You're the girls' mother and you'll care for them as you should.'

'And you're the girls' father and my husband and you'll care for *us* as you should, or I'll take on the job of it.'

Kieran jumped to his feet, making Noreen skitter backwards in alarm. But he grabbed up his dirty work clothes and pulled them on again before storming out.

'You told us ages ago the guvnor was gonna sort things out with them didicois.' Vic had stuck his head around the van's open back door to hiss at Chris. 'We've all had enough of them taking the piss out of us all day long.'

'Guvnor *is* sorting it out,' Chris snapped back. He didn't bother turning around and continued sorting through the tools in the back of the van. 'Just get on with yer work.'

'O'Connor offered me a job last night when I was packing up to go home. Laughed in me face about Stevie's accident and said nobody in their right mind 'ud go up a worm-eaten old ladder. Said your old man should be put out to graze . . .'

Chris sent him a sideways glare. He knew Vic wasn't lying about O'Connor's spite; he also knew his workmate was intentionally trying to wind him up by recounting it all, especially the bit about his father. Vic, Billy and Ted were itching for another showdown with the pikeys and Chris could understand why: never a day went by that they didn't make it their business to cause some problems for Wild Brothers to prevent them working.

123

Now bad feeling was turning inwards and Chris realised it was exactly what O'Connor wanted: he'd be happy to have them sniping at each other, and save him the job of doing it.

'Did you hear what I said?' Vic demanded. 'O'Connor offered me a job with his crew.'

'Well, you takin' him up on it?'

''Course I bleedin' ain't!'

'Well, what yer telling me about it for?' Chris ejected through his teeth. 'If you change yer mind, let me know and I'll have me uncle make up your cards for Friday.' He snapped his head at the house. 'Now get back to work, fer fuck's sake; we're falling right behind.'

Vic stuck two fingers up at a navvy who'd been catcalling at them while picking through salvage he'd dragged out of a house along the road.

Chris jumped off the back of the van and glanced after Vic. He noticed that Ted and Billy were ambling towards him, no doubt for a confab. Chris was aware that the other two often gave Vic bullets to fire because they hadn't got the guts to shoot their mouths off themselves.

'Forget the mother's meeting!' he yelled sarcastically at them. 'Get on with stripping out that back room on the top floor.'

Chris watched until they'd dispersed then turned and carried on unloading equipment from the back of the van onto the pavement. He didn't glimpse O'Connor approaching until he was just a yard or two away. Chris swung towards him, weighing a hammer in his hand. The mood he was in following his run-in with Vic, he was tempted to use it.

O'Connor held out his hands in a gesture of appeal.

'No need for any o' that, son,' he drawled, all Irish blarney. 'Got a few problems with your lads, I see.' He shook his shaggy head in mock sympathy. 'Being the ganger is not all it's cracked up to be now, is it? I know that alright, so I do. I expect you're after wanting your pa back to deal with them; he had a bit more authority about him now, didn't he?'

'You got anything interesting to say, or you just gonna stand there talking crap?' Chris continued tapping the metal hammerhead against an open palm.

'It *was* your dad, wasn't it, who got hurt in that fall? Just come over to ask how he's doing.' O'Connor's concern was as fake as his tobacco stained smile.

'He's doing fine, so now you know, you can piss off.'

'Aw . . . don't be like that when I've come to offer you a bit of help.' Declan swiped a hand about the bristle on his chin, his eyes foxy. 'You'll be one short for a while longer then?'

'You're not gonna ask fer 'is job are you?' Chris enquired dryly.

O'Connor grunted a laugh. 'Not me . . . no . . . no . . . but now I've taken on Murphy I've got a fellow spare I can let you have at a cheap rate. He'll take charge, 'cos you haven't got it in you, have you now, to do a man's work. You're still a wee boy, so y'are . . .'

'If you don't fuck off, O'Connor . . .' Chris muttered threateningly.

O'Connor bared his yellow teeth in a howl of laughter. 'What you gonna do about it, Sonny Jim?' He nodded at the house. 'Now, why don't you all pack up and go, and let a real team take over and do a proper job? Tell you what . . . I'll give you a little something to make it worth your while . . .' He pulled a pound note out of his pocket and waved it mockingly. 'Here . . . buy sweeties . . .'

'What's he saying?'

Vic had stormed out of the house with Ted and Billy close behind.

As much as Chris would have liked to land one on the Irishman he knew that he shouldn't because starting a ruckus was just what O'Connor wanted. He used the same stupid stuff to taunt them with day in, day out, and Chris had learned to let it wash over him.

'You taking up me offer of a job now?' O'Connor riled Vic, deliberately grabbing his shoulder in a vicious pinch to spin him around.

Vic swung a right hook at his jaw but O'Connor had anticipated that. He ducked, jabbing a meaty fist hard in Vic's solar plexus, making him fold over with a heavy grunt. It was the signal for his crew to tumble out of the house along the road and come running. Only Kieran Murphy stayed where he was. He shook his head and disappeared back inside the house where he'd been working.

'Luvly,' Chris heard Billy mutter. 'I'm just about fuckin' ready fer 'em.' He picked up one of the nail bars that Chris had flung onto the ground earlier and took a run and a swing at the closest navvy.

Chris swore under his breath in exasperation but, as O'Connor swiped a shovel and raised his arms high with the intention of putting it over Vic's head, he nipped in and kneed him in the groin. He grabbed at the falling shovel before it crowned him, hurling it aside. Vic was still winded and was having difficulty straightening up enough to turn and deal with the Paddy who'd just jumped on his back. But there were no Queensberry rules here, and as O'Connor staggered, Chris had no qualms about jerking his knee up viciously again, making him shriek in pain. Knuckles raked his cheek and Chris swiftly grabbed his opponent's overalls to haul him forward and nut him before shoving him backwards.

The only way to calm the Micks down was to get their boss to give them the order; Chris had learned that over the months. But he didn't reckon O'Connor was now in any mood to call his boys off. Right now he was clutching his throbbing balls, ambling in a knock-kneed circle, moaning out curses. Chris swung a foot hard at his thick legs, sending him reeling off balance. His second swipe sent the Irishman crashing over. As soon as he was on the ground Chris pounced, planting a boot firmly on his neck.

'Tell them to back off.' He ground his heel harder against O'Connor's Adam's apple. 'Tell them, you Irish bastard, or Vic's gonna keep stamping on yer knackers while I throttle you.'

O'Connor started, waving his arms frantically about and bubbling at the mouth.

'Got the message, have you?' Chris bawled at the Irish gang as they disentangled themselves from their opponents, breathing heavily.

Chris eased his foot off O'Connor's throat. 'Tell them to fuck off back up the road, 'cos I ain't lettin' you up till they're gone.'

O'Connor rasped out the order, and immediately Ted got in a last sly punch, making one of them totter back on his heels. The remainder of the little crew also retreated, sending venomous looks in their wake.

Chris strolled away from O'Connor and resumed unloading his van while Vic brought his breakfast up into the gutter then, rubbing his sore guts, said he felt much better. His two breathless and bruised colleagues stood with their narrowed eyes fixed on the Irishman who was dragging himself up off the floor.

'You're a dead man . . .' O'Connor whispered against the graze on Chris's cheek, his eyes blazing hatred.

'You first,' Chris returned, giving him a despising look and a dismissive jerk of the head.

When peace had broken out, and his colleagues' banging and crashing could be heard coming from the top floor of the tenement house, Chris turned his thoughts to what Vic had said earlier. He shut the van doors and locked them, a frown on his face. He was also starting to worry that his uncle was taking his time about getting rid of the Micks. When Rob said he'd do something, he did it. His uncle was no pushover and certainly wouldn't be frightened of taking on O'Connor and his crew. He'd grown up hearing tales from his relatives of how Rob Wild had seen off rivals, and yet he was also a canny businessman and doting husband who steered clear of anything too drastic that might upset the authorities, or his wife. Chris knew if O'Connor were still around at the end of the week he'd have to bring up the matter with his uncle and find out what was going on.

'I'm onto it, I swear,' Walter Purvis whispered into the phone. 'And you shouldn't have rung me here. How did you get this number?' He was standing in the hallway of his home, throwing nervous glances over his shoulder. His wife poked her head out of the kitchen to frown crossly at him. He gave her a sickly smile and a little wave.

'Never mind about any of that,' Rob said. 'You're

starting to piss me off, Walter. When we last spoke you said you'd need only a few more days to have things under control.'

'I *will* have it under control,' Walter hissed, covering his mouth in panic in case his wife was listening. 'But Kennedy's a slippery character. I've been trying to get him on his own . . . it's a delicate situation . . . as you must appreciate . . . not something that can be brought up in the office with others present . . . I have to investigate then approach him carefully in case he blabs once he knows the game's up . . .'

'Don't give me excuses, Walter,' Rob sighed. 'Give me results. I'm expecting to hear in a couple of days that they're gone 'cos if I don't, I'm getting a mob to shift 'em . . .'

'No, no, don't do that, all hell might break loose,' Walter interrupted.

'I'm sure it will, Walter, that's the idea . . .'

'Coming, dear,' Walter piped as his wife's greying perm appeared again and she mouthed to him that his tea was getting cold. 'I've got to go. I'll speak to you in the week.' He put down the phone with an unsteady hand then used it to push his wispy hair back from his perspiring brow. Pinning a smile to his face he entered the dining room.

The moment he spied his quarry Walter Purvis hastened out from behind the newsvendor's stall where he'd been loitering and strode towards him. He'd known Kennedy was off out on his dinner break as he'd heard him in the office making arrangements on the phone. At last he'd been presented with an opportunity to collar him away from flapping ears and have it out with him.

'Need to speak to you, Kennedy . . .'

The younger man glanced sharply at Walter. 'Oh, hello, sir,' he said. 'I'll pop along to your office this afternoon.' When Walter stepped in front of him to halt him Kennedy added, 'Can't stop now; meeting somebody for lunch.' He tried to step past his stout middle-aged boss.

'That's going to have to wait,' Walter said, grabbing his elbow. 'This is urgent.' When Kennedy gave him an impatient look, Walter decided to use his trump card. 'It's about the Whadcoat Street job,' he said quietly. 'I believe you might have some explaining to do there . . .'

Kennedy's expression transformed immediately and a mix of guilt and defiance narrowed his eyes. 'What about Whadcoat Street?'

'Yes, indeed, what about it?' Walter muttered with a significant raise of his eyebrows. Having glanced about for somewhere private he noticed an unoccupied bench set on a rectangle of green that was screened by trees. 'Let's go over there and have a little chat about things and see what we can come up with.'

Kennedy reluctantly followed him then perched on the edge of the wooden slats, gripping together his hands. To escape Walter's fixed stare he examined his nails. 'I hope this won't take long, Mr Purvis,' he began. 'I'm already late . . .'

The look his boss gave him promised him he'd take as long as he liked. Walter was becoming more confident that he had rattled Kennedy, and that made him sure he was right in thinking he'd been taking backhanders off pikeys. 'Where have you been siphoning the money from to pay O'Connor?' When he got no immediate response, and Kennedy shuffled his feet on the gravel,

130

staring into space, Walter smiled. 'I think you've been booking it down to the Stroud Green job because it's coming in under budget and it'd be a shame to let good money go to waste, wouldn't it?'

Kennedy suddenly coughed and fidgeted as though he might jump up and run. Some of the boys who Walter arranged to meet in clandestine places had the same gauche air about them. He found it rather endearing.

'I'll make it easy for you, Kennedy. I feel responsible, you see, as I recommended you and helped get you promoted.' He patted the young man's knee. 'Now I know you've done wrong but I'm prepared to think you've been foolish rather than corrupt. Besides, I don't want this bouncing back on me any more than you want to feel the full weight of an investigation into false accounting, misappropriation of public funds and so on, and so on. Of course, I'm sure you wouldn't want to perjure yourself either if it went to court, so I'm going to suggest a way around things.'

'Why?' Kennedy croaked after a lengthy silence.

Walter blinked at him. 'I thought I'd explained: I don't want to get my knuckles rapped for singing the praises of a miscreant, neither do I want to see you arrested for taking backhanders and doling out *jobs for the boys* . . .' Walter hoped Kennedy was appreciating the distinction, and who had the most to lose. 'I took a look at your file, you see. I noted your father's family hail from Ireland, although, of course you'd never know it as you have a rather common London accent.' Again he tapped Kennedy's knee, gave it a little squeeze. 'Perhaps you've been doing a favour for an uncle . . . cousin?' Walter's head trembled enquiringly as he waited for an answer.

'Yeah, that's it,' Kennedy muttered.

'Family, eh? Who'd have 'em?' Walter chortled. 'We can put this right,' he soothed. 'Of course, you'll need to tell O'Connor his services are no longer needed. And then hand over to me the cash he's paid you.'

'I've spent it.'

'Oh, dear,' Walter sighed. 'Well, we'll have to think of another way you can repay me for saving your bacon . . .'

'Kind of you, sir.' Kennedy gave his boss a sour look but a moment later placed a hand on his knee.

Walter beamed at him. 'That's the spirit.' He got up and buttoned his mac. 'It would be best if you left the department; perhaps a shift sideways. I'll arrange a transfer for you. Enjoy your lunch.'

CHAPTER TWELVE

'You've not been fighting with the Irishmen again?' Grace frowned at the bruise on Chris's forehead, then brushed a finger along his grazed cheek. It wasn't the first time she'd seen him looking battle-scarred.

'It's nothing; it happened earlier in the week,' Chris replied quietly, as he saw Shirley emerge from the kitchen. 'You ready?'

'Dear me . . . you've been in the wars, Christopher!'

'Had a bit of rubble fall on me at work, Mrs Coleman,' Chris slickly said. He knew Shirley already thought him a rough handful; if she knew the truth of it she'd probably banish him from darkening her doorstep.

'Cup of tea before you go out?' Shirley offered brightly.

It was unusual for Christopher to enter the house. Shirley was aware that Grace normally made sure to be ready and waiting when he pulled up, so she could simply call goodbye when shutting the front door. Her daughter wanted to keep her and Christopher apart to avoid any awkward questions arising. Grace was always telling her to stop prying, because when there was something to know, she'd come out with it.

But Shirley thought she had a right to find out a few things now, seeing as they'd been going steady for months, and her daughter invariably returned home after a night out with Chris looking dishevelled and dreamy-eyed. A bit of kissing and cuddling didn't bother Shirley, so Grace's tousled hair and swollen rosy lips were overlooked. She waited up for her daughter's return to run an eagle eye over her for tell-tale undone buttons and a skew-whiff skirt. Grace was more than old enough to be a mother herself, but to Shirley she was a spinster daughter who was too headstrong to heed advice, and might allow a horny charmer to get her into trouble and ruin her future.

After Hugh had thrown Grace over, Shirley had panicked, wondering if her daughter had been daft enough to go all the way with the two-timing swine before getting the ring that mattered on her finger. She'd had visions of Grace with a swollen belly in a few months' time and no man in sight to marry her.

Eventually Grace had had enough of her nagging and had shouted at her she was still a virgin so she had nothing to worry about, and in future to mind her own business. But that had been some years ago. Grace was now twenty-three and had been left behind by most of her contemporaries. Shirley had seen a wistful look flit over her daughter's face a few weeks ago when they'd bumped into one of her old school chums pushing a pram in Wood Green High Street. Shirley knew such longing could be more dangerous than a randy, determined man, in addling a woman's wits.

Considering Christopher was a handsome rogue, with

a nice line in patter – Shirley remembered his smooth, confident manner the first day she'd seen him at Matilda's – he no doubt attracted lots of girls. Shirley thought it likely he'd been trying it on with her daughter and what she wanted to know was how successful he'd been, and whether he'd yet asked Grace to get engaged. Shirley knew she'd have mixed feelings if he had; she still thought her pretty daughter could do better for herself than a good-looking builder from a notoriously bad family.

Grace worked in an environment teeming with respectable men, with good pay and prospects, who arrived home clean and tidy. Hugh might have been a bad lot but at least he had turned up to take Grace out in a smart Hillman saloon rather than a dirty Bedford van.

For fifteen years Wilf Coleman had came home reeking of raw meat, because he'd worked in a food-processing factory until the war gave him a way out. Shirley had never let him near her until he'd bathed, and even then the odour seemed to cling to his flesh and turn her stomach. She'd had high hopes of Grace doing better for herself . . .

'Where're you two off to then?' Shirley asked, hoping to delay them to slip in a few probing questions.

'Wood Green Gaumont; "The Lavender Hill Mob" is showing.'

'Oh, that's a good film. I saw that with Miriam after work one evening; we did have a laugh.' Shirley came further into the hallway. After doing her shift in a Woolworth's store in Wood Green High Street she occasionally had an evening out at the Gaumont, followed by a bite to eat, with a colleague.

She ran a look of grudging approval over Christopher's

attire. Shirley had to admit he turned up to take Grace out smelling fresh and looking smart though she had noticed bruises on his face a couple of times. Being as he worked on a building site, and his father had recently come a dreadful cropper, she was prepared to give him the benefit of the doubt about the rubble, rather than jump to the conclusion that he'd been brawling.

'Better be off,' Grace said, edging Chris towards the door. She'd noticed her mother scrutinising Chris's face. 'If we don't get going we'll miss the start . . .'

'Don't be late back!' Shirley grimaced disappointment as the couple disappeared. She'd not managed to find out a thing.

'Fancy some chips?'

'No thanks . . . I had a big tea before I came out.' Grace smiled.

They'd just descended the steps of the Gaumont surrounded by the dispersing audience who'd enjoyed the antics of Alec Guinness and the rest of the madcap cast of 'The Lavender Hill Mob'. They started walking in the September dusk towards Turnpike Lane, where Chris had parked the van.

Grace slipped a hand through his arm and gave it a squeeze. 'You're a convincing liar, you know. This evening when you told my mum rubble fell on you I almost believed you myself.'

'Rubble did fall on me earlier in the week,' he insisted, giving her a subtle smile.

'Maybe it did, but I'd put money on it that somebody's knuckles left those marks on your face.'

He stooped to brush a kiss on her cheek. 'Shhh . . . they're almost healed and I've had enough listening to the lads going on about the pikeys all day long. Shall we go for a coffee? Or stop off at a pub?'

Grace shook her head.

'What d'you want to do?'

'Go for a drive?'

He slanted a look at her. 'Right . . . now if I reckoned you'd suggested that 'cos you were gonna ask me to park up somewhere nice and quiet so we could . . .'

Grace gave a tiny laugh and averted her pink face. 'You've got a one-track mind, Christopher Wild. Can't we just park up and have a talk about things?'

'No . . .'

'Why not?'

''Cos I know what *things* you want to talk about,' he said levelly, 'and every time that subject comes up we end up arguing. I had enough nagging off the lads at work today.'

Grace withdrew her arm from his and, halting by a brightly lit shop window, rested her back against the glass. She gazed up indignantly at him, noting impatience in his expression, but choosing to ignore it.

'Don't snap at me; it's not my fault you've got a lot of problems at work,' she said tartly.

'I didn't say it was.'

'And I don't *nag* you about contacting your mum. I just think you should.'

Christopher spun on his heel away from her and took out a packet of Players. He had a cigarette alight in a matter of seconds.

'You can have a fight every day of the week yet you can't find the courage to drive to Bexleyheath to say hello to your mother?'

He walked away a few steps, dragging deeply on the

137

cigarette. 'Come on . . . I fancy a cold beer.' He shot out a hand behind him for her to take.

But Grace stayed where she was despite feeling a bit chilled. She had on a pretty sleeveless summer dress with just a cardigan over it. But the night air was fresher than she'd anticipated. Wrapping her arms about her middle she settled back mutinously. She wasn't going to let him ignore her. Too often he changed the subject, or started kissing and caressing her, when there was an issue he wanted to avoid talking about. If he used the latter method of shutting her up, it worked a treat for him, she realised sourly.

He pivoted about and their eyes clashed across a few separating yards of pavement, both too proud and stubborn to back down or close the gap.

'Why do you go on about it every bloody time we go out?' He sounded angry and frustrated. 'I wish I'd never told you about her at all. I want to relax when I'm with you, Grace, not get an ear-bashing.'

'Is that all you want?' Grace asked tightly.

'No . . . but as there's not much chance of that I'll settle for the cinema and a cold beer,' he said, a touch too sarcastically.

'I wondered when we'd get around to that,' Grace murmured.

'Well, it's not as if you're sweet sixteen, is it?' he muttered.

'I wondered when we'd get around to that too . . .'

Chris stuck the cigarette in his mouth and shoved a hand through his dark hair. 'It doesn't matter . . . swear. I know you've had the dirty done on you by another bloke, and you're gonna be cautious for a while about trusting men.' Spontaneously his hungry eyes roved over her curvy figure and slender, bare legs. 'I promise I'm not like him . . . I won't up 'n' leave . . .'

Grace laughed acidly. 'Only you could turn a conversation about finding your mother into a complaint about me not going all the way with you.'

'That works both ways.' Chris drawled and ground the cigarette butt beneath his shoe. He glanced up, holding her gaze with his dark, sleepy eyes. 'You told me it's my decision whether I go to Bexleyheath to look for her, and I reckon you were right, so back off and leave me alone.'

'Yeah . . . I certainly will . . .' Grace replied in a suffocated voice, pushing away from the window and starting back the way they'd just come.

In a few seconds Christopher was at her side, spinning her about by gripping her arm. 'What game you havin'?'

'I'm not playing, that's the point,' Grace said tremulously, shaking him off and continuing walking briskly. 'You're the one behaving like a sulky kid and I've had enough.'

He crowded her back against a brick wall. '*I'm* the one acting like a kid? You're twenty-three, you've been engaged, and you're acting like a fucking virgin . . .'

'Perhaps that's because I am,' she stormed.

She punched at his arm to move him but he kept her penned while frowning at her.

'Really?' he eventually said hoarsely.

'No . . . I just said it to piss you off, like everything else I come out with.' She ducked beneath one of his braced arms and darted across the road.

He weaved between traffic and caught up with her. This time Grace came to a halt. She knew trying to outrun him was silly and undignified. She waited for a

couple to amble past arm-in-arm before she said, 'I think
. . . it's time we had a break from seeing each other.'

'You're giving me the brush-off?' He sounded incred-
ulous. 'Why? Because I won't let you order me about?'

'I'm not ordering you about.' Grace made a despairing
little gesture. 'Can't you understand that's the problem
. . . you just see it that way?' She swallowed the tears
blocking her throat. 'I think it's best if we have a break,'
she repeated, attempting to smile. 'Perhaps you need
to have some time on your own to work out what to
do . . .' Her voice tailed away then sprang again into
life. 'Before I came along and complicated things you
seemed certain you wanted to contact your mum.'

'It's nothing to do with you coming along and compli-
cating things. Me dad's been in hospital, in case you've
forgotten. He's not long been home and I'm not going
to upset him again by going off looking for someone
who was a lazy slut and didn't want me anyhow . . .'

'You don't know that . . .'

'You think me dad's lying to me?'

'No . . . but things aren't always so cut and dried, and
I think your mum deserves to be heard.'

'She's never bothered to come and find me and ask
me to listen to her side.'

'Perhaps that's because she knew what sort of reception she'd get.'

'I know what fuckin' reception *I'll* get!' he ground
out through his teeth. 'Now I know a bit more about
her, I know she's gonna tell me to get lost and stay out
of her life!'

'Well, at least then you'll know,' Grace reasoned. 'You
said Matilda was encouraging you to find her too; if you
won't listen to me, I know you'll listen to her advice.'

'Me aunt wouldn't have mentioned her name if I hadn't kept on about it. If she thought Pam Plummer was worth finding, she'd have told me to go looking years ago. That's what Matilda's like: all fair 'n' square. The only reason she wants me to meet her is 'cos she knows once I've done it I'll never ask about me mum again.'

Grace raised her glistening eyes heavenwards. 'It's no use, Chris,' she said despairingly. 'Thanks for taking me to the pictures tonight, I can get the bus back home . . .'

He gripped her wrist and dragged her roughly into an alley between two shop-fronts.

'You all right, miss?' A middle-aged man had observed their altercation and was now hovering at the mouth of the narrow opening.

'She's fine, piss off,' Chris growled without turning to look at him.

'I'm fine,' Grace called in a tremulous voice. 'See what I mean about you?' She gave a gulp of humourless laughter while watching the fellow shake his head then disappear.

Chris raised a hand to cup her face. 'I'm sorry . . . it's just you drive me nuts, Grace . . .'

'I'm sorry too, 'cos you drive me nuts . . .' Grace sighed. 'I meant what I said . . . I think it'd be best if we don't see each other for a while . . .'

He plunged his mouth hard on hers, curving a hand about her nape to move her forward and prevent her scalp scraping against the brick. He knew he could have her if he wanted to. He wasn't sure why he hadn't, and always courteously brought her back outside her house to kiss her goodnight and ask if she was ready to stay away somewhere on Saturday. It'd taken him one date

141

to discover she was putty in his hands after a bit of clever petting. He was confident that if he eased them a way further up the alley now, and kept up the onslaught, he could take her against the wall, in the same way he had numerous other girls he barely remembered. But he wouldn't forget Grace . . .

He heard the little moan as he tantalised her mouth and throat with deliberately sweet, seductive kisses. To satisfy his conceit he suddenly twisted them further into darkness and lifted her, wedging himself with practised ease between her parted legs. Her lids flew up and she gazed at him with startled doe eyes. But she didn't struggle and he knew if he was slow and artful he could have her hate him tomorrow.

He tilted his forehead against hers, closing his eyes, then lowered her slowly to the ground. He turned away and shook out his cigarettes so clumsily some scattered on the concrete.

'I'm just going to get the bus home,' Grace said in a husky, quavering voice. She moved a hand as though to touch his arm in farewell but withdrew her fingers again almost immediately.

'I'll see you to the bus stop,' he said and set off towards the High Street, outpacing her along the alley by yards.

They walked in silence and stood at the stop together for no more than a minute before a trolley bus pulled up in a squelch of brakes.

Grace gripped the metal pole and turned to say goodbye but the word withered on her tongue. He was already a distance away, striding swiftly towards Turnpike Lane with his head down and his hands thrust into his pockets.

CHAPTER THIRTEEN

'I reckon it's time you stopped shirking, you lazy sod, and got yerself back into work.'

Faye gave her husband a frown, even though she knew he'd only been ribbing his brother about his convalescence. 'Give poor Stevie a chance, will you! He's not been out of hospital that long.' She passed the bowl of potatoes to Pearl. 'Help yourself. There's more keeping warm in the oven so dig in.'

'I've told him he needs to get himself sorted out. Bored stiff, aren't you, Steve, sitting about doing nothing but reading the newspaper or listening to the wireless all day long.' Pearl liked her food and she took Faye up on her generosity, liberally spooning mashed potatoes onto her plate.

'Well, there's a job waiting to be done in the office. I've only got one pair of hands and an in-tray that's spilling all over me desk.' Rob took the bowl from Pearl and helped himself to spuds.

'Do I get any say in this?' Stevie asked, feigning an

air of injury while pouring himself lashings of thick brown gravy.

'I'm with you, Stevie.' Faye rallied to her brother-in-law's side. 'It's up to you to decide when you're ready to get back to work so don't let Rob push you into it.'

The two couples were sitting around the kitchen table, enjoying a cosy dinner of steak and kidney pudding and mash, with a few beers to wash it down. It was just the four of them at home at Faye and Rob's as Daisy had gone out with her friends for the evening. It was the first time they'd met socially since Stephen had been discharged and naturally enough conversation had quickly turned to the subject of Stevie's employment prospects.

'Seriously, mate, you know the job's there waiting for you as soon as you're feeling up to it.' Rob tucked into his food but continued sending enquiring glances his brother's way.

'Yeah, thanks, I am grateful, it's just . . .' Stevie sighed. 'It's true I'm bored stiff at home, but . . . no offence, I reckon I'll be bored stiff pushing papers around 'n' all. It just ain't me, sitting behind a desk all day long. I know it'll drive me crackers.'

Rob looked surprised. He knew his brother was not in a position financially to give up work altogether. Stephen needed an income more than ever now it looked likely Chris might soon announce he and Grace were setting up home together. But, judging by the way his brother was still limping about, Rob didn't think Stephen was fit enough for manual work. 'You want to go back on the tools?' he asked with a frown.

'Nah . . . don't think I'm up to climbing ladders any more,' Stephen admitted. He forked some tender beef into his mouth, savouring it before adding, 'To be honest the thought of going up a high reach again gives me the shivers.'

'Well, if you make sure this time it's one with rungs that ain't worn through . . .' his brother commented dryly.

'Shut up and leave Steve alone.' Faye pointed her knife at her husband.

'Anyhow, Chris is doing a better job of supervising the lads than me.' Stephen added to his reasons for giving up his job with Wild Brothers. While he'd been at home he'd been doing some thinking and had come up with the idea that he'd like to start a little business of his own. He hadn't yet mentioned anything about it to Pearl because he was still mulling over possibilities. He was an experienced driver and knew he could start doing van deliveries. He had thought of asking Rob to give him a contract for taking some of his merchandise from the warehouse to market pitches. But he knew, much as he appreciated what his older brother had done for him over the years keeping him in cash and sound advice, he'd like to step out from Rob's shadow before he got too much older. He wanted to earn a living in a job where he wasn't relying on his brother for employment but pulled in clients won on his own merit.

'Tell you what,' Pearl suddenly piped up. 'That suet pudding you did earlier in the week were a treat, Stevie. I reckon you could knock 'em up in your kitchen and flog 'em at a profit.' She started to chuckle, tucking into her food.

'I've tasted your suet pud and it ain't half bad.' Rob nodded his head in agreement.

Stephen continued eating, looking thoughtful. He

enjoyed cooking and knew he had a flair for it. Even when rationing had been at its height, he'd been inventive and had managed to knock together some tasty grub for himself and Chris. But it had never occurred to him before that there might be a profit in it.

'That's not a bad suggestion,' Faye suddenly said, taking the words from Stephen's mouth and glancing about at them all. 'I know I'd pay good money to eat something you'd cooked, Steve. You're a natural.'

'Don't want to get stuck indoors tied to yer own kitchen sink, do you?' Rob sounded dubious about the idea.

'No . . . but I wouldn't mind a little premises,' Stephen said slowly, putting down his knife and fork and looking serious. 'Suit me down to the ground, that would, having me own caff. Wouldn't need to be anything big 'n' fancy, just a cosy place to do afternoon teas and perhaps a few plain dinners. Got to keep costs down or no bugger would be able to afford to come in and eat. Except you, of course.' He grinned at his brother.

'Well, if you reckon it's a goer, and you can find a property that seems about right, I'll stump up for the first year's rent while you get on your feet.' Rob noticed Steve about to decline his offer. He hadn't realised until he'd had that talk with Chris following Stevie's accident just how fed up his brother was with feeling beholden to him. Stephen was now keen to be his own man and Rob admired him for it. "Course, it'll be a loan and you can repay me any time you like. Won't charge much in interest.'

Stephen gazed gratefully at his brother. 'I'd pay you something off the loan as soon as I started to make a profit,' he vowed gruffly.

'Yeah, I know,' Rob said, businesslike. 'Can do it official, if you like, through the books.'

'Well, no need to go mad,' Stephen returned, grinning.

'I'm interested, if you want any help,' Pearl suddenly burst out in an enthusiastic tone. 'Me boss in the chemist's is always telling me I'm a natural with the customers. Got the gift of the gab, so he says, and keep 'em coming back.' She barely paused before rattling on, 'If you like, Stevie, you can do the cooking and I'll do the waitressing and clearing up. I could take the orders and man the till. Don't mind doing all the shopping too . . .' Her round pink cheeks were glowing in excitement. 'I've got a little bit saved, and I'd like to invest it if you'll let me.'

Faye got up from the table, smiling serenely. 'Forget about the ales, I think this calls for a bit of a celebratory toast.' She went quickly to the pantry and found a bottle of red wine.

'Never mind that, love,' Rob said, having finished off his beer in a gulp. 'I've got a bottle of champers down in the cellar. Been saving it for a special occasion, and I reckon this is it.'

When Stephen heard his son's key in the lock he turned off the wireless and got to his feet. It didn't occur to him to glance at the clock on the mantelshelf in the back room or he'd have realised it was early for Chris to be home from a night out with Grace.

Stephen had dropped Pearl off earlier and she'd promised she was going to immediately look at her savings books and do some sums. Stephen had headed off home with the intention of doing the same. He knew he had a Building Society passbook with a small amount in it that he had been saving for Christopher. He hadn't told

Chris he'd been putting money by for some years for when he eventually got married. Even had Chris been aware of the little nest egg, Stephen knew his son wouldn't mind him using it on something so important. Besides, Stephen had every intention of replacing it soon from the profits he'd make from his new business venture. And he was bursting to tell Chris all about the exciting plans for a caff that had been discussed that evening at Rob's. He hoped perhaps Chris might take some time at the weekend to look at premises with him, if he wasn't planning to work or be off out with Grace.

Stephen appeared in the hallway, a bright smile on his face. 'How you doing, son? Good night out? How's Grace?'

Chris mumbled something at him and continued towards the stairs. A moment later he was halfway up them with Stephen gawping at his back.

'You lot! Get out here and take a look at this!' Vic crowed, his voice bubbling with glee.

Ted and Billy emerged from the house to join him on the pavement.

Ted's grimy face split into a snaggle-toothed grin. 'Oi! Chris! Come 'n' take a butcher's,' he bellowed. 'Yer can't miss seeing this! If I 'ad me camera I'd take a picture.'

Chris came out of the house, frowning impatiently, but his expression lifted when he saw what was amusing them.

Along the road O'Connor's crew were loading their gear onto an open-backed truck and it was obvious, from their snarling expressions, and the fact that two of them were rolling on the ground, having a scrap, that they were not happy. They appeared to be packing up and leaving for good.

'Looks like the guvnor managed to swing it after all . . . good on 'im.' Vic did a little jig, with much clicking of heels and fingers.

'Guvnor never lets you down, do he?' Ted began nodding his head. 'Might have took him a while but he got there in the end.'

'When he does it, he does it right, see.' Billy added his two penn'orth.

A darkly sardonic glance encompassed his workmates but Chris refrained from reminding them that just yesterday they'd all been chewing his ears off again with complaints about his uncle taking his own sweet time in seeing off the Micks. Instead, he gave Declan O'Connor a jaunty wave. 'Oi! O'Connor! I'll 'ave me ladder back now as you won't be needin' it,' he shouted. 'And while you're at it, I reckon you can leave them two shovels 'n' all. Won't charge you no hire rates . . . ain't my way to put the boot into a man who's down.'

O'Connor tensed rigid on hearing that taunt then swung about and pointed a thick finger at Chris. 'Told you once before, Sonny Jim, you're a fookin' dead man.'

'Yeah . . . and I told you, you'll go down first, mate . . .'

O'Connor turned his back and continued arguing with Kieran Murphy before shoving hard at the man's shoulder, sending him crashing back against some house railings. A moment later he scrambled into the truck, crashing the gears and sending it lurching forward. The way the vehicle was facing he either had to do a three-point turn to head away from them or drive past and endure more jeering.

The truck suddenly screeched down the road, O'Connor deliberately aiming the vehicle at them, sending the Wild

149

Brothers' lot diving behind the railings fronting the house.

'Fuckin' sour grapes, I call that,' Billy scoffed with a two-fingered salute from behind his protective screen.

O'Connor's face was boiling red with rage as he sent them all a hate-filled glare. The gears groaned as he got reverse and disentangled his bumper from the railings.

'You go ahead and have your laughs now while you can,' Declan spat menacingly. 'I'm not a man with a short memory, you fookin' remember that.'

Ted pretended to scrub tears from his eyes with his fists. 'Gonna miss you when you're gone . . .' he boo-hooed.

The rest of the Irish contingent had jumped in a panel van and it came hurtling down the road to shudder to a stop beside their boss's vehicle. The menials seemed to be waiting for a signal from their guvnor to tumble out and get stuck in, but O'Connor appeared reluctant to go for a final tear-up. Chris surreptitiously swooped on an assortment of tools in the hallway of the house and distributed weapons amongst his colleagues, in case Declan decided to give the nod.

O'Connor suddenly let out the clutch and his truck whizzed back, then rammed once more against the railings, buckling them to within inches of Vic's shins. A moment later he'd ground the gears into reverse and, steering manically, he roared on towards Seven Sisters Road with Vic's hammer and snarling curses following him. The other vehicle was soon revving, a mass of faces, spewing filth, bobbing at the side window, then it raced away in the truck's fumy wake.

'You'll never guess who I saw the other day.'

Grace stopped stirring her tea and glanced at her friend Wendy, faint interest lifting her eyebrows.

'Hugh Wilkins,' Wendy said. 'He asked after you.' She took a glance around the café. 'Where's my bun? I'm starving . . .'

'He can go and take a running jump,' Grace muttered sourly.

A Lyons nippy appeared and put down two plates holding aromatic currant buns.

Wendy immediately split hers and began buttering it. 'I was in Bourne & Hollingsworth and he came up to me.' She shook her head. 'Didn't want to give him the time of day but . . .' The bun hovered in front of her mouth. She smiled impishly. 'I made sure I told him you were with a new boyfriend and it looked serious.'

'You shouldn't have lied, Wendy.' Grace chuckled ruefully.

'Is it a lie?' Wendy's eyebrows hovered close to her brunette hairline.

'You know it is,' Grace said quietly and started buttering her bun. 'Serious?' She choked a miserable laugh. 'It's over between us by the looks of it.'

'Chris *still* not been in touch?'

Grace shook her head.

'He'll be back.'

'Was Hugh out with his wife?' Grace could tell her friend was about to pursue that conversation about Chris and, although they were close friends, she didn't want to discuss him with anybody.

At first she'd been confident that in a week or two Chris would pull up outside her house and ask for a second chance, and they'd discuss calmly what to do about his mother. But he hadn't come to see her, or telephoned, and she'd begun to realise she must have

151

been wrong in thinking he'd been on the point of telling her he was in love with her.

He seemed to have easily forgotten her, but, unbearably for her, it seemed there was truth and wisdom in the old saying that absence made the heart grow fonder. Since they'd split up she'd come to realise she'd fallen in love with him. But much as she yearned to see him she knew the problems that made them argue wouldn't go away, not while the spectre of his mother was wedged between them. So she hadn't contacted him to say she'd made a mistake because, deep down, she knew she hadn't, and besides, her pride was smarting and she was unwilling to chase after him.

'Hugh had a girl with him,' Wendy said, having swallowed her mouthful of bun. 'She looked about fourteen and seemed a sulky brat.' Wendy sipped from her tea. 'Hope he's got a hellish life with his stepkids. It's what he deserves after what he did to you.'

Grace shrugged her indifference and bit into her bun. She realised she hadn't given Hugh Wilkins a thought in ages.

'Don't see how anybody could forgive or forget something like that,' Wendy said bluntly. 'What about all the money you lost? I feel bad now that I couldn't afford to pay you for my bridesmaid's dress. It was a beauty and I've worn it a few times.'

'It doesn't matter; in any case, later on you bought me a lovely silk blouse in compensation.' Grace paused, feeling uncharacteristically resentful. 'I'm glad Hugh had laid out as well, at least he didn't get away scot-free.'

'But he ended up marrying a rich woman, so it didn't matter so much to him, did it?'

Grace simply shrugged and gazed out of the corner

café onto an Indian summer afternoon. It was early October and gloriously mild weather. Women were still strolling in summer dresses and open-toed sandals. But appealing as the sunlit scene was, Grace couldn't put from her mind the loss of her little nest egg. After the shock of being jilted by Hugh had subsided a bit, the realisation that she'd wasted her savings on an aborted wedding had come as a huge blow.

She hadn't yet managed to build up her little kitty again. A wistful twist shaped her lips. But there was scant likelihood of needing savings to pay for a wedding any time soon.

'You finished?'

Grace was jolted from her thoughts by her friend's voice. She pushed away her empty cup and plate and nodded.

'Come on, let's go and spend some money,' Wendy said and led the way out of the café and, arm-in-arm, they headed in the direction of the market.

CHAPTER FOURTEEN

'How's things going at work?'

'All right now the pikeys have gone,' Chris informed his dad. 'Feel sorry for Kieran Murphy; he came over and asked again for a job. I spoke to Rob but I knew what his answer would be: there's not enough in the contract to warrant another pay packet. Anyhow, the lads would never have stopped moaning; they're all after overtime, and again Rob says there's nothing doing on that score.' He paused. 'We got a good day in today though and are back on schedule. What's for tea? I'm starving.'

'Doin' a mince 'n' onion pie.' Stevie turned awkwardly on his healing leg to watch his son plonk down at the kitchen table and unfold his newspaper.

'You not getting in the bath?' He ran an eye over Chris's mucky appearance.

'Yeah . . . in a bit.' Chris carried on reading the midweek football scores. 'Fancy coming down the Arsenal Saturday?' he asked his father.

'Yeah . . . don't mind . . .' Stevie continued spearing

sideways glances at Christopher while rolling pastry. 'Going out tonight?'

'Nah . . . gonna listen to the wireless and get an early night.'

Stevie didn't keep tabs on his son's social life, but he was beginning to suspect that Chris hadn't seen Grace for a couple of months. At first he hadn't given it much thought because sometimes a tiff, or family circumstances, just made it work out that way. But now he suspected it was something far more serious than that.

'You used to see Grace most Thursday evenings.' It sounded like an idle observation.

'Don't now,' Christopher said, standing up. 'I'll run me bath. How long's that gonna be?'

'About an hour.' Stevie patted the pastry lid on his pie and started crimping it. 'Grace was right for you, y'know. You want to tell me what's gone wrong?' he asked quietly.

'No,' Chris said and strolled off into the hallway.

Sighing, Stevie shoved the pie in the oven. He wasn't fooled for a moment by Chris's nonchalance. If he were over the girl he'd be out on the pull with his mates, or boozing it up at weekends. The fact that he wasn't, and had spent the past couple of months moping around at home, made Stevie think that his son was behaving himself because he hoped to get her back. But he seemed to be taking his time about doing it for some reason.

When he'd first got discharged, Chris had been like a mother hen, but once his son had realised that, apart from being slow on his pins, he was quite healthy, he'd eased off fussing and they'd fallen back into their old routines.

Stevie reflected on the evening that he had waited up

for Chris to come home so he could tell him the news about his plans for a caff. His son had come in looking shell-shocked and had gone to bed without saying a word. Stevie had guessed immediately he'd got woman troubles; he recalled seeing that vacant expression gazing back at him in the mirror a few times in his life. During his divorce from Pam he'd walked round like a staring-eyed zombie for months.

Having put the potatoes to boil Stevie sat down at the table and frowned sightlessly at the newspaper. He regretted bringing his ex-wife to mind. The thought of the horrible tension he'd caused to exist between him and Chris, just before his accident, now made him feel uneasy and ashamed.

He knew he'd cheated death, and whether it was that humbling knowledge or the hefty bang on the head that had knocked some sense in to him, he couldn't be sure.

While in hospital he'd had ample time to reflect. He couldn't escape his conscience, or the fact that Matilda had been right – as she usually was. He shouldn't have been so hard on his son because he wanted to find his mum. Stevie knew the shock of hearing Matilda's news that day had made his mouth work faster than his brain, but there'd been no excuse for carrying on being stubborn and resentful.

Any proper father would have talked things through like an adult with his only child; instead he'd made both their lives hell with his sullen silences. He understood now that Christopher had the right to know about his past, whether it were good or bad, and it was no longer his job to sift out the stuff that might upset him, because he wasn't a kid any more.

Christopher was a man and he'd fallen in love with

a nice girl. Stevie realised he wished things would come right for Chris and Grace. He wished his son might soon be a father himself. But most of all he wished he'd told Chris he was sorry for what he'd done, and if he still wanted to find his mother, he wouldn't stand in his way.

Since he'd got out of hospital nobody had mentioned Pam, not even Matilda. Having mulled things over in his mind Stevie had come to the conclusion that it would be unwise to dredge it up, even to apologise. Many months had passed since it all blew up so the best thing might be to let sleeping dogs lie and in that way Chris might put all his efforts into getting back with Grace . . .

'Smells good . . . make the gravy, shall I?' Chris came into the kitchen towelling his hair. He pulled a box of Bisto out of the cupboard, dropped it on the table then wandered off into the front room to turn on the wireless.

'Oi! That gravy won't make itself, y'know . . .'

Chris's contribution to the gravy making was always limited to finding the box, leaving it on the table, then disappearing.

Stevie heard his stomach grumble and he realised he was hungry. Pushing aside his troubles, he got stiffly to his feet and opened the oven door. Inside he could see a crisp golden crust, from which was coming a rich, savoury aroma. He smiled wryly wondering why it had only just occurred to him how good it was to be back home.

Chris stopped drumming his fingers on the steering wheel and started tapping his feet instead. Suddenly he thrust back against the seat, dropping his eyes to study his fists clenched on his thighs. Abruptly he hauled open the van door and jumped out. Having carefully locked the vehicle he strode away. He swung about, came back to test the door. It didn't budge. He rubbed a hand across his mouth as he quickly turned to enter an un-gated garden path. He rapped on the door, then clasped his hands behind his back. There was no answer but a middle-aged woman two doors along, sweeping up fallen autumn leaves, straightened wearily from her task and stared at him.

'D'you want me?'

'Er . . . no . . . I'm after Mrs Riley.'

'That's me . . .' She smiled at Chris. 'You've come about the gate, have you? I saw you sitting in your van and wondered if you were the builder I called yesterday. Managed to get here sooner than you thought, did you?'

Chris licked his lips; his voice seemed trapped deep in his throat. Carefully he planted a hand on her red-tiled windowsill to steady himself as he felt his head swim. From his father's, and Matilda's, descriptions of Pam Plummer's looks and character he'd built up an image of his mother now being a blowsy old bottle blonde, about Shirley's age, and with a similar tendency to appear as mutton dressed as lamb. He couldn't have been more wrong. The woman getting slowly to her feet was thin and dowdily dressed in a shapeless cardigan and pleated skirt, her lank, greying hair scraped back into hairgrips fastened either side of her head.

'Oh . . . you're wondering what I'm doing over here.' The woman was now brushing together her palms to get dirt off them. 'It's Mrs Lockley's garden, not mine. She's almost eighty and widowed, you see, and isn't up to a job like this.' She came out onto the pavement, latching her neighbour's gate behind her. 'She had a bit

158

of a tumble on wet leaves last year. Done her hip in, poor old girl.' She was rolling down her cardigan sleeves as she approached. 'Don't mind helping out 'cos we're all gonna be old someday. 'Course you've got a way to go, by the looks of it, but it's catching up on me, I can tell you . . .' She halted by the opening to her property, grimacing at the space where a gate should be. 'So, how much d'you reckon? Doesn't need to be fancy; a plain wooden one with fastenings will do, and I'll paint it myself.'

'I'm not here about the gate.' Christopher barely recognised his own voice and his knuckles showed white against the red tiles.

'Oh? Who are you then?' She looked him up and down. She'd wondered why a builder would turn up in his best clothes to price a job, unless he was going straight out on the razzle, of course. It was only mid-afternoon but he looked the sort of handsome young man who would have a full social life.

'Christopher . . .' Chris ejected his name hoarsely. 'I'm Christopher Wild . . .'

She was still smiling faintly at him, but when her features froze in shock, and she sagged at the knees, he simply watched his mother crumple to the ground. Jerking into action Chris rushed forward with his arms outstretched to help her up. She flapped both hands at him, her eyes screwing shut as though he were an abomination she couldn't bear to gaze upon.

'Go away,' she gritted through her teeth and lowered her head so her chin rested on her chest.

'I just came here . . . wanted to say hello . . . see you . . . that's all,' Chris stuttered quietly. 'Please let me help you up . . .'

'Go away . . . go away and never come back!' his mother hissed into her muffling cardigan.

'I just . . . I'm sorry . . . I just wanted to say . . .'

'Go away!' she screamed, her small hands balling into quivering fists.

Chris stumbled past her cowering figure and hovered on the pavement for a moment, staring at her. He strode to the van, then returned, his hands alternately plunging into his pockets and ripping free again. 'I'm sorry. Let me help you up . . .' His voice was raw with pleading. He glanced to his right and saw that a neighbour was peering out of a window. A moment later the woman was opening her front door and staring open-mouthed at the scene.

'You alright, Pam?' the woman called urgently. 'You got trouble with him? Do you want me to call the police?' Gladys Rathbone came further down her path but halted behind the protection of her gate. 'What's happened to her?' she demanded of Christopher. 'What in God's name have you done to her? I'll get the police on you.'

Pamela Riley slowly hauled herself to her feet, using the privet hedge as support. 'It's nothing,' she told her neighbour. She tottered quickly towards her front door, searching in a pocket. 'My fault . . . Just had a trip, that's all. It's nothing.' Her voice was so low it was virtually inaudible yet it held an unmistakable demand for privacy. A moment later she'd found her key and thrust it into the lock. She barely opened the door but managed to squeeze herself through a tiny aperture, before closing it.

As soon as Christopher found an area that seemed deserted he pulled up and jumped out of the van. He prowled to and fro on weed-strewn concrete outside an

160

ugly brick building that resembled a warehouse. As though comforting himself had just occurred to him he jammed a shaking hand in a pocket and pulled out his cigarettes. He smoked one while pacing then lit another from its butt before halting and remaining motionless till the cigarette clamped between his lips had had the life sucked out of it, and the stub had been shredded beneath his foot. Like a drunk, he weaved a path to the brick wall of the building, turning his back to it for support. Squeezing shut his burning eyes he sank to his haunches then gripped his scalp with both hands as the first sob tore out of him.

CHAPTER FIFTEEN

'Supper's ready . . .'

Grace had known it was suppertime even before she heard her mother calling up the stairs to her. The warm aroma of toast had wafted into her bedroom while she sat, dressed in her pyjamas, legs curled under her on the eiderdown.

It had been a Coleman family ritual, for as long as she could remember, to have a light supper of toast and jam, or toast and dripping, with a hot drink of Ovaltine, just before turning in. As children, she and her brother would draw out their suppers for as long as possible to delay bedtime. Grace didn't really fancy anything else to eat today; however she'd go down and eat a few mouthfuls so her mother would have no reason to again remark that she wasn't herself since breaking up with Chris Wild. The comment was always followed by a heavy hint that it was time she stopped moping over him, because he wasn't worth it, and started going out with friends to find herself a nice fellow this time.

The faded photograph on the coverlet drew Grace's

eyes and she picked it up, placing it back in the shoebox with the other little treasures that Chris had given her when they'd been a couple. There were blackened copper coins, and a tin soldier that he had said had probably been pilfered from the factory in Thane Villas. It might even have come via his father's cousin: Alice had worked there before the First World War when just a girl, straight out of school. There was also a brass belt buckle that Chris had said he believed once belonged to his grandfather. It had been found in a house where Stevie and Rob had lived with their parents for many years. His father had found the buckle and, having stared silently at it for several seconds, had flung it away as far as he could. He'd told Chris afterwards he recalled being thrashed with such force by his rotten father, Jimmy, that a buckle had come loose from his leather belt, and he'd got another swipe because of it.

Even before Chris had told her a bit about his wicked grandfather, her mother had related a few tales about the notorious Jimmy Wild, with pointed references to how bad blood in families passed down the generations. Apparently, Jimmy had been a pimp and a criminal in his time, but what sickened Grace was the knowledge that he'd regularly beaten his wife and children.

As soon as Chris had mentioned to Grace he and his workmates were unearthing odds and ends in the Whadcoat Street houses she had expressed an enthusiastic interest in seeing them. The first item he'd brought her had been a battered old cocoa tin, rusted firmly shut, but containing something – probably coins – that clattered when it was shaken. When Chris had made to force it open, Grace had stopped him for some reason, wanting the treasure to remain safely sealed within.

The tin had been discovered behind loose bricks in a wall. Chris had explained a likely reason it had been put there: when his father was a kid growing up in Campbell Road, his mother, in common with most women, would use hidey holes to conceal money from husbands who drank or gambled. He'd gone on to tell her his dastardly grandfather would loot any small savings his grandmother, Fran, would stash away to buy Christmas treats for Stevie and Rob, as children.

The photo had been found wedged down the back of a drawer in a built-in cupboard, and was badly fissured, but the face of the handsome youth, taken when he was many years younger than she was, Grace guessed, was still brightly smiling. He was dressed in First World War army uniform. Chris had told her that his dad had studied the photo, but hadn't recognised the young private as a neighbour from his days living in The Bunk. But then Stevie had been only seven years old when the Great War started, and the fellow might have perished on the Somme, and never made it back home to Campbell Road.

The last item he'd fetched her, before they'd split up, had been a tattered letter that had brought Grace to tears. A woman called Violet Brewer, living in Lancashire, had sent it in January 1901. In a spidery, uneducated hand the poor wretch had begged her husband, Alfred, to come home, or get some money to her somehow, so she could feed their remaining five children, the baby having recently died of a fever.

Grace touched the stained and crumpled envelope, but didn't take out the note to reread it. She felt guilty for having pried at all into Violet's misery. But she wondered, as she always did, whether Alfred *had* returned to help. Chris had read the letter too, and had said, in his blunt way, he doubted the poor sod would have had any help to give if he'd ended up in one of The Bunk's notorious doss houses . . .

'This is going cold, Grace, and I'm not making more, 'cos there'll be no bread left for breakfast.'

'I'm coming down now,' Grace called in response to her mother's tetchy complaint. She put the lid on the shoebox and returned it to its place in the wardrobe.

'Who on earth's come calling at this time of the evening?' Shirley dropped her jammy toast to her plate and, sucking her sticky fingers, exchanged a look with Grace. The knock on the door had startled them both while they'd been sitting at the kitchen table, enveloped in a comfortable quiet.

Shirley hurried into the hallway and disappeared into the front room. Having twitched aside a curtain to spy outside she whipped back to hiss, 'It's Christopher. Did you know he was coming round?' There was a hint of blame in her voice.

Grace shot to her feet. 'Of course not!' She glanced in dismay at her pyjamas.

'I'll tell him you're already in bed,' Shirley whispered crossly.

Grace suddenly realised that he'd knocked some minutes ago, and hadn't done so again. As nobody had answered, he might have gone away, thinking they'd already retired for the night . . . or were intentionally ignoring him. She dodged past her mother and quickly yanked open the door, hoping he hadn't disappeared, and gazed straight up into his dark features.

'For Heaven's sake, Grace, act with a bit of decorum,' Shirley muttered angrily at her from behind.

165

Grace kept her pyjama-clad figure concealed behind the door as she stared wide-eyed at him.

'Can you come out?' It was a husky plea.

'Well . . . it's a bit late . . . and I'm not dressed . . .' His eyes dropped to her lightly shivering figure.

'I'll wait in the van. Can you get dressed and come out? I need to talk to you.'

'This is a fine time to come calling, I must say,' Shirley directed at him while trying to peer past her daughter. 'No manners,' she sighed out heavily.

'Shut up, Mum,' Grace sent over a shoulder. 'I'm just off out for a while.'

'What?' Shirley barked. 'You'll do no such thing, miss. It's gone ten o'clock . . .'

'I'm twenty-three!' Grace snapped in a suffocated voice. 'If I want to go out for half an hour on a Sunday night, I will.'

'I've said before, you weren't this damned rude to me before you started knocking around with . . .' Her voice tailed off but both her daughter and her unwanted visitor understood what else she'd been about to say.

'Wait for me?' Grace murmured, with a pleading look, and received a nod from Chris in response.

He retreated backwards along the path, muttered, 'Thanks,' before swinging away and closing the gate.

'You in trouble indoors 'cos of me?' Chris asked Grace when she was seated beside him.

She slanted a look at him and gave a rueful smile. 'Oh, yeah . . . but don't worry, I've had enough of her ordering me about and thinking I'm still a kid . . .' She glanced away, feeling bashful. Her mother wasn't the only one who thought her childish: the last time she'd been out with Chris before they broke up he'd implied the same thing . . . but not for any reason her mother would approve of.

'Can't blame her,' Chris said quietly. 'Girl like you's worth protecting from blokes like me, and she knows it.' He smiled wryly. 'I was gonna pop by earlier and ask if it'd be alright to come back this evening.'

'But?'

'Thought you might say don't bother . . . Would you've done?'

'No . . .'

He put the van in gear and set off with a jerk. After taking a few back turnings he pulled up and opened the window. A moment later he got out his cigarettes and, having lit one, he turned to look at her. 'Thought you might like to know I've been to see me mum. Last week I went to Bexleyheath and she was still living at the address you gave me.'

Grace stared through the dusk at him with large, luminous eyes, not daring to ask. 'I'm glad,' she breathed. 'That's good . . .'

'Is it?' he countered. 'Aren't you gonna ask how it went . . . this long-awaited reunion?'

Grace swallowed the aching lump in her throat. She didn't need to ask; she could tell from his tone of voice, from his savagely sardonic expression, that he very much regretted having done what she'd pushed him into doing.

'Are you blaming me?' she asked. 'If you are, I'll apologise. It wasn't ever my business, and I know I was wrong to interfere in the first place . . .'

'No, you were right,' he interrupted, dragging on the cigarette and exhaling a stream of smoke out of the

167

window. 'You're always right, Grace. It's done, it's over and now I can forget about her.'

'Have you told your dad or Matilda that you went to see her?'

'No . . . no point . . . there's nothing to say apart from she told me to piss off. Well, not exactly in those words; I suppose she was as polite as she could be, considering I nearly gave her a heart attack. So, it's done, and now I'm gonna forget all about her.'

'Are you sure you can do that? You sound too wounded to forget her,' Grace reasoned gently.

'I'm not wounded,' he returned immediately, pitching the smoked butt out of the window and pulling the pack of Weights out of his pocket again.

'Is she a horrible woman, like your dad said?' Grace burst out, suddenly fired with an urgent need to know how hurt he'd been. She felt furious with Pamela Riley for rejecting him and was tempted to go to Bexleyheath herself and give his mother a piece of her mind.

'No . . . she was nice . . . nothing like what I was expecting from me dad's description of her,' Chris admitted with a faraway look. 'When I got there she was in a neighbour's front garden, down on her hands and knees, clearing the wet leaves off this old dear's path so she didn't slip over.' He paused, tapping the packet of Weights on the steering wheel. 'So . . . if she was a lazy, good-fer-nuthin' slut at some time, she ain't any more. She'd been watching me sitting in the van, while I was plucking up the courage to get out and knock on her door. She thought I was the builder she'd rung up about fixing her a new gate.' He gazed through the windscreen into the darkness. 'Once I'd gone up her path she came over, smiling and chatting. I liked her straight away. I think she liked me too . . . till I told her who I was.' He tipped his head back and chuckled bitterly at the memory of it. 'Nearly got meself arrested over it.' He glanced at Grace's solemn face. 'As soon as she real-ised why I'd come, she collapsed. One of her neighbours saw her on the ground and rushed out threatening to get the police on me. Must've thought I'd whacked her.'

'What happened?' Grace gasped through her fingers. Her heart was pounding beneath her ribs at the idea that she might have caused him to be in such serious trouble. 'Did your mum say you'd assaulted her?'

'No . . . she told her neighbour she'd tripped over, but I can't deny it was my fault that she ended up on the deck. I thought for a minute she was seriously ill. She wouldn't let me help her up, though; she just got on her feet and went inside, and that was that.'

Grace gave an audible sigh of relief, instinctively reaching out a hand to comfort him. He watched her fingers hover before just brushing his sleeve and with-drawing.

'It's alright, you don't need to worry I'm feeling vindic-tive. I've said I don't blame you. I'm not even going to say I told you so . . .' He held out his hand, inviting her to touch him again.

His reassurance seemed hollow, spoken in such a stinging tone and, for the first time, a little frisson of fear tightened Grace's gut. Even when he'd had her pinned against the wall in an alley, she'd trusted him not to harm her. But this wasn't about a tiff, and a girl telling a boy she wanted a break from seeing him; it was about a lifetime of wishing and dreaming crumbling in an instant, and she knew if she were in his shoes she'd be inconsolable.

'Why didn't you come and tell me straight away you'd gone there?' she asked huskily.

'Weren't up to it,' he admitted brusquely. 'It knocked me for six for a while. Dunno why, 'cos I was sure I'd cope alright with being told to get lost.' He turned his head, protecting a glitter in his eyes. 'Me dad knows something's up with me . . . reckon he thinks it's what's gone on between us, so I've let him believe what he likes.'

He'd been licking his wounds for a whole week, Grace realised, before feeling composed enough to come and tell her that, against his better judgement, he'd done what she'd said, and had his courage rewarded in the way he'd said.

She knew there was nothing she could say to ease his pain, but there was something she could do, and she wasn't sure whether that was what he was expecting and was the reason he'd brought her here: so she could make up for hurting him, his way. Worse, she was wondering if it was the least she owed him . . .

Although she'd honestly wanted things to turn out well between Chris and his mother there had been a selfish reason too that she'd been unwilling to examine till now.

Naively, she'd believed that once a reunion had taken place, Chris wouldn't be so obsessed with Pamela. Grace had had her fill, when engaged to Hugh Wilkins, of competing with an older woman for her boyfriend's attention. But instead of removing a rival, and helping Chris to feel more relaxed about his relationship with his mother, all she'd done was given him more reason to brood about her.

'I'm sorry . . .' she whispered, unable to express her guilt and remorse more fully.

170

'Me too . . .' He withdrew his hand. 'So where does that leave us?'

Grace swallowed. 'I don't know . . .' she croaked. 'Perhaps if you try again in a week or two to see her, she might then understand . . .'

'Fuck's sake . . . !'

The curse exploded beneath his breath but she'd heard it and the violence in his voice made her flinch and swivel away from him.

'I'll come with you, if you want. You don't have to go there alone next time. I promised I would go with you, and it's the least I can do.'

'I'm not going there again, with or without you.' It was a quiet, calm statement.

'Was her husband at home . . . or any children?'

'Don't know . . . never saw anybody else . . . they might've been out, I suppose.'

'I should be getting back . . .' Grace murmured.

He lit another cigarette, settled back against the seat. 'Have you missed me?'

'Yes . . .'

He turned towards her. 'Good, 'cos I've missed you.' He stretched out a hand and stroked the side of her face, trailed his fingers to caress softly beneath the hair at her nape until her eyelids drooped. 'Goodnight kiss?' he asked in a throaty murmur that mingled a challenge with wry pessimism.

She gazed at him with such wariness that he started laughing. A moment later he was leaning forward to turn the ignition. 'I might be pissed off, and sex-starved, Grace, but I haven't turned into a rapist.'

As he flicked the half-smoked cigarette out of the window, and reached for the handbrake, Grace spontaneously slid close to him, hugging him tightly about the waist and burrowing her face in his chest. 'I know . . . I know you wouldn't . . . it's just I can see how sad you are and I don't know what to do to make it right . . .' Her muffled words petered out. She knew she'd said the wrong thing. But he didn't laugh, or make any lewd suggestions. He put an arm about her, then the other, so she was squeezed hard against him and his warm breath stirred her hair.

'It was brave of you to go there,' Grace said after a few quiet minutes, when their hungry embrace had loosened a bit and the atmosphere between them was peaceful. 'If your mum can't be brave too, and meet you halfway, it's her loss. Perhaps, once she's got over the shock of seeing you for the first time . . .' cos it is for the first time, really.' She ran a hand up and down on his sleeve, searching for the right words. 'Last time she saw you, you were just a babe in arms, weren't you? Now you're a man, and perhaps you don't look anything like she imagined you would. But she might feel differently when she's had a chance to calm down.'

'You think so?' He sounded cynical, yet also strangely open to persuasion.

Grace nodded vigorously and edged away from him so she could gaze earnestly into his eyes. 'She must be a kind soul if she helps out her elderly neighbours.'

'That's what I thought.'

'People who are kind sometimes never get thanks, or favours done back. My nan's a bit like that,' Grace said. 'She's sprightly for her age, and does a bit of shopping for a couple of her neighbours who hobble about, yet the old miseries moan if she's gone in the wrong shop and spent a penny too much on their butter.'

'You coming out with me at the weekend?'

Grace nodded and smiled. 'It'll have to be Sunday though 'cos I promised my nan I'd go to Wood Green shopping with her on Saturday, then back to hers for tea.' She suddenly sat up. 'Would you like to come to my nan's for tea?' She read his dubious expression. 'Oh, you needn't worry about my mum, she won't be there, thank goodness. One of her friends is a hairdresser and she's going to give Mum's hair a permanent wave.'

'Right, in that case, I'd like to meet your nan,' Chris said. ''S'long as she don't mind sharing her Victoria sponge with me.'

'How d'you know we have Victoria sponge?'

'Everybody has Victoria sponge according to me dad, now he's an expert on teatime favourites. Oh, by the way, he's opening a caff.' He chuckled on seeing Grace's comically sceptical expression. 'It's true . . . you can ask him . . .' With that he caught her to him for a kiss of tender passion before steering away from the kerb.

'I once met your grandfather, you know.'

Chris put down his teacup and gazed at the small, elderly lady seated across the table from him. 'You knew the Plummers?' he asked hoarsely, darting a look at Grace.

They were seated at Nan Jackson's square dining table with an ample tea of sandwiches and dainty cakes spread out before them on a crisp linen cloth.

'No, not your Plummer grandfather,' Nan Jackson clarified with a smile. 'I have to say I never knew them at all. But I once got introduced to Jimmy Wild in a pub. Me and your granddad Bert.' Nan Jackson looked at Grace who was interestedly listening to this anecdote.

'Well, we'd gone to Islington to see some people, you see. Bert had a job in a factory before he went off to fight in the Great War and he used to work with a fellow by the name of Lenny . . . can't remember his surname . . .' Nan Jackson's lined face puckered further and she gave an impatient little tap on the table. 'Ooh, what was it? Anyway, Lenny and his girlfriend were having a bit of a party in a pub in Holloway Road 'cos they'd got engaged. Nag's Head, it was,' she blurted with a pleased smile on remembering the pub's name. 'Lenny was quite pally with Jimmy Wild 'cos he and his girlfriend lived close to The Bunk. I expect you knew your grandparents used to live in Campbell Road, didn't you, Christopher?'

'I did,' Chris confirmed. He was eager to hear more about his notorious grandfather, and have an outsider's opinion on him. Everybody in the family had seemed to loathe Jimmy Wild because of his wicked ways. 'I know he was unpopular. What did you think of him?'

'Well, he was a handsome devil, I'll give him that,' Nan Jackson said with a chuckle. 'I assumed he was with his wife, your grandma, that night but apparently the pretty blonde woman with him was his fancy piece. Everybody in the Nag's Head was going on about how brazen they were, carrying on like that.'

'I've heard some tales about him.' Chris gave Grace's grandmother a rueful smile. 'I feel sorry for me poor old Nan Fran and what she must've had to put up with.'

'He tried to murder Matilda in the 1920s, you know,' Grace piped up, eyes widening. 'You told me about it, didn't you, Chris.'

'I'd heard a rumour about that . . . dreadful thing to do, wasn't it?' Nan Jackson said but her lips twitched in scandalised humour. 'I've heard about Matilda Keiver

174

too and I reckon it'd take a better man than Jimmy Wild to see her off.'

Chris nodded, his expression making words unnecessary. He helped himself to a piece of sponge oozing butter cream.

''Course Jimmy was young when I met him. You could tell just from looking at him that he was a rogue alright: all swagger and brash as they come. He'd flirt with any woman who was walking past him. I remember his fancy piece . . . Nellie was her name . . . giving him such a look for trying to chat up the barmaid right in front of her eyes.' Nan Jackson stretched out a withered hand and pushed the plate of cakes towards Chris. 'Now come on, take another one, I've not baked this lot to see them go to waste. Eat up, both of you.'

'Mum thinks the Wilds are a rough lot, but I reckon you needed to be to survive in a place like The Bunk.' Grace gave Chris a smile. She was pleased he didn't seem embarrassed at all by this conversation about his evil grandfather, and that he and her nan had seemed to take to one another straight away.

'Good and bad in all families,' Nan Jackson said succinctly. 'And I speak as I find. I can tell from meeting you, Christopher, that you're a good 'un.' She gave her granddaughter a wink and poured herself a fresh cup of tea.

'Well, on a lighter note we're after some chairs to borrow for the Coronation Day party we're having in The Bunk.' Grace chose a cake and put it on her plate. 'Chris's dad is opening a caff so we'll be able to borrow some from him because, of course, he'll be shutting up shop on the big day. But we still don't reckon we'll have enough, do we?' She glanced at Chris for a nod of agreement. 'Do you know if your community centre up the road might have some going spare in June next year?'

'I could ask the committee, if you like,' Nan Jackson said. 'You don't want to take 'em just yet, do you?'

'Oh no, nowhere to store them, but we're trying to get everything organised so it all goes off with a bang.' She turned to Chris. 'We want it to be a great do, don't we. Matilda has already got a few cases of drink stashed away in her room, and a whole list of people she wants to track down and invite.'

'Surprised she ain't drunk the Irish whiskey,' Chris chipped in drolly. 'I've heard a few tales about her 'n' all and how she liked a tipple or two in her time.'

'Living in The Bunk, I reckon she probably needed it,' Nan Jackson said, rolling her eyes.

CHAPTER SIXTEEN

'I've seen you before. You were here a while ago, weren't you?'

'Yeah . . . is Mrs Riley about, d'you know? I've come to do her job.'

Chris already knew she wasn't: for a week he'd secretly investigated his mother's routine to find out if there were days and times when she was regularly away from home. To do so he'd had to take time off work, and he knew his three workmates were getting narked that he kept disappearing. But he didn't care. He wasn't even bothered that they'd fallen behind schedule again in Whadcoat Street, and he had nobody to blame for it but himself. He'd had set in his mind for a long time what he wanted to do, and today he was fired up to go ahead and do it.

Every time he'd passed his mother's house, on a recce, he'd been relieved to see the gate was still missing. He knew any direct offer of help from him would be rejected. Just a glimpse of him might again make her frightened and unwell, and he couldn't bear the thought of that, so he'd made sure to keep out of sight.

Earlier that morning, he'd seen Pamela walking towards the bus stop on the corner of her road. He'd known she'd be away from home for some hours, working as a waitress, because he'd previously checked where she went when she set off in the mornings. On one occasion he'd followed the bus and had noticed her go inside a place called the Greengage Café. A short while later he'd spied her, dressed in white pinafore and cap, serving behind the counter. It had looked the sort of cheap and cheerful place that he and the lads might use during their dinner break to stodge up on pie 'n' mash before going back to work. He knew too that Pamela didn't leave work till after three in the afternoon, and that she seemed to live alone. He'd kept an eye out for her husband, or any other family members who might be living at the address. He'd even knocked once, after she'd set off for work, just in case somebody might be in there. He'd thought it best to find out rather than be spotted hanging about. But there had been no response, and no neighbours had appeared to give him the third degree.

Today he hadn't been so lucky.

After Pamela had got on the bus that morning to go to work he'd pulled off from where he'd parked out of sight, behind a larger vehicle, to halt outside her house.

Unfortunately, just as he'd got out of his van, the neighbour who'd threatened him with the police on the day he'd come to introduce himself to his mother had been on her way out, swinging a shopping bag.

Chris cursed his bad luck but managed a vague smile in response to the woman's barked greeting.

'So you're here to do the gate, are you?' Mrs Rathbone plonked her hands on her hips and cocked her head, eyeing him suspiciously.

Chris nodded and looked busy, shuffling paperwork on his bonnet.

'You must have given her a better price than the other fellow. Disgrace, he was! He wanted a fortune for a little job like that! Mrs Riley only wanted the gate put back to stop the litter blowing up the path. She told me she wasn't going to bother having it done after all . . . she must've changed her mind.'

'I charge reasonable rates,' Chris muttered, and turned his back on her hoping she'd quickly get going.

'She's not in, anyhow, because she works Tuesdays in a caff and won't be back till this afternoon.'

'Yeah, well, don't matter. Can do the job if she's in or out.' Chris strode to the back of his vehicle and started rummaging in it for tools, wishing she'd just piss off so he could get started.

'Shame they never kept the gate that was on there,' Gladys Rathbone remarked, following him to peer inquisitively into the van. 'Nothing wrong with it, but they got rid of it, you see. You could just have fixed that back on for her, and she'd have saved herself a tidy amount.'

'Yeah? What happened to it, then?' Chris slanted a glance at her.

'Gave it to the scrap man after it got taken off because of the wheelchair. Even then it was still a scrape for him getting through the opening.' She nodded at the privet hedge. 'So she had to cut that back quite a bit with the shears, but it's grown over nicely now.'

Chris straightened, turned slightly towards her, frowning enquiringly, but wary of seeming to be prying.

'Mrs Riley's husband lost a leg in the war. He was in a wheelchair from about . . .' she looked heavenwards, calculating the years. 'Say . . . 1942 it must've been

179

when he got invalided home. Died two years later, poor soul . . . infection. Only got married, the two of them, shortly before he joined up, so she ended up his nurse more than his wife . . . no children . . .' Drawing herself to attention, the woman shot him a look, realising she'd spoken very much out of turn. Briskly she buttoned her coat. 'Well, I've got to be off.' She checked inside her shopping bag before marching off up the street.

As soon as she'd gone Chris measured the opening, praying that it would be the right size, or near enough, so he could plane the gate to suit. He'd chosen it with care, driving the merchants mad by making them bring out practically every timber variety they had stocked in the warehouse till he saw one that seemed right. But, as he strode to and fro on the pavement, he was glad to see his one matched well with those hanging on the gateposts of the neighbouring houses.

He quickly went to the back of the van and lifted out the gate then a moment later returned for his tools.

'Bleedin' hell, decided to turn up, have you?' Vic's expression was as sour as his speech. 'I've been coverin' fer you, y'know. We was goin' like the clappers till you started doin' a disappearing act fer days on end. So don't blame us now we're behind again. Where've you been slopin' off to this past week?'

'Mind yer own business, and stop nagging,' Chris replied mildly. 'I'm here now, ain't I?'

Vic went off muttering beneath his breath.

'Where's he been hiding this time?' Billy mouthed, jerking his head Chris's way.

'Gawd knows . . .' Vic grunted and, raising his hammer, brought it down with a crash on a doorframe.

'Bird trouble, bet yer life,' Billy said with a cautious peer towards the door to make sure Chris was out of earshot. 'He ain't been the same since he started seeing Grace Coleman. Don't go out nowhere, 'less it's with her.' He pressed down a thumb onto his open palm. 'That's where she's got him . . . *right* under . . .'

'She is a good-looking sort. I know I would . . .' Ted made a lewd gesture with his fist.

'I don't reckon even he's managed to get a leg over with that one . . . she's a right tight knickers, if you ask me,' Billy replied with a smirk. 'Anyhow, saw Sharon Webb down Tottenham Royal on Saturday and she was asking after Chris.'

The mention of Sharon brought his mates' eyes swivelling his way. She'd always been a favourite with the boys since she had a voluptuous look of Diana Dors about her.

'Chris could be in there again like a shot if he wanted. Dunno whether to tell him about Sharon asking after 'im being as him and Grace seem to be back on . . .'

'He was always a lucky bleeder like that; surprised he puts up with being henpecked.' Vic started stamping his boot against the frame until it splintered and came out in a cloud of dust.

His remark had given Billy and Ted an opportunity to exchange a gleeful look. 'Yeah . . .' cos you make sure you let Deirdre know who wears the trousers in your house, don't yer, Vic?' Billy mocked.

'Yeah . . . and you'll be laughing on the other side of your face once you 'n' Bet get married, mate. Ain't all it's cracked up to be, having a missus 'n' kids.'

'Deirdre ain't dropped her nipper yet, what you moanin' about?'

'Me brother's got two under five and I've seen what goes on, don't worry about that,' Vic returned dolefully.

'When's it due?'

'Five months to go . . .'

'*Five months?* Got ages then to learn how to change dirty nappies.' Ted started chuckling.

'You lot are worse'n a bunch of old women, y'know that.' Chris had come in and dumped down a ten-pound hammer. 'Get that wall down, Ted, and the rest of you . . .'

'Whoa . . . whoa . . . hang on . . .' Billy made a meal of finding his watch up his sleeve then stared at it. 'It's just a couple of minutes to dinnertime. We've been here since quarter to eight, and I'm bleedin' starving, so I'm off to the caff.'

'I'll come 'n' all. Deirdre ain't done me no sandwiches today.'

'That's a result then, Vic,' Ted said drolly and downed tools. He turned to Chris. 'Here . . . some old tramp's been kipping upstairs again.'

Chris glanced around as he picked up the ten-pound hammer, propped against the wall. 'How d'you know that?'

'Couple of old blankets and a few empty bottles are up there. Must be bleedin' desperate to use this place to doss in.'

As Vic started shrugging into his jacket he muttered, 'No harm in it, surely, if someone is making use of some o' the houses.'

'Just half an hour . . .' Chris yelled after them as they all trooped out.

But he was smiling as he took a swing at the wall. He hoped his mum was pleased with her new gate, but if she wasn't, and had it taken off so she could burn it because it came from him, he knew he'd still be glad he'd done it. He doubted she'd contact him, either to thank him, or to have a go about him trespassing and interfering. But he'd thought of a way to do her a favour, and perhaps let her know, despite everything that had gone on between her and his dad, he was his own person, and he only wished her well.

From what her neighbour had said about her losing her husband, it seemed she'd had an unhappy, unlucky life. Chris felt annoyed with his father for having called her names when he knew nothing about her now. Stevie didn't appreciate how fortunate he was. He had Pearl, and a brother who was supporting him in opening up a new business, and a son who took him down the Arsenal and cared about him – even when he was acting like a silly old sod. What did his mother have? A job in a greasy-spoon caff, and an empty house to go home to.

Whatever Pamela Plummer might have done in the past, Chris doubted it had been so bad that she'd deserved to suffer so much since. If his father discovered how it'd turned out for her, he'd probably mutter about what goes round comes round, and think she'd got her just desserts.

Chris knew he wasn't yet completely content; he'd found out that his mother was alive, and he knew he'd like very much to see her again. Perhaps, through her, he'd find out a bit about his Plummer grandparents. If they were dead too, she might have no family at all . . . except him. Next time he went that way, and he knew he would, if the gate was still standing, it'd be a good sign, and he'd take a chance and knock on her door . . .

Chris heard his stomach grumble and realised he was

hungry. He strolled out to the van and rummaged for the big pack of sandwiches and the flask of tea his dad had done him that morning. He went back inside, sat down with his back to what was left of the wall, and started eating. It was a moment before he sensed he wasn't alone. He turned his head to see little Kathleen Murphy staring at him . . . or rather at his cheese and pickle sandwich.

Chris smiled at her, thinking she was a sweet little thing, but wondering what on earth she was doing here. She was shoeless and coatless on a late November day and he realised she was lucky not to have hurt herself climbing over the rubble in the hallway. He pushed himself upright.

'Hello . . . where's your mum?'

The girl pointed outside and then at his sandwich.

'Your name's Kathleen, isn't it?'

'Kathleen Murphy,' she said in a lilting accent.

She pointed again at his sandwich but Chris could tell she was either too polite or shy to ask outright for it.

He rummaged in his lunch box and got out a fresh one and offered it. 'Take you home now,' he said.

She moved towards him for the food, wincing as her tiny feet stepped on grit.

Swinging her up in his arms he said, 'Now, Kathleen, I think we should find your mum.' He felt her cold little body beneath his palms and automatically rubbed at her legs to warm them.

Kathleen grabbed at the sandwich and immediately took a bite out of it.

'Hello . . . Mrs Murphy . . . you in?' Chris had stopped at the bottom of some stairs in a musty hallway to yell out.

A moment later he heard the sound of a baby's cries followed by its hacking cough. He started up the stairs, carrying Kathleen.

Before he reached the top a woman appeared, looking harassed. She halted, gawping at him and turning pale. Chris could tell she'd no idea her daughter had gone missing.

'Kathleen . . . ?' Noreen gasped. 'What . . . where has she been . . . ?'

'She came down the road and into the house we're working on,' Chris explained. 'No harm done,' he reassured her when a look of mingling shame and embarrassment transformed Noreen Murphy's shocked expression.

'Sorry about that . . . I thought she was playing out here on the landing . . . that's where she was . . .' She indicated a doll discarded on dirty bare boards.

'No harm done,' Chris repeated and set the girl down next to her mother. 'She seems a bit cold . . . and hungry.'

Again the woman's face flushed guiltily and she lowered her eyes. 'I was just going to do us a bite to eat.' Noreen knew that for a lie. She'd been waiting for her husband to come home with some groceries, but if Kieran hadn't managed to find Declan O'Connor, and get his wages from the tight-fist, he'd be back with nothing for them to eat.

'What's going on?' Kieran Murphy's voice sounded soft and suspicious as he started up the stairs towards them.

Chris could tell straight away that Mrs Murphy didn't want her husband to find out one of their children had been neglected, and could have got hurt. But he didn't see any way to avoid telling the truth. The last thing he wanted was Kieran jumping to the conclusion that he was making a play for his missus while he was out looking for work. And Noreen was a good-looking young woman despite her dishevelled appearance.

'Your daughter was just outside, I brought her in,' Chris said succinctly.

Kieran's eyes darted to his wife's face as he took the remnant of sandwich from Kathleen's fingers, making her whimper and try to snatch it back.

He thrust the food at Chris then the next moment was roughly steering his wife into their room and dragging his daughter behind him by the hand.

Before Chris had reached the bottom of the stairs he could hear a violent argument in progress and two children crying.

'Done a good job there, hasn't he?'

Pamela glanced up to see Gladys Rathbone strolling towards her, inspecting her new gate. Unable to speak, she nodded and removed her hand from where it had lain, curved softly about the top rail.

'Got a few bits 'n' bobs myself need doing,' the woman added. 'If I wait for Charlie to put me up a few more shelves in the pantry, I'll be waiting for evermore. Perhaps I might give your fellow a call, see if he'll give me a quote. When I spoke to him earlier, he said he does reasonable rates.' She slid Pam an enquiring look, hoping to find out what she'd paid for the job. 'I will say, he's a very handsome young man . . .' She chuckled dirtily and prodded Pam's arm.

Pamela raised her head at last and her neighbour saw her bloodshot eyes were glistening.

'Don't mind me having a joke about your builder,' the woman apologised with a frown. 'You're thinking of your Stan, aren't you, Pam . . . 'course you are. I should've known that getting a new gate would bring back sad memories for you. I'll leave you in peace. But come over a bit later, if you feel like it, and we'll have a cup of tea and a bit of Battenberg before my Charlie gets home.'

Once she was alone, Pamela latched the gate carefully, noting how easily it snapped into place, how well it swung on silent hinges. She turned and went inside to stare at the scrap of paper she'd found on her doormat that afternoon. It now lay on the hall table and, picking it up, she reread for the hundredth time the message neatly written on a page that had been torn from a cheap notebook.

I was going to paint it but don't know what colour you like. Anyhow you might get wet paint on your clothes. You don't owe me anything. Christopher.

A sob swelled in her chest and she sank to sit on the low table clutching her son's note to her heart.

CHAPTER SEVENTEEN

'So it's all back on with you and him, is it?'

'I'm going out with Chris again, if that's what you mean,' Grace confirmed, continuing to brush her hair. As she pinned a section of sleek blonde hair back with a gilt clip she noticed, at the corner of her eye, her mother still hovering by her bedroom doorway. Grace felt like also saying she was sick of hearing Christopher called *him* when Shirley knew his name perfectly well. But she bit her lip, waiting for her mother to leave her in peace, so she could finish getting ready to go out. Unfortunately, her mother seemed content to settle back against the doorframe to watch her, so Grace got up from the little dressing-table stool and picked up from the bed the navy-blue wool-crepe dress she'd got out of her wardrobe earlier. She stepped into it then approached her mother and turned her back for her to do her up.

Her mother jerked up the zip then fiddled with the hook and eye at the collar. 'You need long sleeves on now the weather's got so cold,' Shirley lectured, eyeing her daughter's bare arms. 'You'll need a cardigan on over that if you're not going to catch your death.'

'I'm getting one out of the drawer in a minute,' Grace replied, relieved her mother seemed to have turned her attention away from Chris.

'Your nan tells me that you've taken him round there with you a couple of times.'

Grace muttered beneath her breath and bent down to look for her shoes under the bed. 'Yes, I have. We went for tea and were telling her all about the plans for the Coronation Day party in Whadcoat Street next June. Nan likes Chris; I expect she's told you that.' Grace sat down on the edge of the mattress and misted her wrists with perfume, rubbing them together to fire the warm spicy scent.

Shirley hurrumphed. 'She wouldn't though, would she, if she knew a bit more about him. You're lucky I've kept her in the dark about what sort of family he comes from or he wouldn't get past *my* mother's doorstep.'

'You're wrong about that,' Grace said calmly. 'Nan does know his family were once very hard up because I told her. And when we were there she was talking to Chris about his wicked grandfather Jimmy 'cos once she and Granddad met him. We had a laugh about it. Luckily she's not as prejudiced as you are.'

'I'm not prejudiced! I just don't think he's good enough for you.'

'Why can't you just leave him alone!' Grace swivelled about on the edge of the bed. 'He's done nothing to you!'

'What's he done to you, eh? That's what I want to know, my girl.'

'Oh, here we go again . . .' Grace muttered wearily.

'Yes, miss, here we go again, and with your attitude, and if you're not careful, I can see you ending up just like your cousin Celia . . .'

'Please . . . not the cousin Celia story,' Grace sighed. 'Don't tell it to me again, Mum. I can recite it off by heart.'

'Good! 'Cos if that doesn't put the fear of God into you, I don't know what will.'

'Well, it's certainly put the fear of God into you, Mum!'

'I don't deny it!' Shirley thundered. 'It's enough to scare the wits out of any decent mother! Do you think I want a daughter of mine ending up in a sanatorium?'

Grace raised her eyes heavenwards. One of her cousins – on the Coleman side, naturally, her mother ensured she made that clear to anybody she recounted the tale to – had ended up in an unmarried mother's home after her parents threw her out, and the baby's father did a runner.

A policeman had got Celia pregnant, then resigned from the force, and joined the navy in the latter half of the war, to escape being tied down. Rumour had it he'd come back as hale and hearty as when he'd left, and had moved up to Cumbria without contacting Celia. But by then, with no family willing to help her, the baby had been forcibly taken from Celia for adoption, and the poor girl had attempted suicide twice.

At regular intervals Shirley would remind her daughter of Celia's disgrace, stressing the stupid girl had only herself to blame for giving it away to a rotter before she'd got the marriage lines tucked away in a drawer.

'Where are you off to, then?'

'Just out . . .'

'Where?'

'For God's sake, give over! We're not going to a hotel, and even if we were, it's none of your business.' Grace glared at her mother with a mixture of pity and annoyance. 'Just because you and Dad never had a kind word to say to each other doesn't mean couples who get along want to be at it like rabbits . . .'

'What do you mean *never had a kind word to say to each other*!' Shirley interrupted in a bellow. 'That's a wicked thing to say! We might not have been lovey dovey, but we had *respect* for each other. And your father would never have dreamed of taking liberties with me before he'd paid for his fun with a wedding ring.'

Grace sighed. Her mother obviously had on her rose-tinted spectacles. Sadly, she could bring to mind numerous occasions of bawled insults flying between her parents when mutual respect had been nowhere to be seen or heard. But it hadn't just been a case of Wilf being browbeaten by Shirley's withering looks and sarcasm. Grace had felt sorry for her mother, too, married, as she was, to a man whose passions in life seemed to be a pint of bitter, a game of darts, and the racing pages in the *News of the World*.

Obviously, they'd felt close enough, on at least two occasions, to produce her and her brother, Paul. But, Grace couldn't recall any instances of her parents being openly affectionate. The only time she'd seen them in each other's arms was when they'd danced a waltz at her brother's wedding in the back room of the Red Lion pub in Guildford.

'So let's have a little less backchat from you, my girl . . .' Her mother's nagging was penetrating Grace's reflection. A moment later a loud knock on the front door brought Shirley's lecture to a close, and Grace fully to her senses. But her mother was already heading for the stairs, and was halfway down them before Grace had even collected her handbag.

'Oh, it's you, Christopher,' Shirley said as though his arrival was a surprise. 'Come in; Grace is still upstairs. You've been going out a while now, haven't you, and Grace has introduced you to some of the family.' She immediately launched into the speech she'd rehearsed in her mind. 'Her nan tells me you've been round there for tea. Well, I think it's time for me to say that, as Grace's dad has passed away, you're welcome to speak to me about anything . . . intentions . . . anything like that . . .'

'Mum!' The single word was heard as a suffocated, silencing groan issuing from the landing.

'Evenin', Mrs Coleman,' Chris responded with studied courtesy. 'Thanks for that, I'll bear it all in mind.' Slowly he lifted his eyes, brimming with sultry amusement, to Grace, hovering at the head of the stairs. She'd swung about on the top tread as though she might disappear, then turned slowly back to give him a frown that was, at one and the same time, ashamed and apologetic.

He shook his head slightly, biting his lip to suppress a smile, hoping he'd indicated he wasn't at all bothered by Shirley's pushy behaviour.

With a deep, calming breath Grace descended the stairs, yanked her coat off the peg, and tonelessly said, 'Bye, Mum.' She was halfway down the front garden path before she allowed Chris to help her into the garment. Despite it being dark, and a cold and foggy November evening, she'd simply wanted to get out of the house, and away from her mother, as soon as she could.

They had driven for a few minutes in unbroken quiet

before Grace burst out, 'I'm sorry . . . she's so embarrassing . . . I've not said anything to her to make her think . . .'

'I know,' Chris said, slanting an amused look at her profile. 'Since that idiot you were engaged to slunk off, I suppose she thinks all men are the same. She's just looking out for you, Grace,' he added reasonably.

'She's looking out for herself, more like!' Grace returned. 'It's not just about protecting me, it's about her not wanting to be shown up or gossiped about, like Celia's lot.'

'Who's Celia?'

'My cousin.'

'Got herself in trouble, did she?'

Grace studied her hands while giving Celia some proper thought. 'It is a very sad tale, actually,' she admitted. 'It's just I'm sick of hearing about it.'

'What happened to her?'

'She's more my brother Paul's age than mine, so I never really knew her well,' Grace started. 'When she was nineteen or twenty she got pregnant by a policeman who wouldn't stand by her. So, against her will, her baby was taken away for adoption . . . it sent her mad.' She glanced at him, wondering if it was the sort of thing he'd shrug off, or perhaps he'd applaud the copper's deviousness, being as he was, in his own words, a man who liked to push his luck on a Saturday night.

'What happened to the copper?'

She shrugged. 'Nothing, as far as I know.'

'What . . . he didn't even get a good kicking?'

'He joined up to avoid getting married, and when he came back after the war, he went off to Cumbria. Probably he's Chief Constable by now,' she finished sourly.

'Why didn't Celia's old man go after him with a shotgun? Cumbria's not that far . . .' One of his hands sliced down on the steering wheel. 'Straight up the A1 and you could be there by nightfall.'

A slight grimace lifted Grace's brow. 'I suppose it was too late; the baby had been adopted by then. Is that what your lot would do . . . go after him, even if he was a policeman, and give him a good kicking?'

'Too right, and being as he was a copper, it'd be a pleasure. It's never too late for revenge, not when it's something as bad as that.'

'You'd do that, for your daughter?' Grace asked.

''Course . . .' He glanced at her. 'Your mum thinks you'll let me get you up the duff and then I'll disappear.' He choked a rueful laugh. 'Seems your mum knows me better than she knows you.' He frowned. 'That was a joke, of course . . .'

'Don't worry about her, she's just an old busybody.' Grace turned her head to stare out of the side window into the misty darkness. 'It's getting very foggy out there . . .'

'I had a run-in with one of those today.'

That comment drew an enquiring look from Grace.

'A busybody,' he explained. 'I went over to Bexleyheath again and got chatting to me mum's neighbour. Same old girl as before.' He paused, grinning. 'She didn't threaten to set the police on me this time.'

'You've been to see your mum again?' Grace echoed before her delicate features transformed into a wondrous smile.

'I saw her, but not to speak to. I kept meself hidden in case she caught a glimpse of me and had another turn. I went over there to do her a favour.' He sounded sweetly diffident. 'I'd been giving a bit of thought to what you said about people like her not getting anything done for them, even though they help out others. So I fixed her a new gate while she was at work.'

'What a good idea!' Grace beamed her approval.

'Yeah . . . I thought so too,' he said, feigning conceit. 'Just hope *she* thinks so . . .' He slanted Grace an exaggerated grimace. 'I stuck a note through her letterbox, just telling her she don't owe me nuthin'; didn't want her to think I might be sending in me invoice.'

'I'm sure she'll know, from a kind gesture like that, you just want to be friends with her.' Grace endorsed her praise by hugging his arm.

'I found out she's had a really hard time of it. This is where the busybody neighbour comes in,' he clarified. 'I didn't ask questions, she just started telling me about why the gate got took off in the first place.' He whipped a quick look at Grace as he steered around a corner. 'When me mum's husband got back from the war he'd lost a leg and needed a wheelchair.'

'And he couldn't get in and out of the gate in the wheelchair?' Grace guessed.

Chris nodded.

'What a terrible shame for him to be crippled and for her too, of course . . .' Grace murmured.

She'd heard similar tragic stories of war casualties. It wasn't unusual to see men out and about, trying to cope with life following the loss of limbs, or their sight, in the wake of the Second World War. Grace was often amazed at how jaunty some of them seemed to be as they hobbled along in their neat clothes and polished shoes. She suddenly realised that poor Mr Riley couldn't be amongst those plucky souls. 'So, if your mum wanted the gate put back . . . that means no wheelchair and no Mr Riley. He must've died.'

'Yeah, she's a widow; he passed on a while ago, not long after he got invalided home.'

'Have you got any half-brothers and -sisters?' Grace asked optimistically.

Chris shook his head. 'According to the battleaxe, me mum married Mr Riley just as the war started, and he was wounded a couple of years after. She said Pamela ended up being more his nurse than his wife . . . in which case it ain't surprising they never had kids.'

'Are you disappointed not to have more family?' Grace asked gently.

'Yeah; I am . . . a bit . . .' He fell silent.

'Talking of kids . . . I did another good turn 'n' all today. Little girl from up the road come wandering into the house we're working on. Lucky she didn't come a cropper; she was walking about barefoot on a building site. So I took her home to her mum. They're the people I was telling you about: the Murphys who moved in earlier in the year. Matilda was doing a bit of babysitting for the woman so she could do a cleaning job. But her husband put a stop to that. He won't let her go out and earn a few bob even though he's scratching around for work now he's lost his shifts with the pikeys.'

'That's a daft attitude to have,' Grace said emphatically.

'Kieran Murphy's asked me for a job a couple of times now but we're not taking on.'

'What did the woman say when you took her little girl back?' Grace asked. 'Anything could have happened to her. She might have got bricks fall on her while you were working. How old is she?'

'About three or four, I reckon. Sweet little thing, she is, polite too; her name's Kathleen.' He chuckled. 'She was after me sandwiches. Poor little mite seemed starving hungry, so I gave her one.'

'They must be very hard up . . .'

'I reckon they are, but it seems the old man's one of these too proud fer his own good and doesn't want it known he can't provide for his family. He took the sandwich off the kid and give it me back . . . what was left of it.' Chris frowned. 'Kieran Murphy was out, but he turned up just as I was handing Kathleen over to her mum. The woman looked guilty as hell and knew she'd been wrong in not keeping an eye on the girl. But she's got another kid to look after, and that one's a lot younger and coughing its guts up all the time.' He sighed. 'Kieran had a face like thunder so I just left 'em to it. Wish I hadn't now; wish I'd offered a bit more help. But not a lot you can do for a man won't even let his kid have a cheese sandwich he ain't paid for.'

'At least you tried,' Grace said, feeling proud of him. 'Some people would just walk on by.'

'Felt sorry for his wife; she knew she'd done wrong letting the tot out of her sight. I could hear him tearing a strip off her before I got out of the house. Shame I can't offer the bloke a job, then perhaps they could get themselves out of there, but the guvnor says there's nuthin' doing.'

'Couldn't he make an exception?'

'Nah, not Rob. He's a businessman and he won't jeopardise his profit margin by gettin' all sentimental. Can't blame him really; if he gives Murphy a job one of the others will have to go and that ain't fair. D'you want to see where me dad and Pearl are opening up their caff?' Chris asked abruptly, changing the subject. 'It's in Hornsey Road; got quite a good spot, they have.'

On seeing Grace's enthusiastic nod, he added, 'We'll probably catch them in; me old man said they'll be working late. He's keen to get it all up 'n' running by next week. He's thinking of doing fancy teas as an opening offer, to draw in the customers.'

'Sort of early Christmas cakes?' Grace observed. 'He's obviously got a good business brain, your dad.' She sounded impressed.

'Suppose he has, in his own way.' Chris had always thought his uncle Robert was the smarter of the two of them, and doubtless he was where winning building contracts was concerned. But perhaps now his dad was working at something he enjoyed, instead of felt obliged to do, he might prove to everybody that he could run a successful business as well as his brother, if he put his mind to it.

Stevie might not know a lot about doing paperwork but he knew what people liked to eat. Everybody loved a nice bit of cake, and with Christmas approaching, they were thinking of their stomachs. Chris reflected sombrely on the Murphys, wondering if they'd manage to get themselves somewhere warm and cosy by then, and enjoy a good Christmas Day.

CHAPTER EIGHTEEN

'I saw Vic this evening,' Stevie announced. 'He was just off to the shop to get something for his tea. Unusual for him to do a bit of shopping.'

'Deirdre's playing a blinder there, I'll give her that,' Chris said with a chuckle. 'She'll probably have him burping the baby and changing it after every feed.'

'Nothing wrong with that,' Pearl stated flatly. 'She'll need to put her feet up for a while after it's born. My husband used to change our Calvin's nappy.'

Pearl was the same age as Stevie, forty-five. She'd separated from her husband almost twenty years ago, after producing one son. But neither she nor her husband had ever bothered to put divorce proceedings in place. Pearl knew that if Stevie were to propose she'd get the ball rolling the following day. She'd loved him for years and very much wanted to be his wife.

Her son had lived with her until he was eighteen, although he'd seen his father whenever he wanted to as the marriage had floundered without rancour on either side. But Calvin had his own life now, and was a regular in the army, so Pearl only saw him a couple of times a year.

'You told me he never done nappies willingly,' Stevie protested, frowning at Pearl.

Talk of husbands helping out with their newborn children always made Stevie feel uneasy. He was uncomfortably aware he could have done more to support Pamela when their son had been born, and then things might have turned out differently. When she'd moaned about Christopher's constant crying he'd told her to pull herself together and get on with it. When she'd complained her nerves were playing up, and she couldn't think straight, he'd told her to get off her backside and be a wife and mother, because she was getting fat and lazy.

He'd never seen his father lift a finger to help his mother, whether it was caring for kids or household chores. In fact, Stevie had never seen his father work willingly at anything at all. Jimmy Wild would always skive and sponge if he could.

At the age of twenty-one Stevie had selfishly assumed babies were women's work, and Pamela should naturally be able to cope with hers. But if he'd ever guessed how she'd go about coping with their fretful son, he'd have nursed Christopher to sleep every night rather than risk him being harmed.

For twenty-four years Christopher had been the most precious thing in his life and, although Stevie knew it was time for them to go their separate ways, nobody could take his son's place in the centre of his heart.

Soon they'd not only be working but living apart, and it was the right thing for both of them, Stevie accepted that. Yet still he felt a pang of possessiveness at the thought of somebody else being more important to Christopher than he was.

'My husband might not have liked doing nappies.' Pearl suddenly took up the cudgels again. 'But he did it all the same. And that's what a woman wants: a bit of support now 'n' again without too much of a song 'n' dance going with it.'

'Sounds like you wished you'd stayed with him,' Stevie muttered petulantly.

'Nah . . . couldn't have done that. Couldn't stand that smell no longer.'

Chris and Grace stared at her before exchanging a glance of suppressed amusement.

'He was a taxidermist,' Pearl explained. 'Bleedin' stinky stuffed animals in every room in our house, there was. Five years of it and I'd had enough!' She wafted a hand in front of her nose.

'I think it's a good thing for men to lend a hand with children,' Grace spluttered, to stop herself hooting with laughter. 'It's handy for you both to know about rearing babies just in case one of you gets poorly at some time,' she gasped out. 'Anyway, if you pull together it makes life easier all round . . .'

'Bear that in mind, son,' Stevie said with mock warning, wagging a finger at Chris. But he glanced fondly at Grace, hoping that she *was* his future daughter-in-law. She wasn't just pretty, and nicely spoken, but wise and kind too.

'Anyhow, I've got a problem with me sink out the back, come and take a look.' Stevie pushed back his chair. 'The tap's playing up. Let the girls finish their cups of tea,' he added, as Chris beckoned Grace to accompany him and explore the caff's interior.

Stevie gripped a stiff tap set over an old butler sink in a small storeroom. It wouldn't budge, so he tried the other one next to it but had no luck there either.

'Need to get a pair of Stilson's on them taps,' Chris said, taking over trying to force the brass crossheads to turn.

'Rob's on the warpath,' Stevie said without preamble. He'd wanted to get his son on his own to tell him the bad news. 'He came round this evening, looking for you, just after you went out. Seems you've been taking time off without him knowing and the job's fallen behind again.'

Chris shot a glance at his father. There was no point in denying it. 'Who told him I've been taking time off?'

'Don't need to be told, do he? He's got eyes in his head. He went round Whadcoat Street one afternoon to pop in on Matilda then meet the council wallah and do a valuation. Vic said you'd just that minute gone off up the shop, or something equally daft, trying to cover for you. Rob ain't stupid, son, neither's the council wallah, and if you want to keep your job as foreman for Wild Brothers, you need to bear that very much in mind. Rob pays you a good, regular wage and you're gonna need that if you're thinking of settling down.'

Chris nodded slowly, instinctively glancing Grace's way. He accepted he'd got banged to rights. 'I'll have a word . . . apologise . . .' he said gruffly.

'Yeah, do that. I slipped in that you've been having a spot of woman trouble . . .' Stevie indicated Grace over his shoulder. She and Pearl were still sitting at a table, chatting over a cup of tea. 'I didn't elaborate on any of it, 'cos that's fer you to do, not me.' He watched as his son kept his eyes down, loosening the cold tap enough for a few drips of water to plop into the stained sink. 'All sorted out now? No more need to take time off?' Again Stevie's head jerked backwards at Grace.

'Won't be taking no more time off,' Chris replied, giving a bicep-bulging, final twist to the tap, and sending brownish water spurting into the sink. He turned it off and dried his hands on his sleeves.

His father patted his shoulder before leading him away to show him a shiny new refrigerator.

Chris followed him slowly, feeling guilty on two counts. He'd annoyed his uncle by neglecting his duties as foreman of his building firm, and he'd misled his father by allowing him to believe that Grace was the woman who'd kept him away from work on recent occasions.

He thought of his mother, as he'd first seen her, down on her knees, kindly sweeping up somebody else's path. He reflected on what he knew of her disappointing, depressing life, which nevertheless hadn't knocked the stuffing out of her – he had done that when he'd introduced himself.

Chris knew that if he found out she wanted to see him, he'd take time off work and go to Bexleyheath again tomorrow . . .

'You've made a prat of me, Chris, and I don't like that.' Rob took a swig from his mug of tea. He hadn't offered one to his nephew this morning when he'd turned up in his office to apologise for letting the schedule slip on the Whadcoat Street job. 'I asked you if you could cope with this contract without Stevie, and you said you could. Now, if you ain't up to it I'll get someone else in to run the show.'

'Don't need it . . . it's all fine now.'

'Not according to my man up the Council it ain't. That's why you've made a prat of me. I made a lot of noise about the pikeys being on my patch and he cleared 'em off. Now I'm getting sarcastic comments about perhaps he should get 'em back . . . and deduct it from my money. Weren't just me turned up when you was absent: a council bloke paid a visit too.'

Chris swiped a hand through his hair. 'Yeah, Dad said. It's all back to normal. I'll work late . . . get it back on track.'

'O'Connor'll be laughing his bollocks off, if he finds out it's going sour on us.'

'I'll work late . . . starting tonight,' Chris repeated. He hesitated. 'How about if I let Kieran Murphy have a few days?'

'Up to you, mate,' Rob answered. 'But you'll be paying him out of your own wages.'

'Best be off to work.' Chris looked at his watch, wanting to get away from his irate guvnor as soon as he could.

'It's not like you, Chris, to be missing shifts,' Rob said. 'What's the problem?'

As Chris met his uncle's eyes he realised he'd guessed more than his father had about the identity of the woman involved in keeping him from doing his job.

'Told you to leave things alone, Chris, didn't I?' Rob shook his head. 'Only one way this is going to end up, you know that, don't you . . .'

'I've gotta get going,' Chris said and strode towards the door.

'Yeah, you do that,' Rob turned his back on his nephew.

*   *   *

'You didn't tell me that the guvnor had been round checking up on things with the council jobsworth when I wasn't here.'

Vic dropped his newly lit cigarette and stamped on it. Chris had been a bit late turning up, so he'd thought he was having a morning off again, and there'd be plenty of time for a crafty fag before getting started. 'I *did* tell you I'd been covering for you,' he insisted, narked.

'Yeah, but not that it were covering for me in a *big* way,' Chris bawled.

'I told them you'd just gone up the shop.' Vic shrugged. 'What's wrong with that? They didn't know no different.'

Chris gave him a sour look. 'The guvnor would never buy that. We're talking about Rob Wild, not Joe Muggins.' He locked the van and strode into the shell of a house they were working on.

'You in the shit over it?' Vic had followed him. He knew if Chris got the sack he could be in line for the foreman's job.

'Gonna work late and get things back on track . . .'

'When . . . when you gonna work late?' Vic asked immediately.

'Why, what's it to you?'

'Nuthin'. . . just thought if there's overtime going . . .'

'There ain't. I'll bring it back on track on me own.' He gave Vic a mocking glance. 'But if you fancy turning up 'n' giving a hand out of the goodness of yer heart, Vic . . .'

'Sod that fer a game o' soldiers,' Vic muttered and stomped off.

'Yeah . . . that's what I thought,' Chris drawled, dropping his tool bag on the floor.

CHAPTER NINETEEN

'Going in, luv?'

Pamela Riley shot a look at the fellow who was holding open the door to the Duke of Edinburgh pub.

'You going in?' he repeated as she hesitated then took a step away. 'Who you after?' He'd guessed she'd been looking for somebody inside, and had been peering through the glass panel to see if they were present before entering.

'Matilda Keiver,' Pamela blurted. 'I know she used to drink here a lot.'

'Old Tilly . . .' The man barked a laugh. 'Oh, yeah, she's still a regular. Don't come in now as much as she used to, but she can sink a few, considering she's getting on a bit.' He glanced at his watch, nodding to himself. 'You might be lucky; she could be along for a dinnertime snifter.' He studied Pamela, noting her dull, sensible appearance. She didn't look, or sound, as though she was a friend of Matilda's. She had the air of a middle-aged housewife from a better part of town. He guessed her to be at least twenty years Matilda's junior, but then

206

old Tilly got along with most folk, as long as they hadn't upset her or her family in some way. If they had, she'd be down on them like a ton of bricks.

'Thanks for letting me know she's still about,' Pamela said, noting the man was still holding the door slightly ajar. 'I'll just hang on here a bit longer and if she doesn't turn up . . . I'll be on my way.' She shrugged further into her coat.

He smiled at her, thinking if she made an effort with a bit of make-up, and took that ugly old hat off her hair, she wouldn't be a bad-looking woman for her age. It occurred to him that she might be waiting outside for a friend to get her a drink, because she was on hard times. Matilda was known to be keen to have a drinking pal, and generous in that respect. 'Come on . . . I'll buy you one if you're a bit short.' He pushed the door open.

'No thanks,' Pam returned curtly. 'If I wanted a drink I'd pay for it myself.'

'Suit yerself, luv,' the man replied, unperturbed. He started off, then retraced his steps. 'She don't live that far away, y'know. If you go round Whadcoat Street you'll probably find her in.'

'Don't know it. All I know is she used to live in Campbell Road.'

'Yeah, that's it. Campbell Road. Now it's Whadcoat Street.'

Pamela frowned at him. She'd walked along Seven Sisters Road and glanced at the turning into Campbell Road, seeing nothing but squalid houses and a few workmen in the distance doing slum clearance. The Bunk had always been a dump, but she'd assumed now it was uninhabited. It hadn't occurred to her to check the street name, high up on the wall.

207

'Whadcoat Street?' she said, in surprise. 'Why'd they bother changing its name now they're pulling it all down?'

'Obviously you ain't been back in a while, duck,' the fellow chuckled. 'Street names got altered right back in the thirties. Gawd knows why; didn't make a blind bit of difference to what went on down there. The Bunk's The Bunk . . . always will be.' He rubbed his hands together, then puffed into them.

It was an early December day and there was a bitter breeze blowing. Pamela was also feeling chilled and had half-turned away from him to protect her cold cheeks from a buffeting. She hunched up her shoulders to her ears and continued listening to what he'd got to say.

'Paddington Street's now Biggerstaff Road, see, 'cos that name got changed as well,' the fellow explained. 'Pen pushers with nothing better to do I suppose . . . can't leave nuthin' alone.'

'Matilda still lives down there, even though they're knocking it down?' Pam couldn't disguise her astonishment, or her scepticism.

'Yeah, and she's not on her own neither. Should've seen the crowd they had down there Bonfire Night.' He shook his head in amusement at the memory. 'Weren't as lively as it used to be in its heyday, but had a good time. Bit of a tradition, ain't it, Bonfire Night and The Bunk. Went down there meself November 5th. Never miss it.' He sauntered off, whistling. A moment later he was gesticulating at her and pointing across the road.

It took Pam a moment to realise he was letting her know that Matilda was on her way.

Pamela felt her insides knotting in anxiety despite the fact that the person progressing slowly in her direction

208

seemed quite unintimidating. The Matilda of old had always had a bounce in her stride; this woman had a slight limp and was dumpy of figure rather than solidly built. Her hair was no longer a fiery flaxen shade, but colourless. It was plaited, as Pamela remembered it often had been, and coiled in buns pinned on either side of her head. If the fellow hadn't indicated this elderly woman's identity she would never have known her.

But then she didn't expect Matilda to recognise her either.

Last time they'd spoken, Pamela had been an overweight, fresh-faced blonde in her twenties. She had no illusions as to how she looked now, even before a glance sideways at the pub's windows reflected back at her the thin, lined face of a faded woman who looked older than her forty-four years. Her thick fair hair had once been her pride and joy; now she mostly went out wearing a hat to cover the fact her crowning glory was wispy, and a silvery shade of mouse.

'After you,' Matilda said as she saw a woman hovering in front of her by the pub's door.

'No . . . it's alright . . . I've . . . I'm just waiting . . .'

Matilda squinted at the woman getting in her way, thinking something about her seemed familiar, but she was unsure what it was. Then a fragment of memory made her think of a woman with a small dimple in her chin and a high-pitched voice, who'd once been part of the family. She'd been giving Pamela Plummer some thought lately but even so it seemed hard to believe that . . .

'You're Matilda Kelver, aren't you,' Pamela blurted out. 'You won't remember me . . . it was years and years ago you last spoke to me . . .'

209

'I know you,' Matilda said, cocking her head, her eyes fixing on Pam with fierce directness. 'Bleedin' hell, you're right . . . it was a while ago . . . about twenty-five years if I remember correctly.'

'Twenty-three, and I haven't come to cause trouble,' Pam immediately burst out. Suddenly the years were peeling away. It seemed only yesterday she'd last had those probing eyes on her. A short while after that, Pam had left the Islington area for good, and hadn't been back since.

'What have you come for then, Pamela?' Matilda asked evenly. ''Cos whatever it is, I think you 'n' me know it *is* gonna cause a ruckus of some sort. But that might not be a bad thing.'

Pamela's thin lips twisted into a smile. Matilda might look past it, but her mind seemed as sharp as it had been when she'd been ducking and diving as one of The Bunk's rent collectors.

Pam had hoped to winkle out of Matilda a few titbits of information about Christopher, so she'd know a little about his life, and could hug it close to her, when she went back to her own existence in Bexleyheath. Instead, she fished in her bag and brought out a five-pound note. Matilda was too cute to give away a thing. Pam knew if she found out anything about her son, it would be because Matilda Keiver wanted her to know it.

'Would you give this to Christopher, for me?' Pam asked hoarsely. 'He did a job for me, but went off without getting paid. I don't take charity.'

'Christopher don't give charity, not if I know him,' Matilda returned flatly. 'What he might want to give you, as you're his mother, is a bit of his time and a bit of his help.'

The five-pound note, in Pam's outstretched fingers, wavered then got dropped to her side. 'I want him to have it. He did a good job. But I don't know where he lives to send it.'

'He lives at home with his dad still.'

'Well, in that case . . .'

'In that case, you'd sooner set off back home with your fiver than come face to face with Stevie.'

'I'd sooner you take it and give it to him,' Pam said shortly but shoved the banknote in a pocket. 'I won't be going to Stephen's place. I told you, I haven't come here to cause trouble . . . especially not for Christopher.'

'Caused him enough of that when he was little, didn't you, Pam.'

'Yeah . . .' Pamela immediately set off. She stopped after a few yards and twisted about to find Matilda watching her, but not maliciously. 'Is that what you wanted to hear? I admit I did something terrible, but rest assured I've paid for it.'

Matilda took a few steps after her. 'Usually the way, ain't it, Pam? The lord pays debts without money . . .'

'Does Christopher know . . . has Stephen told him I nearly   hurt him badly?'

Matilda shook her head. 'Stevie started off telling him you was dead. I let him know I didn't think that was right, and in the end he told Chris the truth. But Stevie's said as little about you as he thought he could get away with.'

Pam grimaced a sour acceptance at hearing that. 'You don't seem surprised that I've seen Christopher.'

'I ain't. I knew he'd find you.' Matilda walked back to the pub and pushed the door handle. 'Come on, inside . . . you've come all this way from Bexleyheath to give

211

the boy his fiver, least I can do is get you a drink to warm you on yer way home. Bleedin' freezing again today, ain't it.' When Pam hesitated, Matilda added, 'Lot of water gawn under the bridge, Pam. You needn't think I'm gonna get at you fer what went on.' With a jerk of her head she invited Pam to precede her into the Duke pub.

Matilda gestured for Pam to put away her purse and indicated a little table cosily tucked into a corner. 'Park yerself over there outta the draught and I'll get the drinks. Still a gin 'n' orange fer you is it, Pam?'

'I'll have a small sherry if that's alright,' Pam answered with a twitch of the lips. 'I want to get back to Bexleyheath in one piece.'

'Small sherry it is, and I think I might have one of them 'n' all fer a change,' Matilda said.

It was a popular pub but today there were very few people who'd ventured out in the bitter cold to enjoy a dinnertime snifter. Most of the drinkers were regulars, like Matilda, and greeted her by name as she ambled by on her way to the bar. As she waited for the landlord to fetch the drinks Matilda turned to look at Pam, gazing into space. Her face was careworn and Matilda knew without a shadow of a doubt that life hadn't been kind to her.

''S'pect you got a right surprise on seeing Christopher, didn't you?' Matilda put the drinks down and eased herself into a chair with a contented sigh. 'Nice to get off me feet,' she murmured, giving Pam a moment to consider her reply.

'Knocked me for six when he introduced himself,' Pam admitted quietly and took a sip of sherry. 'Then when I'd calmed down I wished I'd acted differently. But it was too late, he'd driven off.'

'But he must've been back to fix your gate.'

'Came over and did the job when I was out,' Pam said. 'Kind of him to do it, all things considered . . .'

'He is kind,' Matilda said. 'He's grown into a fine young man.'

Pam nodded and turned her head to shield the sudden glisten in her eyes.

After a short silence Matilda asked, 'Did you get married again, Pam?' She had noticed the younger woman absently twisting a gold band on her finger.

'Yeah . . . married Stan in 1939, not long before the war started. He was a good man. Joined up straight away . . . got injured badly.' Pam's brief account of her second marriage tailed off and she blinked. 'Didn't have much luck with husbands one way or another.' She picked up her sherry and took a swallow.

'Survive his injuries?' Matilda enquired, although she'd guessed that he hadn't.

Pam shook her head. 'Buried him in 1944. He was in a wheelchair for a while . . . we didn't have any kids . . .' Her voice faded. 'How about you, Matilda?' she asked. 'I know you lost Jack in the Great War.'

'Yeah . . . lost my Jack, God rest him,' Matilda said gruffly. 'Lost Reg too in 1943. You wouldn't have known him but I was with Reg Donovan for over fifteen years although we never made it official.'

'Is Christopher married? Does he have any children?' Pam suddenly blurted out the thought that had been rotating in her mind for many weeks. The idea of being a granny, even from afar, had coated her insides with warm pleasure.

213

Matilda smiled. 'Not got a wife or kids yet, but he's got a lovely girlfriend called Grace and I reckon it's getting serious.'

'Good,' Pam murmured, smiling at her sherry. She swallowed the small amount left in her glass and drew a five-pound note from her pocket. 'Would you pass this on to him, please?'

''Course . . . if you don't want to give it to him yerself.'

Matilda could tell that Pam was angling to leave, but she had a few more questions she'd like answers to before she let her escape. 'Did you stick around in London after you and Stevie split up?'

Pam glanced up to find Matilda's gimlet eyes on her. 'Stayed with my parents for a while. They moved off to Cambridge and I went as well for a year and helped out in their draper's shop. But it didn't work out so as soon as I could I got myself a job and moved back to London. I worked in a hotel on the Strand as a chambermaid. Pay wasn't up to much but I got board and lodgings.'

'How's yer mum and dad keeping?'

'Dad died a couple of years ago. Mum's got a bungalow in Cambridge. Don't see her very often.'

'They must've been pleased to see you settle down for a second time.'

'Nothing I did pleased them after what happened . . .' Pam pursed her thin lips. 'Another sherry?' she asked quickly, standing up.

'Don't mind if I do,' Matilda answered, upending her glass.

Pam took the empty schooners and went to the bar.

'Not having one yerself?' Matilda asked when Pam returned and put down just one small sherry.

214

'Got quite a journey to make, better get going.' Pam buttoned her coat. 'Gets dark so early this time of year.'

'Yeah,' Matilda said. 'Well, you take care of yerself, won't you.'

Pamela looked at the five-pound note. She put a couple of fingers on it and pushed it across the table close to Matilda's glass. 'I'd be obliged if you'd pass that on.'

'You can give it to Chris yerself, you know. He's just down Whadcoat Street, where I live, doing the demolition on the houses up one end.'

Pam's startled eyes darted to Matilda. A moment later she gave a quick shake of the head. 'I'd be obliged if you'd pass it on,' she repeated before turning to head out of the pub.

Pamela stopped at the top of Whadcoat Street and gazed into the distance. No men were visible now, just parked vans. She realised her son must have gone inside one of the properties to work.

Much as she longed to see Christopher, and talk to him, she couldn't do that. It wasn't just that her unexpected appearance was sure to embarrass him in front of his colleagues: she felt completely drained following her talk with Matilda. Yet Matilda had been true to her word and had avoided bringing up the reason for the bitter split between her and Stephen all those years ago. Pam knew she'd need to replenish her courage before directly approaching her son.

She stood a while longer, hunched into her coat, hoping perhaps he might come out and go to his van, just so she'd get a glimpse of him before she set off home. Somebody did emerge from a house but she knew it wasn't Christopher. The fellow was too short and too plump – nothing like her tall, handsome son. Pamela glanced back the way she'd just come; she knew if she loitered too long she might find Matilda bearing down on her on her way home from the Duke and she'd said all she wanted to say today to Christopher's great-aunt. With a final yearning stare, she turned to walk briskly on towards her transport home.

'Cold enough for you, Mrs K?'

'Taters, ain't it, Ted. Chris in there, is he?' Matilda shuffled on the pavement to keep warm.

'Upstairs, he is. Want him?'

'Tell him to come along 'n' see me when he's got a mo, will you?'

Ted nodded and ambled back inside carrying a shovel on his shoulder.

'Yer aunt's lookin' for you.'

Chris wiped dust from his eyes to blink at Ted.

'She said can you go 'n' see her.'

'Have to be when I finish later. Ain't urgent, is it?'

'Didn't seem like it,' Ted said.

Chris remembered he'd meant to call in and see his aunt when he was halfway home to Crouch End. He'd worked late, as he'd promised his uncle he would, until the generator had packed up and the light had gone. It was seven-thirty when he turned around and returned to Whadcoat Street to bang on his aunt's door.

The sash above his head was shoved up. 'Took yer time, didn't you? Thought you'd gawn off home and forgotten about me.' The sash banged home again.

'Sorry it's late,' Chris said with a smile. 'Trying to get things back on schedule up there.'

'Thought perhaps Ted had forgotten to give you me message.' Matilda stuck the kettle on the hob. 'Not had yer tea yet, then?' She ran a look over his mucky overalls.

Chris shook his head and sat down close to the little stove. It was surprisingly cosy in the room once the door was shut and the many scrappy draught excluders were wedged in place.

'Get stuck into them biscuits then, you must be starving.' Matilda knew she was playing for time. It was unlike her not to come straight out and say what was on her mind. But she didn't want to seem to be prying. Christopher and his mum seemed to be making headway without any help or interference from anybody else.

Chris took two digestives. 'Hope me dad's got a nice hotpot on the go . . . me belly thinks me throat's been cut.'

'Don't know how lucky you are, having a dad like that.'

'Yeah . . . I know . . .' Chris took a bite out of a digestive.

'Saw yer mum today.'

The biscuit hovered in front of Chris's mouth then was dropped to his lap. 'Who d'you see?' he asked in a squeak that betrayed he thought his ears had deceived him.

'Pam came over and had a drink with me in the Duke.'

Chris gawped at his aunt. 'Did she come over to tell you I'm making a nuisance of meself?' he demanded hoarsely. 'Did she say to stop going there?'

'No . . . nuthin' like that. She came over to give me this and ask me to pass it on.' Matilda took the five-pound note off the mantelshelf and placed it down on the table close to Chris's mug of tea. 'Wanted you to be paid for the job you done her.' She smiled at him. 'Fixed her on a gate, didn't you?'

'Didn't want no pay for it. Wrote her a note and told her I didn't want nuthin'.'

'You don't want to be paid, and she says she don't want no charity, so you're gonna have to sort that one out between yourselves. But I reckon that's not the only reason Pam came over to see me. She wanted to find out a little bit about you. Just like you've been wanting to find out a little bit about her.'

Chris lifted his eyes to his aunt, a spark of optimism in their depths. 'She wasn't angry? She didn't tell you to tell me to stay away from her?'

'No, she didn't.'

Chris took the banknote. 'I'll buy her some flowers with it.' He glanced bashfully at his aunt.

'She's had a rough time of it, you know, Chris. Lost her second husband not long after they was married.'

'Yeah . . . I know . . .'

'Who told you? Pam said you've not spoken more'n a couple of words 'cos the shock of seeing you was too much for her at first.'

'One of her neighbours came up and started talking to me when I was working on her gate. I didn't ask no questions, the old girl just told me.'

'Does Stevie know you've been over there?'

Chris shook his head. 'Nobody knew about me going over, only Grace.'

Matilda sipped her tea. 'You'll have to tell him, Chris. I know you probably don't want to upset the apple cart now things are settling down, but it's only fair you tell your dad that you've met your mum.'

'Yeah, I know.'

218

'Him and Pearl are getting stuck into their new business so now might be the right time, while he's occupied elsewhere.'

'Don't know how to go about it.'

'Come straight out and tell him, son. Honesty's the best policy, so they say.'

Chris dwelled on his aunt's advice as he slowly drove home, smiling, enveloped in a sense of thrilling anticipation, the like of which he'd not experienced since he was a boy waiting for Christmas.

He wasn't expecting a wonderful relationship to spring up between himself and his mother; a comfortable atmosphere between them would suffice for now. And it would content him to have a little bit of knowledge about his other relatives, especially his grandparents.

The next time Chris arrived in Bexleyheath he hoped his mum *would* be at home. He took a deep breath, rat-tatted politely, then waited.

He loosened his collar from his bobbing throat when he heard footsteps approaching. Quickly he shoved a hand across his hair to neaten it.

'Got you these to say thanks for the money,' he burst out. 'But I didn't want no pay so I hope you'll take them and not think I'm bothering you.' He thrust the huge bouquet towards Pamela. It had been the best bunch of flowers he could find in Bexleyheath High Street.

'You should have kept the cash, not spent it on me; you paid out for the gate after all,' Pam blurted after a shocked silence in which she'd blanched then flushed in mounting pleasure.

The scent of oriental lilies wafted on the air; her son

had bought hothouse blooms that must have cost most of the five pounds she'd left for him with Matilda. Nobody had ever bought her such beautiful flowers. Neither of her husbands had been romantic or demonstrative men; but then she'd not been married long to either of them . . . certainly not to Christopher's father.

She opened the door to its full extent so she could take hold of the arrangement without squashing it.

'Will you come in for a cup of tea, Christopher?' Her eyes rose to meet his.

'No . . . not today . . . perhaps another time.' Chris felt pleased that she'd used his name. 'I'm in trouble with me boss for missing work recently and don't want to lose me job. So better get going. Just wanted to say thanks for the money, but I didn't want nothing. Just wanted to do you a good turn.'

'Well, you must get off then, of course,' Pam said with maternal concern, almost shooing him away. 'Don't get the sack because of me. Thank you very much for these.' Pamela's smile was strengthening as she became more relaxed. 'They're a beautiful selection . . .'

Chris took a step away, chest expanding in satisfaction. He wanted to stop and talk to her, but had decided on the way over to take things slowly. It wasn't just the valid excuse of not getting into trouble with Rob over missing shifts. He knew it would be best not to overwhelm his mother with his presence after they'd spent such a long time apart. 'I'll come back another time . . . if that's alright . . . ?'

Pam nodded and dragged her eyes from her son as she withdrew into her hallway. 'Off you go then . . .' she said softly, a moment before closing the door.

CHAPTER TWENTY

'You be careful if you're going out there. You can't see a hand in front of yer face.'

'Didn't need this holding the job up . . .' Chris had just opened the front door to peer along the garden path, while covering his nose and mouth with his fingers to prevent the freezing air abrading his throat and lungs. He squinted but couldn't make out the shape of his van parked at the kerb, so solid was the sulphurous atmosphere. On the holly bush close to the house droplets of icy water sparkled incongruously like pretty crystals.

'Never mind the job, son,' Stevie said, peering over his shoulder. 'Ain't worth risking travelling on the roads even short distances in this sort of pea-souper.' Stevie couldn't remember the last time he'd seen such dense, choking fog. 'I'm hoping Pearl's got the sense to stop home today. Bloomin' nuisance it is, just as we get to December and put our special teas on the menu. But then again nobody's gonna be out and about in this so no customers as such . . .' Stevie stood looking morose, mentally calculating his losses.

'Better ho[...]
tomorrow.' Chr[...] know to hold fire till it clears
damp that in ju[...] hut the door against the freezing
into his bones. [...] minutes had seemed to seep

'Better hope too Gr[...] ws you'll see her later in
the week,' Stevie said. 'D[...] nt to be doing that sort
of journey at night time, d[...] u.'

'It might clear by this even[...] ow, Tottenham's
not that far,' Chris said with a smile [f]or his father's moth-
erly clucking.

'If Shirley's got any sense she won't let her daughter
out of the house till it lifts. Give you bronchitis easy as
anything, you stay out too long breathing in that muck.'

Chris knew his father's advice was sound, it was the
worst fog he'd ever seen and he did't relish going to
the end of the road again for a loaf of bread, let alone
setting out for work. He'd been to the local shop early
that morning for milk and tea and even with a scarf
wound about his lower face as protection he'd felt his
chest aching as his lungs made an effort to pump air.
When he'd got back he'd been amused and astonished
in equal part to discover his skin, above the scarf, had
been flecked with black soot.

The following day Chris woke to see the same yellow
haze beyond the windows of his bedroom. But he was
determined not to lose another day's work, and had
managed to get messages to the others that he expected
them to turn up no matter what this morning brought
in the way of weather. So he set off early, at a crawl,
towards Whadcoat Street, glad that a bus was immediately in front of him for most of the way so he could
follow its taillights into Seven Sisters Road.

It took him close to an hour to do a journey that usually lasted a matter of minutes. When he got to the site, Ted and Billy were already there. It was their custom to travel to work together in Billy's old jalopy as they lived close to one another. The car was parked at the kerb and there were four others parked behind in a street that was usually deserted.

'What's going on?' Chris gestured at the strange vehicles.

Ted rubbed his gloved palms together and hunched his shoulders to his ears. He came close to Chris to squint at his face through the filthy mist. 'Bleedin' lark this is!' He appeared torn between amusement and amazement. 'You'll never guess . . .' He nodded in the direction Chris had moments ago pointed. 'They've all followed us here, one behind the other, like sheep. They'd been using Billy's lights to guide 'em. Now none of 'em knows where they are and Billy's been trying to tell 'em how to get back to Holloway Road where we must've got the convoy going.'

'Got a torch?' Billy had materialised beside them. 'Bleedin' battery's gone in mine. I'll have to lead 'em down to the bottom of the road. The two in the middle have already had a prang.'

Chris went to the van and pulled out a heavy rubber torch and immediately switched it on.

'You two get started inside . . .' Chris instructed. 'I'll walk in front of them and get them down to Seven Sisters, after that they're on their own.'

'Got some juice fer the generator? We ain't gonna get much done in there today without a bit of light.'

Chris swore beneath his breath. He'd completely forgotten that the generator was out of fuel, and the can on the van was empty. He had meant to fill it yesterday but had stayed inside all day rather than venture out in the fetid air. He knew by the time he got to a filling station, and got back here, it would be dinnertime. In a way he was wishing he'd not bothered setting out this morning at all. Dejectedly, he realised that nothing much was going to get done.

'Is Vic turning up?' Billy asked.

'Deirdre probably won't let him out in this, in case he accidentally on purpose gets lost and she don't see him fer a month,' Ted quipped.

As though to prove him wrong Vic's stooped figure loomed into view.

'Bus driver took a wrong turning. Stupid sod was following a milk float 'n' we ended up outside the dairy.'

'Just get done what you can till I get back,' Chris said and walked tentatively, hands outstretched to detect obstacles, towards the first vehicle parked behind Billy's car. He swung the torch to and fro to ease his path but the beam seemed to bounce off a solid wall of smog.

He peered in the first car to see a man and woman with a child of about six huddled on the back seat, wearing school uniform.

'We were taking her to school,' the woman said in agitation. 'Now all we want to do is get home again.'

Chris could tell from her nice accent that they were well out of their area. 'Where you from?'

'Hampstead,' the fellow announced. 'You should have let her have a day off,' he said to his wife. 'And I should have just gone into work on time, as usual, on the train,' he added cuttingly, making his wife shoot him a glare.

'Wouldn't have got far, mate,' Chris said. 'I heard on the wireless that nothing much is running. Even the underground is out.'

He turned about as a fellow from another car approached him, feeling his way along the vehicle's coachwork.

'What's down the bottom there?' The man pointed vaguely while squinting a frown at the boarded-up houses he could just make out lining the street.

'Seven Sisters Road,' Chris answered. 'I'll guide you down there with the torch and out into the road. With any luck you can find a bus to follow that might be going your way.'

By the time he got back to the house – led there by the sound of Billy coughing so violently he was in danger of bringing his guts up – Chris realised they might just as well pack up and go home. In winter, the interiors of these properties were dingy in normal conditions. Without doors, or glass in the windows, the foul atmosphere that had descended was swirling everywhere.

Once Vic had joined Ted in clearing his chest every five minutes, and Billy had tripped over the toolbox for the umpteenth time, Chris had had enough. 'That's it . . . let's go . . . wasting time staying . . .'

'Waste o' time coming in the first place,' Vic grumbled.

'Alright with getting a day's pay docked, are you?' Chris shot back.

'Ain't our fault we can't do no work.'

'Ain't the guvnor's fault neither, is it? And he's gotta take the losses.'

'Give us a lift?' Vic meekly asked Chris, after that spiky exchange. 'Be bleedin' midnight time I get home if I wait fer a bus. Be better off walking . . .'

'Yeah, make him walk, Chris, after givin' you lip,' Billy called with a wink at Ted.

'You can shut up 'n' all . . .' Vic snapped narkily. 'You ain't offered to give me a lift, have yer, selfish git.'

225

'Just get packed up, all of yers, and I'll drop Vic off home,' Chris said with a sigh.

Chris was coaxing the old girl's damp engine to start when he saw, through the van's window, a woman coming towards him, head down and hand over her nose and mouth. As she got closer and looked up he realised it was Noreen Murphy. Considering the lack of visibility Chris realised she was moving quickly. He immediately wound down the window to speak to her.

'Have you seen Kieran?' she burst out, looking anxiously up at him.

Chris could see she was very agitated and on the point of tears. 'Haven't seen him this morning. Has he gone out to work?'

'He hasn't found proper work, just a day here and there. Yesterday he bumped into one of O'Connor's men and made him tell him where that cheating divil is now. Kieran set out early to catch him in Camden Town to make him hand over his wages. He says he won't wait a day longer, and he won't come back empty handed either.'

'He hasn't paid Kieran yet?' Chris's voice rose in astonishment. The pikeys had been gone from the street a long while.

Noreen Murphy shook her head and swung a look to and fro. 'O'Connor gave him some, but not all what he was owed. We need it badly. Kieran wouldn't have gone out in this otherwise.' Her teeth started to chatter and she cleared a wet film from her cheeks with shaking fingers.

'He'll be alright, luv, don't worry,' Chris soothed. 'Just take him a while to get himself back here; everything's slowed right up and there's no transport running . . .'

'It's not him I'm worrying over.' She raised her glistening eyes to Chris's face. 'Little Rosie's chest is so bad.' She took a look back the way she'd come as though fretting about leaving the children to come out searching for her husband. 'She's struggling to get her breath, the poor little soul. She needs a doctor . . . where is Kieran? He'll have to take her to hospital, so he will. I can't keep dosing her with linctus. It's no use . . .' She twisted around, muttering about having left the children alone for too long.

With a sigh Chris turned off the engine and jumped out of the van. Noreen was again striding so swiftly towards home that she was already lost to view. As he followed her he almost collided with Vic coming towards him, pulling his balaclava down over his head.

'We off then . . . ?' Vic mumbled through the wool.

'You'll have to get Billy to drop you off,' Chris told Vic as his face appeared. 'I'm gonna offer to give Mrs Murphy a lift to the hospital. Her youngest has got a bad chest. I know she ain't exaggerating 'cos I've heard the little mite coughing all week. Now this fog's come down . . .' Chris's words tailed off as he shook his head.

He caught up with Noreen as she was running up the stairs. The sound of a child's whimpering could be heard.

'I'll give you a lift to the hospital if you want,' Chris called after her.

Noreen came down a few steps and gave him a grateful look. 'Will you? Thank you . . . I'll bring them down. Kathleen will have to come too I suppose . . . not that I want her out in this, but I can't leave her on her own . . .'

'Me aunt'll watch her while I get you to the hospital,' Chris said. He knew Matilda was a diamond at giving

227

assistance when it was needed – especially where children's welfare was concerned. And he knew she was very fond of little Kathleen.

Chris didn't bother bawling up to Matilda to announce himself today. He went straight in and up the stairs with Kathleen in his arms to bang on his aunt's door.

Matilda opened up and gawped at him. 'Where you found her?' she asked. 'Under a gooseberry bush?'

'Can you look after Kathleen for a bit for Mrs Murphy?' Chris asked without preamble but with an appreciative little chuckle for his aunt's drollery. 'The baby needs to go to hospital and Kieran ain't about to take her.'

Even if Noreen's husband had returned from tackling O'Connor over his wages, Kieran hadn't any transport, and would have needed to beg a lift rather than carry the child through the streets to the hospital.

''Course I can.' Matilda held out her arms and Chris handed the child over.

'Cor, you're getting a big girl, ain't yer, Kathleen,' Matilda said with a huff and a grimace at the cold, slight figure in her arms. 'See if we can find a few biscuits, shall we, and a nice hot cup of tea to warm you up.'

Kathleen nodded and, as Matilda put her to the floor, she scampered to where she knew the biscuit box was kept on a shelf and gazed at it expectantly.

'How's little Rosie, did you say?' Matilda whispered when sure Kathleen was out of earshot. The tot might only just have turned four years old but she was bright as a button and Matilda didn't want to make her fret over her baby sister. 'I know the poor little mite's chest's been rattling for weeks. Thought it might be Rosie's teeth worrying her 'cos I know Noreen said she teeths with bronchitis.' Her nephew's bleak expression made Matilda give a heavy sigh.

'She's coughing all the time and is as white as a ghost,' Chris said. 'Can see why Noreen's anxious to get her to the hospital as soon as she can.'

'You'd best get off then.' Matilda shooed him on his way.

'Kieran's got a nice welcome home, ain't he.' Chris shook his head. 'I hope the poor sod has at least managed to get his wages out of that thieving git, O'Connor.'

'I'll keep an eye out for him and give him a shout out me window if I manage to spot him through the fog.'

'Right; won't be too long, I hope,' Chris said, moving towards the door. 'But can't see a hand in front of your face out there. D'you want anything brought in today, Auntie? Bread? Milk? Save you going out later.'

'Could do with a loaf and a bottle of milk, Chris.' Matilda spoke while getting the lid off the biscuit box. 'You get going and make sure you drive carefully. Kathleen's gonna be fine here with me so make sure you tell Noreen that 'cos it sounds as though she's got more'n enough on her plate to worry about.'

Chris reckoned Noreen *did* have enough to worry about too. As the van crept along slowly through the fog he could hear Rosie's laboured breathing interspersed with pathetic little mewing sounds. It seemed the baby was too weak even to cry properly and Chris felt anxious and frustrated as the bus in front braked, forcing him again to a stop. He turned his head and squinted through the misty half-light at Noreen. Her face was dipped close to the precious bundle in her arms and Chris glimpsed the tears dripping from the end of her nose as she wept silently. Cursing beneath his breath at their snail-like progress, he took a chance and pulled out to overtake the bus in front. The road ahead seemed empty of vehicles so he put his foot down, praying for a clear run the remainder of the way to the hospital.

CHAPTER TWENTY-ONE

''Ere, Vic, I ain't sure about this . . .' The woman's voice sounded whiny. 'I think I wanna go home.'

'Just keep hold of me hand.' Vic Wilson was picking his way through debris, dragging her with him. His foot knocked against a chunk of rubble and he sent it skittering sideways with his boot and started up the stairs. On reaching the landing he turned right and fumbled in his pocket for candles and matches. He got the light going and led the way to a pile of dustsheets beneath which were stashed a couple of old blankets. He dripped wax onto boards then stuck the burning candle on the floor. Its flame elongated, throwing leaping shadows on the walls of the derelict property.

'It's too cold 'n' creepy, Vic, I wanna go home.' The woman started retreating towards the door.

Vic leapt up and grabbed her hand. 'You was alright last week, Sandra. Just 'cos there's a bit of fog about don't mean you need to get all frightened. Ain't Halloween is it, you silly mare? Come 'n' see what I got under the floorboards.' He tugged her back with him to the dustsheets and prised up a loose board to reveal a bottle of gin and a few brown ales. With a flourish he produced a couple of dusty tumblers from the same place.

'Don't suppose you've brought any orange to go with that gin.' It was a peevish complaint but Sandra was already cleaning out the glass with the sleeve of her coat.

'Do us a favour . . .' Vic muttered, spearing her a sour look. He lunged for her, pulling her down beside him on the makeshift bed. 'What more could any gel want, eh? Candlelight . . . nice drink . . . even got you some chocolate . . .' He drew from his pocket a bar of Dairy Milk and broke it in half.

She snuggled up to him, unwrapping her share of the chocolate to take a bite. 'Pour us a gin then, Vic.'

He half-filled her glass then got the top off his brown ale and took a swig. 'Bottoms up.'

'What you said to Deirdre?' Sandra wound a dark curl about a finger while sliding a sly look at him.

'None o' yer business, I've told you that before.' Vic took another gulp of beer and put down the bottle.

'Your wife ain't gonna believe you've gone out with mates on a night like this.'

Vic took Sandra's glass of gin and put it down on the boards then rolled on top of her buxom body. 'Never mind about her . . .' he growled, sinking his hot mouth against her throat and drawing deeply. 'Thinkin' about you now, ain't I, and it's about time we got you out o' them clothes . . .'

'It's bleedin' freezin',' Sandra protested, trying to hang onto her coat as he shoved it roughly off her shoulders.

'I'll soon warm you up gel, don't you worry about that.'

*   *   *

'What was that?' Sandra struggled to sit up, snatching at her coat to cover her plump bare breasts.

Vic had heard the noise too. He scrambled onto his knees and went on all fours towards the door. Through the cloudy darkness he could just make out a pinprick of light moving down below. He sped back to retrieve his trousers and yank them up, thinking all the while he was glad he'd had the foresight to bring a weapon of some sorts with him, just in case they were disturbed.

'Who's that?' he roared out. 'Show yer fucking self before I come down and put a crowbar over yer crust.'

Sandra was soon at his side, pulling on his arm, terrified. 'Who is it, Vic? Has some dirty old sod been spying on us at it?'

'Wouldn't have seen much, would he, in this?' Vic snarled, shaking her off. He crept out onto the landing, feeling his way, and peered over the banister into the opaque blackness. He heard a few whispered words then and the accents were unmistakable. 'If that's you, O'Connor, I'm on me way down to break yer fuckin' neck.' In fact Vic knew he was going to do nothing of the sort. He was shaking like a leaf. He didn't mind a tear-up with the pikeys when he was mob-handed, but he didn't fancy taking them on alone, especially with Sandra cramping his style.

But it seemed he wasn't going to need to worry about defending them. He heard a few more guttural mutterings, and somebody stumbling and cursing, before an engine roared. He fumbled back past Sandra to peer out of the front window at the street. It was impossible to see any more than a shifting shadow as the vehicle pulled away but he'd recognised the sound of Declan's cranky old motor.

The pikies had been back under cover of the fog, no doubt to see what they could pinch. Vic knew that thankfully nothing was left behind in the way of tools in the evening. Everything got cleared out and taken away on the vans. He knew there'd be no reason to mention this little episode to anybody. No harm was done. He let out a sigh of sheer relief and turned to give Sandra a winning smile. Overlooking the fact that a mop of brown curls was sticking to the tears streaming down her face, and she was vibrating from head to toe in shock, he said jauntily, 'Scared 'em away, see, now . . . where was we?'

'Thank Christ fer that.' Stevie had opened the door to a bright clear day. 'Come 'n' take a look, Chris.' He turned, smiling happily, to see his son coming along the passage eating a piece of toast.

'About bleedin' time too,' Chris said with a relieved sigh. He'd been bored stiff cooped up at home while waiting for the dreadful smog that had blighted the capital for four days to disperse. During that time London had come to a virtual standstill due to the hazardous atmosphere.

When he got to Whadcoat Street the first person he saw was Kieran Murphy. Chris realised the man had been loitering by the railings, waiting for him to turn up, so he could talk to him.

'Need to thank you very much for what you did for us the other day.' Kieran bashfully rubbed a hand across the back of his neck. 'Already said thank you to your aunt Matilda for looking after Kathleen while you took Rosie to the hospital. Mrs Keiver's a fine woman.'

'Yeah, she is,' Chris said. 'And I was pleased to help get the little 'un to a doctor. How is Rosie?'

'She's fine and back home, thank you for asking.'

Chris noticed Kieran's eyes filling up and he gave his arm a small comforting shake. 'I know the poor little mite's had a cough for a while, so it's good to know she's better.'

'They kept her in the hospital overnight and dosed her with strong medicine,' Kieran gruffly explained. 'Noreen has the bottle and must give Rosie some every day this week. A lot of people had the same complaint because of the terrible smog. A very busy place, it was . . .' He paused, looking bashful. 'We should have taken Rosie to a doctor sooner but we were worried they'd find out we lived here . . .' Kieran glanced at the slum behind him.

'Right . . . got you . . .' Chris said, immediately understanding the couple's fears. He'd heard his aunt recounting tales of Bunk children being forcibly removed from their parents when the authorities deemed them in danger of neglect.

'I thank the lord the hospital was as busy as it was, for few questions were asked of us. I thank the lord we have the National Health Service too,' Kieran admitted with a grimace.

'Don't know how we managed before without it,' Chris agreed. 'You still lookin' fer work?' he asked abruptly in an attempt to buck Kieran up.

Kieran nodded and shuffled his feet. 'Noreen told you that I'd gone after O'Connor for my pay on that day.'

'Did you get your money?'

Kieran shook his head. He angled his face to show Chris the bruise on a profile he'd been keeping averted. 'Got that instead. He's an evil man.'

'He's that alright. No work in Ireland for you?'

'I had work but . . .' Kieran sighed. 'There was a lot of bitterness between my kin and Noreen's. We come from different sides of the troubles and we didn't want our children in the middle of a feud. Better that Kathleen and Rosie have just the two of us than know a lot of uncles and cousins who hate one another.'

'Right . . . I'm with you . . .' Chris said sympathetically. 'Well, I can let you have a day a week for about a month, that's all though. Guvnor won't wear more'n that 'cos there's nothing in the price, y'see. But you might be able to pick up a bit elsewhere and make yer money up, and it'll get you past Christmas.'

Kieran's drawn expression transformed into a smile. 'That's grand, thank you. When can I start?'

'No time like the present,' Chris answered.

Kieran pumped one of Chris's hands then turned to rush back towards his house to tell Noreen the good news.

Chris grimaced ruefully to himself. He knew his uncle wouldn't pay out another penny on the job – he was going to have to dock his own pay to give Kieran his wages. Yet he didn't regret doing it, although he knew he'd keep his generosity to himself. The lads wouldn't understand. But Grace would; she'd know why he'd had to help out a man who wanted desperately to provide for his family when Christmas was coming for two little girls . . .

'You've got a damned cheek, d'you know that?'

'Just wanted to speak to you, that's all.'

Grace shot a look at her friend Wendy. But Wendy shrugged and rolled her eyes, letting Grace know she was equally astonished at this unexpected meeting with Hugh Wilkins. She had seen Grace's ex-fiancé some months ago when out shopping, but she'd not bumped into him since.

Grace had just been returning from her dinner break with her friend when Hugh had called to her before she'd entered their office building. He'd obviously been loitering in the vicinity with the intention of ambushing her.

'I'll just go on up, shall I?' Wendy was letting her friend know she'd stick around if Grace wanted her to.

'It's alright,' Grace sighed and tipped her head towards the door of the building, indicating Wendy should get back to work on time.

'I'll cover for you if you're a bit late back,' Wendy called from halfway up the steps towards the entrance.

'I'll be right behind you, don't worry,' Grace said pithily, whipping around to confront Hugh.

'Don't go mad, Grace,' he said quietly, putting out his hands in supplication. 'I just wanted to speak to you.'

'Don't go mad? Just wanted to speak to me?' she hissed. 'Why shouldn't I go mad? And why d'you want to speak to me? What could we possibly have to say to one another now?'

'Well, I could say sorry . . .'

'Sorry! It's a bit bloody late for that isn't it!'

'I want to make it up to you . . .' he continued, shoving a hand through his light brown hair.

Enlightenment suddenly transformed Grace's expression of fury and incomprehension into one of cynicism. 'You've broken up with her already, haven't you? Chucked you out, did she, when she discovered you were only interested in her money?'

Grace tried to whip past him and enter the building but he gripped her arm.

'I knew getting married was a mistake from the start, but she kept on about it. I should never have left you, I know that now . . .'

Grace shook off his fingers. 'Go and whine to somebody else, Hugh. I'm really not interested.'

'I know you lost a lot of money when everything was cancelled.'

Grace spun about on a step. 'Going to offer to reimburse me, are you?' she asked sarcastically.

'If you want, I'll pay you back.' He gave her a crooked smile. 'We could have a drink after work. I'm still working at Carruther's in Moorgate. We could meet up and discuss it, if you like.'

'Get stuffed.' Grace enunciated the phrase quietly and hurried on up the steps to the entrance.

By the time she'd settled at her desk and loaded her typewriter with several sheets of paper, interleaved with carbon for the flimsy copies, she'd calmed down a bit. She could see Wendy peering sideways at her from her desk and she simply shook her head, implying there was nothing urgent or interesting to report.

But hard as Grace tried, she couldn't put from her mind that it had taken her many years to amass the savings that Hugh Wilkins had wasted for her overnight when he'd jilted her. A tiny part of her believed he *owed* her that money, and if there was a way she could get it back without having to pander to the swine, she knew she'd be very keen to hear about it.

'If that was me I'd meet the rat like a shot and get every penny I could out of him. He owes you it.'

238

'He's probably lying about reimbursing me just as he lied about everything else.'

Grace and Wendy were in the ladies' washroom getting ready to leave work. Wendy had kept on about what had gone on with Hugh until Grace had told her. She'd also let her know that it seemed Hugh's marriage was in trouble already and he was sniffing around her again.

'You going to tell Chris that Hugh lay in wait for you today?'

Grace shook her head. 'He's got enough on his plate with his work and his moth . . .' She bit back what she'd been about to say. She never discussed with anybody that Chris was hoping to be reconciled with his mum. Grace had been overjoyed on hearing the news that Pamela had accepted Chris's bouquet of flowers and had let him know she didn't object to seeing him again.

Knowing Chris the way she did, he'd probably offer to meet Hugh for her, just so he could ram the two-timing swine's money back down his throat.

'What you looking so broody about?'

'Sorry . . .' Grace smiled. 'Didn't know I was.'

'Want another drink?'

Grace shook her head. 'How's your dad's fancy teas going?' she asked conversationally, determinedly putting Hugh Wilkins from her mind.

Chris put down his tankard and smiled. 'Sold out of scones the other day. He reckons those are firm favourites, so are home-baked biscuits, and if he could get a bit more sugar he could double his takings.'

'Has he done any dinners?'

'A few pies and Spam fritters with mash and cabbage.

But he says people are careful with their cash and sticking to afternoon teas is best 'cos there's more profit.'

'You're making me feel hungry . . .'

'Fancy a bite to eat?'

Grace shook her head. 'Best be getting back; work tomorrow.' She emptied her glass and put it down, frowning, wondering if Hugh would again materialise outside her office in the morning. He'd been there yesterday when she'd arrived in Lombard Street and she was sure she'd seen him hovering on the opposite pavement when she and Wendy went for their dinner breaks, despite the fact she'd told him earlier to clear off and leave her alone.

'What's up?' Chris asked quietly as he helped her out of the van outside her house.

'Nothing . . .' Grace smiled up at him, giving him a final kiss on the lips.

'You might as well tell me; you will in the end, you know that,' Chris persuaded huskily.

Grace sighed. 'It's just that . . . Hugh's been making a nuisance of himself, but I'm not bothered,' she quickly added, having sensed a sudden tension in the muscled arms enclosing her. 'I can handle the creep.'

'Yeah . . . but I reckon I can probably handle him better. Where does he live?'

'That's why I haven't told you,' Grace said immediately. 'It's not a big deal . . .'

'It is to me.'

'Well, it doesn't have to be, you know. I don't want you causing any trouble.'

'Sounds like he's causing trouble, not me. What's he want? I thought you said he was married now.'

'He is, but it looks like things are going sour there,

and serves him right. I expect his wife's found out he's a money-grabbing bastard.'

Chris looked thoughtful as he stepped away from her to lean back against the van. 'Why haven't you told me before?'

'I said. I don't want any trouble.'

'Has he said he wants to get back with you?'

'Not in so many words.'

'What words has he used?'

'He said sorry . . . and that he knows I lost a lot of money when all the wedding preparations were cancelled. I did too. I lost nearly every penny of my savings.' Grace frowned and stuffed her hands in her pockets. She knew she'd sounded too grasping. 'Forget about him. I asked Mum about Christmas Day.' She quickly changed subject.

'What did she say?'

'Well, she had a moan as she always does, but in the end she said she'd like to come over to your uncle and aunt's. I knew she'd agree, even if it is just to be nosy and have a look about their big house.' Grace bit her lip. 'The thing is . . . I don't like to think of my nan being on her own. She usually comes to us for her Christmas dinner, you see.'

''Course she can come as well.' Chris said.

'Hadn't you better ask your aunt and uncle first, if it's all right.' Grace sounded doubtful.

'I'll ask them, but I know what Faye and Rob'll say . . . the more the merrier.'

CHAPTER TWENTY-TWO

'I didn't think we'd all fit in to the dining room . . .'

Faye, looking slightly hot and harassed, sat down at the table, the last to do so, and glanced about with a satisfied smile at the festive scene. The snowy-white linen cloths were decorated with flaming tapers and sprigs of holly and ivy. Just in front of her husband, seated at one end, was an enormous turkey that had one side carved down close to the bone. The other succulent breast was still protected by crisp bronze skin. Bowls filled with roasted vegetables, stuffing and other yuletide trimmings were lined along the centre of the table and the air was heavy with savoury scent.

'I've had more people than this in my couple of rooms back in The Bunk,' Matilda proudly proclaimed, straightening her paper hat before digging in to her Christmas dinner once more.

'We did too, back in the old day, didn't we, Mum.' Alice Chaplin gave her mother a grin as she also cut into her turkey and stuffing. 'Remember the sing-songs we used to have on a Saturday night round the piano?'

'Remember it like it were yesterday,' Matilda replied gruffly. 'Yer dad bashing away on the old joeyanna and all the neighbours singing and jigging about in a space where you wouldn't think you could swing a cat.'

'And old Twitch, the copper, yelling up to us to keep the noise down, or he'd come and sort us out,' Sophy Lovat, Matilda's eldest daughter, chipped in. She glanced at her husband, Danny. In the olden days the Lovats had lived next door to the Keivers in Campbell Road and they'd been childhood sweethearts. 'Remember it, Dan?'

Danny grinned. 'Couldn't ever forget it. I'd've liked to see that old sod Twitch try to put a stop to those Saturday shindigs. Geoff, God rest him, used to enjoy those nights.' His voice sounded full of gravel as he remembered his younger brother, lost to the Great War.

'On that note, I reckon it's time for a toast,' Rob said. He picked up his wine, waiting for the assembled company to join him in raising their glasses before solemnly announcing, 'Absent friends . . .'

'Absent friends . . .' rippled as a single murmur through the room.

'Has everybody got enough turkey?' Ever the vigilant hostess, Faye rose slightly in her chair to take a look around at the numerous plates, to spot where a refill might be needed. 'You look as though you're ready for seconds, Chris. Rob, carve a few more slices in case anybody wants some more.'

Robert and Faye Wild's usually spacious and elegant dining room was crammed with furniture and people. The main long table had several others coming off it at right angles to accommodate the crowd of kith and kin who had gathered for a big Christmas get-together in Islington.

Matilda and her four daughters were present with their husbands, although her grandchildren and great-grandchildren were spending most of their Christmas Day in their own homes. Many of the extended family would turn up in the evening for the boozy party that went on into the small hours of Boxing Day.

Daisy Wild was sitting next to her brother Adam and it was the first time Grace had met him. When they'd been introduced earlier she'd thought him a handsome, amiable young man with a quiet, slightly reserved manner, unlike his father's boisterous side of the family, but the spitting image of his mum.

Grace had been made to feel very welcome by everybody, as had her mother and grandmother. Nan Jackson got on with most people and had settled comfortably into her plush surroundings. Grace knew her mother was a bit overwhelmed by evidence of the Wilds' luxurious lifestyle, but was trying hard not to show it. When they got home later, no doubt Shirley would attempt to nitpick over their faultless hospitality despite the fact that Grace had observed her fluttering her eyelashes at Rob on a couple of occasions. The *pash* her mother had admitted having for him as a young woman had obviously not completely withered away. He was a charming host to everybody but quite clearly besotted with his wife.

'Pull a cracker?' Chris leaned across the table and held out a shiny red cracker towards Grace.

'Reckon you've already pulled one there, son,' Stevie said with a wink at Grace that made her blush. Stevie and Pearl were seated next to one another, steadily sipping festive spirit, and already quite merry.

'Stop embarrassing the girl, Stevie,' Lucy rebuked her cousin.

244

Lucy was Matilda's youngest daughter and still youthfully attractive despite having turned forty. She gamely tried to draw Shirley into the conversation.

'You live in Tottenham, don't you, Shirley? Are your family Tottenham Hotspur supporters?'

'We only support Arsenal in this house,' Stevie warned, wagging a finger.

'My Wilf used to support the Arsenal,' Shirley said, putting down her sherry. 'Me and Grace aren't really keen on football, are we, Grace?'

'You know your dad was a staunch Tottenham man, Shirley.' Nan Jackson neatly placed down her knife and fork with a pat on her full stomach. 'He had no truck with the Arsenal, I'm afraid to say . . .'

'That's fighting talk!' Stevie adopted a fierce expression for the tiny elderly lady.

'Enough about bloody football,' Beth said. She was another of Matilda's daughters and had married a man from The Bunk. She glanced at her husband. George was a staunch Gunners fan, as were most men who had grown up in Campbell Road, and all of them were still smarting at having lost the Cup Final that year.

'Talking about religion and politics used to be taboo in company; now it's football as well.' Faye shook her head in mock despair. 'Turn on the wireless, Rob, and let's listen to some carols before things get heated.'

'Queen's making her first Christmas speech,' Matilda announced. 'We can't miss listening to that.'

A general opinion undulated around the room that the new queen's first Christmas speech was undoubtedly the highlight of the day.

'And talking of the queen we've got a few plans to put in place for our big Coronation Day party next June.'

'Plenty of time for that,' Stevie said. 'Ain't got Christmas over with yet.'

'We should make it a good street party; it'll be the last.' Faye's comment started off much solemn nodding and grimacing from the assembled company. Everybody knew that The Bunk would soon be no more.

'Will you be home, son?' Rob asked Adam. 'Be good if you were about and could come to the Coronation Day do.'

'Hope I don't miss it, Dad, but too soon to tell if I'll get leave or not.'

'And you must bring Geraldine.' Faye mentioned her future daughter-in-law who today had gone home to spend Christmas with her folks in Kent.

'I'm getting together a list of addresses for you two gels.' Matilda pointed at Daisy and Grace. 'You're the clever ones in the family and can do the honours when it comes to writing to old acquaintances to let them know what's going on. I've never been no great shakes at me letters but I don't mind using one of you lot's telephones and making a call if I've got the number.'

'Saw Sarah Whitton the other day, Mum, and told her what you're planning,' Alice chipped in.

'Still with that layabout Herbert, is she?' Matilda asked. Sarah Whitton and Herbert Banks had been on and off as a couple since schooldays. They were now in their fifties and no closer to tying the knot than they had been as teenagers.

'I said she could bring him along, if she wants,' Alice replied. 'And she's asking her sisters too.'

'I reckon Jeannie Robertson's still going strong with Johnny Blake though I ain't spoke to her in a while.' Matilda mentioned a woman who had once been a

246

neighbour, and a very close friend. 'We sort of lost touch during the last war, but I've got an address in Mayfair for the two of 'em. I reckon they're still living there, if the house survived the bombing. Beautiful place that were; good as yours, Rob,' she said, glancing around at her stylish surroundings. 'Went there a few times to see Jeannie; you visited her once too, didn't you, Al?' Matilda paused to reflect on that time in her youth when her husband Jack had been fighting on the Somme.

'Me and Sarah Whitton went to visit her,' Alice replied.

'And I've roped Beattie Evans in to help with the party preparations.' Matilda's thoughts had quickly returned to her favourite subject. 'She's got a few people to contact. And of course, Margaret's gonna pitch in.' She grinned at Danny as she mentioned his mum. 'Numbers could run into the hundreds if everybody who's asked turns up.'

'I'm planning on going up The Mall on the big day and wave me flag as the queen's coach goes by,' Pearl announced. 'We'll shut up shop that day,' she told Stevie.

'Stevie ain't allowed to go.' Matilda winked at her nephew. 'He's doing all the grub for the party so will be busy all day long in the street.'

'Who's paying for all this?' Stevie suddenly enquired.

Index fingers suddenly appeared from all sides of the tables. Most were pointing at their host.

'Thanks fer that,' Rob said, exceedingly dryly.

'Shouldn't we have a whip round?' Grace had piped up with that, conscious of the injustice of expecting Chris's uncle to stump up for all of it.

''Course we'll have a whip round, love,' Rob told her gently. 'They always like to pull my leg.'

'We weren't,' was chorused back at him with much laughter.

'Right, who's for Christmas pud and mince pies?' Faye asked brightly, noticing Grace looking bashful for not understanding a longstanding family joke. Rob was wealthy and the family, without rancour, often brought it to his attention.

'Need a bit of a blow first.' Matilda leaned forward to spear a Yorkshire pudding from the bowl on the table. 'I will say, gel, you do make a decent bit of batter,' she told Faye. 'Can't let these go to waste. I reckon I'll have my plum pud by the wireless in the front room, while I'm listening to the queen. And I'd like a sixpence in my bit, please . . .'

After dinner, when everybody was crammed into the front room, seated in a semi-circle, awaiting the start of Queen Elizabeth's first Christmas speech, Chris beckoned to Grace to join him at the back of the gathering.

'Want to speak to you,' he whispered in her ear, then followed up by brushing his lips against her rosy cheek. He took her hand and they slipped from the room, along the hallway, and into a kitchen that was filled with washed and stacked crockery, baking trays, and an aroma of sage and onion stuffing.

'I'm gonna go and see me mum this afternoon and wish her a Happy Christmas.'

Grace stared at him with wide, shining eyes, a hesitant smile on her lips. 'Does your dad know?' she whispered.

Chris shook his head. 'Don't want to ruin his Christmas by saying nuthin' about it. But don't want to think of me mum all on her own for the whole day, neither.'

'She might not be,' Grace said. 'Perhaps she's had some friends over?'

'I know she might have company of some sorts, but

no family, I reckon. Anyhow I've got her a present. Ain't much; just some chocolates and perfume. But I think she'll like it.'

Grace gave him a spontaneous, rewarding hug. ''Course she'll like it,' she murmured gruffly. 'She'll be so pleased you've not forgotten her.'

'Ain't forgotten you either . . .' He looked on the point of blurting something out, but instead drew from his pockct a box. 'Go down on one knee if you want . . .' He sounded nervous but his adoring dark eyes roved her face as he asked huskily, 'Will you marry me, Grace?' He opened the little box to show her a solitaire diamond ring. 'Ain't as fancy as I'd have liked to get you, but now me wages have dropped back a bit since I took on Kieran Murphy, I thought no point waiting longer to try and save a bit more . . .'

Grace threw her arms about him and kissed him full on the lips. 'Of course, I'll marry you,' she breathed against his mouth. 'I thought you'd never ask.' She blinked, sniffed back tears, fiddled with his new tie. 'I only got you this . . .'

'It's enough,' he said, stroking a few fingers on the slubbed silk, 'cos we've got to start saving now.'

'I know,' she said softly 'And I'm glad you didn't put Kieran off before Christmas just to spend more on mc.' She took the little box to study her engagement ring. 'It's beautiful . . . just right. Hope it's a perfect fit too . . .' Gently she eased the gem from its velvet bed and, having turned it this way and that to watch its rainbow sparkle, let Christopher slip it on her finger.

'Made to measure,' he said with a pleased chuckle. His hands cupped her face. 'Will you come to see me mum with me? I'd like to introduce you as my future wife, 'cos I love you and I want her to know.'

'I love you too,' Grace returned softly. 'But how are we going to escape?' Her eyes were glittering with happiness and excitement. 'And . . . are we going to tell them all we're engaged? Don't know how my mum'll react; but I'm sure my nan will be very pleased.'

'Perhaps we should announce it tomorrow in case Shirley causes an atmosphere. I'll come over in the morning and we'll tell her then.'

'She's already tucked away a few sherries, so it could go either way,' Grace admitted. 'Never know with Mum, when she's had a few, if she'll nod off or start a war.'

'When shall we get married?' Chris asked.

'Tomorrow?' Grace returned, achingly softly.

He drew her into his arms and kissed her. 'If only we could. Soon as I've got the money together, we'll do it. Can't ask for me dad's help now he's got pressure on him with this new business. And it ain't fair to expect your mum to help either, being as she's a widow.'

'I'll save as much as I can,' Grace said. 'If I can get overtime I'll do it. Where will we live?'

'Don't mind . . . Tottenham if you want. Don't care so long as we're together.' He hugged her tightly to him, dropping a kiss on her soft fair hair.

'I've thought of an excuse to escape!' Grace exclaimed in a whisper, pushing back from him a bit. 'These new shoes are killing me. It's not a fib; Mum knows I've got blisters.' She eased off one of her new leather courts with a pained grimace. 'We can say you're taking me home to get a comfortable pair to put on. If me mum and nan don't want to stay for tea we can take them home at the same time, then go and see Pamela.' Grace not only wanted to accompany Chris to see his mother, she yearned for some private time with her fiancé so they could discuss their exciting future plans.

"Course it's an excuse,' Matilda growled at Stevie, who'd just frowningly watched his son and Grace leave the room. 'Young love, ain't it. Those two want a little bit of time on their own . . . only natural.' She turned to Shirley, seated next to her on a sumptuous velvet settee. 'Credit to you, that gel.' Following her pronouncement Matilda took a sip of Irish whiskey and smacked her lips.

Shirley graciously accepted the compliment by dipping her head.

'Glad you're stopping for a bit longer, Shirley, and yer mum 'n' all. You wouldn't want to miss the spread we'll have, come teatime,' Matilda told her, settling back comfortably. 'If you're partial to a sausage roll, or turkey sandwich, then you'll be in luck later. Afterwards, there's jellies and fruit and a sherry trifle. And when you've had yer fill of all o' that lot, I can promise you Faye bakes a lovely fruitcake . . .'

'Shhh . . .' Faye begged for hush from the assembled company as the queen's crisp, clear tones were heard. They listened in silence until the speech had ended.

'Well . . . that was nice,' Faye said to break the quiet.

'Didn't forget to mention them serving abroad, did she.' Rob nodded. 'And quite right too.'

'Gracious as you like, weren't she, bless her. And she mentioned the Coronation Day next summer, so that's made me even more determined to make it a great party.' Matilda hoisted her whiskey. 'A toast to our new queen.' Glasses were raised and Matilda's words were echoed by one and all.

Shirley took another sip of sherry. 'Having such a nice time,' she slurred. A moment later her eyelids had fallen closed and her chin was sagging towards her shoulder.

'That's it, gel, get yer head down fer a while.' Matilda gave Shirley's knee a pat. 'Serious drinkin' starts after teatime . . .'

Matilda took Shirley's half-empty sherry glass, and put it safely on a table.

CHAPTER TWENTY-THREE

'Lights are on, so someone's home.'

Grace nodded and her eyes veered from the little terraced house to collide with Chris's in the twilight. 'Do you want to go and knock on your own, or shall I come with you now?'

'Better go on me own first in case she's entertaining and gets embarrassed to see me. Don't want to upset her at all. If she seems a bit flustered I'll just give her the present and come away.' He turned in his seat and drew forth from the back of the van a neatly wrapped gift topped by a small bow. A moment later he was walking quickly away from the vehicle.

Grace watched with bated breath as he knocked then turned back to give her a nervous smile while shuffling from foot to foot. A moment later the door was opened and Chris was bathed in muted coral light. But Grace couldn't see who was standing in the hallway.

Suddenly he turned and beckoned, evidently relieved,

and with a deep breath Grace fought to slide open the van door and jump out.

'Sorry, I've nothing else to offer you, but I usually treat myself to this at Christmas as I quite like it.' Pamela gave a small smile, approaching Grace with the bottle of ginger wine.

'Oh, that's fine, thank you,' Grace said quickly. 'But I won't have more than just a little drop.' She didn't want to take too much out of what looked to be Pamela's solitary bottle of Christmas cheer.

Pam returned to her chair, her eyes darting back to her son, clinging to him, before she unconsciously brushed her fingers over the gift he'd brought her, placed on the table at her side. 'I shall open it when you're gone, if that's alright. I'm sorry, I haven't got something for you . . . I didn't think I'd see . . .'

'Don't worry, please, 'course you didn't know I'd come over today,' Chris burst out over her apology. He was seated opposite his mother in a chair close to the hearth. 'So . . . you had a Christmas drink earlier with Mrs Rathbone and her husband, that was nice.' He sounded jolly.

'They're good neighbours, but she can be a little bit . . . inquisitive.' Pam gave her son a tiny private smile, knowing he'd remember her neighbour's threat to get the police on him on the first occasion he'd come to see her. 'I only stay for an hour, but it's enough. They've got their kids and the grandchildren over today, so they've got a houseful.' She paused. 'Oh, and tomorrow they'll come in to me for a Boxing Day drink once they've seen off their family.'

Pam glanced at the bottle of beer she'd given to Chris.

She knew she'd now only a couple left to offer Mr Rathbone, and very little ginger wine left to share with Gladys, but she didn't care. She knew she'd be overjoyed if Christopher would stay long enough to drink the whole lot this evening.

Continually her eyes were drawn like magnets to her son although she tried hard not to stare in case she embarrassed him.

'Your tree looks very nice,' Grace said into the silence. She looked at the small fir adorned with baubles and tinsel. It seemed to be the only concession to Christmas. There were no other decorations up in the room and very few Christmas cards on the mantel.

'They make a bit of a mess when the needles drop, don't they?' Pam clucked her tongue.

'But I like the nice fresh scent, don't you?' Grace replied with a smile.

'Are your mum and dad in good health?' Chris asked huskily. He desperately wanted to know about his grandparents. He thought his mother looked startled by his question but eventually she answered him.

'My father is dead . . . my mother . . . I don't see her much,' Pam said and took a sip of ginger wine. She suddenly put it down. 'Would you like a bite to eat? I could do a sandwich . . . or there's some Dundee cake if you'd prefer . . .'

'No, thank you all the same, we've had a big blow-out dinner at me uncle and aunt's . . .' Chris's voice tailed off. He wished he'd not mentioned that. There was no hint of turkey and stuffing here, just the faint scent of lavender polish and the smoky aroma of burning logs coming from the fireplace. He felt a stabbing pain in his guts because his mother had probably not bothered with a Christmas dinner at all. He wished now he'd come over to see her on Christmas Eve and offered to spend the day with her. If she'd wanted his company he'd have foregone his big merry Christmas with his father's family despite the war that would have started at home when he told Stevie where he'd be going.

Grace watched Pam as she sipped her drink and flicked constant glances at Chris. The woman was trying hard to be amiable to them both but Grace could tell Pam wanted to have her son to herself for a while. And Grace thought that was right. Besides, Chris probably had personal things he'd like to ask Pamela, but he wouldn't want to make his mother feel uneasy by voicing them now, in front of his fiancée.

'May I use your bathroom?' Grace asked quietly, placing down her glass.

'Oh . . . of course. Top of the stairs, first door. Shall I show you?'

'No need. I'll find it, thank you.'

'So, when will you get married?' Pam burst out cheerfully when the door had closed behind Grace. 'Have you set a date?'

'Not sure when it'll be,' Chris admitted diffidently. 'Only got engaged today.' He grinned boyishly. 'Nobody knows . . . except you . . .'

'You've told me first? Before your father?'

Chris nodded. 'But I came here to give you your present as well.'

'Thank you.' Pam returned his smile, eyes glowing. She swallowed the lump in her throat. 'She's a lovely girl, you'll be happy . . . I know you will . . .'

'Grace is a diamond. She's encouraged me to come and find you right from the start.'

'Does . . . does your father know you're here?'

Chris shook his head and gulped at his beer.

'Does he know that you've been here at all?'

'No,' Chris admitted. 'But I told him I wanted to find you a while ago.'

'He was angry when you told him,' Pam guessed. 'I knew he would be.'

'It's up to me what I do, not him,' Chris gently replied. 'If he doesn't like it, it's too bad.'

'Don't fall out with your father because of me,' Pam said. 'I'm not worth it.'

''Course you are!' Chris jumped up and in two strides was dropping to his knees in front of his mother's chair. ''Course you're worth it! You're me mum . . .' He gazed earnestly at her lined features.

'And he's your dad, and he's brought you up his way . . .' Pam quietly championed her ex-husband without glancing away from her lap.

'Are you ashamed of me?' Chris asked hoarsely. ''Cos I'm one of the Wilds and they're a rough lot?'

'No! *Ashamed of you?*' Pam raised her glistening eyes to the ceiling. 'How could anyone be ashamed of having a son like you?' She placed a quivering hand on his dark hair and smoothed his cheek before returning it to her lap. 'Look at you! You're handsome, polite and kind . . . you're everything . . .' She knuckled her moist eyes. 'Stephen's done a fine job bringing you up, so don't you go falling out with him because of me.'

Chris got to his feet. 'Did you regret having me, is that why you went off and left me behind?'

'No . . . it's just . . .' Pam hesitated. 'I wasn't a good mother . . . I couldn't cope, so it was best your father looked after you.'

'Did you try and see me when I was little?'

Pam nodded.

'But he wouldn't let you?'

Again she nodded.

'That weren't fair.' Chris sounded angry.

'It was . . . don't blame him,' Pam interjected. 'Although I didn't think so at the time, it was fair. I deserved to be punished . . .'

'Why? What did you do?' Chris asked hoarsely.

A long silence preceded her admission.

Immediately after losing Christopher Pamela had tried to prepare for this talk a thousand times or more, so sure had she been that she could persuade Stephen she was fit to have her baby back. She'd understood she might have to account to Christopher for her cruelty at some time. But her pleas, and her optimism, had fallen on Stephen's deaf ears and so had withered away over the years, together with, so she'd believed, the necessity to explain herself. It was only recently she'd again gone over in her mind how she might mitigate once having almost killed her only child. But she wouldn't lie to him . . . it was too precious, too pure a moment to sully it with cowardly deceit.

'I gave you . . . something to quieten you because I couldn't cope. I was too selfish and stupid to try hard enough to cope. So I gave you something to quieten you . . .' she whispered and stared at the fire.

'What was it?'

'A drug . . . laudanum . . . don't hear that name often now . . . gave you too much. It was dangerous . . . far too much . . .'

Chris was frowning in silence at her strained, white profile as she watched the flames.

'You nearly poisoned me to death?'

She gave a single nod while staring at the blaze with tears trickling down her cheeks.

Chris remained still and silent for almost a minute before leaving the room. He found Grace hovering on the stairs. 'Ready?' he asked hoarsely.

'Are we saying goodbye?' she whispered and glanced at the front room.

'Nothing more to say.' He opened the front door then waited for her to precede him into the street.

CHAPTER TWENTY-FOUR

'You promised to give me back fifty pounds today.'

Grace was finding it difficult to contain her temper. She glanced around the pub interior, already regretting agreeing to meet Hugh. He'd contacted her several times about returning her some money as a gesture of good-will, even going so far as to hand a note, begging for a meeting, to the porter at her office. The old fellow had slipped it to her while she'd been pounding away on her typewriter.

Yesterday Hugh had caught her after she'd finished for the day and was on her way to the tube station. She'd been walking with Wendy and, as soon as her friend had spied his lofty, smartly suited presence heading in their direction, she'd prodded Grace to get what she could from the low-down rat.

Now Grace was wishing she'd not listened to anything but an inner voice that had been warning her Hugh Wilkins was callous and only out for himself.

From the first time he'd ambushed her outside her office she'd had an instinct that he was spinning her a line in order to get back with her now his wife had realised he was a chancer. Even knowing she'd got engaged a month ago hadn't put Hugh off his pursuit. Grace wasn't surprised that he hadn't turned a hair when she told him she was engaged. Considering he was a man who'd easily jilted her close to their wedding day and now didn't seem to value his own marriage, he was acting true to form. She felt a fool for having ever in her life got involved with such a nasty character. It was no valid excuse that she'd been young and gullible, and he'd been a plausible liar; she should have known better.

'I did try to get fifty pounds for you.' Hugh shrugged, took a swig of beer while looking around the pub's clientele. He was always keen to spot a bigwig to ingratiate himself with. And now it looked as though his main meal ticket might soon be whipped away he could do with giving his career a boost. 'Val's watching me like a hawk and I don't want to end up getting arrested.'

'What's *she* got to do with it?' Grace impatiently stood up. 'This is between you and me and nothing to do with your wife. Why would you get arrested?'

'She holds the purse strings; or in this case the key to the bureau where the cash is kept.' Hugh's mouth thinned in annoyance. 'The old cow would get the law on me too, if she caught me, but she won't, trust me.'

Grace abruptly sat down again in the chair opposite him, her complexion turning white. 'Well, you kept that quiet, didn't you!' she hissed in shock. 'You implied you were going to pay me from your salary at the end of the month because your conscience was pricking you. Now you tell me you were going to give me money stolen from your wife's bureau?' She glared at him, her expression quickly displaying her disgust. 'You're a thief as well as a liar. I feel sorry for her; I hope she does set the law on you.'

Hugh lunged for one of her arms, gripping it tightly as she would have yanked it away. He glanced furtively about to make sure nobody was watching them tussle.

'Get your hand off me, and don't you dare contact me again, do you hear?' Grace spat in an undertone. She jerked herself free with such force that she knocked her half-full glass onto the floor where it shattered.

Ignoring the stares she strode out of the pub and headed back towards her place of work.

Tears of rage and frustration were glittering in her eyes as she marched on. She'd thought that when she saw Chris later she'd have some good news for him. She'd known all along he'd be angry when he found out she'd met Hugh, but had hoped he'd understand why she'd done it when she produced fifty pounds to be put in their wedding kitty.

Christopher was still paying Kieran from his wages and doing any overtime he could get hold of to try and make up the shortfall. They were trying hard to save for a deposit on a property, but Grace felt guilty that she'd contributed very little to the pot. Once she gave her mother some housekeeping money, and laid out for her fares and dinners, there was little left from her pay to contribute towards their future. Christopher told her he didn't mind, and it was his job to provide for them both. Neither of them wanted a long engagement, yet they were both adamant they'd rather wait till they had enough for their own place than start married life living with either of their parents. Dejectedly, Grace realised the wedding was going to be some way off yet.

Once they'd announced their engagement on Boxing Day both Shirley and Stevie had offered to house them on hearing they wanted to get married as soon as possible. Grace had understood her mum's proposal had been prompted more by economics than generosity. Shirley would be able to supplement her small income with their rent, and Grace didn't blame her for being practical about it.

Stevie had said they could have the second bedroom in his place free of charge, but Grace had known from Pearl's strained smile that only conflict would ensue from that situation. In any case, neither offer had tempted her and Chris because they remained determined to start off married life in their own little home . . .

'Piss off,' Grace muttered, her voice dripping with disdain. Hugh had sped up and tried to halt her by swerving in front of her. She shoved him aside and carried on.

'This bloke you're with hasn't done you any favours, you know.' Hugh loped after her again. 'You sound common as muck, you know that?' he jeered.

Grace sent a shout of laughter over a shoulder. 'Good. I hope I'm *just* like him. He's the only reason I met you today. Know why? 'Cos I love him and can't wait to be his wife, and I'm damned if I'll let a good, decent man like him work his fingers to the bone to get the money for us to get married when I ought to have had savings to chip in.'

'Managed to get you into bed, has he? Or are you still frigid?'

Grace whirled about and cracked a hand against his cheek, unaware of a blue Bedford van pulling up at the kerb.

Chris leapt out and was by her side in a matter of a few seconds.

'Don't think I need to ask you who you are, pal,' he ejected through his teeth. His hand snaked to Hugh's throat, squeezing, before he shoved him forcefully away.

'This him?' he asked Grace.

She nodded, whitening in shock at his sudden appearance before a guilty blush stole across her cheeks.

'She's told you to leave her alone. Now I'm telling you. Bother her again and it'll be the last thing you do . . . understand?'

'She met me for a drink of her own free will. Ask her . . .' Hugh gasped out, rubbing his grazed throat. His expression was vindictive and pinned on Grace. Then he looked Chris up and down, a sneer on his face, as he took in his grubby workman's overalls. With deliberate contempt he straightened his tie then started brushing down his dark suit as though to rid it of contamination. 'Don't worry, mate, you're welcome to my leftovers,' Hugh drawled, then with a laugh he turned to walk off.

Chris yanked him back by a shoulder and gave him a short sharp one to the jaw. 'Need to learn a bit of respect when you're speaking to my fiancée, mate.'

Hugh staggered back against a wall clutching his aching face but he didn't retaliate even though Chris allowed him time to get his balance and throw a punch. Hugh wasn't looking so superior a few seconds later when he slunk off, ignoring the few bystanders who were gawping at the scene.

Chris pivoted about to stare at Grace. 'That true, what he said? You've had a drink with him?'

'It's not like that . . .'

'What is it like?'

264

'What are you doing here at this time of the day?' Grace blurted out. Chris never came to her office during her dinner break although he had picked her up after work on occasions when he had to visit a merchant's in the area. It had always been a lovely surprise to see his blue van parked at the kerb when she came down the steps.

'Come to tell you me uncle Rob knows of a house going cheap. He said to look at it straight away when we finish work today 'cos it's going to auction this week. So I got off work to tell you but . . .' He gave her a hard stare. 'Perhaps we won't bother, eh?' he finished softly.

'You've not let me explain,' Grace started. 'You don't understand what's gone on.'

'I'm listening,' Chris said quietly.

'I did go for a drink with him but only 'cos he said he'd give me fifty pounds.'

'Yeah? And what was he expecting in return?' Chris sounded viciously sardonic.

Grace felt her temper rising. Everything she'd done, she'd done while thinking about him, so he wouldn't need to work so hard, because she felt it was only fair that she contributed towards their future. Now he was allowing stupid jealousy to make him lewd and nasty. She noticed Wendy a way along the street, waving to her and pointing to her watch.

'I've got to go; me dinner break's over and I need to get back.'

'You've not told me why you've been for a drink with him.'

'You know why; I've told you before he's promised to give me back some of the money I lost when we cancelled our wedding.'

265

'Yeah, and I thought we'd agreed you'd let it go and never see him again. You're engaged to me now, or so I thought . . .'

'You're being daft, Chris.' Grace looked close to tears. 'I just want us to get the money together so we can get married. It's not fair you do it all on your own. I want to be able to help us set up home.'

'You saying you think I can't support you and that you'll have to carry on working after we're married?'

'I don't mind carrying on working till we start a family, I've told you I think that's a good idea.' Grace spun on the spot, looking harassed. 'We can't talk about it now. I've got to get back to the office, but I'd love to look at this house after work with you. Where is it?'

He walked away from her then stopped a few yards from the van to lob over a shoulder, 'Don't matter. Seems to me we've got a lot of things to iron out before we take the plunge on a property. I'll tell me uncle Rob we're gonna give this one a miss.'

'Hello there, Kathleen,' Matilda called out in greeting as she approached Smithie's shop. The Murphys' little girl was loitering outside. 'Where's your mum? Getting something for your tea, is she?'

Kathleen nodded and pointed to the door, indicating Noreen was inside.

'Reckon I might find a couple of pennies fer sweeties. Been good fer yer mummy, have you?'

Kathleen grinned up at Matilda. It was a bitterly cold February day and as Matilda took hold of Kathleen's hand she could feel her small, icy fingers clutching tightly at her glove. Matilda entered the shop to find Noreen with baby Rosie, swaddled in a shawl, in her arms. It seemed she'd been unsuccessfully asking old Smithie for stuff on the strap.

'Gotta pay up something for what you've already had, Mrs Murphy, before I let you take more,' he grumbled with much head-shaking. He dragged her groceries back towards him on the counter. 'Only doin' it fer yer own good, y'know. Yer husband's gonna be after me if I let you chalk up a long tab he can't settle.'

'There's no need to tell him. I can bring in something Friday, so I can,' Noreen pleaded in a whisper, turning about at hearing the doorbell's clatter. She grew red on seeing Matilda leading her daughter in from the cold.

'Kathleen! I told you to stay here with me. Thought she was behind me there,' she told Matilda. 'She must've followed Beattie Evans out a short while ago.'

'Give her the stuff she needs, you miserable old git,' Matilda growled at Smithie.

Matilda had known the Smith family for a long while and spoke to Peter Smith in the same way she'd addressed his father, Godfrey, half a century previously: in any way she pleased. Godfrey had not been such a stickler for weekly payments from creditors as was his son.

Before the Great War, when Matilda's darling Jack had been alive, and her middle-aged daughters were still schoolgirls, the majority of families living in Campbell Road had lived hand-to-mouth. Godfrey had kept the Keivers and the Wilds afloat by allowing them groceries on tick. In those tough times – that Matilda nevertheless reflected on nostalgically – finding a forgotten farthing was akin to unearthing treasure. Godfrey would dole out small amounts of tea or jam or broken biscuits in return for the tiny copper to assist the destitute in their fight for survival.

'Listen 'ere, Tilly, I've got a business ter run . . .' Smithie started moaning.

'You can afford it,' Matilda muttered. 'Made yourself a tidy amount out of what I've bought off yer over the years, don't say you ain't,' she mocked. 'And I'll have a bag o' sweets fer that.' She plonked down her two pennies.

'It's alright, you don't have to do that,' Noreen said in her soft Irish tone. She still seemed embarrassed at having been overheard begging for credit.

'Fill it up . . . that ain't two penn'orth . . .' Matilda grumbled as Smithie held out a brown paper bag containing an assortment of liquorice and sherbet and chews.

'You'll be the ruin of me, Matilda Keiver,' Smithie complained, winding more black bootlaces into the bag.

'Yeah . . . you told me that more'n twenty year ago,' Matilda returned dryly. 'And since then you've had two new cars, and a new wife, so don't you go pleadin' poverty.'

Noreen was about to forget her groceries and slip out of the shop while Matilda was engaged in a verbal duel with the shopkeeper.

Matilda caught at one of her thin arms and gave Smithie a significant stare.

'Just this lot then, Mrs Murphy . . . but bring in something before the weekend.' Peter Smith sighed.

Noreen quickly put Rosie on her unsteady little feet. She started loading bread and tea and milk into her shopping bag and mumbled her gratitude before quickly whipping her youngest up, settling her on her hip and heading for the door in case he changed his mind.

When they were outside, being buffeted by a bitter breeze, Noreen again tucked the wool shawl about Rosie's shoulders to protect her from the cold.

'Why don't you come over mine fer a cup of tea before you head home,' Matilda said kindly.

Noreen gave a brief nod and a grateful smile. She knew Matilda's room was little better than her own but at least it was a different dump. Besides, it was somebody to talk to and, ashamed as she was to acknowledge it, she knew her neighbour would ply the children with biscuits to fill them up for a while and save her the necessity of doing it. She could present her husband with a fresh uncut loaf when he came in for his tea later.

'She's looking bonny now. Wouldn't think you'd had that scare with her in the dreadful smog.' Matilda nodded at Noreen's youngest. Little Rosie's cheeks were pink with cold but at the moment she was toddling, giggling, from one to the other of Matilda's battered old chairs to clutch at the seats. 'How old is she now?' Matilda asked, shaking the kettle to judge what was in it.

'Sixteen months,' Noreen said, gathering her daughters to her side to prevent them chasing about in Matilda's home.

'Let 'em play,' Matilda said gruffly. 'Not doing any harm and I like to see kids enjoying themselves.' She put the kettle to boil on the hob and set two cups. 'Now I reckon I might find something nice for two good little gels. Know any gels who's been good?' she bent down to ask Kathleen.

'Me 'n' Rosie's been good . . .' Kathleen piped up, glancing shyly at Matilda's biscuit box on the shelf. 'Your Kieran not managed to turn up some more work?'

Matilda asked bluntly as they sat sipping from their cups and Rosie and Kathleen sat side by side on Matilda's bed, eagerly chewing digestives.

'He's out now looking,' Noreen said on a sigh.

'Not working along the road today?'

Noreen shook her head. 'He's got nothing. Christopher put him off last week . . .' She glanced quickly at Matilda. 'Oh, I'm not complaining, neither is Kieran. Not at all. It was good of your nephew to give Kieran work to get us over Christmas. And he kept Kieran on longer than he said he would; he was good to us because he knew that divil O'Connor had kept hold of Kieran's pay.' She paused. 'He was a cheat and a liar and those other Irish fellows who were working in the road were always looking for trouble with Christopher and his men. Kieran fretted at first that we'd be thought of as trouble as well after he got a job with O'Connor. But you've all been kind. We're grateful to you for helping.'

'Don't mind doin' good turns fer them wot deserve it,' Matilda announced. 'And that O'Connor'll get what's coming to him sooner or later. But I didn't know Chris had put yer husband off 'cos I ain't seen much of him fer a few weeks.'

Yesterday she'd spied her nephew at a distance and had given him a wave. As they'd barely had an opportunity to speak since Christmas, Matilda had expected him to jog over and have a quick natter. But he'd simply raised a hand then gone back to work.

Matilda had a nose for trouble brewing and she was wondering if perhaps she ought to amble down the road later and have a word . . .

From the start she'd had an inkling that Chris might

270

have taken Kieran Murphy on off his own back. At Christmas she'd mentioned to Rob that Kieran seemed to get along alright with the other lads in the firm. She'd noticed Chris shoot her a quelling look, and Rob frown in puzzlement, so she'd said no more on the subject because Christmas was a time for putting work aside and concentrating on family. But Matilda was cute enough to put two and two together and come up with a bit of a problem.

Despite the short, freezing-cold days putting folk off loitering to chat Matilda knew it was unlike Chris not to pop by. He usually poked his head in to say hello at least once a week. Previously she'd not given it much thought because she knew he now had Grace to think about, and lots of exciting plans to make with his future wife.

Of course, there was also Pamela still in the background. Matilda wondered if Christopher had yet found the right opportunity to tell Stevie that he'd managed to contact his mum and, following a tricky start, there had been an improvement in their relationship.

Matilda hadn't questioned Chris because she accepted it was his business whether he kept her informed about how things were progressing with his mother. Besides, Matilda reasoned the less she knew, the less she'd have to own up to if Stevie should try to cross-examine her on the subject.

After Noreen had gone home with her children, filled to the gills with tea and biscuits, Matilda got her coat and headed off down the road in the gathering twilight. She could see Chris's van parked so knew he was still about somewhere.

'Ain't been up to see me in a while. You alright?' she

271

called up to Chris as he stuck his head out of a window to talk to her.

'Yeah . . . I'm alright. Sorry I've not been in; been a bit busy. I'll pop along when I knock off.'

CHAPTER TWENTY-FIVE

'Saw Noreen Murphy earlier. She says you've put Kieran off.'

As soon as Matilda saw Chris heading up the stairs towards her she let him know what was on her mind.

She'd been filling the kettle at the sink on the landing. When done, she followed her nephew into her room and closed the door against the gloomy cold. Having kicked back into place the sausage of rags that served as a draught excluder, she set the kettle on the hob.

'Had to . . .' Chris sighed a reply as he sat down. 'Didn't want to, but . . .' His voice tailed away.

'Rob know, does he?'

Chris gave a noncommittal shrug.

'Your uncle never knew you took him on, did he? You've been paying Kieran outta yer own wages 'cos that bastard O'Connor wouldn't settle up with him, and the Murphys didn't have a pot ter piss in over Christmas.' She gave Chris an admiring smile. 'That's a fine and generous thing to do fer someone you hardly know.'

'Wish I could've done more, but I can't . . . not now . . .'

'Can't be expected to. Things have changed for you in a big way.'

Chris planted his elbows on the battered table and cupped his face in his hands. 'Feel bad about taking back all me pay but . . . never gonna get enough saved to get married otherwise.'

'Grace been on to you to get shot of Kieran?' There was no accusation in Matilda's tone. It was sensible and acceptable in her estimation for a young woman to scrape together every penny she could get hold of to set up her own home with her future husband.

'No.' He grunted a laugh. 'If she knew she'd be upset I'd done it.'

'Not told her then?'

Chris shook his head.

'Seen yer mum lately?' Matilda fired off another question that had been niggling at her.

'Saw her Christmas Day. Took her a present. Ain't seen her since,' Chris stated, staccato-voiced, avoiding Matilda's astute gaze.

'Sounded like you wanted to add, and don't want to see her neither . . .' Matilda set his tea in front of him.

Chris took a sip and turned his head. He held out a palm to the warmth coming off the small stove.

'What's up, Chris? You had a big barney with Stevie about seeing Pam over Christmas?'

'He still don't know I've found her. I've not told him anything, and he's not asked. S'pect he's been too busy with the caff to bring it to mind.'

'Well something's eating away at yer, I can see that.'

After a short silence Chris straightened in his chair and gazed at his aunt.

'Remember you said, ages ago when I first started talking about finding her, that it was up to me mum to have an honest talk with me about the reason they split up?'

Matilda nodded. 'Yeah, I do. It were the day I come over to Crouch End to speak to Stevie about it all.'

'She did tell me; she said she nearly poisoned me 'cos she couldn't cope with me when I was a baby, but s'pose you already knew that.'

Matilda remained quiet, mulling over how hurt Chris must have been to hear it. But admiration for Pam for having the guts to admit to it dominated her mind. 'Were brave of her to tell you something like that,' she stressed gently. 'She could easily have lied. Tell you the truth, I thought she would.'

Chris gave a sour smile. 'That's what Grace said, more or less. Seems women stick together on these things.'

'Ain't sticking together, son, it's understanding that being a wife and a mother ain't all hearts and flowers. You should be glad your Grace already knows it.'

'Yeah . . .' Chris stood up. 'Gotta be off, now . . .'

'Seeing Grace later?'

'Dunno. Doubt it. We had a bit of a row last week.'

'Got it coming from all sides then, ain't yer?' Matilda said.

As Chris trudged towards the door, fiddling with opening a pack of cigarettes, she said, 'Look at yer: tall, strong as an ox, handsome with it. No lasting harm done, Chris; no need to get bitter over it now and let it sour all the good things you got to look forward to.' She waited till he turned towards her before adding, 'Yer mother's paid her dues, you can't say she ain't, knowing the life she's had. Let it go.' She gave him a smile as he got a cigarette alight and immediately started to cough. ''Course you could cut down on them 'n' give yerself a few more years.' She took the packet and dropped it back in his overalls' pocket. 'Choke up chicken . . .' she added, patting his back. 'How long you been barking like that?'

'Ain't nothing . . . just caught it off Dad; he's got a bad cold he can't shake off.'

'Didn't need that on top of all the rest, did yer?' She gripped his arm comfortingly. 'It'll all come right, you mark my words. Come Coronation Day you'll be dancing in the street with your lovely fiancée.'

'Well, this is a nice surprise,' Matilda called out of the window, beaming in pleasure. 'Come on up . . . door ain't locked.'

It was the first time Grace had been alone to Whadcoat Street. She hadn't told Chris she was planning on visiting his aunt, not because she didn't want him to know, but because she hadn't seen much of him. The cough he'd had had worsened enough to take him to the doctor's last week. But Grace knew it wasn't just a bout of bronchitis keeping them apart. He was using illness as an excuse to see her less often. Chris had been distant and cool ever since the incident with Hugh outside her office.

When Grace had seen Matilda during the Christmas holiday she'd promised her she'd write out Coronation Day invitations before Easter. But with the friction between her and Chris worsening she'd forgotten all about starting on the task. Yet it wasn't just duty that had brought her to Whadcoat Street on a chilly Saturday afternoon in March. On the way to Islington on the bus she'd mulled over whether to ask Matilda if Chris had confided in her that he wanted to break off their engagement. If anybody had Chris's trust, it was his great-aunt Matilda.

'Weeks are marching on; it'll soon be Easter and we need to get them invitations sent out about now, I reckon. Then if some people choose to stick close to home for their Coronation Day dos we can get by with less grub and booze, or ask a few more folk over to make up the numbers.' Matilda had fired that at Grace before the young woman had fully explained the reason for her visit and was properly seated at her old table. 'I reckon everybody'll come, y'know.' Matilda stuck the kettle on the hob and set two cups and saucers.

'Hope so,' Grace replied with a bright smile. She took the pieces of folded paper that Matilda had pulled from the drawer in the table and was now holding out to her, and put them in her handbag.

'Faye writ that list out for me so you'll be able to understand it. Got a beautiful hand, she has.' Matilda spooned tea into the pot while giving Grace a closer look. She guessed the girl had something on her mind and had an idea of what it might be. Stevie had told her that Chris was suffering with bronchitis and had hardly seen Grace. But Matilda had spotted her great-nephew, at a distance, working along the road. She knew that if Chris was fit enough to work, he was fit enough to see the woman he loved. If he wanted to, and still loved her. Matilda hoped that *was* the case because she'd grown fond of Grace and was sad to think something bad had blown up between the young couple. 'Had a word with Rob about the trestle tables we're gonna need fer the kids' tea party,' she said, stirring the brew, and pondering on the wisdom of sticking her oar into this problem. 'He's got a few decorators' trestles in the yard down Holloway Road but we'll need more than that. I expect Stevie'll let us have some tables out of his caff.'

'That's a good idea,' Grace said, injecting enthusiasm into her voice. 'I'll start on the invitations tomorrow,' she promised, taking the cup of tea Matilda had poured for her.

'Penny for 'em . . .' Matilda sat down opposite Grace, having decided to have her say.

'Oh . . . it's nothing . . .' Grace blurted. She was always startled by Matilda's blunt approach and hadn't yet worked out how to go about asking for the woman's advice.

'You 'n' Chris had words?'

After a moment Grace nodded, blinking back tears that had started immediately to her eyes. 'Had a row a while ago and things haven't been right since,' she croaked.

'Will it patch up eventually?'

'Don't know . . .' Grace admitted huskily. 'He won't say much about it or tell me how he's feeling. I've said sorry . . .'

'So what've you got to be sorry about?'

Grace fiddled with the handle on her cup. 'I . . . I went for a drink with an old boyfriend and Chris found out.'

'So, he's jealous, you mean. Does he need to be?'

'No!' Grace insisted. 'I only met Hugh because . . .' She tailed off. She didn't want Matilda to think her greedy and mercenary, and yet sometimes that's how she saw herself. She'd stupidly risked her happiness with Chris for money.

'Yer mum told me once that you was going to get married before but your fiancé did the dirty on you. Same fellow, is it?' Matilda enquired.

Grace nodded. 'He's a creep and Chris knows it 'cos I've told him all about Hugh. And I've explained why I met him that day. But he doesn't seem to want to believe the truth.' She raked her fingers through her fringe of fair hair before owning up, 'I wanted to get some money to put towards our wedding savings.' Grace took a quick gulp of tea before elaborating. 'When Hugh broke off our engagement I lost money I'd put down as deposits on the wedding. I admit I've felt resentful over it and would have liked it back. Then when Hugh started pestering me at work saying he felt guilty and wanted to pay back some of what I lost, I thought . . . why not? So I agreed to see him one dinnertime . . .' Her eyes narrowed. 'But I should have known the swine was lying, as usual.'

'More interested in getting cosy with you than clearing his conscience, was he?' Matilda cackled a laugh.

'Exactly!' Grace sighed. 'And Chris won't believe that's all it was.'

Matilda patted Grace's fingers curled on the tabletop. 'If it's meant to work out, it'll work out. And if you want my opinion, I think it will 'cos Chris ain't a fool, and if he lets you slip through his fingers, that's what he'll be.' Matilda stood up and shook the kettle. 'More tea?'

'I'd best get back,' Grace said huskily. She gathered up her bag and buttoned her coat.

'We're gonna have the time of our lives in a few months on Coronation Day, Grace . . . all of us . . .'

'Thanks for tea . . . and everything.' Grace suddenly felt rather shy, and unsure whether it had been wise to disclose quite so much. She knew Chris wouldn't have told a soul about their personal troubles.

Matilda heard Grace clattering down her rickety stairs and went to the window, watching the young woman pulling up her collar against the cold before hurrying away. A sigh escaped Matilda's withered lips. Much as she felt like going after her great-nephew to talk some sense into him, she knew she wouldn't. If Chris was getting cold feet, and using Grace's old flame as an excuse to call off a wedding he was unsure about, that was his business. It would be better for everybody if he wriggled free now than went ahead and regretted getting married. No doubt his father would also want to impress that on him.

Later that evening, Grace could no longer contain her frustrations. 'I can't stand these silences between us. If you think you've made a mistake and want to call the engagement off, just say so.'

'Has he contacted you again?'

'No! I've told you no a thousand times, why won't you listen to me?' Grace cried in a muted voice. 'I haven't seen Hugh Wilkins in weeks and weeks and I'm not expecting to.'

Chris drew out his cigarette pack and opened it, about to light another, despite him giving a sudden, hacking cough.

In exasperation Grace snatched at the carton and threw it into the back of the van. 'And it's no use moaning you don't feel well and haven't any money when you're spending out every day on those and making yourself cough!' She covered her face with her hands, muttering bitterly through her fingers, 'Sorry! It's up to you if you want to smoke fifty a day and waste money rather than save for a deposit on a house.'

Chris sank back into his seat, suppressing another tickle in his throat. 'Perhaps we should have a proper break from each other, till I can . . .'

'Till you can what?' Grace let her hands fall to her lap. Her eyes darted to him and instinctively she twisted the diamond ring on her finger. 'Till you can trust me? Is that what you were about to say?'

'No . . . I wasn't going to say that. I was going to say . . . till I can sort out the mess in my head.' He glanced at her, inwardly wincing at the hurt and confusion in her eyes, but he couldn't find the right words to comfort her while his thoughts were scrambled. He couldn't seem to control his anger or his jealousy. He wanted to track down Hugh Wilkins and properly ram his teeth down his throat this time. But it wasn't just his rival unsettling him. Thoughts of Pamela were constantly niggling at the back of his mind too. 'It's not just about us, Grace, or that prick you were engaged to before. One minute I think I hate her and never want to see her again, the next I think I'll go over there so she can explain why she hated me so much.'

'Your mother didn't *hate* you, Chris,' Grace said wearily. 'If she had she wouldn't have tried to see you after your father took you away. She made a mistake, a dreadful mistake, and she's owned up to it. I wish I'd not interfered . . .' Her husky voice petered out before springing back to life. 'It's my own fault. I kept on at you about seeing her. Everything was alright between us till you went to see your mother on Christmas Day and got to know her better.'

Chris gazed sombrely into the darkness. He knew he

shouldn't keep sniping at Grace about her ex-fiancé when in his heart he understood more than jealousy was gnawing at his guts. He also knew it was best they stayed away from each other for a while or he risked destroying the finest thing that had ever come into his life. And he couldn't bear the thought of losing her.

'The lads are going down Harringay Stadium at the end of the week. They've asked me if I want to go . . .'

'Go. You deserve a night out. Go,' Grace said and forced a smile before she quickly got out of the van and went indoors.

CHAPTER TWENTY-SIX

'That's O'Connor over there, ain't it?'

'Where?' Billy plonked down his tankard and glanced about the room. He spotted the stocky middle-aged Irishman at a table, guffawing with two of his work colleagues, and a couple of brassy-looking women. 'Oi, Chris, that bastard O'Connor's over there.' Billy nudged Chris in the ribs.

Chris had been lounging against the bar, talking to Vic about the odds-on favourite in the next race. Now he straightened and turned immediately in the direction Billy and Ted were jerking their heads. He stared intently at the Irishman; O'Connor looked different done up to the nines in his shiny suit, with his hair, usually a wild black frizz, sleeked down flat. Chris felt his back teeth grind together. No doubt the thieving pikey was having a good time spending Kieran Murphy's money on booze and bets. He could feel his temper rising and on impulse he pushed away from his support. Weaving between tables, he strolled over.

Declan O'Connor noticed him approaching and his

laughing expression froze in recognition. A moment later he'd pushed himself upright and jutted his chin belligerently.

'What is it you want, Sonny Jim?' he snarled in an undertone.

'Kieran Murphy's wages. I told him if I bumped into you I'd collect 'em for him.'

O'Connor hadn't been expecting to hear that and he blinked, taken aback. His tongue slithered over his fleshy red lips, aware that the others seated about his table were gawping, awaiting his response.

'Don't know what you're talking about, Sonny Jim, so why don't you run along back to yer little pals.' He flicked some thick fingers, gesturing for Chris to go away.

'Yeah, I will . . . with Kieran's wages in me pocket.' Chris stuck out a hand, aware that Vic and Ted and Billy had stopped observing from yards away and now come to join him. They stood in a semi-circle behind his back. He knew that because the men in O'Connor's group had got to their feet and were looking over his shoulder in anticipation of a fight starting.

'Come on, don't need to be no trouble,' Chris jibed softly. 'Just do the decent thing fer once and give it here.' His fingers beckoned impatiently but he felt the pent-up anger and frustration that had been bubbling in his guts since Christmas Day calming down. Obliquely, he understood that getting Kieran his money wouldn't set everything straight, but it would be a step in the right direction.

'Fook off,' O'Connor spat through his teeth. 'Oi don't know what you're talking about.' He half-sank back into his seat.

'Think you do.' Chris took a step closer. 'Now why

284

don't yer be a big man and hand over what you owe, 'cos if yer don't these ladies are gonna twig they're on a hiding to nuthin' come the end of the night.' He glanced at the fat blonde. 'He ain't gonna pay you, luv. Want to join us instead?'

'I told you once before you're a dead man, Sonny Jim . . .' O'Connor's lips flattened against his teeth and he suddenly crashed around the table making the women shriek and his two comrades spring into action.

'Deirdre's gonna go mental soon as she cops a look at the state of me.' Despite his comment, Vic started chuckling and dusting down his torn jacket with a hand.

Ted and Billy were also trying to neaten their rumpled clothes while guffawing.

'You got us fuckin' barred from a dog track, Chris,' Ted complained with a smile. 'Can't believe it . . .'

'Done you a favour then, ain't I? Money you was losing down there every week, you could do with a break.' Chris grinned behind the fag in his mouth.

They were walking back towards where their vehicles were parked, having got thrown out of the stadium for brawling. The Irish crew had been ejected too but had sensibly taken off in the opposite direction, having received a drubbing before the bouncers raced to intervene.

Chris had managed to get a tenner out of O'Connor's pocket before he'd removed his knee from his windpipe and let him up off the floor. Before he headed home he was going to Whadcoat Street to give it to Kieran just in case he was in desperate need of it. Old Smithie in the shop could always be knocked up for emergency supplies. If the old miser got a sniff of a tenner in the offing, he'd probably deliver the stuff personally.

'Give us a lift back, will yer, Chris?' Vic asked.

'You'd be better off jumping in with Bill, he's going your way.'

'Ain't goin' home, it's too early,' Vic said. 'Gonna go round a mate's, see if they want a drink,' he mumbled.

'I'll come fer a drink with you,' Ted offered. He wasn't keen on heading home early either. He knew he'd only finish the night stuck on the sofa between his warring parents, listening to the wireless. Besides, after the evening's events they'd got a good tale to tell in the pub.

'Nah . . .' s'alright . . .' Vic discouraged him quickly. When Ted looked huffy he added shortly, 'Ain't that sort of mate.'

'You're gonna get yerself hung, Vic, you keep on,' Billy warned with a laugh. 'Deirdre's old man finds out you're still playing away even though she's up the duff, he'll have yer guts fer garters.'

'No need fer anyone to find out if you all keep yer mouths shut.' Vic sounded peevish. He knew that his bit on the side wouldn't give him earache about the state he looked. He could feel a lump coming up on one of his cheekbones and taste blood on his lip. Sandra would be happy enough to see him so long as he had a bottle of gin to offer her, and he'd be glad to see her because the night's excitement had got him aroused and he knew his pregnant wife wasn't going to be any help there. She never was lately . . .

'What's happened? Has there been bad trouble?'

Kieran had answered the door in his pants and vest then whipped outside onto the landing and stood shivering and staring at the bruising on Chris's face.

Absently Chris touched the swelling by his eye. He knew it'd be black by tomorrow.

'Nah . . . nothing much. Just run into O'Connor when I was out with the lads tonight.' He fished in a pocket and drew out the banknote. 'He gave me this for you . . . yer wages.'

Kieran stared at the money as though it were a mirage. He made to take it then quickly withdrew his fingers.

'Take it. Won't be no trouble, promise. He owes you it, he knows that.'

'You had a fight with that divil to get this for me and Noreen?' Kieran raised astonished eyes to Chris's face.

'Would have had a fight anyhow,' Chris ruefully admitted. 'Just the mood I was in.' He took one of Kieran's hands and slapped the tenner in it. 'Better get inside. You look bleedin' freezing standing out here . . .'

'What's going on?' Noreen, with an old coat over her nightdress, had joined her husband at the door.

'Christopher has brought us this . . . from O'Connor . . .'

Aware that he was in for another round of questions Chris backed away a few steps. He just wanted to get home. He felt exhausted. 'Right, I'll let you two get back to bed, then.' He started along the landing just as a baby's wail was heard. 'Sorry . . .' He pivoted about, gesturing he hadn't meant to disturb them all.

'Thank you,' Kieran called and took a few paces after him.

'Can I get you something? A cup of tea before you go?' Noreen blurted.

'No, thanks . . . gotta get off . . .'

Chris turned quickly and clattered down the stairs. He was walking swiftly towards his van when he spotted his aunt coming towards him in the gloom, looking a bit unsteady on her feet.

'What you doing up 'n' about this time o' night?' he asked, a smile in his tone.

'Could ask you the same thing.' Matilda chuckled, sounding merry.

'Been round the Duke?' Chris had caught a whiff of intoxication about his aunt.

'Nah . . . been over old Beattie's. Her son fetched her over a bottle of port for her birthday so I offered to help her polish it off. We've been making plans for our Coronation Day party.' She waved a bit of paper at him. 'See, between us we've writ out a list of grub. Spellin' might not be up ter much . . .' She grabbed her nephew's elbow. 'Gonna help me up the stairs, son? Me old legs are playing up something chronic tonight, can't hardly stand up 'cos of me arthritis.'

'Don't suppose the port's helped much there either,' Chris muttered wryly. He assisted her over the threshold and the two of them went stumbling up the stairs in a journey that took twice as long as it should have. He was glad of the darkness concealing his damaged face from his aunt because he didn't feel up to another round of questions.

'What was that?' He spun about as they reached the landing.

'What was what?' Matilda echoed on a yawn.

'Sounded like an explosion.' Chris hesitated for a moment, frowning, then raced down the stairs and into the street. Instinctively he gazed back the way he'd come, towards the Murphys' house, and saw an ominous orange

288

glow. He took one step in the direction of the fire – before sprinting as fast as he could towards it.

'What is it?' Matilda had wobbled back down the stairs to yell at Chris from her doorway, but he was already too far away to hear her.

As he got closer Chris could see that the fire wasn't at the Murphys' place, as he'd dreaded it might be, but further along the street, in one of the empty houses Wild Brothers had been working on.

Flooded with intense relief he diverted to Smithie's shop and pounded on the door while bawling up at Peter Smith to phone for the brigade. He heard the sash being shoved up and, angling back his head, saw Smithie's frowning face appear.

The shopkeeper didn't need any more telling; he'd seen the flames licking through a glassless window diagonally opposite. 'I'll call for help,' he immediately shouted down, before disappearing.

Chris hurtled on down the street. He thanked heaven the Murphys were safe, but he knew this could be a disaster for Wild Brothers if all the firm's future work was destroyed. And he had no doubt who had tried to finish them off: O'Connor was behind it. The pikey had come here tonight to take revenge and, despite knowing the seriousness of the situation, Chris still praised the lord that the vicious bastard had turned his spite on him instead of Kieran. The thought of two little girls trapped behind a wall of flames . . .

Chris slowed to a walk as he neared the inferno, blinking in astonishment to clear his vision, because smoke was stinging his eyes and he couldn't believe his mate, Vic, was really waving frantically to him from the first-floor window of the burning house.

'What are you doin', you fuckin' maniac?' Chris roared at him, snapping out of his trance. 'Get out of there now!' He raced to the railings fronting the house and stared up, horrified, at Vic.

'Can't . . . can't . . . tried . . . can't . . . too late . . .' Vic was babbling in terror. 'Stairs are alight and Sandra won't try and go down 'em.' He turned to glance over a shoulder. 'Silly cow won't go down, 'case she gets burned . . . shall I leave her here, Chris? Shall I?'

'Fuck's sake, jump then,' Chris thundered. He opened his arms and braced his legs, grounding himself. 'Chuck her out first. You got to jump, you stupid bastard. I'll try 'n' break yer falls a bit. Jump!'

Chris was obliquely aware that people were emerging from houses and rushing towards him with offers of help. He glanced back up the road and saw his aunt hobbling closer, frenziedly waving. He knew she was signalling at him not to do anything daft. He spun on the spot looking for an able-bodied man to help; but most of the people who still lived in the street were elderly, like his aunt. Even Peter Smith looked to be in his late fifties. Chris spotted Kieran coming out of his house at a run while trying to jump into his trousers.

Vic's head had disappeared; a moment later he'd dragged Sandra into view, shoving her forward while trying to lift her over the sash so she could escape. She was hysterical with fear, shaking her head and beating at him with her fists.

'What you doing up there anyhow, you bleedin' nutter?' Chris had bellowed that out needlessly; he could easily guess what Vic had been doing camped out with a woman in a slum. His adulterous colleague had reckoned on being safe from disturbance or detection. Chris realised he now knew the identities of the tramps who'd been squatting overnight on site.

'Shall I leave her, Chris? Shall I?' Vic whimpered.

'Anybody got a ladder?' Chris whipped around to shout that out to the gathering crowd. 'Anybody got a high-reach ladder?' He had one himself on his van parked along the road, but the ladder was padlocked down on the top. The key to the padlock was at home in his overalls' pocket. By the time he'd wrenched the ladder free it might be too late . . .

'I've got one,' Peter Smith cried out.

'I'll help you get it.' Kieran Murphy was doing up his belt. 'Quick, let's bring it.' He set off at a run in the direction of Smithie's shop, the older man puffing in his wake.

'I'm gonna jump . . . ain't waiting . . .' Vic tottered about by the open window. He'd just watched, mesmerised, as flames curled around the banisters on the landing. Sandra screamed as he got a leg over the sill and tried to hold onto him. He shook her off and pushed away from the stone ledge, landing on Chris and two other fellows who'd linked arms trying to buffer his fall while at the same time twisting sideways to avoid serious harm. Vic rolled on the ground, groaning and clutching at a shin, while his saviours tried to get their wind back.

'Where the fuck's she gone?' Chris gasped, when he'd breath enough to do so. He was blinking up through a screen of acrid smoke at the open sash. There was no sign now of Sandra's shaggy dark head poking out; she'd disappeared.

'Stupid cow . . . I told her you'd catch her . . .' Vic moaned from his prostrate position.

Chris pointed a threatening finger at him and drew back a fist as though tempted to whack him. But his attention jerked to Smithie and Kieran, who were jogging back with a ladder.

'Sandra, get to the window!' Chris shouted, trying to shake off his aunt who was hanging on his arm telling him to wait for the brigade. But there was no sound of a fire engine approaching yet.

The ladder was whacked against the wall in preparation for someone to brave the danger and drag Sandra out. Chris exchanged a bleak look with Kieran. They were the only two youngish men present, apart from Vic who was still rolling about in pain, and no use whatsoever.

'I'll go,' Kieran said.

'You fuckin' won't.' Chris shoved him away from the ladder. 'You've got a family.' With a thudding heart and a deep breath he started up the ladder, aware of the heat and smoke increasing as he approached the open window. Despite his lungs feeling as though they were being squeezed in a vice, he fell over the sill and squinted into a fog. He saw Sandra cowering against the wall clutching a bottle of gin, peeping at him through a tumble of tangled curls.

He stumbled towards her and yanked her arm, tugging her towards the window on her backside because she wouldn't get up. Suddenly she sprang into life and started clawing at his face, and because he felt breathless and panicky, he punched her as lightly as he could. As she sagged he hoisted her onto a shoulder then struggled to get himself through the opening and onto the ladder without dropping her or coughing his guts up. The roar of an approaching inferno focused his thoughts. He was fumbling his way down the first rung when he heard the fire engine's bell. Having taken a wobbly peek over his shoulder he was aware too that Kieran was coming towards him, arms outstretched to offer assistance. His head was swimming and his nostrils felt on fire so he breathed through his mouth although it increased his coughing. He'd descended a few more rungs before he lost consciousness and crashed down on top of Kieran, sending them all tumbling in a jumble of limbs to the ground.

CHAPTER TWENTY-SEVEN

'Where's Grace?'

'She's outside,' Stevie croaked. 'She's been waiting outside all night.'

'Want her . . .' Chris murmured and moved his tongue about his arid mouth.

'How you feeling?' Stevie asked while patting his son's hand, lying on the coverlet. 'Give me a fright, you did. Brave you were doing that. Why d'you do it?' Stevie choked out, squeezing shut his eyes. 'Could've got killed . . . you stupid sod.'

'Get Grace for me, Dad . . .'

Stevie nodded and rose stiffly from his bedside chair. He went out into the hospital corridor.

'Chris's woken up,' he announced with a wavering smile for the family who were keen to know how the hero was doing, and to hear the doctor's verdict this morning after yesterday's dreadful incident.

The initial diagnosis had been that Chris's lungs had been badly affected by inhaling smoke from the fire.

'He seems . . . alright . . . normal . . .' Stevie croaked

before gesturing he felt overcome. He sank down onto the chair next to Matilda's and propped his forehead in his palms. His aunt pressed his shoulder with a rough red hand and murmured comfortingly to him while trying to blink back her own tears.

Smithie had arrived late yesterday evening at Stevie's house to give him the devastating news that Chris had been hurt in an accident and had been taken to hospital. Stevie had immediately got in touch with his brother Rob, as he always did when he needed urgent help. Between them they'd decided it best to let Grace know straight away, in case things took a turn for the worse. Rob had gone to Tottenham to break the news and bring her to the hospital while Stevie had headed straight to his son's bedside.

'Wants to see you, Grace.' Stevie looked up with a composed smile.

Grace had dozed for a while in the small hours in a hard-backed chair, but since dawn she'd been mostly on her feet, restlessly pacing, awaiting her turn to go and sit with Chris while he was sleeping. For a moment she stared at Stevie with thumping heart, her eyes glittering with tears of relief. Their recent bickering over money, and Hugh Wilkins, now all seemed to Grace like so much pathetic trivia. All she wanted was to know that Chris was on the mend and would be home soon. A moment later she was walking quickly through the swing doors towards the side ward.

'That's the last time I let you out with your mates,' Grace said softly as she approached Chris's bed and sat down. She folded her quivering hands in her lap so he wouldn't see them and know how badly shaken she was.

Chris smiled weakly. 'Didn't want to go down the dogs anyhow. I'd sooner have gone out with you.'

'We don't go out much, do we, since we got engaged? Perhaps we should enjoy ourselves more and forget about saving for a big wedding.' Grace took his soot-blackened fingers between her trembling palms and raised them to her warm lips.

'Thought you wanted to get married as soon as possible.'

'Yeah, I do,' she sniffed, blinking rapidly. 'But can't always have what we want, can we? All I want now is for you to get well enough to come home.'

'What's up with me then?'

'Doctor said your lungs got inflamed by breathing in smoke. You already had a bad chest, didn't you, so that didn't help. But you'll be alright . . .'

'Yeah . . . strong as an ox, me . . . me aunt told me that, so I must be.'

'You look good,' Grace said, gently touching a hand to his dirt-smudged face.

'So do you,' he replied wolfishly and drew back the coverlet a bit. 'Fancy getting in?'

Grace chuckled and leaned forward to peck his lips. 'You definitely *are* feeling better.'

'What happened to Vic?'

'Broke his leg.'

'That all?' Chris feigned disappointment.

'Billy came by the hospital earlier to see how you're doing and told us Deirdre's already gone home to live with her mum and dad. So, I doubt Vic's going to get off lightly this time.'

'What about Sandra?'

'She escaped with a few cuts and bruises, and so did

Kieran. I saw him earlier,' Grace added. 'He was one of the first to come here to find out how you are. He told me that O'Connor has been arrested. One of his men turned him in.' Her eyebrows drew together in surprise. 'Apparently they weren't all in on it. It was only O'Connor involved in setting the fire; his friends were disgusted by what he did because they knew it could spread and people still live in the street.' Grace shuddered. 'Thank God the brigade got it out quickly.' She leaned close to caress her cheek against Chris's bristly jaw. 'It was very brave of you to do what you did. Bit of a hero, aren't you?'

'I'm glad that bastard got arrested,' Chris said. 'I hope he gets a long stretch. In fact, hearing about it's cheered me up so much I reckon I'm well enough to go home. Where's me clothes?'

'You've got to wait till the doctor says you can,' Grace said firmly. 'No point going too soon then having to come back again.'

She relaxed back in the chair and gazed tenderly at him while her fingers stroked to and fro on the back of his hand.

'I've been acting like a prat lately and want to say I'm sorry,' Chris mumbled gruffly

Grace dropped to her knees by the bed and cuddled him through the blankets. 'There's never been any need for you to be jealous, I swear.'

'I know . . .' Chris stroked her crown of silky fair hair with his mucky fingers. 'I'm just a bloody fool who doesn't deserve you.'

Grace sniffed and raised her head to look at him. 'You've had a lot on your mind, what with your mum and so on,' she said graciously.

'Yeah, she has been on me mind. Would you do something for me, Grace?' Chris asked hoarsely.

''Course . . .'

'Would you go and tell me mum that I'm in hospital but I'm alright and nothing to worry about. I want her to know . . . just in case . . .'

'You'll be home soon,' Grace reassured him softly.

'Yeah, I know, but I want her to know what's happened. Wouldn't want her to feel left out . . . just in case . . .' He gazed at Grace earnestly. 'Had weird dreams while I've been asleep and I was worried it meant I might not ever see her again.'

'You will . . . if you want to . . .'

'Weren't me in danger in me dreams, it was her. She was stuck somewhere behind the flames, and I was trying to get to her, not Sandra, but I couldn't reach her and she was just looking at me whispering it didn't matter 'cos it was what she deserved . . .' His voice cracked as tormenting images vividly assaulted his mind once more.

Quickly Grace renewed her fierce cuddling, comforting him through the blankets. 'It was just a dream . . . s'pect the doctors gave you something to help you sleep and it made you hallucinate a bit.'

'Yeah, but I want to see her, just in case . . .' he insisted and turned solemn deep brown eyes on her. 'Can't ask me dad to go to Bexleyheath; got nobody else to ask, and I want her to know I've been in an accident but I'm alright.'

''Course I'll go and tell her,' Grace promised softly. 'I'll go this afternoon.'

Chris stared at her then raised his eyes to the slowly whirring fan on the ceiling. 'But don't say nuthin' to me dad. Can see he's worried about me and don't want to put more on him just now.'

'Yeah . . . plenty of time to tell him about you and Pam, but you will have to tell him, you know.'

Chris nodded, turning his head to welcome Grace's cool soft lips as they approached his mouth for a farewell kiss. He watched as she quietly left the room with a final fond glance back at him before closing the door.

Chris gazed at the rotating blades above his bed, soothed by the soft whirring sound and feeling oddly at peace, despite knowing he had a war ahead of him with his father when he told him he was in touch with his mother, and it was staying that way for good.

'Where are you off to in such a hurry? Have you got to get to work?' Faye had just parked her car and, having caught sight of Grace hurrying down the hospital steps, she'd quickly intercepted her.

'I won't be going to work today; as soon as I could this morning I phoned in and told my boss what had happened and booked this week off as leave.' Grace gave Chris's aunt a breathless account and a welcoming smile. 'Wouldn't be able to concentrate on anything anyway, not until Chris is home and we're all back to normal.'

'I've just come along to find out how Chris is.' Faye looked eagerly at Grace, then at the hospital building behind her. 'Is he awake?'

Grace nodded and smiled. 'He seems in good spirits and is breathing quite easily.'

A deep sigh of relief escaped Faye. 'In that case I won't go in till later today. I expect there's a crowd round his bed. Can I give you a lift home?'

'I'm not going home, I'm off to . . .' Grace's

explanation faded away. 'Chris asked me to do something for him,' she finished lamely.

'Oh, well, wherever you're going I'll give you a lift.' Faye approached the smart saloon at the kerb and opened the passenger door.

Grace bit her lip. She liked Faye very much and felt she was a woman anybody could trust but . . .

A look of enlightenment flitted over Faye's features. 'Were you on your way to Bexleyheath?' she asked gently.

Grace had guessed that Rob had probably told his wife about Chris's search for his mother; she knew too that Rob had warned Chris to stay away from Pam if he wanted to avoid stirring up trouble.

'It's alright,' Faye said gently. 'If Chris wants to see his mum, that's his business. I've already told Rob how I feel on that score. I'll give you a lift. It'll save time if I take you. I've got a free afternoon.'

'Thanks,' Grace said quietly as she got into the car.

CHAPTER TWENTY-EIGHT

'I used to envy you, you know.'

Pam had come out with that while swiftly buttoning her coat. She had believed Grace's reassurances that Christopher was on the mend in hospital, but nevertheless she'd instinctively recognised her son's summons, and had insisted on being taken to see him. Grace had readily agreed to it as she'd had an inkling it was what Chris really wanted: to talk to his mother rather than have a message relayed to her.

'We all act daft when we're young: I've got plenty to own up to . . .' Faye had been surprised by Pam's frankness and responded kindly to her admission of jealousy. She'd been aware that in the early days Pamela had fancied Rob rather than her own husband. But it was all a long time ago, when they were little more than teenagers, and in Faye's opinion bygones should be bygones.

'I know now I was a fool.' A rueful smile twisted Pam's lips. 'I always thought Robert was the one to catch out of the two brothers, being as he seemed to have everything. But Stephen had hidden strengths . . . just couldn't see them at the time . . .'

Faye understood her meaning. 'He's been a good father,' she agreed simply then fell silent as Grace returned to the front room, having used the bathroom before they set off on the journey back to Islington.

As they trooped down the hall Grace closed her eyes and inwardly sighed. She knew Stephen would still be at the hospital when they arrived there, and trouble was bound to ensue when he clapped eyes on Pamela. But this argument was long overdue and, in a way, she welcomed getting it over and done with because it was another rut on the path to her and Chris's future together.

'Who told you? You've no right . . . God's sake! What are *you* doing here?'

Stephen had angrily hissed that out while gawping in astonishment at the frail-looking woman confronting him. He wouldn't have recognised his ex-wife but for Matilda having greeted Pamela by name. A moment later his aunt had declared she was off out to the caff for a cup of tea before ambling away.

Rob and Faye exchanged a glance.

'Right . . . time I was off. I promised to meet Daisy and take her shopping for new shoes.' Diplomatically Faye started after Matilda, having given her husband a significant look.

'Better check on the lads,' Rob told his brother. 'The sods might be shirking now there's just the two of them. And seeing as we're lucky the whole terrace didn't catch light and put 'em out of work . . .' He tailed off, aware that his brother wasn't even listening to him. Stephen's fierce gaze was fixed on Pamela's careworn face.

'Anyhow, the police are expecting me to go in and give them a statement now they've got O'Connor under arrest. They've already spoken to the lads, and Chris'll be next in line for an interview, when he's well enough.' Rob smiled breezily, gave Grace a very respectful wink, then wandered in his wife's wake.

As the silence lengthened and Stephen continued glowering at his ex-wife, Grace blurted out, 'I brought Pamela here.'

Stephen swung his angry gaze on his future daughter-in-law. 'Wouldn't have said it was the right time for troublemaking, miss, being as Chris is so poorly . . .'

'Chris asked me to contact his mum,' Grace replied firmly. She wasn't going to be intimidated, or made to feel guilty by dirty looks or harsh words. 'Chris wants to see his mum, I know he does.'

'I know what's best for him,' Stephen growled out through stretched lips. 'And it ain't her . . .' He jerked a sideways nod at Pam.

'Don't you talk to Grace like that!' Pamela stepped forward to plant her slight figure between her ex-husband and Grace. 'I'm here to see my son and nothing you've got to say is going to make a blind bit of difference.' She levelled a steady stare at him. 'I listened to you once telling me I wasn't fit to be near him and I believed you,' she said in a flat tone. 'I listened to my parents too, nagging at me to keep up appearances, and keep secrets, rather than fight on to get their grandson back.' Her lips twitched at the shameful memory. 'Terrified them, you did, with your threats to get the police on us all 'cos of what I did. My father never got over it; brought it up on his deathbed just the other year.' She tilted up her chin. 'Now I'm listening to nobody; I'm frightened of nobody. I'm seeing my son. That's where I'm going, in there . . .' She pointed at the door. 'And I'll fight you, or anybody else, who tries to stop me.' With that Pam marched past Stephen and disappeared into Chris's room.

'Just wanted you to know, I'm sorry . . .'

'What've you got to be sorry about?' Pam returned gently.

'Went off at Christmas without saying a proper goodbye to you, or wishing you a Happy New Year. It were rude of me.'

Pam plucked his hand from the coverlet and cradled it in hers. 'It's alright . . . I'd told you something that must've given you a real shock.' Her eyes glistened with penitent tears. 'I'm the one should be saying sorry . . . and I am. I've been sorry for what I did to you for so long it's been a constant torment, so it's a relief to get the words out at last.'

'Well, now we've both said sorry, that's that. All in the past,' Chris mumbled gruffly. 'Clean slate for both of us and when I'm out of here I'll come over again and see you. Saturdays we could do something, like go shopping, or I could have a look over yer place and see what needs tidying up. Done the gate, but I expect there's other bits of work cropping up all the time.'

Pam nodded, keeping her face averted while blinking rapidly. 'Your Grace is a good girl,' she croaked. 'She's strong and confident. She stood up to your father just now.' Pam nodded her admiration.

'So did you,' Chris returned with a wry chuckle. 'I could hear you.' He frowned at their clasped fingers. 'I should have told Dad a while ago that I'd been in touch with you. I've been a bit of a coward about it, I'm afraid . . .'

'You're no coward!' Pam jumped to her son's defence, squeezing his fingers in emphasis. 'Grace told me all about your heroics, saving that girl from the fire.' She patted his hand before letting it go. 'Deserve a medal, you do . . .' She broke off as a nurse poked her head round the door.

'Doctor's doing his rounds, not that there seems to be much wrong with you, young man.'

'This is me mum.' Chris proudly introduced Pam with a jerk of his head.

'Well, he's doing fine, Mrs Wild.' The young sister gave a bright smile before disappearing.

'Better be off now; don't want to get in the doctor's way.' Pam rose from the chair, collecting her bag from the floor.

'I'll come and see you, promise . . . soon as I'm home . . .'

'I know you will, son,' Pam answered softly in a trembling voice replete with love and trust.

'I don't mind travelling back to Bexleyheath with you, honest . . .'

'No!' Pamela smiled at Grace. 'It's kind of you to offer to accompany me, but I'll be fine. I don't mind a journey on my own, and I've brought enough money for the fare.'

Grace and Pamela were conversing in low voices in the hospital corridor; Stephen was sitting still and silent in a chair against the wall. His chin was dropped close to his chest and he seemed to be studying his hands. He hadn't uttered a word to a soul since Pam had entered Chris's room. Suddenly he got up; but he didn't head towards the side ward, he approached them.

305

'I'll give you a lift.'

Grace and Pamela stared at him in surprise.

'Things to say,' he muttered awkwardly. 'Best get it off me chest . . . got the car outside . . .'

'Thank you.' Pamela sounded calm and collected. 'I'll take you up on your offer.'

'Your dad's giving your mum a lift home to Bexleyheath.' Grace gave Chris a rueful smile as she settled down in the chair beside his bed.

Chris gawped at her. Suddenly a dry laugh scratched at his throat. 'I was getting used to having two parents. Might be I won't have even one if they end up stranglin' one another . . .'

As Pam directed Stephen, with a pointing finger, to turn in at the top of her road she was sourly thinking that if he had things to say he was leaving it a bit late to air them. So far the journey across London had passed in silence.

'Thanks for the lift.' Stephen had pulled up outside her house and immediately Pam reached for the door handle.

'I won't stop Chris seeing you if that's what he wants,' Stephen blurted.

'Good; 'cos I wasn't going to let you,' Pam returned. She met his eyes unflinchingly. 'So that's best all round for Christopher.'

'I know it weren't all your fault. I could've done more when he was little. I remember you being . . . sort of depressed, asking me fer a bit o' help just after Chris was born.' The words had spouted forth unrehearsed and Stephen rubbed a finger along the bridge of his nose, wondering whether to continue delving into hurtful memories, or whether to put the car in gear and drive off. 'Just didn't seem to be the thing for blokes to care fer kids,' he continued, gazing through the windscreen. 'Didn't think I'd know how to do it.' He grimaced at his fingers gripping the steering wheel. 'Then I found out I knew alright, 'cos I didn't have a choice in it.'

'You had a choice in it,' Pam responded bitterly. 'You could have let me give a hand bringing Christopher up.'

'I know,' Stephen admitted bleakly. 'But you shocked the sense out o' me for a while with what you did. After that . . .'

'After that you just thought you'd carry on being vindictive.'

Stephen swung a savage glance at her. 'You deserved a hard time of it for being so wicked, you can't say that ain't true.'

'Yeah, well, I've had a hard time of it, hard enough to satisfy even a spiteful sod like you.' Pam made to shove open the car door.

'I never gave you a chance to explain at the time. That were wrong of me.' Stephen put a hand on her arm to delay her then immediately withdrew it. 'You should have got your say about why you did what you did.'

A silence developed between them as the years peeled away and they relived the time they'd endured together.

'I felt alone, even though we were married and I had my parents, and Christopher, and a few friends, I felt it was just me up against it all.' Pam had meant to tell him to get lost because it was twenty years too late to pick it over now, but an explanation simply tumbled out of her. 'I tried to speak to my mum about how I felt . . . but she had nothing to say apart from *you've made your bed, now lie on it.'* Pam grimaced a smile at a passing car. 'Heard that regularly once a week at least; more when I went over to beg her to have Christopher for a few hours to give me a break.' She glanced at Stephen. 'They were disgusted when they found out I was already pregnant when we got wed. They pretended they didn't know. But, the baby was too big to be premature, and the family started to gossip. Mum never forgave me for being a disgrace on that score either.'

'You said your dad had died . . .'

'Yeah . . . he's gone . . .'

Stephen continued staring expectantly at her.

'I do my duty and visit mum a couple of times a year. Neither of us makes much of an effort.' Pam offered up a short answer to his unspoken question.

'You should have told me at the time you felt like it were all getting on top of you . . .'

'Why?' Pam snorted. 'What bloody use were you?' She threw back her head to shout a mirthless laugh. *'Where's me tea . . . you couldn't keep a rabbit hutch you fat cow . . . I'm off out . . .* that's all I ever got out of you!' She relished the guilt that flitted over his features before whipping her face away. 'Soon realised it was just me, on me own. So I liked to quieten Christopher and lose myself in stories in magazines. It was wrong, I know, but from the moment we said our vows it was wrong . . .' She scrambled out of the car as she felt tears pricking her eyelids.

Stephen got out too and met her by the kerb.

'I just want to say, I know things might have been different, if I'd been different.' He'd rattled that off quietly before she could disappear indoors. He had an urgent need to acknowledge his part in the misery that had been their brief marriage. Instinctively he understood that if he didn't his relationship with Christopher would suffer in the future. And earning his son's love and respect had been his life's work.

Pam halted by the hedge and muttered, 'Thanks for saying so. I know you didn't have to tell me, but I've always hoped you might. Always hoped you might say I could see Christopher too.'

'Well, I'm saying it now . . . bit late in the day, I know . . .' Stephen added hoarsely.

Pam glanced at him with eyes that were defeated rather than despising. 'Yeah . . . bit late in the day,' she echoed before opening her front gate.

CHAPTER TWENTY-NINE

2 June 1953

'Can you see our queen, Kathleen?' Kieran hoisted his eldest daughter higher on his shoulders then grinned up at her.

'I can see everything, Daddy,' Kathleen cried out in delight while bobbing her dark head to and fro to get a look over the mass of people in front of her. 'There's a coach and white horses going by and it's gold and shiny.' Kathleen frantically waved both small hands. 'A lady is waving at me, Daddy. Is she our queen, Daddy?' Kathleen giggled, jiggling excitedly on her father's shoulders.

Kieran grinned at his wife, carrying Rosie in her arms in an attempt to protect her from the heaving throng. The toddler was squirming to get down but Noreen held onto her, shushing her. People were good-naturedly jostling for position but the Murphys had managed to find, and hang on to, a good spot in The Mall from which to watch the coronation coaches proceed towards Westminster Abbey.

'It's a wonderful day for us, Noreen.' Kieran sighed contentedly as he lowered Kathleen safely to the ground.

His wife affectionately hugged his arm. 'It's a long while since I felt so happy. If you get the job tomorrow it'll be a new start for us. It's a fine day, so it is.' She slanted up a rueful glance at an overcast sky. 'Even if it does come on to rain later . . . nothing can spoil it.'

After many, many months scratching around for odd jobs Kieran finally had an interview for a permanent post as a driver for a haulage company. They both knew such an opportunity would give them the means to move out of The Bunk at last.

''Ere! I thought you two were staying behind in the street to put up bunting.' That gruff, jovial complaint made the couple swing about to find Matilda weaving through the crowd, accompanied by two of her daughters.

'And I thought you were staying behind to do all the organising for our grand party,' Noreen saucily came back at her. She'd raised her voice to be heard over renewed cheering.

Coaches carrying members of the royal family, and foreign dignitaries, were following on sedately behind the Gold State Coach towards Westminster Abbey. The crowd was surging forward at intervals, flags flapping noisily in the air.

'I *was* intending to set to early,' Matilda admitted. 'But couldn't miss this, could I? I'm glad I didn't. What a glorious sight.' She happily observed the jubilant scene before remembering to introduce the Murphys to Bethany and Alice. 'Plenty o' time to get the party started. The queen's gone by so we've seen the best of it here, and what we'll miss we can watch tomorrow, on the television set round at Rob's. So we'll be getting off home in a mo.' Matilda sighed in satisfaction. 'Turned out a lovely day, ain't it? And didn't Elizabeth look a sight fer sore eyes in her furs and jewels? What a get up.'

'Could see all the stones in her crown sparkling from where I was standing,' Bethany said.

'*I* saw the queen with her crown,' Kathleen piped up, making them all smile down at her. 'She waved at me,' she added shyly.

'My Lilian has got a good spot at the front with some of her kids,' Alice chipped in. 'Oh, well . . . Come on, Mum, no point putting it off longer. We'd better get going and get the tables laid out. The little 'uns will be ready for something to eat after all the excitement.' She crouched down to speak to Kathleen. 'Bet you're ready for some jelly and cake, aren't you?'

Kathleen nodded and bashfully clasped her mother's legs.

Matilda ruffled the little girl's dark locks. 'Make sure to be back in good time for the kids' feed-up this afternoon,' she reminded Noreen. 'I'm expecting to see Rosie and Kathleen tucking in.' She gave Kieran a wink. 'Then later on the adults will have a bit of a knees-up.'

'Is Christopher here somewhere?' Kieran asked Matilda, glancing about. He owed his thanks to Chris for having put him forward for the job at the haulage company. Vince's father was due to retire and Chris had made it his business to tell Kieran about the vacancy coming up. Kieran had been able to get an interview date arranged before the job was advertised.

'Ain't seen Chris for a few days,' Matilda said. 'S'pect him 'n' Grace are busy arranging stuff now they're gonna set a date fer the wedding in September.'

312

'Better get a move on,' Bethany warned her mother and sister, checking her watch. 'Sophy and Danny will be arriving soon and I haven't yet told George what time to meet them when they get off the train.' Beth knew her eldest sister would be disappointed if nobody turned up to give them a lift from the station when they arrived from Essex. Her husband George usually did the honours as they still lived locally.

'We'll see you lot back at home a bit later.' Matilda and her daughters headed off in the direction of the bus stop.

'He doesn't look too steady up there. Go and give him a hand, Josh?' Alice asked her husband. She'd been watching her brother-in-law, Danny, up a ladder, tying a banner made from an old sheet to a lamppost. Painted in bold black letters along its length was GOD SAVE THE QUEEN. Sophy's husband was stretching to tighten the cord and wobbling precariously while shouting instructions at a fellow on the opposite pavement who had hold of the other end of the string.

Josh put down the trestle table he'd been erecting and hurried over to give Danny some assistance while Alice continued setting out chairs.

'They look good enough to eat, Stevie.' Lucy had appeared with an armful of paper tablecloths just as Stephen emerged from Matilda's house carrying a huge platter brimming with sausage rolls. He'd made them earlier at the café and had been keeping them warm on Matilda's little stove.

The savoury aroma wafted temptingly around and the chef had to playfully smack away several hands that snaked out before he could land the plate on the table.

'Kids first, you greedy lot,' Stephen amiably told the adults who'd tried to snaffle a pastry in between positioning chairs for the children's tea party.

Once the tables were covered in their colourful cloths, paper hats and streamers were scattered along their centres. Union Jacks were already anchored in several sash windows on either side of the road and chains of flags crisscrossed high above their heads, fluttering in the light breeze.

'Where's Chris?' Rob had come up behind his brother and wolfed down a cheese straw with much smacking of his lips. 'Not bad,' he said, in praise of Stephen's culinary skills. 'I thought Chris was in charge of making the bonfire.'

Stephen glanced over to where Vince, Billy and Ted, with much larking about, were stacking up a pile of old timbers. The wood had been collected over the previous weeks from the demolished houses at the other end of the street. Close by, and gently rocking a pram in which slept a baby girl, was Deirdre, keeping a beady eye on her husband.

'Not seen Chris since yesterday,' Stephen said. 'He didn't come home last night . . . the dirty dog . . .'

'Stayed with Grace, d'you reckon?' Rob grinned at Stephen.

'Wouldn't be at all surprised,' Stephen answered. 'Like a couple of turtle doves, they are; and now they're talking about a date in September . . .' He gave his brother a wink before adding, more seriously, 'Think that business with O'Connor setting light to the houses shook him up. He's been acting a bit different. I was the same after I had me own accident,' he mocked himself. 'Makes you start to think . . . life's too short to hang about waiting and hoping; just get on and do it's my motto. That's why I jumped in with both feet on the caff. Turned out the best thing me 'n' Pearl ever did.'

'Yeah . . .' It was the sum of Rob's agreement to his brother's theory. 'Chris'll be coming along tonight, though?'

'He'd better!' Stephen laughed. 'Or I reckon Matilda'll have his guts fer garters.'

'What about Pam?' Rob asked, plunging his hands in his pockets while waiting for his brother's response.

'She got invited; up to her if she turns up. Can't do no more'n ask.'

It had been a blunt statement, as though Stephen didn't care either way. In fact he knew he'd appreciate it if his ex-wife put in an appearance; that way Christopher would know he meant it when he said there was no lingering animosity there on his part. He'd make sure he and Pearl made Pamela feel welcome if she came along. But he had a feeling it would be some time yet before his ex-wife's wounds were healed by the strengthening connection to her son. Stephen knew that it wasn't just duty, or a sense of something lacking in his life that took Chris regularly to Bexleyheath. His son was growing to love the mother he'd never known and, oddly, Stephen felt a quiet contentment because of it.

Briskly Stephen stepped back from the table he'd been piling with food and, before his brother could pursue the subject of his ex-wife, he turned on the spot to watch industrious people intent on making this last Bunk party the best ever. 'We've had some shindigs here, ain't we?' he said. 'I can remember as a kid marching up and down at the end of the Great War, banging a spoon on a pot on Armistice Day. Must've

315

been at least a hundred kids in that procession. We all ended up jigging about round the barrel organ . . . went on for a few days, as I recall.'

'Then we had a right good celebration in 1935 for King George's Silver Jubilee and another on VE Day.' Rob voiced his own reminiscences, his eyes distant.

'Stop slacking there, Stevie, and bring out the fairy cakes.' Matilda had come up behind her nephews. 'And where's Pearl with the jellies?'

'She's on her way. She was waiting for 'em to set properly. She didn't get back from Trafalgar Square till late. Don't worry, I've torn a strip off her,' he joked. 'Warned the silly cow she'd get caught in the crush and it'd make her late getting back here.'

'Can't blame her for hanging about in town. Once in a lifetime opportunity to see the queen on the way to get crowned,' Matilda said. 'Ooh, Elizabeth did look lovely . . .'

'Oi, Tilly!'

Matilda twisted about at that familiar, raucous voice and immediately her wrinkled face lifted in a delighted grin.

'Would've recognised you anywhere. Ain't changed a bit, have yer?' Matilda boomed out, hugging her grey-haired old friend.

Jeannie Robertson gave her an old-fashioned look. 'Yeah . . . you 'n' all,' she answered dryly. They both laughed. They were very different people now to those youthful, feisty women who once had fought – against and with – one another while scraping by, living as neighbours in The Bunk's heyday.

'Johnny with you?' Matilda asked while glancing about for Jeannie's fellow. She put down on the table the bottles of pop she'd been nursing while talking to her nephews.

Jeannie pointed to a tall, balding man standing with a group of people. Jeannie and Johnnie Blake had been together, on and off, since childhood, despite Jeannie having married someone else and had children with him.

'And how's your Peter doing?' Matilda went on. Jeannie's adult son still lived at home with his mother having suffered terribly, and never fully recovered, from shellshock in the Great War.

'Yeah, he's alright. Got himself a lady friend,' Jeannie said proudly. 'She's a nice woman. Lost her husband in 1944 so she's quite a bit younger . . .' She broke off to exclaim, 'Bleedin' hell! That's Connie Whitton over there, ain't it?' Jeannie was gazing at a buxom middle-aged bottle blonde who was sauntering along arm-in-arm with a stooped, shrunken-looking fellow. Connie had been a notorious prostitute in her time, when living in The Bunk, although she'd always been quite popular with her neighbours – women as well as men.

'Reckon it *is* Connie,' Matilda said. 'And that must be Ralph Franks with her; now I wouldn't have recognised *him*. He ain't aged at all well – not like us . . .' She chuckled as Jeannie swung an astonished glance at her.

'Ralph Franks? *Not* the rozzer who used to do the beat about The Bunk with old Twitch?' Twitch had been the nickname for Sidney Bickerstaff who had been well-respected by the Bunk community, considering policemen had been universally disliked and distrusted.

'That's Ralph alright,' Matilda confirmed. 'I heard Connie got back with him. Don't think they've ever made it official, though.' Matilda pointed to where her daughter Alice was standing talking to a couple of women. 'And over there's my Alice – good-looking one with dark hair – and I reckon that's Connie's sisters standing with her, Sarah and Louisa. Ain't seen either of them in . . .' Matilda gave up trying to calculate the years. 'Bleedin' hell, too long to remember when I last saw 'em. Before the last war, I know that.' She paused for breath. 'And Sarah's still knocking about with her childhood sweetheart. Not that Herbert Banks is any more use now than he was as a kid. Sarah still ain't married him, and I reckon that's wise . . . but shame she ain't got any children.'

'Wc had some times, didn't we, Til?' Jeannie sighed out.

Matilda nodded and for a moment their eyes closed as they remembered the worst of it. Then wry smiles appeared simultaneously to tug at their lips.

'Lot o' water under the bridge and mighty glad to see most of it flow on by,' Matilda said gruffly. 'But good times 'n' all. Specially when my Jack were alive, God rest him.' She sniffed and chuckled to cheer herself up. 'Anyhow, today we remember all them good times and ferget about the bad. And after the kids are stuffed fit ter burst, I'm gonna get the tables pushed back and remind you all how we used to do a shindig in The Bunk.'

'And I'm ready fer it, don't you worry about that,' Jeannie said with an emphatic little jig on the spot. 'But fer now I'm gonna mosey over and say hello to Connie . . . Oh, look who's here! There's old Beattie, talking to Lou Perkins, 'less me sight's gone along with the rest o' me.' She exaggeratedly patted into style her salt-and-pepper-coloured hair that once had been a rich chestnut brown.

'You're not so bad fer yer age,' Tilly ribbed her. ''Course you're a bit older'n me, so naturally I look better.'

'Bleedin' cheek! I know you're seventy if you're a day and I ain't yet turned sixty-five.'

'Must've had your Peter when you was still at school then.' Matilda roared with laughter before clasping Jeannie to her bosom.

'Right . . . need any help with anything before I disappear?' Jeannie nodded her head at the tables being piled up with platefuls of tasty food.

'Nah, you go off and have a natter. Got me daughters and grandkids giving a hand with all the preparations.'

'Fetch us some more serviettes will you, Sophy, when you get a minute?'

Sophy nodded at Alice and dived into a cardboard box to pull out some napkins printed with colourful Union Jacks. She started distributing them along the table by each plate. 'Kids are getting hungry.' Sophy pointed to a party of children, dressed in their Sunday best, hovering by the table, their eyes wide as they assessed the wonderful spread being laid out.

'Time to get them seated,' Bethany declared and started walking up and down the table pulling out chairs for excited youngsters.

CHAPTER THIRTY

'Adam! You managed to get time off and come to our party!' Faye plonked down the basin of jelly she'd been ladling out to the kids, and rushed towards her son to greet him with a fierce hug. 'I'm so glad you're here. Is Geraldine with you?' She was always happy to see her son's fiancée.

'She's gone to central London with some friends to see the coronation parade. But she's hoping to come along later.'

'Daisy will be thrilled to see you.' Faye waved at her daughter, drawing her attention and, with a delighted grin, the young woman sped over to them. A dapper youth began trailing uncertainly in Daisy's wake.

Daisy launched herself at her brother with such energy she almost knocked him off his feet. 'Chris'll be glad you made it.' Daisy knew her brother and her cousin got on like a house on fire.

'Where is Chris by the way?' Daisy took a squint about. 'And Grace, too. I've not seen either of them yet.' A moment later she'd remembered her hovering boyfriend and urged him forward to introduce him to Adam.

'This is Richard. I've told him all about you, and how brave you were in the war.' She gave her brother a prideful beam.

Adam politely shook the nervous young man's hand. 'Pleased to meet you, Richard . . . she exaggerates,' he added modestly, patting the boy on the shoulder.

'I saw Shirley Coleman turn up a little while ago. I'll go and have a word with her and see if she knows where Grace and Chris have got to.' Faye glanced away from her children with a frown. Her nephew's absence was starting to niggle at her. 'I expect something's held them up, that's all it is.'

Faye left her son and daughter chatting and went off to speak to Grace's mother. She knew Chris wouldn't intentionally miss this party. He and Grace had been talking about the preparations, along with everybody else, for months past. Grace had written invitations to many ex-Bunk residents for Matilda, and had been involved in planning today's celebration. At the beginning of the week the young couple had been to the wholesaler's to fetch back in the van the boxes of souvenir paper plates, tablecloths and serviettes.

'Have you seen my Grace?' On noticing Faye approaching, Shirley had immediately fired that at her, then glanced around, her lips pursed. 'I can't believe she'd not let me know she was stopping out last night.'

'Didn't come home then?' Faye gave a little grimace.

'I only came along to this party to give Grace a piece of my mind for worrying me so. I thought I might find her and Chris already here. But I've just had a word with Matilda and she's not seen either of them for days. Didn't say too much 'cos it looks like everybody's having

321

a good time and I didn't want to spoil the atmosphere.' Shirley again swept the company with a searching gaze.

'Grace didn't give you a clue where she was off to?'

'She had the day off work yesterday to do *wedding things* with Chris; that's what she told me they were up to. Dolled up to the nines, she was. I'm just hoping she didn't get too carried away with *wedding things with Chris*, if you get my drift.' Shirley's eyes narrowed. 'I'm not going to be best pleased if any trouble comes out of this in nine months' time, and I'll make no bones about telling his father so when I clap eyes on him.'

'They're setting the big day for some time in September, so not too far off, is it,' Faye quickly soothed Shirley.

'Grace was engaged before, you know, and the rotter did the dirty on her. As far as I'm concerned, till a girl's got a wedding ring on her finger, anything can happen.'

'Chris idolises Grace,' Faye quickly reassured her. She could tell Shirley was becomingly increasingly agitated by the thought of an unplanned pregnancy arising from the couple's unexplained absence. 'They'll be along soon, I'm sure of it. Now come and meet some people; most of Matilda's grandchildren and great-grandchildren are here. They're a lovely bunch . . .'

Shirley allowed herself to be lead away, grumbling.

'Now who wants more jelly?' Pearl held up the glass bowl. A few hands went up but most of the children were too full to indulge in more. After Pearl had doled out seconds to those who wanted it, Stevie relieved her of the remainder.

'I don't mind a bit of jelly when I'm hungry.' He immediately dug a spoon into it.

Pearl gave him a fond smile. 'You've worked hard, so

I'll let you get away with that one.' She glanced at the table; the children were slowly drifting away now they had eaten their fills. 'Get the empties cleared away, shall we, then we can put out some fresh sandwiches and sausage rolls for the adults to dive into.' She leaned forward to whisper, 'Have you hidden the cake?'

Stephen nodded. Just that afternoon he'd iced a large sponge in the shape and colours of the Union Jack. He chuckled. 'I've made a gold crown for Tilly to wear 'n' all when we come to cut it. She can do the honours as she's our Queen of The Bunk.'

Pearl guffawed. 'She'll like that, Stevie.'

'Let's make a bit of dancing space, shall we?'

Alice and Sophy had started to move back chairs to clear some room in the centre of the street.

Suddenly they stopped and stared as a van pulled up and Rob and Josh tumbled out to open the back doors. Alice burst out laughing. 'I wondered where Josh had got to!' She clapped a hand to her mouth. 'I told him we could do with a bit of music but I didn't dream he'd bring the piano from home.' She weaved through the throng towards him. 'You gone nuts, Josh Chaplin?' She was shaking her head in amazement as he and Rob lifted the piano onto the pavement. 'I was only expecting the Italian fellow to turn up and do a turn on his barrel organ.'

'You can't do the conga properly without someone bashing it out on the piano, Al,' Josh soothed her in his gentle way. 'Anyhow, you know you like a good sing-song, with me tinkling the ivories. And George has fetched over his banjo, so we're all set for a night of it.'

As the light faded, and the bonfire shed a warm glow on the street scene, Alice wandered away into the shadows. Planting her hands on her hips she sighed, realising she felt pleasantly exhausted. She'd moments ago danced the hokey cokey with Sarah Whitton, the pair of them singing their lungs out, and laughing hard enough to make their jaws and ribs ache. Now Alice hoped to find a chair to relax on, and take a breather; but sleepy-headed kids occupied every one.

Instinctively she perched down on her mother's front step, and contentedly let the sights and sounds of the celebration wash over her. Her Josh was bashing out 'If You Were the Only Girl in the World' in between sending her significant little glances. She gesticulated at him not to be daft. That made him laugh and adopt an even more sentimental air, simply to tease her.

Alice settled her back against her mother's door and sipped from her glass. Her eyelids closed and she let the June night air refresh her as her mind retreated through decades to remember herself as a girl, crouching outside with friends on balmy Saturday nights, while above, in their decrepit rooms, the adults would sing and jig to the tunes belted out on the piano by her dad.

It was the same piano that Josh was playing now, Alice realised, and the thought of her dad's fingers flying over those battered keys, forty years previously, filled her with poignant pleasure. In a way it made her content that he was here enjoying this final Bunk party with them today.

Almost simultaneously, Alice's three sisters spotted her quietly relaxing and ambled over to join her. They stood, smiling, watching waltzing couples, before they too settled down on the step or kerb, as they once had congregated together as children.

'You know, I never understood what Mum saw in this

324

place. I couldn't wait to get out and get on . . .' Alice paused, glanced towards Seven Sisters Road. 'Yet . . . it's got something, hasn't it. In a daft way it's special and I've only just realised I wish the street wasn't being pulled down. I know I'm going to miss it when it's gone.'

'Me too,' Sophy said. 'Met my Danny here, didn't I, so there are some fine memories for me. Remember, do you, Al, the day the Lovats turned up to move in next door?'

'Was only twelve at the time, but I won't ever forget it,' Alice vowed. 'I still think about Geoff . . .' she added huskily as she remembered Danny's younger brother. She'd been fond of him, had classed him as her best friend, and he'd proved his worth with his caring, self-less behaviour. His life had ended tragically and far too soon on a Somme battlefield.

'Couldn't ever forget Geoff,' Bethany echoed. 'He was a hero.'

'We had some larks when we were young,' Lucy chipped in nostalgically. 'Might not have thought it was good at the time but they were diamond days. Bloody good job Mum didn't find out about some of it though.'

'Nearly got skinned alive by Mum a few times for misbehaving,' Sophy added distantly.

'We all know you've got a few racy tales to tell your grandkids, when you have some, little Luce.' Alice turned the attention away from her eldest to her youngest sister.

'She'd better not tell 'em!' Beth declared. 'She'll scare the living daylights out of the poor little mites.'

'Best not let on,' Lucy agreed ruefully. 'If any of me grandkids find out I've got a bit of a dodgy past they might not take a blind bit of notice of me when I tell 'em off.'

'In that case, we'd all do well to guard our tongues

about what we got up to as kids. Mind you, I wouldn't mind hearing your stories again, Luce. The antics you got up to!'

'Best leave it for another time, Al,' Lucy answered with a wry chuckle. 'But I *will* tell you . . .'

Alice gave a contented sigh, glancing about at the fire-daubed festivities where generations of their kith and kin were having fun. 'We've got a smashing family, haven't we?'

'Wish Dad was here to see it,' Sophy said.

'Wish Chris and Grace were here to see it,' Lucy suddenly chipped in. 'Where on earth have those two got to? Stevie's been waiting for them to turn up before he brings out his cake.' She grinned at the sight of Matilda, waltzing past with Jeannie Roberts.

'Now I'm down here on this step, I'm not sure I'm gonna be able to get up again, Al.' Sophy stuck out an arm. 'Give an old 'un a hand up, will you, sis?'

'That is a beautiful bit of icing, Stevie. It's a real treat to have such a lovely surprise.'

Matilda was standing, arms akimbo, assessing the Coronation Day cake with a proud expression.

Stevie had decided not to wait any longer for his son and future daughter-in-law to make an appearance before unveiling his masterpiece. A short while after Shirley had arrived at the party, Faye had given him a whispered warning that Grace's mum was in high dudgeon because her daughter had stayed out with Chris. Since having accepted a few drinks, Shirley had mellowed and now seemed more willing to join in the fun. In Faye's opinion – and Stephen had agreed with his sister-in-law – the young couple were probably now sober and feeling a bit bashful about turning up and getting ribbed, and rebuked, because of what they'd been up to last night.

Stephen was disappointed to think the couple might miss the last ever Bunk celebration. He also thought his son's timing pretty bad, being as Chris had known for ages that this party was coming up. But he'd been young himself once, and knew that the urge to spend the night with an attractive woman could easily override good sense. It had happened to him, with Pamela, and had led to his beloved Christopher's birth.

''Ere, everybody come and take a look at this.' Matilda spun on the spot to holler that out.

People started to congregate around the table to admire the large cake Stephen had placed right in the centre.

He whipped out the gold-coloured crown that had been hidden behind his back and placed it gently on his aunt's silver hair.

'Now, being as Elizabeth couldn't make it here today – I hear she's busy elsewhere but she don't know what she's missing . . .' Stevie gave a droll shrug. 'You're our queen, Matilda, and you have to make the first cut in the ceremonial cake.' He handed his aunt a knife.

Matilda looked about. 'Everybody ready?' Having received a chorus of yes, she called, 'Three, two, one,' and plunged the knife into the sponge to an ear-splitting cheer.

'You don't want to go eating too much of that or you'll lose yer figure.'

Jeannie Robertson had come up behind Matilda and given her ample backside a pat.

Matilda wiped her mouth of cake crumbs then screwed

up her paper serviette. 'Stevie do make a decent bit of cake, I'll give him that. I wouldn't mind another bit.'

'Turned into a couple of fine men, your nephews Robert and Stephen, considering who their father was.' Jeannie glanced to where the two brothers were laughing with a group of people.

'Took after me sister Fran, both of them,' Matilda said with gruff pride. 'Nothing like that . . .' She swallowed the swearword, pursing her lips.

'How you been keeping health-wise?' Jeannie knew about her friend's lucky escape from death. She also knew that Matilda's injuries had continued giving her gyp following Jimmy Wild's attempt to murder her.

'Not bad, all things considered. Get a bit of arthritis in me legs . . .'

'Me too,' Jeannie said on a chuckle. 'And I never got shoved out a window. So you come out of it alright, didn't yer? Someone must've been watching over yer that night, Til.'

'Jack . . . dear Jack was me guardian angel,' Matilda whispered. 'He was with me, I know it.'

Jeannie heard the watery gurgle in Matilda's voice and gave her a quick cuddle. 'Got a lovely family, ain't yer, Til. I've met a lot of 'em tonight. That's what I miss, having grandkids. I know Peter won't give me none.'

It was Matilda's turn to offer comfort. 'You never know, now he's got this young lady, he just might surprise you.' She nodded at a young blonde woman who'd just arrived who was holding a baby in her arms. 'That's my granddaughter Lilian there,' she announced proudly. 'Looker like her mum, ain't she? She's Alice's gel. She's holding little Beryl, one of me great-grand-daughters . . . just a few months old.'

'Remember when Lilian was born in The Bunk, I do. Where's all them years gone, Til?'

'Gawd knows, but I remember 'em all like it were yesterday.'

'First sign yer losing yer marbles, ain't it, Til, when you can remember stuff that long ago?'

Matilda roared with laughter and wiped her streaming eyes. 'Glad you come over, Jeannie, you always do give me a good laugh.'

Jeannie patted Matilda's back. 'And there were times when we needed that laugh, Til, else we might have got found swingin' from them banisters.' She cocked her head in the direction of the houses.

'No more talk about bad times,' Matilda said briskly, dusting herself down. 'This is gonna be the best night to remember. I'm gonna jig about till me knees give out.'

'Come on then . . . I'll hold you up, old 'un . . .' Jeannie said, linking arms with her friend and leading her towards the dancing.

CHAPTER THIRTY-ONE

'We're gonna be in trouble, you know that, don't you?'

Grace turned in the circle of Chris's arms to see him smiling ruefully at her. 'Yeah . . . we're going to get a rocket, no doubt about it,' she sighed out in agreement.

From beyond the shelter of the roaring bonfire, they were loitering, watching the Coronation Day celebration while garnering the courage to face their families and explain their absence.

'Shirley's turned up. Look . . . she's over there dancing with Pearl.'

Grace bobbed her head, her eyes following Chris's pointing finger. She smiled at the sight of her mother doing what looked like the cancan as she was shaking her skirt and twirling an ankle. 'Can't see my nan anywhere; I didn't think Mum would come along on her own.' She'd sounded surprised. 'But I'm glad she's here and enjoying herself.'

'I reckon the others must have told her that wherever you are, you're bound to be with me so you'll be alright.' A self-mocking smile tilted his lips. 'Your mum's fine,' he reassured Grace, stroking fingertips on her flame-flushed cheek. 'Look, she's jigging about fit to bust with a pint glass in her hand.'

'Yeah, she's got a drink, so she'll have calmed down by now.' Grace didn't sound wholly convinced that was the case. 'I should have warned her I wouldn't be home. She'll have been worried about me, Chris.' A tinge of guilt had entered her tone.

'Do you regret what we've done?' Chris asked gently.

'No . . .' Grace turned again to gaze earnestly at him. 'No, not at all, it's just, I know we've disappointed people by being selfish. Perhaps it wasn't fair to go off like that.'

'We've not been selfish,' Chris insisted. 'We said, didn't we, we've been thinking about other people too much, for too long, and that wasn't fair on us. Now it's time to concentrate on our future and our happiness.' He emphasised his point of view by tightening his arms about her, and encouraged her to brighten up by dropping one kiss, then another, on her soft hair.

'Can't see *my* mum anywhere,' Chris remarked. 'But that ain't a surprise. She's probably gone out with Roger.'

'Do you reckon poor Roger will stick around with you giving him the third degree all the time?'

''Course he will! If he's made of the right stuff.' Chris grinned. 'Only natural a son would want to make sure his mum's not getting involved with a chancer.' He sounded serious when he added, ''Cos if he *is* a wrong 'un he'll have me to answer to.'

Pamela had been seeing her boyfriend, Roger, for a few weeks. She'd reassured her son that he was a regular in the café where she worked, and she'd grown to think him a nice enough chap over some months. Before she'd introduced him to Chris last week she'd agreed to a few trips to the pictures with Roger, just to make certain he was the kind of gentleman her beloved son would take to.

'She could have brought Roger here with her this evening,' Grace remarked, looking up at him over a shoulder.

'I knew she wouldn't come here, with or without him; she'd have felt awkward . . . an outsider . . . no matter how hard Aunt Tilly and the rest of 'em tried to welcome her. It's best to leave things be now.'

'You're happy with the way things are between your mum and dad?' Grace asked, surprised. Over the past weeks they'd talked in depth about wedding plans and she'd picked up on Chris's frustration about the tricky relationship between his parents.

'I'm happier than I've ever been, but that's because of you, not them. If me mum and dad can keep being a bit civil to one another it's enough for me. Can't expect things to be any better'n that between them considering what's gone on, I know that now. It was pie in the sky expecting the three of us to start playing happy families.'

'Nobody would blame you for wanting that,' Grace replied huskily.

'I've got what I want.' He turned her about to cup her face in his hands. 'And if we'd waited and had a big do with all the trimmings and all the family, just to please them, I reckon we might not have been so happy as we are today.' He smiled wryly. 'We'd have been broke, for a start. And it's said weddings and funerals can bring out the best, and worst, in people. I'm glad we went off and did it quietly, just the two of us, and didn't risk it all falling flat.' Grace still looked a bit subdued, so he added, 'We didn't want any slanging matches, did we, about who sits where and who gets up and says what?'

'No,' Grace said with a wry chuckle. 'We certainly didn't want any of that.'

They had talked for hours during the past month or so about the cost of a wedding, and the organisation needed to get everything planned within a short time so they could be man and wife by the end of September. Finally, they'd realised that getting married and getting their own place was what they wanted, but everything else was negotiable.

Scrimping for a cheap do hadn't appealed to either of them; they'd sooner put their meagre savings towards a deposit on a house. Neither had they wanted to ask either of their families for financial help. And constantly niggling at them was the worrying thought that, once the drink started to flow at their wedding reception, bitterness might float to the surface bringing trouble with it. Chris knew very well that the Wilds were no strangers to blunt speaking, or family tear-ups.

So, caught up in the excitement of the imminent Coronation Day celebration, they had both simply agreed to do it, without telling a soul, because they realised people would try and talk them out of it and make them stick to tradition. They had arranged for the banns to be read and then yesterday had gone to the Town Hall and emerged at three-thirty as man and wife.

'We had a perfect day, didn't we?'

Grace nodded then jokingly complained, 'Not much of a honeymoon though . . . a couple of nights in a hotel.' After the brief wedding ceremony, with two strangers acting as witnesses, they'd had an elegant afternoon tea, followed by a wonderfully sleepless night in a Piccadilly hotel. They had a room booked there for this evening, but after that they weren't sure where they'd be staying.

'Once we get sorted out in our own place, I'll take you somewhere really nice for a week.' The promise was whispered against her lips.

'Where *is* our own place?' Grace asked with a frown. The practicalities of their situation were constantly niggling at her. She hadn't changed her mind about being reluctant to camp out with either of their families, and she knew Chris felt the same way.

'We'll have to rent for a while,' Chris said on a sigh. 'I'll get straight onto finding somewhere tomorrow morning. If we get a cheap room we might be able to keep on saving for a deposit. I don't want to waste too much on rent though. Dead money, is rent. I want us to buy our own house, with a mortgage.'

'Me too,' Grace said emphatically. 'You know I've always wanted to own my own little home.' She paused, staring at the revellers, and beyond. 'If you think I'm talking rubbish go ahead and say so and I won't mention it again but . . .' She twisted about to face him. 'How about if we set up home here, just while we save. Won't get anywhere cheaper to stay than The Bunk.'

Chris stared at her in astonishment. 'You want to live here?' he asked hoarsely.

'No, I don't *want* to, but I will for a few months if need be while we save for our deposit. If we're not paying out for our lodgings we can save almost everything we earn.' She sounded enthusiastic. 'If your Aunt Matilda doesn't mind roughing it a bit, at her age, I'm sure I can do it.'

Chris's eyes were glimmering with a sort of wonderment. 'You mean you really would live here . . . in one of those dumps . . . with me?' he croaked.

'Live anywhere with you,' she said shortly. 'And I know you'll tidy it up the best you can for us. I'll help,' she offered immediately. 'I don't mind doing a bit of painting and decorating.' She started to giggle. 'Besides, it'll suit you down to the ground. You've got no excuse to be late for work . . .'

Chris jerked her against him and kissed her hard on the mouth. 'You're bloody wonderful, know that? Not many girls would even dream of . . .'

'Never mind about other people,' she said briskly. 'I reckon I could just about stand six months living here, if you can.'

'I can, Grace. And I'll find the best room there is and turn it into a little palace for you,' he vowed.

'Good. That's settled then.' She gave him a serene smile.

'It's time to go and tell them,' Chris murmured against her forehead. 'Ready, Mrs Wild?'

Grace nodded and took a deep, inspiriting breath. Suddenly her smile wilted a bit. 'We're not going to ruin their party, are we, by telling them now? I'd sooner own up tomorrow if we might put a dampener on things.'

As Chris stepped out from behind the fire, Grace nibbled at her lower lip and remained in the shadows.

'We could just say we've been held up somewhere then come clean another time,' she reasoned.

Chris held out his hand, beckoned. 'Come on. Time to do it,' he gently urged. 'They've spotted us, anyhow.' He raised a hand to his father who'd stopped dancing with Pearl to squint at him. Stephen began striding towards him, his face splitting into a joyous grin of recognition. Suddenly Stephen turned to bawl out news of the couple's arrival to the others.

'No going back, Grace,' Chris teased. 'You've got to pretend you're ten again and just jump with me, straight in at the deep end. Come on . . . sink or swim together.' With her hand in his they went, laughing, to join their family.

CORONATION DAY

THE WAY WE WERE . . .

East End woman cleaning up on the eve of Coronation Day.

Sweets being given to children to celebrate the
Queen's coronation.

A group of women dancing in East London.

Children playing in the streets during Coronation Day celebrations.

Dancing in the street.

Londoners dressed in their finest.

Coronation Day parade.